Raven's Song

Book One T1 Generation

Lucinda Moebius

Raven's Song

Copyright ©2011 by Lucinda Moebius

Haven Novels 2011
Haven Novels
Boise ID 83713
www.lucindamoebius.com
First Hardcover Edition: 2011
First Paperback Edition: 2011
First E-Book Edition: 2011
The characters and events portrayed in this
book are fictitious.
Any similarity to a real person, living or dead
is coincidental and not intended by the author.
Raven's Song:
a novel by Lucinda Moebius. -1st. ed. p.cm.
ISBN-13: 978-0615570716
Cover design by Danny Avery
Printed in the United States of America

Haven Novels

Prologue

And ye shall hear of wars and rumors of wars:
see that ye be not troubled:
for all these things must come to pass,
but the end is not yet.
For nation shall rise against nation,
and kingdom against kingdom:
and there shall be famines,
and pestilences, and earthquakes in divers places.
All these are the beginning of sorrows.

Matthew 24: 6-8

Chapter One

STORM CLOUDS DARKENED THE SKY, rolling in inky darkness across the horizon, obscuring the full moon. Lightning flashed, highlighting the tips of the mountains, but it was too far away to deliver the promised rolling drum of thunder. The infant in Raven's arm stirred, forcing her eyes away from the storm to the tiny bundle in her arms. He looked so tiny and delicate as he slept. It was hard for Raven to believe this tiny creature came from her. This little baby was all she had left of Billy and yet when she looked at him it was like she was looking into a void.

Raven just couldn't bring herself to love this child. Every time she looked at him it was like losing Billy all over again. She just couldn't go through the pain. The tiny infant in her arms squirmed and she tried to maneuver him into a more comfortable position. It just wasn't working. She just couldn't get him situated comfortably. It wasn't like she didn't have experience with infants. She'd been working in the surrogate program for the past three years and dealt with infants on a daily basis. Caring for babies was second nature to her and she usually loved the job, but now going into the nursery caused her chest to tighten and pressure to build up behind her eyes.

She named her child William Lakota Travis Etu Taylor, wanting to give him a name to remember where he came from. She had kept the last name Taylor despite her marriage, wanting to keep the connection to her mother. Something tying her and her child to the woman who gave her a chance at life. Her child was living in tumultuous times. She remembered the minister at church lecturing about the last days leading up to the Second Coming of Christ and the world being thrown into turmoil and war. If there was any credence to the prophecies then this had to be the last days.

The image of her mother appeared in the darkened glass of the window, walking towards her. Raven could see the limp her mother couldn't quite hide, especially when she was tired. Her mother was beautiful. The scars on her face barely visible, only pulling the right corner of her mouth into a slight frown. Raven turned and watched as the tall, blonde woman approached.

Raven knew the story behind her birth, life, whatever people wanted to call it. Her natural mother was fourteen years old when she was the victim of a vicious rape, resulting in an unwanted pregnancy. Raven would have been doomed if Kai had asked for another doctor instead of Savanna when she had returned to the hospital three weeks into her pregnancy. Savanna had performed an embryonic transplant, genetically altering the fetus destined to become Raven before she implanted it into herself. Savanna was the only mother Raven knew, the only one she wanted to know.

Her mother was so beautiful, even at forty. The scars didn't detract from her physical beauty. If anything they made her even more mysterious. When Raven was a child she loved touching her mother's pale arms and feeling her soft skin. Raven's own skin was a silky brown with a golden undertone. Her younger brother's skin tone was more of a blend of her mother's milk-white skin and the dark coffee color of his father, resulting in a creamy chocolate brown. Despite the genetic alterations to her basic DNA structure, Raven was full Navaho. She matched her mother in height and build, but her face was round to her mother's oval. The most noticeable difference between her and her mother was their eyes.

Tiger eyes, that's what Billy used to call them. The cat DNA her mother used to repair damages to her ocular nerves caused her to develop a tapetum lucidum in the back of the eye. In low light, when a beam hit her eye just right, they would glow just like a cat's. The effect, combined with her eyes' golden-brown color, is what first drew Billy to her.

Raven could actually see farther and better than anyone she ever met, and she could see in the dark. She always felt this made up for being born deaf. Her cochlear implant gave her exceptional hearing, allowing her to serve in the National Guard. If it wasn't for the implant she would have been deemed unfit for service. It was hard to get used to this new implant, though. This one was completely embedded under her skin, not giving her the option of turning it off like she could her old one, but the only way the Guard would allow her to sign up was if she had her old transplant replaced. She hated the constant humming the implant drilled through her head. The effect was completely psychosomatic, but she wasn't quite able to shut it out completely.

Her mother moved to stand beside her. Savanna's honey-blond hair was down and flowing about her shoulders and her back, in stark contrast to Raven's straight black tresses. Raven turned back to the window and stood silently for a few minutes, watching the storm expend itself over the mountains.

"I need to leave, mother," she said.

Savanna didn't respond. Raven turned to face her, catching the confusion in her mother's face.

"I volunteered for active duty and I'm leaving Lakota with you." Raven could hear the hopelessness in her voice.

"No, Raven. You're needed here." Savanna said.

Raven knew her mother worried about her. Savanna often expressed her fear and concern for her, Caleb and the lost children Emily had taken with her when she ran away from Haven. It was strange to think about having brothers and sisters she never met trying to survive in a land torn apart by war. She knew at least one of her mother's children was safe. It wasn't hard to see the reflection of her mother's face in the child Michelle had brought into Haven. Even though the child's parentage had been confirmed through DNA no one said anything to Michelle.

"Mom, I'm leaving." She felt the need to explain her feelings to the woman who had borne and cared for her all her life.

"You have a calling. You help people, here. I need to help people out there." Raven placed her son in Savanna's arms. "I call him Lakota so he'll never forget where he comes from." Raven brushed her hand over the infant's forehead. "Goodbye, my son." She turned and walked down the corridor.

Raven walked into the changing room leading outside. Residents rarely wore their Haven uniforms outside the stone walls of the complex, instead changing into work clothes, or in Raven's case, her National Guard uniform, before leaving the gates. Since she knew she had no intention of ever returning to her mother's compound in the mountains, Raven decided she would take all of her personal belongings with her when she left. She had the bin containing the things she had collected over the years brought to her. The container was nearly empty, holding the clothing she was wearing when she entered Haven fifteen years ago, a pair of hand woven, hemp sandals and a bead necklace her husband had made for her when they were married.

The necklace was created out of handmade, rice-shaped beads of blue and white. There was one green bead intermingled with the others, so the necklace wouldn't be perfect; after all, only the Gods could be perfect. Raven placed the beads around her neck, making sure they were hidden under her uniform. Once she made it to her new assignment the necklace would be placed in the bottom of her footlocker. The jumpsuit went into the recycle bin and she was about to toss the shoes in after, but something stayed her hand.

A memory came to her, one so far distant she wasn't sure if she was even remembering it correctly. The long drive when she was a child, her first taste of soda, her mother in pain in a white hospital bed and a woman. A gentle, kind woman, who washed her feet and gave her a pair of shoes when hers were soiled.

Raven placed the shoes back in the bin and sent it back down the conveyer to be stored on a shelf. She needed to hurry, the transport was leaving Haven in fifteen minutes and she needed to be on board.

Raven walked out of the compound and headed towards the row of transports. She was slated to ride in the gunner's chair on the top of the cab of the lead truck. Climbing inside, she made her way up to the dome on the top of the cab. The reinforced plastic shield would protect her from most attacks while allowing her a bird's eye view of the surrounding terrain. Adjusting her position slightly, she settled into the padded seat, allowing the cushions to support her hips. The rotating cockpit was designed after the bird's nest on old fighter jets and allowed her to spray the area in a 360 degree pattern with armor-piercing rounds from the gun mounted on the roof. Most insurgent militia groups didn't have the equipment to fight against this type of armament, so Raven felt relatively safe and comfortable in the padded seat. She strapped herself in and locked her gun in place.

The convoy started to roll as Raven put her headgear in place. Her helmet fit snug over her tightly braided and coiled hair and the goggles she positioned over her eyes fed data from the cameras positioned around the perimeter of the convoy. She adjusted the focus of the lenses to fit her acute sight parameters and turned on the heat-seeking capabilities. One by one she identified the heat signatures of her companions and turned them off.

The weight of the gun array rested on her thighs. She was glad it wasn't on her stomach and hips since she still hadn't fully recovered from giving birth and was still slightly sore. It helped that the weapon was lightweight, and she knew there wouldn't be much kickback if she did need to shoot.

Raven realized her commanding officer was giving her the cushiest job in the convoy since she wasn't quite back to her pre-pregnancy conditioning and was thankful she wasn't riding the cycles around the perimeter. She gave a salute to the guard at post as the metal gates opened to allow the convoy's egress.

Heat signatures popped up in front of Raven's eyes as they passed through Little Haven. She automatically filtered out the animals and small children, focusing on anything over one meter. It didn't take long for the convoy to roll past the huddle of longhouses built outside the gate. She breathed a sigh of relief as the last heat signature faded from range. Populated areas were always the worst. Insurgents liked to hide in the crowds and throw surprise attacks, unconcerned for the civilians and innocents in the way. Little Haven facilities were usually safe. Travis' guard force worked hard to protect the residents of the communities.

Cycles crossed beside, in front of and behind the convoy. Raven listened to the static of the calls as the riders spoke to each other. She missed the freedom of riding in the phalanx surrounding the trucks, her usual assignment. When she joined the Guard she had her choice of fields. The most logical one would have been medical, but when her husband signed on as infantry she followed suite. At first it was awkward to be around the powerful weaponry and assault weapons. Now though, there was something comforting in being able to strap forty pounds of metal loaded with hundreds of armor-piercing bullets to her body and knowing she was in an impenetrable shield. Nothing could harm her as long as she was locked in this bubble. She was in complete control, a feeling she hadn't had for months.

"Crow's nest," the captain's voice crackled in Raven's earpiece, "be prepared. Approximately thirty individuals in a field by the side of the road."

Raven could feel her lips curling into a smile. Tightening her grip on the double stock, she flipped the safety covers off the triggers. She positioned her thumbs above the red trigger pads to prepare to activate the firing mechanism. An electrical impulse flowed through her, causing her heart to palpate. Every nerve in her body tingled. She actually felt alive. Clenching her teeth together, she focused her scope on the tent city ahead. The heat signatures appeared as red masses in her view. As the convoy approached the tent city, the heat signatures suddenly started to collapse in on themselves. Raven realized the signatures weren't disappearing; the residents were ducking into tents and flattening themselves to the ground.

This gypsy group posed no threat to the highly armed Guard unit passing by. Raven relaxed into her seat and waited for the stand down order. It wasn't long in coming. She flipped the covers over the trigger pads and unclenched her fists from the grips. It took a moment to massage the feeling back into her fingers, clenching and unclenching her hands to relieve the tingling. Slow breathing calmed her heartbeat and allowed her to refocus on scanning the horizon.

The trip to the freeway was uneventful. Few people were willing to risk hiding in canyons and barrows after a storm. Flashfloods had a tendency to be more devastating than a National Guard unit. Once the convoy was on the freeway the trucks pulled side by side with the cycles scouting ahead and behind. The phalanx was so tight no other vehicle was able to insinuate its way between the vehicles. When the lanes widened from three to four the transport trucks spread into a diamond pattern surrounded by cycles.

The convoy crawled to almost a stop as they approached the Boise city limits. Raven's transport took the lead, allowing her to run recon as the scouts cleared traffic on all sides. Current traffic regulations required all non-military vehicles to maintain at least fifty yard clearance from military transports. Not being able to announce times of transport due to insurgent attacks created traffic havoc. The city was the most hazardous point in the journey.

The trucks camera feeds looked for any break in traffic patterns. Most cars exited the freeway when they saw the vehicles coming, wanting to avoid any run-in with the military convoy. Raven watched as the freeway cleared in front of the massive transport truck and the exits jammed with vehicles scrambling to get out of the way. She could see cars stacked up on side roads at a complete standstill. Many of the occupants exited to stand by their vehicles. Raven knew they were watching the olive colored transports glide by, knowing they wouldn't be going anywhere until the convoy passed.

The freeway was almost completely clear by the time they reached the Broadway exit. Raven studied the stone sound barrier on either side of the roadway. She looked south, trying to imagine the white house with a magic room, its ceiling covered in stars. Her brother was probably just coming home from football practice and Travis was returning from his office where he now managed a private security force. Rose must have had dinner waiting on the table. A happy family tableau, if not a very common one, in these tumultuous times. At least her little brother was safe, for now.

Raven knew the fifteen year old had just signed his letter of intent with the Marine Corps last week. He started training next year, so he would be ready to enter combat when he turned nineteen.

For the first time in five years Raven offered a prayer, *"Please, God,"* she whispered, *"if you're really there, protect him. My mother can't go through what I just did. She's been through so much; she can't lose another of her children."* She didn't give any thought to going to combat herself.

Chapter Two

THE CONVOY CRESTED THE HILL on the outskirts of town and Raven allowed the thoughts of her little brother to fade away. He was cloistered behind chain link fence and brick walls, safe for now. She would be back from the Sandbox before he went to Basic. The mission in the Middle East was still the same as it was twenty years ago, when the Big-Five diseases were first released. Find terrorists' nests and find the labs producing the killer viruses. The terrorists just knew their desert too well and finding the labs seemed to be an impossible feat. Raven adjusted in her seat. Her hips and back were starting to ache and she knew it would be another hour before they reached the base. She needed to be alert.

White clouds danced across the horizon, reminding her of a journey she made as a child. The tune to *Puff the Magic Dragon* started playing in her head, dancing in her mind. Trying to find shapes in the clouds would be too much of a distraction, so Raven tore her eyes away from the sky and scanned the horizon. All was quiet.

One of the bikes buzzed past the lead truck, zigzagging across the path. Raven could make out the gun strapped across the soldier's back, within easy reach. A flash reflected in the corner of her eye and she turned to look. Something was on the hill to the right. Pushing the alert button, Raven applied her thumb to the scanner, unlocking her own gun. She scrolled to the rocket launcher setting and pressed the icon. Feeling the gun chamber vibrate and rumble while the launcher rolled into place gave her a sense of security and she relaxed back into the seat. The cycles tightened their formation and slowed, allowing the convoy to pull close.

A spark and a plume of smoke from far back on the hill, followed by a cloud of white and grey, warned of the ensuing danger. A rumbling sound reverberated in Raven's head and she braced for impact. She felt the truck slam to a stop. The body of a soldier flew past the dome above her head. The hill seem to spring to life as bodies rose from the ground. Hot spots appeared on the periphery of her vision as movement counteracted the effect of the heat signature deflectors being used by the attackers. Raven scanned the crowd, looking for the most significant attacker. There, on the hill, a form carrying a rocket launcher. That had to be where the fist attack came from. The first rocket was to test the launcher's range, it was SOP. She zeroed in on the hilltop, sighting the insurgent in her crosshairs, and fired. A cloud of pink mist and an empty hilltop testified to her perfect aim.

By the time she rolled the gun back around and aimed at the bodies rolling from the hill the insurgents were intermingling with the cycles. Raven couldn't safely shoot at the insurgents without hitting her own men. The convoy had rolled to a stop in front of a smoking, gaping hole in the middle of the road. Reaching above her head, she pushed the button releasing the top of the nest. Pushing the gun off her lap and unbuckling her harness, she grabbed her sniper rifle from the rack behind her and belly-crawled on top of the reinforced cab of the truck. The roof of the truck contained a sniper's nest with steel walls rising to create a shield around her. A rotating turret controlled by foot pedals allowed her to rotate and find targets. She had less directional control in this sheltered turret, but it was easier to aim at individual insurgents from the crow's nest. Raven took aim at the invaders closest to the trucks. Only a few had made it past the scout cycles. Raven picked them off with quick, easy shots. The insurgents, those still alive or uninjured, were quickly captured or had turned tail and fled back into the hills.

The cycles took off to pursue the insurgents, but Raven could hear the Captain's voice calling them back. It was more important to guard the convoy than to pursue a ragtag gang who made the hills their home and probably had hideouts peppered in the mountains. Calls of 'medic' rang in Raven's ears from the bodies scattered on the ground and she knew she needed to crawl down and help. As she peeled her body off the top of the truck she took stock. Her hips and thighs were a little stiff, but she felt in pretty good shape. Making her way down the ladder, she grabbed a medic kit from the side of the truck and ran to the first body. A quick glimpse revealed exposed grey matter and, even though the man's breath was coming in short, quick gasps, Raven gave him a black tag and moved on to the next victim.

Raven was applying a field dressing to a sucking chest wound of an insurgent when she felt the down draft of a chopper. She sealed the dressing, allowing one end to flap, expelling air from the chest. She signaled the lead medic to let him know her victim needed to be evacuated and moved to find the next. Two medics approached with a gurney as she stepped away.

As intense as the few moments of battle were, there was very little carnage apparent on the roadside. Seventeen bodies, sixteen of them insurgents, were laid out and covered with white sheets on the side of the road. The only fatality in the unit was the scout who had flown by Raven's truck. A rocket had hit the front of his cycle, propelling him into the air and shredding the road under his tires. Captured insurgents were kneeling along the side of the road, hands on their head. Soldiers were standing guard, one eye on the prisoners, the other on the perimeter, looking for other attackers.

The prisoners were trussed and hobbled, kneeling on the side of the road. Five of them, all injured. Raven treated their wounds as they were sitting on the side of the road. The smell of hot tar mingled with blood and dirt, caused her eyes to water. The deep blue eyes of the boy in front of her reminded her of her mother. Raven studied his face, wondering if he could be one of the lost ones. He looked to be about twelve, too old to be one of the embryos Emily had taken. The oldest of the missing children was presumed to be about nine, but it didn't stop Raven from looking into every face she saw, searching for indications they were one of her brothers or sisters.

When Raven cut the ragged shirt from the boy's wound he rolled his shoulders forward, pulling away from her. He barely flinched as she washed the blood from his arm and gently probed the edges of the wound. Raven could make out each of his ribs as they curved around his back and attached to his sternum. The child didn't have any subcutaneous layers of muscle or fat. There was no way his condition came from a healthy lifestyle of diet and exercise. This child was starving. From the condition of his body, he was starving to death. Raven leaned close as she applied gauze to the oozing wound.

"What's your name?" she asked, quietly.

"Joseph." The word was said in such a low whisper Raven had to lean forward to hear.

"How old are you?"

A hiss from the prisoner beside him silenced the boy before he could answer and Raven could feel him pull away as he ducked his head. The muscle in his jaw flexed as he sealed his lips and Raven knew he wasn't going to volunteer any more information. The prisoners were escorted to the back of a transport truck. They were forced to lay face down on the bed of the truck as soldiers climbed in behind them. Raven helped lock the tailgate in place glancing at the boy before locking the gate. His tiny shoulders were quivering and when he turned his head Raven could see tears creeping down his face.

Raven ensconced herself back in the crow's nest. The perspective allowed her to see the cleanup effort underway as crews came in to eradicate any evidence of the battle. She turned her head away from the work crews placing the fatalities in the body bags. Swallowing bile, she refused to think about how many of them she was responsible for putting there. This wasn't the first time she had taken a life, but she was sickened by the idea. She never mentioned her feelings to her mother, even refusing to talk about it in her counseling sessions at Haven. The only time she mentioned it at all, outside of mandated personnel counseling, was in her letters to Billy.

Although she knew Billy was gone and her letters would never reach him, Raven still wrote to him faithfully. She ached so much for him. The letters allowed her to assuage some of her grief and express her deepest feelings without fear of repercussion. She kept each of the letters in an encrypted file on her personal data pad, hidden away from prying eyes.

Raven hummed a tune as the truck pulled away from the carnage. She found the simple, rhythmic pattern helped close out the horrible scene she just witnessed. A whole litany of music was filed away in her brain and she drew on the melody of a spiritual, learned as a child, to assuage her mind. She needed to focus on her job. The food in the transport trucks was needed to support the squadrons of genetically altered soldiers currently in training at the Mountain Home base. Despite this attack, Raven needed to regroup and focus on completing the task at hand.

The black shadows of two helicopters flanking the convoy flitted across the dull brown of the hills. The rhythmic beat of the propellers matched the tempo of Raven's heartbeat. She felt heaviness in her chest and tears burned her eyes, but she forced them back. This was no time to get emotional. She had a job to do. The supplies needed to make it to base. She couldn't help thinking about the prisoners in the back of the truck. They had to have been desperate to attempt an attack on a military transport convoy.

Most attacks happened at night, when the insurgents had the cover of darkness to hide and assist in escape. Only the most desperate or most skilled dared attempt an attack on a fully armed convoy. Raven pictured Joseph, with his exposed ribs and small frame. There was no doubt in her mind from where this group's motivation stemmed. She only hoped her work in the guard could help alleviate some of this desperation. If she could only help people understand there were other ways to obtain the necessities of life without resorting to attacks and loss of life, her sacrifices would be worth it. Even Billy's sacrifice would mean something.

The sun was approaching its zenith as the convoy pulled off the exit and onto the two lane road headed to the base. The bikes and convoy spread out to take both lanes of the highway. No other vehicle would be on this road. All patrols spread out to cover the desert terrain and access roads, blocking traffic until the convoy passed. Raven didn't relax her guard. Insurgent attacks were becoming more bold and, even within this thirty mile stretch of road, they were known to happen. She continually checked her weapon status and scanned the horizon for any indication of attackers. She didn't relax until the convoy rolled past the metal gates of the base.

Raven was dispatched to help offload the prisoners as soon as she disembarked from the crow's nest. All she needed to do was stand guard as the men were off-loaded. Most of them were able to climb down on their own, but Joseph lay on the floor of the truck, his tiny frame trembling. Raven pulled herself into the back of the truck and approached his huddled form, crouching to avoid the canvas covering held in place by metal crossbars.

The boy was breathing, Raven could see the expansion of his ribcage, but he wasn't moving. Raven put her hand on his shoulder and rolled him on his back. A pool of liquid had formed under his head. From the viscous quality of the pool it was obvious he had regurgitated the contents of his stomach. Raven was able to see a few blades of grass combined with what looked like some sort of fruit. She realized she was seeing evidence of the child's last meal.

Raven leaned close to the boy's head and whispered his name, "Joseph." The only response she received was a low groan.

His skin felt warm and slightly clammy. She rubbed the knuckles of her fist against his chest, trying to elicit a response to pain stimuli. Joseph groaned and opened his eyes. His eyes lacked focus and rolled back in his head before they closed again. Raven picked him up off the bed of the truck and carried him to the back. Another soldier reached up to help her down, but she didn't let go of the boy. He was surprisingly light, despite the length of his long, lanky body. A number of medics and service personnel were gathered around, triaging injured soldiers and assisting them onto stretchers and gurneys.

"I need a stretcher over here!" she called out.

The soldiers close by just looked at her. None of them seemed to move very fast.

"I need a medic and a stretcher," she yelled. "This child needs help."

At a gesture from an officer, a medic brought a stretcher. Raven had to help carry the stretcher into the infirmary. She made sure Joseph was settled into a cot and another medic had taken over for her before she left to report for debriefing.

Chapter Three

HER FEET DRAGGED IN THE gravel as she walked across the sidewalk to the white command building across the courtyard of the base. Exhaustion flowed over her in waves. The last thing she wanted to do was go to debriefing, but she still joined the rest of her crew in the auditorium. Her captain handed her a data pad as she walked in the low-roofed building.

"Fill out this form." He gestured to a row of chairs.

It didn't take long for her to fill out the form. This wasn't her first debriefing. She knew the shrink wouldn't be happy with her saying she was fine and was ready to get back to work. She filtered through the events, trying to decide which ones to talk about and which ones she would keep to herself. She decided not to mention the pink mist, saying she witnessed a bike flying past her and aimed to where she thought she saw the blast originate. She signed the report and handed the data pad to the receptionist. Moving back to the seats, she took a moment to stretch the kinks out of her back and legs before she sat down to wait for her turn with the shrink.

Raven was shown to a small room containing a desk, a leather office chair and a plush, fabric-covered couch. The short, non-descript, mousy-looking man in the room motioned her to take a seat on the couch. She sat on the edge, wanting to minimize contact with the fabric.

"Lieutenant Taylor, why don't you sit back and relax. We're going to be here for a little while. You might as well be comfortable." He had the same disingenuous smile all the therapists at Haven had on their faces when they were trying to soothe the fears of the women living there. Raven always hated the way they smiled.

"It's okay, Sir. It's not that I don't want to relax, I'm just concerned about all the germs fabric couches like these harbor." She wanted the psychiatrist to think she was concerned about germs and not anxious about this interview.

"Well, I guess that's to be expected since you grew up at Haven. I've noticed a certain level of germaphobia present in the residents of that community." He paused a moment to make a notation on his data pad. "I read your report on the insurgent incident. Is there anything you would like to add before the final report is sent to your commanding officer?"

Raven looked around the room, pretending to think for a minute. Her experience at Haven taught her shrinks liked their patients to think about what they were going to say before they said it. It showed the patient reaction was based on an intellectual level, not an emotional one. Raven looked up, into the pale brown eyes of the psychologist.

"There's not a whole lot more to add." She paused for effect. "I know I killed some of those men today and that's horrible. I also know if I didn't act, more men than Johnson would be dead right now. These supplies needed to get through or people here would suffer. I'm sorry those men died, but I acted within my training and we got the supplies here. We all did what we had to do."

"It says here you lost your husband in Korea and you left your son with your mother. How do you feel about that?" The question wasn't unexpected so Raven was able to keep her face passive despite the wrenching pain she felt in her chest.

She swallowed before she answered, trying to moisten her dry throat. "My husband's death was devastating. I'm not going to pretend it wasn't." She always felt it was best to be honest when asked about Billy. "My son is safer with my mother than he will be anywhere else in the world. I'm here because of Billy. He died trying to bring peace and order to the world. I owe it to him to fight in his place."

He asked a few more questions and Raven gave him her carefully prepared answers. As he dismissed her, he ordered her to report to the base commanding officer.

As Raven walked out of the office she glanced over at the group of soldiers waiting for their turn with the shrink. She knew she would be sitting in bi-monthly counseling sessions with the group over the next three months. Shaking her head, she left the center and walked across to the command center. A Corporal was sitting at a desk. He gestured for her to have a seat and continued entering data in a computer. Raven sat in the blue, plastic chair, trying not to squirm or show any discomfort. She didn't want anyone to find an excuse to take her off active duty.

It wasn't long before the Corporal motioned her to enter. Raven schooled her features before she walked into the office. She tried to appear as calm as possible. A red-headed officer sat at a desk, studying a data pad in front of her. As Raven entered the room she looked up and smiled. The officer stood and Raven saluted and stood at attention.

"At ease, Lieutenant." The officer motioned for Raven to take a seat.

"Lieutenant Taylor, I'm Colonel Egan. I don't know if you know this, but I met your mother once." Colonel Egan paused as if waiting for Raven to respond. Raven didn't recognize the name, so she sat silently waiting for the officer to continue. "It was in Old Vegas, years ago. She had followed someone into the Fringe and ended up being attacked. Do you remember?"

An edge of a memory nipped at the corner of her mind. Her mother, in pain, saying something about Kai. Raven felt herself frowning at the memory. Shaking her head, she pushed the memory away, smoothing her features before she looked back at her commanding officer.

"I vaguely remember our trip through Vegas," she said. "I was only four at the time. I think I was more interested in the sights on the journey than the few hours we spent in the city."

Egan studied Raven's face for a few minutes. Raven kept her features blank, looking steadily into the colonel's eyes. She knew the woman was looking for any crack in her defenses. Egan broke eye contact first, but left Raven with the impression the conversation about her mother wasn't over.

"I read the report on the attacks from this afternoon. It looks like you saw something long before any of your unit." Egan glanced up. "Your quick actions saved a number of your fellow soldiers. We estimate the insurgents had at least two other missiles ready to launch when your rocket hit. They were probably counting on the rockets providing enough cover to get their men inside the defenses."

Raven adjusted slightly as she listened to Egan's assessment of the attack. She didn't want to talk about the attack to this woman, anymore than she wanted to talk to the psychiatrist. Egan put the data pad down and locked eyes with Raven.

"I understand you performed medic duty after the attack," she said.

It took a moment for Raven to figure out what Egan was asking. When Raven first signed up for the service she went in as a medic. She had her RN license before she entered and, after her basic training at eighteen, went back to school and obtained her physician's assistance license. Not long after she married Billy she had the opportunity to go to officer's candidate school. It seemed like a good idea at the time, a few weeks away from her new husband and the chance for a promotion. When she returned Grey put her to work in the Surrogate program taking care of the prenatal needs of the pregnant women. After Billy died, she requested a transfer to infantry. She couldn't stand the thought of seeing one more baby being born to be turned into a soldier to possibly die on foreign soil. She frequently had nightmares about her own developing child during her pregnancy. It took time to convince her commander to approve the transfer. Grey wanted to send her to a M.A.S.H. unit at first, but she persisted in her request. Finally, the overwhelming need for infantry soldiers convinced Grey to approve the transfer. Raven wanted to be on the front line and she knew she would always use her medic skills, but the thought of sitting in a hospital caring for injured soldiers when she couldn't be there for her husband when he need her, filled her with a sense of dread. Egan was staring at her with an expectant expression. Raven cleared her throat, trying to form an answer in her mind.

"My training kicked in, I guess." Raven knew what was coming next. There was no way she was going to get out of medic duty. It was in her blood. She might as well resign herself to the job.

"We need more medics here. We have one of the highest casualty rates of any states' unit and we have the detention facility here as well. While you're stationed here I'm going to assign you to the hospital. It'll only be for a few months." Egan made an entry on her computer and signed it with her thumbprint. Raven could feel the aura of dismissal in her mannerisms.

"Ma'am," she tried to make her voice as calm as possible. "Respectfully, I'd much rather be patrolling the perimeter. I have had extensive training in hand-to-hand combat, weaponry and strategy. My strengths---"Egan held up her hand, forestalling any further comments.

"I'm well aware of your training, Lieutenant. I also know where I have the biggest need. I need you in the hospital. Your belongings have already been placed in your barracks. Go get some sleep. You'll report to Captain Garcia at 0600 hours tomorrow. You're dismissed." This time Raven couldn't ignore the dismissal and stood to leave.

She offered a crisp salute and strode from the office.

It didn't take her long to find her barracks. Outside of the long, white structure soldiers lounged in different stages of relaxation. Raven heard the buzz of conversation and the throaty vibration of laughter as she moved through the doors.

"Taylor!" She turned at her name. A soldier covered with road dust and still in full gear was motioning to her. Raven took a few steps toward him.

"Great reflexes out there today," the soldier said. "I thought we were goners when I saw that rocket hit Johnson. We're all headed over to Mess as soon as we get cleaned up. Wanna join us?"

Raven lifted her shoulder in a half shrug and nodded. She might as well make an effort to be friendly. This crew would be her unit while she was stationed here. She would expect them to have her back as much as she had theirs.

"Great, we'll meet back here in twenty and head over together. I'm Lieutenant Jayden Fitch, by the way." Raven acknowledged the introduction before she headed into the building.

It only took a few minutes to shower and change into a clean uniform. She was able to make it back to the rendezvous before the rest of the crew. At first she paced in the courtyard, but she didn't want to appear anxious so she sat on a bench with a clear view of the front door. Before long, Fitch came out of the building, followed by a small crowd. He gestured for Raven to follow. Falling into step, Raven realized she was taller than every member of the group. All of them were slim, with wiry muscles clearly outlined under their shirts. They all moved with the same unconscious grace as they marched across the compound.

The raised voices in the mess hall assaulted Raven's ears as the group moved through the chow line. She made a motion to turn down her implant, but she remembered in time she no longer had access to volume control. Smoothing her hair back, she tried to disguise the motion by pretending she was fixing an errant strand.

Once through the chow-line, Fitch led the team to an empty table near the center of the room. The food was rich and full of proteins. It was also cooked to the consistency of mush. The taste didn't even come close to the food offered at Haven. Raven managed to choke down half the meal before she had to push the bowl away.

Fitch reached across the table and tipped the bowl, looking at the congealed mass at the bottom. "Is your palate so sensitive you can't even stand good army food, Taylor?"

Raven studied his face, trying to discern if he was being malicious or just teasing her. She decided he was just trying to see if he could get a rise from her. She smirked as she responded.

"No, I just filled up on a big breakfast this morning. Gotta keep my girlish figure." She patted the hard muscles of her abdomen. Raven had kept her physical conditioning up as long as she could during her pregnancy, so it wasn't difficult to bounce back to her pre-pregnancy shape.

"I heard you grew up at Haven. Are you a Gen or a Natch?"

Raven's confusion must have shown in her face. She didn't know how to respond to the question.

"Are you genetically altered like the ones coming out of the Haven Program or are you completely natural?" Fitch continued.

"I'm not one of the program's children, if that's what you're asking." Raven picked up an apple from her tray and bit into it. She chewed for a minute, trying to decide what to tell Fitch about her background. "I was genetically altered as an embryo, but not to the same extent as the children in the program. My mother enhanced my immune modifications and strengthened my cellular structure."

Fitch nodded. "You're pretty much a Gen. Everyone in our crew are Gens, too. We all have the same genetic markers and DNA in common. In a sense we're all brothers and sisters."

Raven studied the faces of the five people sitting at the table. Each one carried a strong familial stamp. Straight brows, long narrow noses above thin lips. Their faces were small and they all had the same olive cast to their skin. There was very little to distinguish the males from the females. Raven realized she was sitting with three men and two women, although the way each of them carried themselves it was almost impossible to tell.

"How did you all get stationed in the same unit? Wouldn't it be unusual for sibling groups to be stationed together?" Raven gave up on her food, but since the others were still eating she decided it was safe to sit and continue talking.

"If we had been raised as a sibling group we would have probably been stationed separately. We were raised as part of the Smith project. Thousands of us were created and trained as soldiers. You should know about that project. The Haven unit is part of it." Fitch's voice had a low, glottal timber and Raven could tell other soldiers were listening in on the conversation.

One of the other members of the group spoke. "We may all have the same core genetic markers, but we all have different modifications. All of us have enhanced immunity, strength, reflexes and a few other enhancements, but we have all been given specialty traits unique to each individual. I am enhanced with simian DNA to give me strength and flexibility. I'm PFC Katrina Jorgenson by the way."

A piece of a roll landed on the table in front of her. Raven looked down the table to see if she could spot who threw it. A blocky, muscular soldier was grinning at her. He offered Raven a cocky salute with the hand holding the other half of the roll.

"When you get tired of hanging out with the monkeys, you could always come hang out with us." His grin split his round face and reached his eyes.

Fitch picked up the bread and chucked it back to him. "Shut up, dog. No one wants to hear your barking."

The soldier laughed and shoved the rest of the roll in his mouth. He grabbed his tray from the table and marched to the depository. Raven watched as he dropped his tray on the conveyer and walked out of the cafeteria.

"Just ignore Flager." Fitch picked up his tray and the others followed suit. Raven gathered her own half-finished food and walked with the rest of them to the conveyer. "He was bred to be aggressive and assertive. If his type weren't imprinted with the predisposition to be pack animals there wouldn't be any cohesion in their unit."

Raven was exhausted by the time she made it back to her barracks. She barely noticed the two women she had sat with at dinner were also assigned to her quarters. They smiled at her as she past them, toothbrush in hand. Pulling down her hair from the quick knot she had tied it into after her shower she fluffed it out to let it dry, then brushed her teeth before making her way back to her cot. She wanted to plug her headphones in and listen to her music as she drifted off, but since it was against regulations she settled for quietly humming a few bars of Beethoven's Moonlight Sonata. The rhythm soothed her to a deep, dreamless sleep.

Chapter Four

THE SUN WAS JUST CRESTING the hills as Raven finished her run the next morning. She barely had enough time to shower, pin her hair up and dress before she had to report for duty at the hospital. She didn't want to give herself any lag time before her shift started so she wouldn't have to think about it. The glass doors of the hospital beckoned and she couldn't put off entering any longer. The whisper of the doors opening preceded the overwhelming antiseptic odor Raven knew was omnipresent in every hospital. The aroma could never disguise the odor of death permeating the halls. Raven took a deep breath of fresh air before entering the brick building.

The feeling was different. Raven was used to the brightly lit halls and pale painted walls of Haven. Children born at Haven were brought into a gentle, quiet environment, so different from the world they were created to defend. The noise of this hospital was completely different from Haven. Low moans and deep-throated cries came from behind white-draped curtains. Raven was used to walking down halls full of screaming women and crying babies. Voices much higher pitched than the ones she was hearing now. She was used to treating wounded soldiers, but that was during her medic training over two years ago. Treating wounded adults was much different than delivering and caring for infants.

The clock above the nurse's station showed 0555 hours. She had five minutes before she had to report for duty. The duty nurse looked up and smiled as Raven approached.

"Lieutenant Taylor, we've been expecting you." The nurse's smile brightened her face. "Captain Garcia is waiting for you. Follow me."

The nurse led Raven to a cramped office tucked in the corner of the hospital. A Captain was sitting behind a desk, reviewing medical records. The nurse turned and walked away, leaving Raven by herself to meet the doctor. Raven stepped into the room and stood at attention, offering the man behind the desk a crisp salute.

" Lieutenant Taylor, at ease. Come in and take a seat." He motioned to one of the padded chairs. "I want to go over a few things with you before I release you to your duties."

Raven moved to the chair across from the desk and sat, her back stiff and eyes forward on the Captain. He finished what he was doing on his data pad and set it aside.

"Taylor, I'm assigning you to the detention ward," he said, without any preamble. "We have the highest burnout rate with the orderlies and nurses on that unit and we need someone there with a strong background. I've reviewed your record and believe you have the skills we need for this unit."

Dr. Garcia stood and moved around the desk. He positioned himself so he was leaning on the corner of the desk, looking down at her. Raven recognized the strategic move for what it was, a position meant to put the other person at ease and yet still maintain the aura of authority by forcing her to look up at him. She doubted the Captain even realized what he was doing by the move.

"Sir, I don't know why you are sending me into the detention ward. I don't have much experience working with prisoners." Raven refused to be intimidated by this man. She looked steadily into his eyes without flinching.

"I've read your jacket, Lieutenant." Garcia's tone let Raven know she wasn't going to get away with any deception. "Your background as a resident of Haven has exposed you to both sides of this war. You have extensive weapons training and hand-to-hand combat experience. You have more medical experience than I do, even though you're a physician's assistant and I am a doctor, and you are compassionate and strong." He paused and locked eyes with Raven. "I'm surprised you opted to join the military instead of staying and taking over Haven. That facility is the safest place in the world right now."

Raven waved his comment off. She didn't want to think about the walls of Haven right now. "I want to help make the world as safe as Haven. My mother has things under control there. I'm needed here."

Garcia nodded and picked up a data pad from the desk. "I'm putting you in charge of the detention unit. I'm glad we can take advantage of your skills while we have you. I'm putting you in charge of the toughest unit in this hospital. I need you to clean house." He handed her the pad. Glancing at it she saw it was loaded with data about the detention unit.

Raven stiffened in her seat, already anticipating problems with the others under her command once she took over the unit. She was young to be a Lieutenant and she knew it. There was a certain sense of bitterness in her mind when she thought of her officer's training. It was four weeks she spent away from Billy not long after they were first married. At the time it seemed like a good idea. The two of them figured she could get the training out of the way and work as an officer in the army hospital and he could do a couple tours before coming home and going through the training himself. A few weeks apart in their lifetime together. She could feel her throat tighten as she thought of him. Shaking her head to dispel the tears before they could betray her, she cleared her throat and swallowed hard.

"I'm not looking forward to this." She held up the data pad containing the stats of the detention unit. "I thought my tour of duty would take me in a different direction. I specifically requested non-medical duty."

"I'm sorry to disappoint you, Lieutenant." Garcia moved back to his position behind the desk. "We need you here. Take some time to look through the information on the data pad. The duty nurse is expecting you at 0700 hours. He'll orientate you to the floor. Your duties are outlined in the data pad. You're dismissed, Lieutenant."

Raven stood, offered another salute and walked out of the office. The detention ward was segregated from the main floor of the hospital. As she walked through the long, narrow halls leading to the locked double doors she tried to clear her mind from thoughts of Billy. The records describing how he died were sealed. All she knew was he was injured in the line of duty, evacuated to a M.A.S.H. unit and died on the operating table. She had no way of knowing if there was a compassionate nurse holding his hand as he died or if he passed from this life empty and cold. Her eyes tightened with unshed tears.

She paused for a moment before she turned the corner to enter the unit. Pushing all thoughts of Billy aside she approached the guards standing on either side of the door. Both men snapped to attention and saluted. Raven acknowledged the salute before she offered her palm to be scanned. The light on the monitor flashed from red to green and the doors slid open with a hiss. Raven stepped into the alcove separating the detention unit from the rest of the hospital. The doors behind her closed, leaving her facing a second set of white doors. She could feel the hum of the magnetic lock sealing the doors behind and in front of her. Placing her hand on the locking mechanism of the second doors, she waited while the scanner read the micro-chip in her palm and the DNA sampler analyzed her sweat. It only took a few moments for the scanner to acknowledge her and for the doors to slide open.

A heavy weight seemed to press down on her shoulders and settle in her chest as she stepped through the entrance and into the ward. The antiseptic aroma couldn't disguise the stench of festering flesh and unclean bodies. Raven couldn't identify exactly where the stench was coming from, but there was no doubt the patients were not receiving care up to needed standards. As she approached the nurse's station she passed three orderlies standing near the wall. Their eyes followed her as she moved past, causing the muscle between her shoulder blades to tighten into a knot. She placed her data pad on the nurse's station and ran her hand across the surface of the desk. Despite the clean appearance she could feel a dusty, sticky residue. She gestured to the orderlies standing by the wall. As they sauntered over she realized they lacked the bearing of military personnel. The three men stood in front of the station, staring at her with slightly blank expressions. She held up her sticky fingers so they could see the grime.

"This unit is not even close to being up to code," she kept her tone low and steady. "I want maintenance up here now. We are going to clean this unit from top to bottom."

The men's eyes narrowed and lips pursed, eliminating the blank expressions. One of them stepped forward, his black eyes flashing a challenge. The man was a few inches taller than Raven. He was lean and wiry and his cheekbones and chin cut a fine line in his chiseled features. If it wasn't for the flash of anger in his eyes he would have been extremely handsome. He put his hands on the desk and leaned across, apparently attempting to stare her down. Raven mirrored his posture and stared right back.

"We keep this facility up as best we can. The military hired us as private contractors to run this place." The hair on his knuckles stood on end as he balled his hand into a fist. "We're short-handed and trying to keep these insurgents contained takes most of our time."

Raven leaned forward; putting her face so close to his she could feel his hot breath against her cheeks. "You will get a crew up here and you will get this unit scrubbed from top to bottom, starting now!" Raven didn't change the tone of her voice, but she knew there was no doubting the intensity of her instructions. "I can smell the stench of infection in here. I run this facility now and if you want to keep your jobs you will follow my orders. I want to meet with all the department heads from all shifts in my office in one hour."

The man made a sound in his throat, indicating he was about to interrupt. Raven held up a finger.

"One hour." She picked up the data pad and held it steady in front of her eyes, trying to maintain a dismissive stance. It was a posture she observed her mother use when she was asserting her authority. It took a few moments for the men to realize she wasn't budging. She could hear them grumble as they walked away, but had no doubt she would have all the department heads in the conference room in less than an hour.

The huge oval table took up the biggest portion of the conference room. Seven people were seated in the black padded chairs and each watched as Raven took her place at the head of the table. She looked over each of them before she spoke. Four women and three men, all significantly older than her. She wasn't worried, though. She had grown up hearing how her mother had been in charge of an entire team of researchers before she was twenty. Raven was a year older than her mother was when the first outbreaks of genetically altered plagues were released by terrorists. Being in charge of one medical unit would be nothing compared to what her mother did.

Raven pulled information from her data pad and projected it onto the screen behind her. Highlighting details, she turned to the crew sitting around the table. She could see the reactions on their faces as they read the information she displayed. They were all shifting uncomfortably, refusing to make eye contact with her. A quick tap on the pad brought up the statistics Raven wanted to show everyone.

"I have never seen such an abysmal mess as the information I see here." The group continued to squirm. "There is no reason to have this high rate of staph infection. There are bed sores and restraint injuries on almost every patient. It's unacceptable to have patients in this condition."

One of the women, a petite blond, leaned forward. Her lipstick made her mouth look like a red slash across her pale features. "We do the best we can with the resources we have." Her voice was high pitched and nasal, grating on Raven's nerves.

"Then get better resources." Raven was accepting no excuses. "I am not going to run a hospital where people end up sicker inside than they were on the outside."

"These criminals are enemies of the United States." This time it was one of the men. His florid face seemed to radiate his anger. "They take enough of our resources as it is."

Raven stood to forestall the man's tirade. "Kevin Terimen, is it?" The man nodded. "You're fired. Security is waiting outside the door to escort you off the property."

Kevin stood and attempted to stare Raven down. She held her ground, but kept her finger above the icon on her pad, prepared to push it and call the security force standing guard just outside the door. The man's face changed from red to white and back to red before he expelled an explosive breath. He turned without saying a word and stomped out of the room. Raven almost released her breath in a gasp, but she realized the others in the room were looking at her. She pulled up the list of duties she had organized on her pad and displayed them on the screen.

"We will be having trainees from the units coming in to help with these duties. Each of you will be assigned a crew and you are to make sure they are doing their jobs, if you value yours." Raven looked around the table at her remaining staff. As her eyes paused on each one they glanced away. "Your duties are all outlined and will be sent to your data pads within the hour. You're all dismissed."

The remaining six staff members filed out of the room. None of them looked back at her. Raven waited until the door closed behind the last one before she sat down. She could feel her hands shaking and she hid them under the table in case one of them came back in unexpectedly. Taking a few deep breaths, she turned her focus to her data pad. The information scrolled past: lists of patients with staph infections, lack of basic immunizations, diseases running rampant through the cesspool of a ward. Raven placed the data pad in her jacket pocket and pushed herself away from the table. It was time to get to work.

Chapter Five

RAVEN SLID THE CURTAIN BACK revealing the emaciated form of the boy on the bed. Soft restraints were buckled to his wrists and ankles, tying him to the bed. His muscles were slack and his eyes were closed, but Raven could tell he was awake. The muscle in his cheek was twitching and his eyelids were squeezing together too tight. She closed the curtain and slowly approached the shivering form of the boy. The stench of sweat, blood and other bodily fluids assailed her nostrils as she approached the bed. Yellow rings on the sheet attested to the other odors she smelled. Raven placed her hand on the boy's arm and he flinched away without opening his eyes. She leaned down close to his ear.

"Joseph," his eyes closed even tighter. "Joseph, I know you can hear me. I'm here to help."

A tear glistened in the corner of his eye just before it rolled down the side of his face, moistening his hair. Raven used a washcloth to gently wipe the dampness away. The cloth came away covered in grime.

"Joseph, I'll be right back. I want to go get some clean sheets and some water." Raven placed the washcloth on the bedside table. "I am going to give you a proper bath."

Raven checked the IV drip before leaving the curtained area. She pulled up the boy's medical chart on her data pad before walking back to the nurse's desk. An aide was scrubbing down the desk, her face screwed up in a scowl. The girl looked up as Raven approached.

"Why is that child strapped to the bed?"

"It's protocol. All prisoners are to be strapped to the bed to protect the safety of the staff." The girl went back to scrubbing the counters.

"He's a child and he's nearly starving to death." Raven spoke in a low, even tone. There was no way to disguise her anger. "His restraints are to be removed and, unless he shows he is a credible threat, they are to stay off."

The aide stared at her, her mouth hanging slightly open. She had stopped wiping the counter and the rag was hanging limp in her hand. "We can't do that," her voice was a hoarse whisper. "Liability—"

"I'll take responsibility," Raven interrupted. "Go get a couple of basins of warm water and some clean linen. Meet me in his room. We need to give him a bath."

Raven had removed the buckles and straps from Joseph's wrists and was moving down to his ankles when the squeal of the curtain announced the arrival of the aide. The girl was pushing a cart with basins of water and a stack of white towels, sheets and bedclothes. Captain Garcia followed close behind.

"How's it going, Lieutenant? He moved to Joseph's other leg and started to work the buckle loose. "I understand you're shaking things up here."

"You did put me in charge of this ward." Raven didn't take her eyes off the restraint she was trying to unhook. The leather was stiff and Joseph's ankle was swollen under the padding. She was gently turning the limb to alleviate the pressure. The buckle sprang open and Raven removed the leather band and massaged the red marks on the boy's ankle. Joseph still hadn't moved. The aide was moving the water basin from the cart and placing it on the bedside table. Sliding it across the table caused the water to soak the edge of the bed and splash down Raven's scrubs. The girl froze, staring at the growing dark spot as it spread down Raven's legs. She pulled her hands away from the basin and stepped back as Raven made eye contact with her. Raven took a deep breath and looked at the young boy on the bed. He had finally opened his eyes as he flinched away

37

from the pool of water. Raven moved up to the head of the bed and put her hand on his shoulder. He looked up at her, fear humming in his eyes.

"You may go," she said, without looking up. "I'll take care of this young man."

She heard the footsteps of the girl as she backed out of the room. Captain Garcia slid the curtain closed and approached the bed again.

"Let me help you," he said. "I haven't given a bed bath since medical school, this'll be good practice."

The pain in Joseph's eyes bore into Raven's soul, beating past the defenses she had built around her heart. As she set up the clean bed linens and bath supplies she started humming a low, rhythmic chant deep in her chest. Even though she was wearing vinyl gloves she could still feel the warmth of the water flow over her hands. As she brought the cloth to his face she expected him to pull away, but he didn't move as she gently washed the tear streaks off his cheeks.

She put her face close to his ear. "Close your eyes," she whispered. "I'm going to put a warm cloth over them. It will help soothe the burning."

He followed her prompting with ease, rolling when she asked, lifting limbs and offering them to receive her ministrations. The entire time Raven chanted under her breath. A simple rhythmic chant she learned years ago from her grandfather. Joseph seemed to respond to the chant, the beat of his pulse slowing as she continued the care.

When she was done, and Joseph was swathed in clean linens, she raised the head of his bed and adjusted his blankets. The water in the basins was grey from the dirt she had removed from his body, but he seemed to shine. His pale skin was slightly pink where it had been scrubbed and his white-blonde hair stood up in straight stalks around his head. Garcia watched her the entire time she was tending him, quietly following her directions.

Joseph's eyes were closed, the muscle in his check relaxed. Raven placed the call light in his hand. "Joseph, if you need me, push this button. I will come right away."

The boy opened his eyes and looked at her. Raven could see he was assessing to see if he should believe her. She brushed her hand down his arm, feeling the smooth skin.

"I don't care what time you need me. I'll leave orders for them to call me any time."

Joseph relaxed back on the bed and closed his eyes. Raven smoothed the bedding one more time and followed Garcia out of the curtained area. After they both washed their hands they walked to the nurse's station together. Raven inspected the now clean surface. Running her hand over the counter, she felt for any residue.

"It's better. We need to get work crews in here to clean and repair some of the wards."

Raven pointed to some peeling tiles and dirt-encrusted corners.

"This ward has the highest infection rate of any ward in the hospital," Dr. Garcia picked up her data pad and scrolled through the information. "I like your plan to bring soldiers in here to clean and make repairs. As long as we can keep the soldiers and the prisoners segregated we should be fine. Most of the prisoners are just desperate, hungry men, trying to do what is right for their families."

Raven took her pad and pulled up Joseph's file. There wasn't much there, just the information she had been able to extract from him while they were on the road. There was a first name, an approximate age and a medical history consisting of a report on malnutrition and parasites found in his body. It appeared he had dodged the bullet so far on any of the Big Five, the mutated plagues the terrorists had released over twenty years before and were still rearing their heads in various populations. Raven looked up to find Garcia studying her expression. She handed him the data pad.

"Why don't we have any more information on this boy?"

Garcia scanned through the information on the data pad. "It's more information than we have on many of these patients in here." He leaned forward, resting his hands on the desk. "Most of the prisoners refuse medical care. The only time we can get them in here is when they are so far gone they can't object. Even then we sometimes need to go into the cells, past their friends, and drag them out. This detention center is a holding station for prisoners being shipped to Texas or Ohio. We don't have the resources to care for them long-term. Until the prisoners are processed through the system we have no way of identifying them. Most of them are ghosts in the system. They were born into political groups with no ties to the government. No birth certificate, social security number, no record they exist anywhere." Garcia shook his head. "There are too many of them. We don't have the man power to take care of them all."

"I don't know how much help I'm going to be." Raven placed the data pad on the now clean nurse's station. "I'm headed to Afghanistan in a few months. It's going to take that long just to get the facility up to standards. How did it get so bad?"

"No budget, no manpower, turning the facility over to private companies." Garcia rested against the station. "I was hoping you could use some of your influence to bring in more resources."

Raven knew exactly what influences he was asking about. Despite her mother's civilian status she had more power and influence than many of the high-ranked officers Raven had worked with over the past few years. Everyone knew who her mother was, so Garcia's comment wasn't unexpected. Ducking her head, she stifled a sigh. She wondered what Garcia wanted. Requests usually ranged anywhere from asking her to help get wives and children inside the protective walls of Haven to opening supply lines or finding black market drugs. Her mother's work was omnipresent in Raven's life. It seemed she couldn't get out of the shadow of Haven's walls.

"My mother does not have unlimited supplies at her disposal." Raven tried to keep the bitterness out of her voice. "Haven is self-sufficient, but its resources aren't infinite."

Garcia leaned forward and lowered his voice. "What we really need is manpower. I know Haven has a huge staff of medical personnel. We just need your mother to send a few of them here. We can protect them. The only attacks we've had here are on the supply warehouses. None of the attacks have been able to penetrate the inner sanctum and the hospital. Please, just talk to your mother."

Raven stayed silent for a few minutes. She kept her eyes downcast to avoid looking directly at Garcia. Her mind ran through the women and children of Haven. Her mother had managed to keep the facility safe for the past five years, despite the turmoil roiling around the walls. Very few people made it through the security barrier to attack the facility since Grey brought his surrogate program to the grounds. The facility housed nearly three thousand people, most of them women and children. Another two thousand lived in the surrogate barracks on the perimeter of the grounds.

Raven picked up the data pad before looking up at Garcia. She closed out of Joseph's medical record as she met the Captain's eyes.

"I'll talk to my mother," she said. "Haven is tightly regulated. She may not be able to send anyone out."

"We have a number of women here who were being held captive by the insurgents." Garcia said. "They need a safe place to stay and heal from their injuries. I was hoping we could send them to your mother to replace those she would be sending here." He pulled a file up on the pad. "Look here, my plan is all outlined. My request has been approved by the Colonel. All I need is for you to talk to your mother. It would solve a lot of problems if she approves."

Garcia smiled as if he had just won a battle. "I'm getting back to my rounds. Let me know what your mother says."

He turned and walked away before Raven could respond. She watched the white tails of his jacket disappear around the corner before she picked up the data pad and scrolled through the list of about a hundred names Garcia provided. Raven had no doubt her mother would want to accept these women into the already overflowing walls of Haven. She wondered if her mother would be willing to let any of the women at Haven go. Some of the travel restrictions had been lifted over the past five years and residents of Haven had been able to leave and a few women had entered the program. Studying the list of names in front of her, Raven tried to picture how each of them would fit into the world of Haven.

She tucked the pad into a pocket of her lab coat and started her rounds. Most of the men tied to the bed were in advanced stages of illness. As Raven crossed into the cordoned off areas separated by dingy, white curtains she was assaulted by the odors of rotting flesh and bodily fluids. The men and women in the beds all looked at her through glazed, drug-shadowed eyes. Raven knew she didn't have the time to give them all the care they needed.

Twenty-seven patients altogether, including Joseph and two others injured during the failed raid on the convoy. All the patients' records, except the new admissions, showed secondary staph infections manifesting after they were admitted to the hospital. Raven was standing outside the last curtain, reviewing the patient's chart when Garcia found her again. His lips were curled into a slight grin as he approached

"Hey, I just wanted to let you know I talked to Colonel Egan about bringing in some units to get this hospital cleaned and arranging transport of the women to Haven." He said. "We can't have the prisoners in here while the cleaning is going on, but I think we can double up prisoners and if we're creative we can find space for them while construction is going on. We should be able to transfer the women early this week, if your mother okays it."

The smile he gave Raven was pregnant with expectation. Raven finished sealing the patient record and put her pad away before looking up to meet Garcia's eyes. She repressed her sigh before she answered.

"I'll talk to my mother." Garcia's smile got even bigger. "I can't make any promises. My mother is very protective of her women."

Garcia didn't seem to hear anything past the promise Raven made to talk to her mother. He patted her shoulder before turning and walking back down the hall. Raven took a deep breath and started humming as she entered the curtain. She found by humming she was able to control her respirations and she didn't have to breathe deeply and smell the putridity of the patient's odor.

Chapter Six

RAVEN DROPPED ONTO HER COT and buried her head in her hands. She smoothed the stress from her temples and forehead, trying to force her headache away. Garcia was expecting her call her mother and she decided it would be better to call now rather than wait for morning. She liked to get her exercise out of the way first thing in the morning because she was always more alert after a run and, not wanting to feel rushed in the morning, she reached for her pad and dialed her mother's personal connection. Her mother's eyes looked tired when she answered, but Raven noticed her smile was warm and full of love. She couldn't help but reciprocate the smile as her mother greeted her.

"Raven, I am so glad you called. I wasn't expecting to hear from you so soon." Savanna sat back in her chair and Raven saw she was holding Lakota in her arms. Although her mother said she wasn't expecting her to call so soon Raven knew if she didn't check in at least once a week her mother would be calling and harassing her. "I thought you would be so caught up in your training you wouldn't be able to call for at least another week."

Raven swallowed back the question bubbling on the tip of her tongue. It was too soon to ask about her child. He couldn't have changed much in two days. Looking past the dark hair on the tiny head, Raven studied her mother's eyes.

"Hey, Mom." Raven sighed and relaxed back on her cot. She had about half an hour before anyone came in from maneuvers, but she wanted to hurry so the conversation wouldn't be overheard. "I wasn't expecting to call so soon either. Some things came up, though. I think you need to hear this."

Raven outlined the situation Garcia had presented, forwarding the list of names Garcia had given her directly to her mother's private link. Savanna's brow furrowed as Raven talked and the concern was apparent on her face. Lakota started to fuss and Savanna turned to the baby, breaking eye contact. Raven looked at the top of her mother's head while waiting for her to calm him. It only took a moment to calm the infant and her mother turned back to the screen. Raven could see the softening around the edges of her mother's eyes when she looked away from the baby, but they were still hooded with concern.

"Raven, this is a big order." Savanna's voice was rich with concern. "You know how crowded Haven is right now and I'm not sure there are many women here willing to leave the safety of these walls. I don't want to expose them to any unnecessary dangers." The hesitancy in Savanna's voice came through, despite the lowered tone intended to soothe the infant.

"I know," Raven moved so she was cross-legged on the cot, placing her data pad in front of her. She hated having her hands restricted as she subconsciously signed to punctuate her speech. She probably wouldn't be having this conversation with her mother if she hadn't stopped by the fenced-off enclosure holding the women and children held captive by the insurgents. "Mom, we need to get these women and children out of here. There's no room to house them. They can't be mainstreamed and the enclosure they are kept in is little better than a horse barn. They won't survive the winter."

Concern flooded her mother's eyes. Lakota disappeared below the screen and Raven realized her mother was putting down the baby so she could pull up Haven records.

"Send me the records of the women and I'll see what I can do," Savanna said.

Raven knew the problem was off her shoulders now. Her mother would take over and the women and children would be at Haven within the week. Rubbing her face, she tried to push exhaustion away. It didn't work.

"Raven, you need to sleep." The tone of Savanna's voice let Raven know she wasn't fooling her mother. She lifted Lakota into the frame and directly into Raven's line of sight. "Say goodnight to your son."

Not trusting her voice, Raven signed "I love you, my son."

"Raven, take care of yourself." Savanna's voice was gentle, soothing. "I love you."

Raven knew her voice wouldn't pass the lump in her throat, so she signed her farewell. Her mother's smile was tired and Raven didn't want to see the pain in her eyes any more. She signed off, hoping her mother didn't see the longing in her own eyes. Her arms and legs felt robotic as she went through the motions preparing for bed. She crawled under the rough cotton sheets and pulled her blanket around her shoulders hoping to get to sleep before the rest of her team returned from maneuvers.

Raven didn't even realize when she drifted off to sleep, but revile startled her awake in the early morning hours. The rhythm of the trumpet caused her heart to palpitate as she sat up on the edge of the cot. Taking a few deep breaths, she slowed the pounding in her chest and stood and stretched. All around her the other women assigned to her unit were rising and stretching as they prepared for their morning routine. PFC Jorgenson smiled at her from across the room. Raven realized she hadn't spent much time with the members of her unit, something she knew she needed to do to build the trust relationship necessary to be an effective unit. Working in the hospital was taking her away from training maneuvers. She hoped it wouldn't take long for arrangements for more staff members to be transferred from Haven. As she pulled on her shoes for her morning run she noticed Jorgenson was pulling on hers. It was still an hour before muster and chow. A silent nod across the room was the only invitation Raven needed to give for the long, lean woman to cross the room and address her.

"Taylor, we've wondered where you've got off to. Have you permanently transferred to the hospital?" Jorgenson asked.

Raven shook her head. "I'm just there for a few more weeks. I'll be back with you guys for pre-deployment training as soon as they get staffing from Haven."

"We were wondering if medical absconded with you." Jorgenson leaned against the locker at the foot of the cot as Raven squared the corner of her blankets and smoothed the surface to crisp perfection. "We wouldn't want to lose someone with your reflexes and instincts. I'll see you at chow."

The woman bounded across the room and made her cot so fast she seemed to be a blur. Raven tightened the laces on her shoes and headed for the track.

The quiet impact of rubber soles rebounding on the red clay track vibrated in Raven's ears. The cadence of the unit across the field carried and matched the rhythm of her footsteps. She wanted to race across the field and join the unit in their morning calisthenics, but she couldn't push herself to total body failure and still work a full twelve hour shift at the hospital. As it was, she stayed on the track until the first rays of sunrise burst over the mountains and the birds started singing their carol to the morning. She showered and made sure she had chow with her new friends before heading to the hospital for her shift.

Joseph was sitting up in bed attempting to spoon a liquid, white gruel into his mouth. His hand was shaking to the point most of the food was dripping back into the bowl. Raven pulled a chair to the side of the bed and sat beside him. Joseph's pale cheek turned slightly pink as Raven leaned in to speak. He didn't make eye contact. Raven smoothed the blankets around the boy and then gently removed the spoon from his hand.

"Let me help you with that," she said. "It's going to take a while to get your strength back."

"You were there, weren't you?" Joseph asked.

Raven had to lean in close to hear what he was saying. She knew what he was asking about, the only place he could be talking about.

"Yeah, I was there." She scooped up some of the gruel and held it up for Joseph to take a bite.

Raven could see the tears forming at the corner of his eyes. "It was my first battle. I was supposed to prove myself so I could enter the ranks." He ducked his head and turned away, forcing Raven to pause in her feeding. "I think my dad was killed. He was with the rocket launcher. The Elders told us it was too risky to attack a military transport, but we needed food. Military transports almost always have food and medical supplies. I wish my father listened to the Elders. I wish---"

Raven didn't need to ask what Joseph wished for. Too many people these days had the same wish. Food raids were becoming more prevalent as resources were stretched thin. She filled the spoon with more gruel and held it up. "As long as I'm here I'll make sure you have enough food."

Joseph turned and looked at her with a steady gaze. His blue eyes welled with tears, none of them fell. Raven was able to get him to eat a few more bites, but she could tell he was getting full and was having a difficult time forcing the food down. There were just a few lumps of white gruel in the bottom of the bowl when Raven finally stopped. She put the bowl on the bedside table and pushed it aside. Joseph was smoothing the blankets around him, not meeting Raven's eyes.

"Joseph, how old are you?" Raven asked.

He stopped fiddling and looked up. "I'll be sixteen this winter. We don't really keep track of exact birthdays. The elders tell us birthdates are one way for the government to keep track of us."

The boy's small frame and underdeveloped body mass had to be a result of malnutrition. Raven realized she would need to run some bone density tests and test for anemia. His tiny frame did not reflect his biological age. She couldn't help wondering what was going to happen to him when he was released from medical. The detention yard was little more than a jumbled pile of tents overcrowded with a sea of humanity. There was no doubt in Raven's mind Joseph wouldn't thrive in that environment.

"What about your mother?" Raven asked. "Does she know you were part of this attack?"

"Ma'am, I don't know. I mean, I don't know who my mother is." He was back to fidgeting with the blanket. Raven could see this line of questioning was making him uncomfortable. "We are not allowed to form emotional bonds with the women in the clan. All women are our mothers, our wives, our sisters. This way we're not tempted to hold back for one woman or another. When we bring food to the table it is for the good of all. Medicine is there for all to use, not just the one we love above the others."

So many questions flashed through Raven's head. She had never heard of a clan that did not survive without the traditional familial unit. There were many women who came through Haven from the tribal groups that had been formed in the past twenty to thirty years and yet all of them had some form of familial order, usually with the male as some sort of figurehead. Raven wanted to ask questions, but she realized this young boy had been through so much trauma drilling him would only add to his stress. She stood up and took the tray of leftover food.

"I'm going to order a few more tests," she said. "In the meantime I'm starting you on a high protein diet. We need to build your body mass. Have you been out of bed and walking around yet?"

Joseph blushed to the roots of his hair. "No, the nurses won't let me up. They say it's bad enough I'm untied from the bed. They---They made me use a bed pan." He refused to meet her eyes with this last statement.

Raven nodded her acknowledgement without speaking. She knew he was embarrassed and she didn't want to exacerbate the situation. "I'll let them know I want you up and walking around. We can put you in a private room for a while. We're going to need to for the cleaning anyway."

Raven carried the tray to the kitchen cart and slid it onto the track. She documented Joseph's intake and placed the order for his high protein diet. The aide Raven met the day before was walking towards the station carrying a stack of towels. Raven knew the moment the aide spotted her because the girl stopped in her tracks and started looking around as if to find the closest bolt-hole. Raven motioned for her to approach. The girl took a few tentative steps toward the nurse's station.

"What are you working on right now?" Raven asked.

The girl stuttered as she tried to answer. Raven held back a sigh, knowing any impatience would send the girl running. She waited a few moments for the girl to calm herself and answer.

"I'm bringing these to the shower room," the girl's voice still quivered, but at least she had stopped shaking. "The guards are bringing the men into the showers one at a time so they can get cleaned up while we strip their beds. The units are coming in tomorrow to start the deep cleaning and document needed repairs. We're still trying to figure out where to put all the prisoners while the cleanup is happening."

Raven allowed the girl to continue on her way. There was no use telling her what to do with the prisoners, as she wouldn't be here long enough to do anything. The women from Haven would be transported to the facility in two days. Raven was surprised by the response from her mother's facility. Once the women had been assured their safety and security would be seen to in this new facility many of them had volunteered to be a part of this new crew. Garcia was already planning his new work schedule and had given the agency staffing the hospital notice. A tension Raven had noticed when she first entered the hospital was beginning to dissipate, although there was a definite sense of resentment from many members of the staff. Raven was looking forward to the change in regime.

Chapter Seven

IT DIDN"T TAKE LONG FOR the women of Haven to settle into work at the base hospital. The structured work schedule of Haven melded perfectly with the expectations of the hospital. Raven was able to send culture swabs of patient infections as well as swabs from the floors, furniture, beds, curtains, walls and various other surfaces to be analyzed in Haven's lab. By the time Raven had been working at the hospital for a few weeks she had heard most of the patients' stories. The men talked of choosing a life of personal freedom and viewed the government as an enemy to liberty. Slowly, a picture of desperation began to form from the conversations with the men. They talked of living on the edge of starvation, of watching their women sacrifice food so their children wouldn't go to bed hungry. Each of them talked of losing loved ones to the plagues or the great machine that was the government.

It had been weeks and Raven was still assigned to hospital duty. The rest of her unit had started their pre-deployment training. She watched them file out of the barracks in the predawn hours and crawl back filthy, exhausted and ready to collapse long after dark. Her morning exercise routine was keeping her physically strong, but she knew she wouldn't be mentally prepared for combat. The newly implemented hospital staff was integrated into their duties and Raven was becoming increasingly frustrated with the slowly grinding wheels of bureaucracy. It seemed they had no problem transferring her where they think they needed her instantaneously, but when the need was no longer there she was stuck in red tape.

Cutting her morning run short, Raven headed to the hospital earlier than usual. She was hoping to catch Garcia before he started his morning rounds. A young nurse Raven recognized as a former resident of Haven was sitting at the main nurse's station. The woman smiled as Raven approached and stood to meet her.

"Raven, it's good to see you."

Raven nodded her acknowledgement. "Is Captain Garcia in his office?"

"He's doing rounds in the prisoner section." The woman pointed towards the dividing doors. "He said he wanted to make sure everything is in order. Some of the prisoners are ready to be transferred back to the cell blocks and he wants to give them one more physical."

Raven's heartbeat increased its tempo. She realized one of the prisoners making steady improvement was the young Joseph. Although the young man was improving, Raven wasn't sure if he would be strong enough to thrive in the overcrowded, unsanitary corral. The detention center was a temporary set up of tents and less than sanitary latrines and shower facilities and the thought of sending the young boy into the sea of humanity locked inside the chain-linked, razor-wired enclosure tore at her sense of well-being.

When the detention center was first established it was supposed to be a temporary holding cell, used to confine home grown insurgents until they could be put on trial for their crimes. The court system soon became clogged with defendants accused of terrorism and the temporary detention centers soon became long term holdings. Raven knew some of the prisoners had been encamped in the Corral, as it had been termed, for five years or more.

Raven took a deep breath and schooled her features before she went in search of Garcia. Joseph had been much on her mind lately and she realized it was more important for her to have a conversation with the Commander about him than it was to push her transfer back to the unit.

Despite her concerns she couldn't help but feel a sense of pride as she walked into the detention ward of the hospital. All around her was evidence of changes she was instrumental in implementing. Within the first week of taking charge of the unit the walls, floors and surfaces had been scrubbed and sanitized. Holes in walls had been repaired and painted with bacteria-resistant paint. Purified air now circulated through the unit, scrubbed clean by the air filters. Raven recognized all the workers in the unit. Everyone of them, even the ones who built and repaired the walls, came from Haven. There were still areas of the hospital under construction, but the main work had slowed as many of the builders worked on creating a barracks for the former residents of Haven. The miniature town built at the edge of the base was Savanna's idea. She had felt it would be safer for the hospital workers to have a secure facility near the edge of the base than to allow them to live in the town twenty miles away and transport in every day. The stone walls and iron gate built to contain the new buildings had already been erected and now construction was started on the long, low walls of the living structures that would mimic Haven's angular design on a much smaller scale. Plans were in the works to start construction on an underground tunnel that would allow hospital workers to travel from the enclosure of the barracks to the reinforced walls of the hospital. The only difference the new facility didn't have compared to Haven was the acres of fertile fields to grow a safe and stable food supply. However, Haven facilities were producing much more food than the shelter needed and Savanna had arranged to provide the new community food and supplies.

The atmosphere in the hospital was charged with a different type of energy than the one present when she had first walked through the doors a month before. Nurses and aides walked the halls with a sense of determination and purpose. The overwhelming odor of disease and decay was gone, replaced by the smell of antiseptic, fresh paint and sawdust. Women smiled at her as she passed, nodding their acknowledgement at her presence.

Raven picked up a data pad from the front desk and started scrolling through patient records. She pulled up Joseph's chart and looked at the latest round of tests. All the infections in his system had been cleared and he had put on nearly seventeen pounds. Technically he should have been released two days ago, but she had managed to keep him in the hospital, explaining his immune system had been compromised and he would be at risk for contracting another infection if he was released into the main prison population. Bed space was at a premium and she knew she wouldn't be able to keep him in very much longer.

She approached the corridor containing the curtain-cordoned section of the wing. Security guards roamed the halls, another addition since Raven took over. She refused to allow the prisoners to be restrained, so security personnel were now mainstays of the facility. At first they had brought in soldiers from the base to cover security, but after a few too many confrontations between the prisoners and the guards, Colonel Egan decided to try private security forces. Raven was instrumental in bringing in these guards as well. She told Egan about Travis' security personnel and the careful background checks he performed on all employees as well as the intense physical training they had to undergo, so Egan contracted with Travis to staff the detention center. All of the new security guards were well trained in non-lethal force, much the same way Travis trained her and the other members of Haven.

Raven marched down the hall with a determined gait, a habit she picked up from watching her mother. No one interrupted her when she walked towards Joseph's bed. The curtain was pushed back and she could see the bed was empty. Turning to see if there was someone at the nurse's station, she saw Joseph walking down the hall. His slightly bowed legs, a side effect of rickets, protruded from the bottom of his gown. The pale white legs had a slight down of hair shimmering in the light. Joseph grinned as he approached and it took a moment for Raven to notice the figure walking beside him. Garcia took Joseph's arm and guided him back to the bed.

"I just wanted to see how well he was walking. He seems to be pretty steady on his feet," Garcia said.

Raven could feel the heat on her cheeks. She knew she had been caught in the act and it wouldn't be long until Joseph would be in the corral with the other prisoners. Raven didn't speak until Garcia closed the curtain and they walked to the nurse's station. Garcia was looking over her charts, scrolling through the notes she had made about Joseph over the weeks.

"I know he is ready to be released. I just can't see putting him in the detention center." Raven kept her voice low, but she could feel the power behind her words. "He's not like the others. The only reason he was involved in the attack at all was because he was desperate for food."

Garcia placed the pad on the counter and put his hand on her shoulder. Raven was sure he meant to be reassuring so she tried not to cringe away from his touch.

"The courts have been petitioned to release him into the custody of the state." Garcia dropped his hand off her shoulder. "I am waiting to hear back from the lawyers next week. The court is trying to decide if they should try him as an adult. The problem we are facing is coming up with a place for him. Not many foster homes will accept a child with his background."

Relief flooded through Raven, filling her with a sense of peace. She had Garcia on her side. She couldn't help smiling a bit before she responded. Pulling up a file on her pad, she handed it to him.

"What would you say if I told you I know of a place for him?" she asked. "A place where he can live among the stars?"

"I'll turn this over to the defense attorneys. I'm sure the judge will be easy on him if he has a place to go where he can be watched and be safe." Garcia handed the pad back and smiled. "Oh, and one other thing. I know you are anxious to get back to your unit. I have the transfer orders on Colonel Egan's desk. You'll be back with them by the end of the week. You'll have to go in as their medic, just so you know. We can't waste all your medical expertise by allowing you to be a common foot soldier."

Tightening her grip on her pad, Raven ducked her head, attempting to hide the flash of frustration she knew crossed her face. The joy she used to feel as she was working as a nurse and later as a physician's assistant just wasn't there for her any more. She had helped fix Billy up when she first met him. He became healthy and strong and then he went to war and died. Helping at Haven and her mother's clinic in Garden City showed the effects of the devastating plagues still wreaking havoc on the world. Even here, in the medical unit of the hospital, soldiers missing fingers, toes, even limbs or dealing with traumatic head injuries or PTSD spilled out of rooms and lined the hallways. Victims of the many conflicts scattered all over the globe. It seemed the entire world was at war and the hub of soldiers created to fight these wars ended up in her hospital. Raven walked past the white-sheeted beds every day making her way back to the detention ward. The eyes following her as she paced the halls seemed to be empty, as if part of their souls were missing along with parts of their damaged bodies.

After Garcia left, Raven typed a quick message to Travis, updating him on the situation. Travis had met Joseph, briefly, when he had first come to the base to assess the security needs for the hospital. Raven had filled her stepfather in on as much of Joseph's case as she could and explained her concerns for the young boy. It was in the initial conversations with Travis that Raven realized one of the reasons she was so concerned about Joseph was because he was so close in age to her own younger brother.

Her fears for Caleb's safety were transferring to Joseph. She couldn't imagine her brother being cold and hungry and fighting for survival with no one to help him. Caleb was healthy and strong, but he had never had to fight for his next meal or wonder if he would be attacked in the night for his jacket and blanket. Raven knew enough of these newly formed tribal bands to know survival of the fittest was one of their many mottos. Joseph had battle scars and physical ailments enough to prove he wasn't one of the most fit members of his tribe.

Hopefully things would work to her advantage, now. Travis had agreed to take Joseph if the courts released him. She would be able to keep her promise to make sure he always had enough to eat as long as she was watching over him. It seemed ironic that her mother and Travis had both become foster parents as a way to care for children and perhaps protect them when many of Savanna's own children were scattered to the winds. Now she was grateful Travis was so willing to help this lost child. The only question now was whether or not Joseph would accept the help. Raven hoped the courts were willing to be lenient on this child.

Chapter Eight

THE SQUEAL OF THE CURTAINS grated on Raven's nerves as she pulled them back. Even with all of the advanced construction her mother's work crews had put into updating both units of the hospital, there wasn't anything anyone could do about the distinctive high-pitched song of the privacy curtains. Joseph was relaxing on the bed, playing some sort of video game on the pad consol attached to a swinging arm of his bed. The volume was turned down low, but Raven could still hear the simplistic music chiming from the device, announcing his progress as he advanced levels. As soon as Raven crossed the threshold into the curtained off room he tapped an icon and the music stopped.

"You don't have to turn off the game, Joseph." Raven close the curtain and crossed to stand next to him. "I just want to do one last check-up. I received new orders today. I'm going back to my unit by the end of the week. It's a good thing we got you all fixed up; it looks like you'll be checking out about the same time I am."

Raven tried to keep her voice light and cheery. She knew a patient's mental status was as important to their physical well-being as their health. He had been through quite a few upheavals in his life lately and she was concerned about Joseph's reaction to this latest change. As she predicted it didn't take long for his face to change. She could tell he was trying to fight back tears, his chin was quivering and his legs were shaking. Raven placed her hand on his shoulder noting, with some degree of satisfaction, she could no longer feel the bones through his skin.

"Hey, I have some good news." Joseph's eyes didn't quite meet hers and Raven hoped he was listening. "Do you remember my stepfather? He came in a couple of weeks ago. He's agreed to take you in as a foster child. He's been a foster parent for a while now.

It's one of the ways we were able help some of the youngest members of Haven. I know it's kind of strange, not being with your real mom and dad, but I can promise you living in the star house is an amazing experience. My brother loves it there and it's where my mom grew up."

Raven allowed her voice to trail off since it seemed as if Joseph wasn't listening. She began her assessment of the boy, starting at his feet. The open sores on his feet had healed nicely, no scarring or deformities. His legs were still slightly bowed, accounting for an undocumented case of childhood Rickets. His weight gain was apparent from the now rounded muscles covering his bones. Raven was checking the wound track on his arm when he finally spoke. His voice was low, barely a whisper. Raven doubted she would have heard him if it wasn't for her subcutaneous cochlear implant.

"What's it like to have a mother?" His voice quavered a moment and Raven wondered if he even meant to ask the question. Her fingers paused briefly at the L5 vertebrae as she pondered the question. Her mother was such an integral part of her life, she didn't quite know how to answer. After a moment she continued her assessment of his spine. She had him roll on his back as she formulated her answer.

"My mother was a powerhouse." Raven didn't even know how to start describing the woman who took her on as an embryo and showered her with more than enough love to last a lifetime. "When I was young I didn't think there was anything my mother couldn't do. And when she joined forces with Travis those two were unstoppable. Even when she got hurt, she fought back so hard I don't think she ever gave up on anything. I know there is a certain amount of hero worship when I think about my mom, but she can do just about anything she sets her mind to. I just hope I can be half the woman she is." Raven felt a tightness in her throat and her eyes tingled from unshed tears. She had Joseph sit up and she tested his reflexes. "What about you, tell me about your mother."

Joseph closed his eyes and whispered his answers. "I don't know, we aren't allowed to know who our mothers are. We are taken away and given to a wet nurse at birth. Our mothers aren't even allowed to see us. When I was young, there was one woman. She was so kind to me, making sure I always had enough food, teaching me what to look for when scavenging, coming between me and the other boys when there were fights. But they sold her away to another tribe. They said she coddled us too much. They said if we showed too much compassion for only one person we would forget the tribe and we couldn't stand together as one. All we would be concerned about is protecting that one person. I always liked to think that woman was my mother. I would be willing to die for a woman like that."

Raven pulled her hands away from Joseph as he spoke. There was an intensity in his words, an intensity she usually only heard in her mother's voice when she was talking about defending Haven. She wondered if Joseph wouldn't be better off in Haven itself, but it was difficult for older children to assimilate into the structure of Haven, even with the support of a family. He just wouldn't fit into the shelter.

The day was almost done and Raven headed back to her barracks. There wouldn't be much time before the rest of her unit showed up and she wanted to take a look at her new duty roster before the others showed up. Starting Monday she was joining her unit in PT. She was looking forward to the intense physical training, although she still wasn't thrilled about being the medic for the unit. In addition to carrying her gun and fifty pounds of gear, she would also be humping a twenty-pound medic kit.

The meatball medical aspect of her job as a medic tied her stomach in knots. Grab and dash, get the patient stabilized, get them in the chopper, pray that they will be all right. It all rushed by so fast. In three days she would be starting drills with her unit. They were going to start looking to her for their lives. She could save them, or they could die. She could be the difference between someone's family receiving a message saying their loved one was injured but coming home or their husband, brother, sister, wife would be transported with full honors to be interred next to their great-grandfather in Arlington. She rolled over and punched her pillow. Burying her face in the soft form, she clenched her teeth to prevent any noise from escaping. She wanted to scream, but held back, only allowing silent, choking sobs to escape. After a moment she rolled on her back and stared at the ceiling. Blackness greeted her. Ashamed of her weakness, she tried to surreptitiously look around the room. Her enhanced vision allowed her to make out the huddled forms of her unit. None of them seemed to be awake. The heavy, even breathing attested to her companions' exhaustion. Confident no one had witnessed her outburst she rolled to her side, attempting to get comfortable. Matching the rhythm of her breathing to the woman on the cot beside her, she drifted into oblivion.

Sleep was a welcome reprieve over the next few weeks. Raven knew she was in top physical shape, had been since she was a child at Haven, but the physical training she endured to prepare for deployment pushed even her physical capabilities. Calisthenics until total body failure, ten-mile runs, live ammo drills, crawling through the mud in the rain, sitting staring at the wall in the blistering sun, locked in a cellar experiencing complete sensory deprivation, all as a way to prepare for any eventuality while deployed. She was getting used to the extra weight of the med-pack. Her unit was starting to look to her for their pains and minor injuries brought on by the intense training.

It was late afternoon and the unit was in full gear, hunkered down behind a hill. Raven could feel the sweat dripping from under her helmet as the late afternoon sun beat down on her head. Shale was raining down on her head, shattered by the live rounds being fired on the hillside behind them. Raven glanced at the man beside her. Fitch grinned at her as he slung his grenade launcher from his shoulder. A quick hand signal let her know his intentions and she signaled for the flank to offer cover as he made his way up the hill. The hand signals she had adapted from the primary language she learned as a child were becoming the primary method of communication with her unit when they were in close combat scenarios. She could hear the whipping of helicopter blades in the distance, but she knew they were too far away to reach the unit before they ran out of ammo. Fitch and his battle buddy crept as close as they could to the top of the hill. The battle buddy positioned the shield at the top of the hill. Fitch pulled himself up behind the shield, inserted his weapon into the launcher space and balanced his shoulder against it, allowing his battle buddy to drop a grenade in the chamber. A puff of smoke from the launcher announced the release of the grenade. The sharp ping of bullets striking the shield continued for a moment, then sudden silence shadowed the mountains. Whipping chopper blades washed them with biting grit as it flew by, but the backup was too late. Already ear pieces were buzzing with orders for all units to return to base.

It was difficult to keep the grin off her face as they rode back to the base. Looking around at the occupants of the truck showed a number of matching grins. Fitch could barely maintain his seat as he relived the final moments of the battle. He barely paid attention to the icepack slipping off his shoulder, stopping his chattering only long enough to push the pack back into place. Raven knew he was going to be stiff in the morning. The recoil of the launcher blast had pushed the shield into Fitch's shoulder, causing a massive hematoma to form. He would need to have an MRI of his shoulder to assess the damage, but at this point it didn't look like the injury was hindering his movements. He turned to Raven and winked at her.

"Great job out there, boss." He turned his body to face her. "I'd follow your orders any day. I had no idea the shield would work so well."

He pulled the shield around so Raven could see the front of the device. The concept of a personal shield was not new, but it was hardly practical to carry a large, heavy metal barrier into battle. This new device was designed to be lightweight and collapsible. A simple push of a button would cause the shield to expand enough to shelter two soldiers, as long as they crouched almost on top of each other. Today was the first time the device had been tested under live-round conditions. Raven had been chosen to lead the team in this exercise, a role she threw herself into wholeheartedly. As a medic she didn't have the opportunity to lead very often. She was expected to stay near the middle of the pack in a sheltered position, prepared to assist the injured if she was needed.

Raven glanced at the group huddled at the back of the truck. Flager was attempting to wipe blue dye from his hair with a dirty rag. Others were attempting to scrub splashes of blue and orange dye from their skin or uniforms. The dye markings showed the direct hit made by Raven's team. Flager glanced up and looked across the truck, meeting Raven's eyes. She was taken back for a moment by the anger flashing across his face as their eyes met. Her first instinct was to duck her head and glance away, but she realized as his eyes bore into her he was trying to show dominance. Raven stared steadily back and grinned before she looked away. Her group was laughing at something Jorgenson had said. Fitch started a short, barking victory cheer. Raven joined in the howl as the volume increased. Soon the truck was echoing with cheers and laughter.

Flager's group piled out as soon as the truck rolled to a stop. Raven and her crew were quick to follow. The unit lined up in formation as they exited. Raven took her place in line as her crew filed past, many of them patting her on the back and shoulder as they crossed behind her. Colonel Egan was approaching from across the grounds so Raven motioned them to get into formation. The sergeant called them to attention as soon as Egan took her position. Raven kept her eyes forward despite the energy and tension she felt emanating from the soldiers around her. Working hard to maintain a straight face, she watched as Egan scanned the unit. Egan's glance stopped when her eyes connected with Raven's. Giving a half grin, she gestured for the shield to be brought forward.

Jorgenson double-timed it forward and handed over the now-collapsed shield. Egan inspected the shield, running her fingers over the scratches and dents formed by the live rounds. "It looks like it passed."

Raven had to bite the inside of her cheek to keep from cheering. Behind her one of her teammates didn't have her self-control. A "Hooah" carried from the back of the rows of soldiers. Egan allowed the ripple of sound caused by the cheer to filter through the group. A few more of the soldiers gave the traditional chant while others expressed their emotions with disarticulated howls. Flager's crew didn't join in the chants. Raven could see them standing at the edge of the unit out of the corner of her eye. Despite standing at stiff attention, each member of the defeated team had an aura of dejection about them.

The training and discipline instilled in the soldiers soon took over and silence again reigned the field. Egan held the shield above her head.

"We have the tools to defeat our enemies." Egan's voice rang with passion. "You will be the army to bring peace to this land. Your hearts and your souls are dedicated to this fight. You have proven yourselves and it's time to prove yourselves in battle. Orders are in. You ship out in three days."

Her dismissal was drowned out by the cheers of the unit. Even Flager's crew joined in the sing-song chant.

Chapter Nine

THE WIND PICKED UP MINISCULE bits of sand, spun it around in a whirlwind and pelted Raven with stinging accuracy. A storm was coming out of the mountains, bringing in a wave of billowing sand. Tightening the cloth across her face, Raven ducked her head and headed towards the row of dun colored tents. Soldiers scurried between structures, tightening flaps and covering trucks and equipment. Raven bee-lined it straight to the medical tent. She needed to be inside to make sure there were plenty of supplies stocked.

The flap fell heavily as Raven entered the cavernous tent. Turning around she tied the flap closed, shutting out the winds. Sand still filtered in from outside, drifting around the bottom of the tent. Raven pulled a felt rug close to the opening and pushed the edge against the bottom of the flap. Reaching up she pulled the strings of another flap, this one from the top of the opening. Rolling it down to meet the felt rug, Raven effectively sealed the opening from incoming sand.

There was no way to completely seal the desert out of the tent. A fine dusting of sand sifted down, sprinkling her head and shoulders. Raven removed her helmet and unwound the shemagh covering her head and mouth. Using a bottle of water she rinsed her mouth and spit the water into a basin. Sand floated down and glittered in the bottom of the yellow, plastic bowl. Shedding her outer gear and dropping it into the laundry hamper freed her from the worst of the grit. She could still feel the scratching of the sand as it trickled beneath her collar and mingled with the sweat coursing down her back. A shower would be great right now, but in this desert water was a rare commodity. The best she was able to manage was a wipe down with a damp, disposable towel.

Pulling on a clean uniform, Raven changed into a clean pair of boots and tightened the laces. The felt carpeting grated against the soles, but at least it kept the spiders and scorpions out of the tent. Taking her hair down, she brushed as much of the sand out of the waist length mass as she could. She braided it and tucked and pinned it into a tight roll. It only took a few minutes to prepare herself for her duty shift, at least she looked prepared. She still didn't want to spend the next twelve hours on hospital duty and, with the way the storm was coming in, it was possible she would be locked into the hospital for the next three days. All the patrols had been pulled into the base and hatches had been battened down. No one wanted to be caught in 100 mile an hour winds hurling bits of sand capable of shredding skin from bone. Even desert nomads familiar with the climate of the region locked themselves down in this kind of weather. Arizona summers were tame compared to what Raven was experiencing in the Sandbox.

The tent enclosed a metal, sectional building. The structure offered a layer of protection from the sand. Raven's hard soled boots reverberated against the tile of the treatment room. This camp was semi-permanent so the expense of the tile floor in a tented enclose greatly out-weighed the cost of treating infections. The main drawback was the deep gouges in the tile caused by sand dragged in from the desert. A series of small robotic vacuums constantly buzzed around the floor, always underfoot, and there were always at least two privates on duty scrubbing and polishing every surface and piece of equipment free of any grit. As Raven past the first bed, the private clearing sand from a cleaning robot looked at her and smiled. An easy friendship had developed between Raven and the other members of her unit. The only person who rubbed her wrong was the big, beefy man who had thrown the roll at her when they first met. Even now, though, Flager had developed a grudging respect for her as everyone came to her for treatment of the minor injuries and complaints that seemed to develop as part of camp life and filled the time between major rushes of combat injury.

Scanning the patients in the beds as she past, Raven assessed them for any changes in breathing, skin color or restlessness. There were only five occupied beds-two soldiers with injuries from roadside incendiary devices and three local children recovering from multiple symptoms from the plagues. The children had been brought in by their mothers. Both women had succumbed to the effects of diseases, dying within hours of bringing their children. One of the women had the wherewithal to explain how they had all became sick before she succumbed to the illnesses and died.

She explained her tribe was part of a nomad group traveling from the desert to the city. They had been captured by a group of armed men and had been promised food and medicine if they agreed to hide two of their soldiers in the tribe and sneak them into the city. The elders of the tribe objected, but they knew if they refused the soldiers would slaughter the entire tribe. All the tribe members were told they would be vaccinated against the city diseases and were subjected to a number of injections they were told contained the vaccines. The soldiers travelled to the city with the tribe, but left when they were two days out of the city, leaving two rough young men behind. The children in the tribe admired their brash, wild ways and tried to emulate them. The young men would tell stories of the infidels. According to these boys, invaders from across the ocean brought more than just diseases of the body, they brought diseases of the mind. The young men told of the infidels' goal to convert, by words, the children of Islam to the God of Israel and if words wouldn't work they would convert them by the sword, for their souls to find salvation.

Before long the children were playing at a new game. The boy soldiers taught the children to find ways to touch the infidels. Calling the game the Sand Spider, the children were taught to lick the palms of their hands and sneak up on pale-faced soldiers and touch any part of the body. Bare skin was the preferable target, accruing the most points, while anything the infidel soldier might come contact with was worth a decreasing number of points. The women were suspicious of the game and wanted to put a stop to it, but fear of the boys' wild ways stayed their hands. After the tribe's visit to the city the two boys walked into the desert and disappeared. Within just a few days, the children of the tribe started to get sick. Not long after other members of the tribe began to exhibit symptoms of the city diseases the nomads had been warned about.

Raven had listened to the women explain in a strained, harsh voice that she and her sister knew there was no hope for the young children in the tribe. They knew the boys had exposed their children to the diseases with no thought to the suffering they would leave behind. The city wouldn't let the tribe back in the gates and no one would come near them to help assuage their suffering. With no other options, the tribe gathered together and headed to the desert. By the time they were found by an outlying patrol the two women and three of their children were all that was left of the tribe of nearly thirty.

The children were recovering, finally, after a few touch-and-go moments. Despite the traumatic loss of life, Raven was thankful she wasn't there when the members of the tribe first became ill. She remembered the haunted look her mother's eyes carried through most of Raven's childhood as a result of the loss of life from the genetically altered diseases. Now, in this hell on earth, thirty people lost their lives, their bodies left out in the desert. By now scavengers and sand had scoured their bones clean and scattered them throughout the desert. The unit commander reported the incident to the local authorities, but no one wanted to take responsibility for the sick children. Despite the treatments they received at the base clinic, the children were still considered carriers of some of the more resistant diseases.

Raven walked past the beds as silently as she could, an almost impossible task with the drumming of her boots against the floor. The two injured soldiers didn't budge. Morphine induced comas kept them asleep. All three of the children were sitting up in their beds; their dark eyes following Raven as she past. Taking foil-wrapped bits chocolate out of her pocket, she handed the bite-sized bars to the children. She could feel the soft edges of the quickly melting candy as the children quickly snatched them from her fingers. The children didn't seem to mind the slightly liquid consistency of the candy as attested to by how quickly it disappeared, except for a few slight traces of creamy chocolate on the tiny, dark faces.

The littlest one, a girl estimated to be about three years old, crawled out of the bed and followed Raven to her work station. Raven sat at the desk and pulled up the charts on the computer. She missed the touch screen capabilities of her data pad from Haven, but the delicate screens were not desert proof. She waited patiently for the details of the patient logs to come up as the tiny girl leaned on Raven's legs. In an unconscious gesture developed from working in the surrogate unit, Raven reached down and pulled the little girl onto her lap. The child nestled into Raven's chest and stuck her thumb in her mouth. Raven used her free hand to brush the child's hair out of her face.

It didn't take long to pull up the patient charts and assess their status. Nothing new or surprising. The two soldiers were scheduled to fly out the next day, or whenever the storm cleared, to connect with the transport to Germany and then back to the United States. As Raven was looking through the charts she could feel the child in her arms getting heavier. Before long the girl's breathing deepened and became the long, regular breaths of a sleeper. Raven kissed the top of the sleeping girl's head and carried her back to her bed.

The child woke as Raven pulled the sheet over her tiny body. She reached up and brushed Raven's cheek. Her finger lingered at the corner of her eye. Raven pulled the tiny hand to her mouth and kissed her fingers. Guiding the little girl's finger, she started the game.

"Eye?"

The girl used her other hand to point to her own eye.

"Eye," she repeated.

Raven pointed to the center of her face.

"Nose?"

Again the girl pointed to her own tiny nose.

"Nose." The child giggled and continued the game. Raven played along for a few minutes. As the little girl pointed to things Raven gave her the English word and followed it up with the same word in Sign. She had been trying to teach the children English, but each time she taught the children a new word she had been following the spoken word with the word in Sign Language. The children had been treating the learning as a game and had been picking up Sign much faster than English. Raven was finding herself relying on her other language more to communicate over the past weeks than she had in the past five years.

As she was playing with the child a med tech approached. The man handed Raven a pad with a medical chart displayed on the screen.

"It looks like her lungs are finally clear." Raven could hear the relief harmonizing with the exhaustion in his voice. "The other two are lucky they didn't get tuberculosis, too."

"I don't know how lucky they are. Smallpox is a harsh disease. I'm surprised this one survived both infections." Raven smoothed the blanket around the child and signed for her to close her eyes and go to sleep. She gestured for the tech to move away from the sleeping patients to give his report.

Raven heard the whistle of the wind and realized someone had braved the storm to enter the building. Moving to the nurse's station, she looked for the security screen showing the entrance. Fitch, her commanding officer, was shedding his outer layers and scrubbing the sand off his face. He flashed a grin at the camera before moving out of range to change his clothes. Raven knew she had a few minutes before he finished changing and making sure the entrance was sealed from the storm, so she moved to the storage room to check the stock of supplies against the record in her data pad. There was no way of knowing how long the storm would last. Moving from the supply tent to the hospital would be a dangerous endeavor for anyone to undertake and Raven wanted to make sure the hospital was well-stocked. The rhythmic tap of leather soles on tile announced Fitch's arrival and Raven moved to greet him.

Fitch was standing beside the oldest child's bed. The best estimate was the boy was six years old. He was the one who had provided the names of the three surviving children. His name was Hamasa and his sister was Asal. Raven assessed her age to be about four. The youngest, Marwa, was the one Raven was the most concerned about. Hamasa and Asal had contracted Smallpox, but were both recovering well from the viral infection. Test results showed they were free from any other infections despite Raven's suspicion the entire tribe had been exposed to more than one of the five plagues. In addition to Smallpox, Marwa had contracted tuberculosis. The double whammy of infections nearly killed the little girl. Every lifesaving drug Raven had administered in the battle had been developed by her mother. Watching the up and down struggle of the tiny girl as she fought for life gave Raven an even greater respect for her own mother. Raven couldn't imagine having to go through what she did with Marwa thousands of times, fighting a constant battle against disease.

Chapter Ten

RAVEN WAITED FOR FITCH TO leave the children's bedside before speaking. She kept her voice low, hoping Fitch would pick up the cue to stay as quiet as possible. He pulled a stool close to the station where Raven was working.

"Taylor, it looks like the children are doing good." His natural exuberance was tamped down, but Raven could tell he was excited about something. "I have news."

"I thought you might." Raven was used to Fitch's grand announcements. "Why else would you risk being trapped in the hospital during a wind storm instead of calling?"

"Well, I thought you would like to hear all this in person." Fitch's grin stretched across his entire face. "We found a place for Hamasa and Asal. There's an orphanage in Kandahar willing to take them."

Raven's relief was tempered with concern. No mention was made of Marwa and she had a feeling Fitch wasn't finished doling out his news. Looking over at the beds, she could see the patients were all resting, undisturbed by the quiet conversation. Fitch's eyes followed her glance and his gaze rested on Marwa. The smile faded from his features as he turned his focus back to Raven.

"We can't find placement for Marwa. The fear is she is still a carrier even though she is symptom free. There are a few TB hospitals willing to take her, but they are overcrowded and not the healthiest place for a three year old." Fitch shook his head, frustration carrying into his voice. "We're not equipped for this. We're a military base, not an orphanage. I know you have developed an attachment to the children, but we need to find a safe place for them."

"Marwa is no longer contagious." Raven struggled to keep her voice low. "We were able to treat her with the medicine we keep in case of accidental exposure. She will always have the antibodies in her system, but she can no longer infect anyone."

"I know that, you know that, but it is difficult to convince any of the relief workers of that," Fitch said. "It's hard when the victims of the war are so young."

"The worst part is they weren't civilians caught in the crossfire." Raven felt the catch in her voice. "These children were deliberately used as weapons and you're asking me to return them to the same people who exposed them to these diseases. I wish I could send them to my mother. She would take care of them."

"Captain, we're doing the best we can." He placed his hand on Raven's arm. "We're here to find the terrorists who released these diseases into the world and to shut down any labs. It's been over twenty years and not only are the labs still in operation, but the diseases are still being modified and spread throughout the world. Not everyone in this country is a terrorist. Many of them are normal people trying to live a normal life in an ugly world. The children will be safe in the hospitals and orphanages. Besides, your mother has done enough. I swear she has more connections than the President. I think she's been able to provide more vaccines and medicine for the inhabitants of this country than even the humanitarian groups across the border. Don't worry, Taylor, we'll find someone to take Marwa."

Raven nodded, tucking a loose tendril of hair behind her ear. She tried to focus on what her commander was saying, but her thoughts travelled to the humanitarian groups camped around the edges of the Afghanistan borders. It wasn't unusual for refugees to make their way across the border and find their way to these camps. Raven knew there was a camp set up about a hundred miles from the base, just across the Pakistani border. Refugees passed by all the time, trying to find the safest route to the border. Maybe she could slip Marwa into one of these groups. The child would have a better chance of survival across the border. Shaking the thoughts away, she focused her attention on her commanding officer.

"What's your other message?" she asked.

"I need you to lead a mission."

Stunned, Raven studied Fitch's face. He had to be joking. The unit had been at this base for the past year working to defend the border town that was a major export/import hub. The protection of this major artery was the main focus of this force.

He leaned forward, whispering even lower. "Report to my office at 0830. I'll give you the details then." He looked at the security screen, now showing a blur of sand. "I better get back to my office before the storm gets too bad. I'll get one of the med techs to let me out and reseal the opening."

Raven barely had the wherewithal to salute the Captain as he left. She waited until she was sure he was gone and then assigned tasks to the med techs and cleaning crew that would take them out of the main hospital wing. As soon as the room was clear she walked to the cabinet holding the microchip machine. The cabinet contained a palm-sized computer used to program microchips and insert them under the skin. It was used to replace microchips in soldiers due to loss of limbs. They also had permission from the Afghan officials to mark prisoners of war, and if any of the locals requested a chip they were authorized to mark them as well. Raven knew what she was about to do would be pushing the bounds of ethics but she couldn't stand the thought of sending Marwa into the sea of sand and never knowing what happened to her.

She sat at the nurse's station, holding the device below the lip of the desk. It only took a few moments to transfer Marwa's and the other children's medical information into the device. She slipped the machine into the pocket of her lab coat and walked over to

Marwa's bed. She looked around the room, making sure no one was watching.

As she lowered herself to sit on the edge of the bed the child woke up. Raven cupped the child's hand in hers, and with a quick motion she pressed the device to the meaty part of Marwa's palm and pushed the button. A click let her know the chip found a home under the child's skin. Marwa's lip quivered in response the pinch of pain. Raven wiped the tiny droplet of blood from the girl's skin and kissed the child's palm, soothing away the hurt. She kissed the girl's cheek and hummed a soothing whisper into her ear. It only took a moment to assuage the child's hurt and rock her back to sleep.

Raven cleaned the equipment and moved to the next child. Within minutes all three children's information was imbedded in the palms of their hands and recorded forever in the database. She would probably be reprimanded for her actions and a mark would be put on her permanent record, but it was worth it if it meant knowing what happened to the children. She cleaned the equipment and returned the device to the cabinet. Groans from across the room let her know one of the burned soldiers was waking up. Calling for one of the med techs to help her, she pulled on a pair of gloves, dragged the burn treatment cart across the room and lined up gauze and ointment to do a bandage change.

The tech pulled on a pair of vinyl gloves and prepared to help. He placed the virtual reality device over the soldier's eyes and pressed the on button. Raven carefully removed the bandages swathing the soldier's hands and arms. As gently as she could, she probed the deep burns, focusing on the joints on the fingers and wrists, looking for any sign of infection. The second and third degree burns seem to be infection-free, but Raven wasn't taking any chances. She spread the ointment over all the burnt skin and covered the injuries with clean, white gauze. Both soldiers needed skin grafts and reconstructive surgery, procedures beyond the scope of practice at this facility. The sand storms had shut down the medevac choppers, so Raven had to treat the injured soldiers with what she had. She gently removed the virtual reality device from the soldier's head. The young man blinked and gave a wan smile.

"Private." Raven whispered. "Can you tell me what your pain level is on a scale of one to ten?"

Raven leaned close to hear the whispered answer.

"It stings more than anything. My skin is tingling all over. I feel like I'm floating about six inches above my body."

"That's the morphine." Raven used a square of gauze to wipe drool from the corner of his mouth. "We'll have you on a chopper and out of here as soon as we can. In the meantime we're going to need to continue these bandage changes every few hours. I'll give you another dose of morphine in an hour."

Raven smoothed the blanket over the soldier before she removed her gloves and washed her hands. Hesitating slightly, she moved over to the second soldier. There would be no VR device for this soldier. Her night vision goggles had malfunctioned during the explosion and the resulting flash had burned her retinas. Burns covered her right arm, shoulder, neck and the entire right side of her face. Shrapnel from the explosion was so deeply embedded in her flesh there was no way for the surgeons to remove it in the meatball surgery suites. Raven was doing constant battle, fighting infection and trying to balance the pain threshold for the young woman. Too much pain medication and the woman would slip into a deep coma, one she probably wouldn't wake up from, not enough and the pain would overwhelm her bodily functions, putting undue stress on her heart and lungs.

It took nearly an hour to remove the soldier's bandages, clean the wounds, apply ointment and wrap her in new gauze. Despite Raven's attempt to be gentle, the soldier moaned in pain as the procedure was completed. Tears flowed from the woman's left eye. The right eye socket was so damaged the tear duct was unable to function. Raven squeezed a moistening gel into the woman's eyes before covering both with gauze. When she was finished the woman's head and torso were completely covered in white, filmy gauze, not the best covering for burns, but Raven had to work with what she had. Raven really hoped she would be able to fly these soldiers out the next day.

A med tech was leaning over Hamasa's bedside, whispering in a language Raven didn't understand. She realized he was speaking in one of the local dialects. Hamasa was responding, but didn't seem to understand everything the man was saying. Raven approached, drawing the attention of the tech. He smiled and stepped towards her, after gently ruffling Hamasa's hair. His file was one of the many Raven had studied when she was assigned to this unit nearly a year before. This tech, Corporal Salinger, had been raised in the surrogate program. Although they had never met, the common bond of being raised around the Haven complex was enough to help her develop a strong relationship that soon developed into a close friendship. Like many of the members of the unit, Salinger was specifically designed to be deployed to CENTCOM. His training included learning the many languages and dialects of the nations of people he in which he would serve. He was even genetically designed to look like a resident of the country, with dark features generic enough he would be able to fit into many of the tribes without even creating a ripple.

As Raven walked back to her desk an idea was percolating in her mind. If it worked out she may be able to keep the three children together. She guided Salinger back to the nurse's station, not wanting to disturb the patients with their conversation.

Raven pulled up a series of schematics on her data pad. There was a hundred miles of desert between the base and the Pakistan border. A path fraught with danger from the elements and insurgents. She knew there was a man in the village who transported refugees across the sand in his beat-up, gasoline-powered truck, for a price. These refugees were desperate enough to do anything to survive. She thought about what these people needed most; what would they accept in exchange for saving these children. Locked away in a footlocker in her room were bags and bags of dehydrated and freeze-dried food. Her mother sent her care packages frequently. Packages filed with more food than she could ever eat. With this food and some water all she would need was a little money, just enough to bribe the border guards. Enough to give whomever took the children the chance at a new life.

Raven knew she had enough money to cover the children's escape. The military always made sure soldiers received some of their pay in local currency, hoping soldiers spending money in local marketplaces would stimulate the economy and facilitate feelings of goodwill. Raven didn't spend much money in the local village and had developed a substantial bundle of coins tucked in the corner of the locker. Once the children were across the border into Pakistan it would be easier to bring humanitarian aid to them, as long as they could be found again.

She gestured to Salinger she would be back in a moment. Salinger had picked up quite a bit of the sign language Raven had been teaching the children. He had a real affinity for languages. Raven opened the video device on her pad and walked to the children's bed. She filmed each one of their sleeping faces, lingering a few extra moments on Marwa.

Returning to the desk, Raven glanced at the security screens. She knew there was a camera right above the nurse's station. If she discussed any of this here she would be in trouble. There were a couple of places in the building without cameras. People would think it was strange if she brought one of the male med techs into the bathroom. She realized the showers in the prep room didn't have a camera and with the storm raging outside it would be difficult for the microphones to pick up voices. Raven motioned for Salinger to follow her.

"We need to clean the showers and make sure the towels are put in the laundry." Even though it was said in a whisper, there was no mistaking her tone. Salinger stood at the order. Medics tended to pitch in when the cleaning staff was overwhelmed, so Raven's order wasn't unusual.

Once the door to the shower room closed behind them Raven motioned Salinger to move closer. The wind whistled, whipping the fabric of the tent. Using Sign and whispering only when necessary to clarify points, Raven outlined her plan. A smile spread across Salinger's face as the plan came together.

Salinger was familiar with many of the people in the town. They trusted him and often told him information they wouldn't tell anyone else. Raven knew him well enough to know this about him. This was the crux of her plan. Salinger would find out when the next group of refugees was coming through. He would convince one of the women to claim to be the aunt of the children and explain she wanted to take them with her to a refugee camp. In exchange she would receive food, water and a few coins. More money would be given to the driver to cover his fees and to bribe the border guards. This was a risky maneuver. She needed to make sure Salinger was completely on board with the plan.

Chapter Eleven

THE STORM LASTED WELL INTO the night, finally clearing up just before sunrise. The silence was deafening after the constant hum of the wind against the canvas of the tent. Raven made her final rounds, checking each patient and ensuring they were clean and comfortable before the next shift change. The security monitors showed sand piled around the edges of the tent and abutting the opening. It would take a while to remove the sand from the opening of the tent by workers outside and as long as they were working Raven wouldn't be able to leave, but the wait would be worth it. Every effort needed to be made to keep the desert out of the med tent.

As soon as she was relieved from duty, Raven headed straight to her tent and the locker at the foot of her cot. There was a package sitting on top of the buff-colored metal cube. It had to be another package from home, more goods to add to her already burgeoning supplies. As an officer, Raven had a little bit of storage room allotted for personal items and so she was able to tuck away much of the food her mother was sending her. Raven picked up the package, hefting it for weight. Using the knife of her multi-tool to slice the tape she peeled back the layers of packaging material to reveal the goods beneath. Tossing aside the customs claim slip, Raven took her mother's letter out of the box. She held it for a moment, deciding whether to open it now or wait until she saw what was in the package.

A glance at the clock told her Salinger was going to be at her tent in half an hour. They planned on walking to breakfast together, giving Raven an opportunity to give him some of the food and her money. After breakfast she would bring him to her locker so he could load up bags with the food she had stored away. There was enough to keep the children fed for at least two weeks. Salinger had already planned on going into town with a group of soldiers after breakfast, giving him a chance to make some initial probes and put Raven's plan into effect. It was 0700, Raven had to hurry.

Salinger was the official liaison between the soldiers and the residents of the village, less than a mile from the base. He was scheduled to bring a few coins to a villager named Arman. His goat had been hit by a transport truck a few days before and the man had asked for the money to replace his animal. It took a few days to establish the worth of the animal, an event in which the entire village had become involved. Raven had been present during most of the negotiations, observing the subtle by-play of the game everyone, villager and soldier alike, used to alleviate boredom.

Arman claimed the goat was a young, healthy ram used for breeding purposes. Another villager said it was a dried up nanny giving nothing but sour milk. There was no reason for the man to contradict Arman. It just gave the villagers a chance to sit around and debate. The body of the animal had been decimated by the impact so there was no way to verify its status previous to the accident. Raven was there when a settlement was reached. She didn't understand all the words, but she knew enough of the local economy to know the money promised would buy two healthy young goats and the smile on the villagers' faces showed the satisfaction of being the winner of a game. Salinger had allowed the game to be played out, enjoying it as much as the villagers.

Raven wanted to go into the village with him to see what he could find out about caring for the children, but she was expected in Fitch's office right after breakfast. She dumped the contents of the care package on her cot. Her bunkmate entered just as she started to sort the palm-sized, brown-paper packages. Jorgenson kicked sand off her boots at the entrance and stripped out of her jacket. She tipped her helmet off and placed it on the shelf by the door. Grinning at Raven, her eyes rolled over the package on the bed.

"Package from home?" Her voice had a hopeful tone. "Third one this week."

Raven picked up a package labeled 'apricot' and tossed it across the room. "My footlocker is overstuffed. I'm going to have Salinger bring some of it to the village to give to the children."

Jorgenson smiled as she popped a dried apricot in her mouth and started sucking to soften it up. The fruit would keep her occupied for awhile, leaving Raven in silence to sort through her goods. She pulled the bin containing the backlog of food her mother had been sending over the past few months. Each package Savanna had sent contained at least five to ten pounds of food as well as numerous personal care items. Even though Raven kept assuring her mother she was well cared for and didn't need all the food she was being sent, the packages didn't slow down. Raven couldn't find enough containers to store the food to keep the desert critters away. She ended up giving most of it away to her bunkmates or the children of the village.

It didn't take long to gather a variety of food and place the packages in a linen bag. She removed the sock filled with local currency from under her spare socks and placed it on top of the food. Turning her attention to the most recent care package, she sorted the foodstuff from the personal care items. She had enough toothpaste and baby wipes to last months and she knew her mother would send even more in the next package. She pulled toothpaste, toothbrushes and the wipes out of her locker and placed them in the already stuffed bag and pulled the drawstring closed. Placing the leftover food into the plastic bin and sealing it shut, she replaced the bin in her footlocker. She closed the lid and swung the linen bag over her shoulder. Salinger was waiting for her outside her tent when she stepped out. Raven handed the bag to him and he slung it over his shoulder, letting it rest next to his pack.

"We're going to head into the village right after breakfast, unless you want us to wait for you."

Raven shook her head. "No, I'm on duty tonight. I'm going to crash before it gets too hot in the tent to sleep. Wake me up when you get back and tell me what you find out."

After breakfast Raven led Salinger to her storage locker and helped him unload all the bins containing the dried foods and toiletries her mother had sent her over the past months. They carried three bulging sacks to his tent and placed them in his footlocker. He then shouldered his pack and joined the group headed into the village. Raven waved to him as he walked past and then turned and headed toward the command tent. Fitch motioned her to sit as she soon as she stepped into the building. Five other soldiers were seated around the small conference table. Fitch motioned for her to take a seat near the head of the table. Flager grinned at her as she moved past and sat next to Fitch.

As soon as Raven sat down, Fitch leaned over and tapped the top of the table. A schematic chart pulled up in the middle of the table, and then projected into a three-dimensional diagram. When the picture stopped spinning Raven could make out the form of a squat building sitting in a valley. A few more taps on the computer embedded in the table brought up a blue highlighted section and a red path leading down from a hill. Raven's chest tightened and excitement bubbled up from her gut. She knew this was going to be something big.

"You six need to study this map. In twelve hours you'll head out. You'll be dropped here." A point on the map glowed briefly. "Follow this exact path into a village." The red path brightened. "Once you're at the rendezvous, you'll meet two men. They will deliver a package to you. You'll meet at these coordinates. The code word is 'crescendo' your response will be 'tempo.' Once you retrieve the package, skirt the village, follow this path and rendezvous at this point."

Another point on the map glowed. "You'll be dropped in the hot zone at 0100 hours. It's a two mile march to the village. You'll make entry at 0200 and complete the extraction at 0215. Follow this road to this abandoned village to meet your extraction team at 0245. Things are going to heat up at exactly 0246 so, if you're not out by then, you won't be getting out."

Silence filled the tent. Raven studied the map, still rotating above the table.

"Taylor!" Raven pulled her eyes away from the map and focused her attention on Fitch. "You're leading this mission. You're uniquely qualified for this job. We're going in the back door, but there'll still be dangers." Fitch paused. Raven figured he was giving her time to process the information. It wasn't sinking in. "You're vision allows you to see any trip wires or hidden dangers. The others will have night vision goggles, but their vision will still be limited. I have the next room set up with everything you need for the next twelve hours. Until deployment you're in seclusion. We're counting on you all. Taylor, I'm ordering you to get at least six hours of shut-eye." Fitch tapped the console a few times and the display disappeared. "The coordinates will be on your personal data pads. You're dismissed."

Raven's new team members stood and started to file from the room. She noticed Flager led the group. He nodded as he passed. There didn't seem to be any lasting animosity since Raven's team had defeated his in the war games, but he hadn't gone out of his way to befriend anyone in the unit either. Raven realized the safety of this group of people was going to be placed in her hands. They needed to trust her to get them all back in one piece. The door closed behind the last soldier before Raven even realized she hadn't looked closely at the team. Feeling eyes on her, she turned back to Fitch.

"I know this is your first official mission, but it's vitally important you succeed." Raven didn't need him to tell her this, but she listened without interruption. "You'll be back within forty-eight hours. Corporal Salinger says he has a lead on a relative of the children. I won't send the older two to the orphanage 'til you get back. This'll give you the chance to say goodbye and it will give him more time to find this relative."

Raven ducked her head, hiding her smile. Hopefully this would give Salinger the time he needed to put the plan in motion. She pushed away from the table and stood up.

"I'll get some sleep." Even to her ears her voice sounded worn and tired.

Stepping through the door to the seclusion ward, Raven glanced at her team. The five of them were huddled around a small table holding palm-sized devices. Raven pulled up a chair to see what they were discussing. She picked up the one remaining data pad and scrolled through the map. There wasn't much more information, but the coordinates and orders were vocalized. Her crew was all listening closely to the slightly digitized voice, pausing and discussing the different points and analyzing how each of their specializations would come into play.

Raven studied the faces of her new unit. She was familiar with each one of them, although she didn't know each of their specialties. A flashing icon on her pad drew her attention. Using a stylus she tapped the folder. Five names flashed on the screen letting her know the file contained the statistics she needed about each of her crew. The red line on the map blurred and seemed to dominate her vision. Realizing exhaustion was settling in, Raven decided she needed to get some sleep before reading the files. She stood up and addressed her unit.

"You're all to get at least six hours of shut-eye before deployment," she said. "I'm going to get sleep now. We have twelve hours. We will meet here at 1900 hours to finalize strategy. Make sure you are well rested and had plenty to eat." She looked at each of them in the eye, offered a salute and headed to the cots lined up against the far wall.

A white envelope was lying on the cot next to a small pile of personal care items. Raven realized it was the letter her mother sent with the care package. The last time she had seen the letter it was still sitting, unopened, on her cot. She picked it up and turned it over. The envelope had a little weight to it. Slipping her finger under the flap she tore it open. When she pulled out the contents a picture fell out. She picked it up and looked at the five faces smiling back at her. For a moment her vision blurred. She blinked a couple of times to try to clear her sight. When that didn't work she rubbed her eyes with her palm. Feeling moisture, she drew her hand away and grabbed a baby wipe to clean her face and wipe away tears, turning her face to the wall so the others wouldn't see.

The picture made an interesting tableau. Her mother was sitting in the center, holding Lakota in her lap. Travis was at her right shoulder, Joseph on her left. Caleb was sitting beside her, one arm around her shoulders. Savanna had a strained smile on her face. It must have taken a herculean effort to get the family together for the picture. Raven relaxed onto the cot, placed the picture face down on her chest and proceeded to read the letter.

My Dearest Raven:

I wish I could talk to you face to face instead of through writing. I miss you, my daughter. I hope you are doing well and staying safe. This computer communication blackout is one of the scariest things I have ever experienced. I look forward to your letters and cannot wait until you are allowed to call.

I thought you would like to see the most recent picture of our family. Travis and I have resigned a commitment contract. Travis is able to run his security company from Haven and Joseph and Caleb are adjusting well to living at the compound. It's nice to know we are all safe again in Haven. Caleb and Joseph are joining in the training with the surrogate units. I don't think I could keep your little brother away from them. I'm just glad I don't have to send him to war quite yet. Caleb loves having Joseph around and they are staying in your old room together. Joseph is considering joining the Marines and, since he and Caleb are close to the same age, they may be able to go in together.

Lakota is growing so fast. I had forgotten what it was like to have a baby around. Your son is always so happy. His laughter brightens the room. I show him your picture every day and tell him stories about you. I want him to be able to recognize you when you come home.

We all miss you. You made quite an impression on Joseph in just the short time you knew him. He has become quite strong and healthy.

I love you so much. Please write back as soon as you can.

> *Love always,*
>
> *Mother*

Raven clutched the letter to her chest, closing her eyes she attempted to get her emotions under control. Wrapping the letter around the picture, she tucked it under her pillow. She plugged a specially made ear piece into her ear and programmed her data pad to read the personnel files and mission coordinates to her while she slept and set her alarm to wake her in six hours before curling up on the cot to sleep.

Chapter Twelve

THE WHIPPING OF THE HELICOPTER blades drowned out all other sound. Even the headphones didn't muffle the reverberation of the blades slicing the air and Raven could feel the vibration of the machine throughout her entire body. She grinned at Flager and received an answering grin in response. The rest of the team was sitting in the seats around her, each one chosen for their specialties. She had reviewed their bios and talked with them in the hours while preparing for this mission. Flager was there for muscle. He was an expert in close combat, hand to hand combat and demolitions. PFC Simmons was a bomb expert. She could identify and deactivate just about any bombs from IEDs to a nuclear missile. PFCs Crew, twin brother and sister, were weapons experts. Raven had seen them in action; there was a connection between them beyond anything Raven had ever seen. Between the two of them they knew how to operate every weapon ever created. They could make entry into a building and cover every square inch of it in less than five minutes, all without saying a word. The final member of the team was a linguistics expert, Corporal Sandoval. He was going to be the one talking to their contact person. He was also their communication officer. Sandoval carried an extra fifteen pounds of radio equipment in addition to his fifty pound pack full of gear. The unit would be under communication blackout for most of the mission, but he still carried a homing device and radio equipment that would be used if anything went wrong.

The six of them had spent the last sixteen hours in close quarters, going over every inch of the plan, writing messages home to loved ones they hoped would never need to be sent, sleeping, eating and in general doing all the things soldiers would do before sent on a high risk mission. Raven wrote a letter to her mother, carefully avoiding any mention of her mission, where she was stationed and what was happening in the desert. The message wouldn't be sent unless she didn't return from her mission. Raven wanted to tell her mother about the children and to tell her about the microchip, but there was no way of explaining it to her without compromising her unit and her own safety. She filled the letter with all her love and hope and promised to stay safe.

The chopper snaked its way through the canyon, its blades nearly touching the canyon walls in some places. Raven looked at her watch. The numbers were barely legible, discernable only to her eyes. 0055 hours. The drop should happen any second. She signaled her team to gear up. They put on their night vision goggles, tightened straps and double-checked weapons. All of them had matching grins, their white teeth glowing against their camouflaged, night-blackened skin. Once they dropped from their chopper their black paint and clothing would make them part of the night.

The chopper slowed and hovered over a flat piece of earth. The signal was given and the team stood as one. Raven locked her carabineer in place and started her descent. The rest of her team followed. The ropes sang against her hands as she sped down the fifty feet to the ground. Raven felt the friction of the rope against her gloves as she slowed just before her feet hit the ground. Unhooking the carabineer she allowed her body to drop the last few inches to sand. The rest of the team hit the ground at almost the same time. Raven looked at her watch.

0100 exactly.

The countdown started. Getting to the extraction point in the allotted time in the dark was going to be a challenge. Raven motioned for the crew to fall in and led them to the foot of a steep hill. Scanning the path in front of her, Raven looked for any disturbance that might indicate hidden IEDs.

A glint showed a wire crossing the most accessible path up the mountain. She drew her team's attention to the trip wire. One of the twins--Raven couldn't tell the difference between the two when they were covered from head to toe in black--pulled a palm-sized device out of a bag and placed it on the ground. The probe flipped out a metal arm that attached itself to the wire. It rolled along the wire until it reached the hidden device. Metal legs flipped out and surrounded the IED. Within seconds the device was disarmed and the team marched past. The twin stopped to retrieve the probe.

According to the intel this should be the only booby trap between here and the contact point, but Raven knew better than to trust intel completely. She kept her eyes peeled for any deviation in the path. A bright glowing creature skittered from under a rock. The creature was more interested in finding a hiding place away from the six prodigious monsters approaching his lair than in attacking. She watched as the glowing scorpion skittered under a rock. The march up the hill was intense and challenging, eating up nearly forty-five minutes.

Raven scanned the hill, looking for any bright spots that would indicate body heat from a human. The ridge was clear. Raven and her team scurried over the top, staying low behind outcroppings of rock. She could see the glow of yellow lights coming from the buildings in the valley below. Noting the position of the brightest lights, Raven turned to the south. A smaller building lay about five-hundred yards from the main compound. Tall smokestacks attested to its purpose. Hundreds of thousands of crematories had cropped up in all nations since the terrorists attacks over twenty years ago. Cremation was now the common method of body disposal to reduce the risk of spreading disease.

The descent was much faster than the ascent. The glow of lights from the facility made the path easier to see, although it also increased the chances of being spotted by outlying patrols. Raven's team skirted the edges of the light, keeping to the outcroppings of rock so as not to betray their presence. They headed towards the crematory, far away from the brightest buildings. About twenty yards from the entrance to the crematory was a low wall, a crumbling remnant of an ancient village. Raven's team backed up against the wall, crouching low. The twins crouched back to back, one keeping eyes on the trail behind them, the other watching the road just beyond the wall. Raven kept Sandoval right next to her and the twins, sending the others fifteen paces down the wall on either side. Her watch showed 0159. Twin headlights appeared on the road traveling from the direction of the facility. This had to be the contact, but Raven wasn't taking any chances. Motioning her team to stay down she drew a bead on the lights, the butt of her weapon against her shoulder, the muzzle pointing through a niche in the wall. The other members of her team took up similar defensive positions.

The vehicle became a huge, amorphous shape as it came closer. As it solidified into view Raven could make out the shape of two men in the cab of a transport truck. It stopped directly in front of Raven. Motioning her team to stay down, she aimed at the driver, keeping her finger on the trigger. The driver exited the vehicle, keeping his hands extended to his side in the universal sign he was unarmed. His white robe billowed in the wind, the only brightness in the blackness. He whistled a complicated tune. Sandoval called out the code word in a local dialect. The response was immediate and sharp.

"It's them," he whispered.

Raven nodded her response and gestured for the team to stay down. Shouldering her rifle, but keeping it loose just in case, she led Sandoval and Flager over the wall. The truck's passenger slid across the seat and exited the driver's side as she approached. He moved to stand next to the driver, his hands extended.

"We need to hurry." The low hiss was spoken in perfect English, without a trace of accent. "I'll ride in the back with the package and most of your team. Your driver and mine will sit in the cab."

Gesturing for the men to turn around, she ordered Sandoval and Flager to search them. Once her men determined they were clean, Raven motioned the rest of the team over the wall. The twins searched the cab while Flager and Sandoval moved to the back. The 'all clear' was given and the team moved to the truck. Flager took the driver's seat while the rest piled into the back with the twins taking up position at the tailgate.

The truck was enclosed by a canvas covering so common with military vehicles, but Raven was missing the armor plating usually found on medical transports. She felt completely exposed. The only thing separating the cab of the truck from the bed was the back of the bench seat. Raven sat directly behind the driver, her gun resting across her lap and her right hand gripping the stock near the trigger. Sandoval sat beside her, his gun in much the same position. The muzzle of his gun wasn't quite pointing at the white-robed man sitting directly across from him. Simmons was facing Raven, not even bothering to hide the fact he was keeping his gun trained on the man in white. A large cloth bag rested on the bed of the truck. Raven could make out the shape of a body within the outlines of the sack. Next to the body was a squat, square metal container sealed with a keypad and marked with a universal medical hazardous material symbol. The truck seemed to hum with repressed tension.

As they passed the crematory, Flager turned off all the lights in the truck. Raven would have liked to been the one driving. Her natural vision was better than the night vision goggles Flager was wearing, but she needed to focus on multiple tasks at once and couldn't be locked into driving. Flager pushed the accelerator as they passed the shadowy towers spewing oily smoke into the unrelenting stars.

"There's no reason to fear pursuit." Raven turned her attention to the man sitting across from her. "Everyone at the facility fears us. We destroy death. We are unclean. No one follows us out here when we do our work. That's why we are going to get away." He smiled, revealing a row of perfectly healthy, white teeth.

Raven didn't relax, despite his reassurance. They reached the rendezvous point without incident. The village was supposed to be deserted, but with the instability of the region Raven wasn't taking any chances.

"Stay on high alert." The command was whispered, but the veracity in her voice was unmistakable.

The twins opened the tailgate and jumped out, weapons at the ready. Once they signaled the all clear, Raven gave the signal for the others to egress. Sandoval helped her pull the sack out of the back of the truck. They lowered it gently to the ground. Raven could feel the shape of a man within the sack, warm, breathing, but obviously by the limp, yielding movement of the bag, unconscious. Simmons carried out the metal box.

Raven could feel the vibration of the choppers moving across the desert before she heard them. These new Black Hawks were smaller and quieter than their ancient counterparts and much more maneuverable. Two of them were approaching the hiding place of the unit. Staying below the detection grid, the twin machines hovered just above the ground, spraying the unit with gritty down draft.

The closest chopper lowered a basket along with a retrieval team descending on ropes. Sandoval helped Raven strap the lumpy white sack into the basket while Simmons strapped the metal box at the feet. The two men who had delivered the packages were strapped to the retrieval team and reeled into the chopper with the basket. Before the forms were completely in the cargo bay the chopper was rising into the air and floating across the desert.

Raven strapped herself into the retrieval harnesses of the second chopper. The comforting cradle of the harness pulled at her waist and hips as the winch pulled her towards the cargo bay. She could see her team rising from the ground all around her. The down draft of the chopper whipped around her, driving grit into the exposed flesh of her face. The whistle of the wind drowned out every other sound. Suddenly the air beside her ear exploded with sound. Recognizing the song of a bullet as it passed by her head, she felt heat explode past her cheek. Suddenly hands were on her, pulling her into the belly of the chopper, the musical ping of bullets off metal rebounding around her.

She felt hands all around her, unbuckling straps, forcing her into a seat, more straps being pulled around her shoulders and hips. Managing to grab the buckle, Raven forced the latch closed. The helicopter rose smoothly at first, but as they gained altitude Raven could feel it start to buck and shudder. From where she was sitting she had a clear view of the pilot. He seemed to be struggling with the controls, both hands pulling in the stick. Raven pulled on her headsets. The pilot's voice cracked through the static.

"Prepare for hard landing. We lost rudder control."

Raven could feel the helicopter shuddering as the tail whipped uncontrollably. The sand seemed to flash with a thousand stars as the lights from the chopper grazed it. All Raven could see was sand and the ground seemed to be approaching fast. She wanted to relax her body, knowing a relaxed posture absorbed impact better than a tense one. The skids hit the ground with a scream of twisting metal. For a brief flash Raven thought they had come to rest, but the chopper picked itself off the sand and twisting, rolled to its side. Sand flew into the belly of the machine, covering Raven in a fine grit as blades sliced into the desert. The blades hoisted the chopper out of the sand and flipped it upside down. For a few seconds the body of the machine spun before the main rotor ground to a halt.

It took Raven a minute to realize they had come to a stop. She heard the thud of bodies as everyone around her stripped off their straps and fell to the roof. Releasing the catch on her belt, she slid out of her seat and onto the roof of the chopper. Her shoulder made a dull thud on the metal as she made contact. The chopper tilted and her body naturally started to roll and slid down the hot metal. A strap slid by her hand and she reached out, grabbing onto it. For a second it felt as if her arm was ripped from its socket the stop was so abrupt. The strap managed to stop her fall and she pulled herself into a stable position.

Raven pulled herself to the seat using the strap as leverage. Hanging onto the back of the seat, she looked around the belly of the chopper. She could see movement and bright spots as her unit moved all around her, exiting the downed chopper. No other heat signatures remained in the hold. She knew everyone was out because even if they were dead there would still be enough residual body heat for Raven to be able to see them. Using the seat to pull herself forward, she moved to the cockpit. Shattered glass crunched under her feet. She could see the radiant heat of the pilot hanging upside-down in his seat.

Chapter Thirteen

RAVEN PULLED HERSELF FORWARD UNTIL she reached the back of the pilot's seat. His head was hanging limp. One hand was still curled around the joy stick, the other flung above his head and swaying gently. Reaching around, Raven felt the side of his face, trying to trace to his throat, feeling for a pulse. His skin was cooling, stiffening. She felt the sticky wetness of blood and knew the soldier was gone.

The co-pilot's door was partially open, the edge digging into the sandy soil. Raven squeezed her body through the door and dropped to the ground. Crouching low, she scanned the horizon, looking for the source of the attack. A flash of light and popping noise drew her attention to the low hills to the west. The buzz of the bullet passing by her ear forced her to the ground. She belly crawled across the sand, looking for shelter from the shower of bullets. A sudden, solid thunk and a glint of metal landed beside her. She looked into the grinning face of Flager only inches from hers. The metal shield covered both of them as she pulled herself from the sand.

It was difficult to stay behind the shield and keep pace with Flager. After a few moments they caught their stride together and managed to make it to the wall. Flager was so large the shield barely covered both of them and she had to stay within the shadow of his shoulders to maintain cover. When they got to the wall he balanced the shield with one arm and offered Raven a leg to boost herself over. The top of the wall was about six inches above Raven's head. She would be exposed for the brief seconds it would take to scramble over the top. Reaching up she put her hands on the top of the wall and, with the boost of Flager's hand on her backside, she scrambled over the top. A burning fire hit her hip, but Raven knew she wasn't dropping over the wall until her entire team was safe. Pressing her body against the wall, she reached down and grabbed the shield and held it steady while Flager scrambled over the wall.

Raven dropped to the ground, giving a grunt as the air whooshed from her lungs. It took her a moment to catch her breath so she could take in her surroundings. They were back in the village where they had parked the truck. Most of the buildings behind the wall were crumbling and offered no protection. Their best bet was to stay behind the wall.

Raven looked for the rest of her team. The twins were crouched side by side; their rifles set up to take advantage of a crumbling divot in the wall. Simmons was crouched beside the co-pilot from the chopper, her pistol in one hand as she worked on opening her pack. Raven knew she had a portable grenade launcher inside; it would just take a few minutes to set it up.

"Flager, cover Simmons!" Raven realized shouting the order probably wasn't necessary, the crack of gunfire wasn't overbearing.

Flager crouched to stay below the wall and moved next to Simmons. The co-pilot didn't move even though Flager almost tripped over him. He was still alive by what Raven could see of his body temperature and breathing rate, but his lack of movement worried her. Sandoval wasn't anywhere along the line of the wall. Raven looked into the village but didn't see any sign of him. A whistle and a gesture from one of the twins drew Raven's sight back to the desert. A form was crawling between the chopper and the wall. It was Sandoval and Raven could see he wasn't going to make it without help. Someone needed to go back over the wall.

Picking up the personal shield, Raven thrust it in front of her. She motioned for the others to cover her and leapt over the wall. The ping of bullets ricocheting off the shield pounded out a rhythm in her head. It was only a few yards from the wall to where Sandoval was crouched. Raven reached him quickly, grabbed his jacket with her free hand and pulled him from the sand. He stumbled and staggered beside her, all the way back to the wall. Flager was there to help pull Sandoval and then her back over to shelter behind the crumbling stone. Sandoval rolled into a ball and pushed himself against the wall. Raven reached over and grabbed him by the backpack, shaking him until he focused on her.

"The communication gear is in your bag-get it out!" He stared at her, obviously not comprehending her words. "Get out the gear! Send a distress signal!"

Sandoval shook himself as if he was trying to wake up. Pulling open his bag, he grabbed the radio. He flipped the switch, sending a distress signal on a closed circuit. Across the horizon the sky suddenly lit up, bright flashes of red and white fires turned the night to day. Raven could see the shape of jets against the black sky, stealth bombers deep in enemy territory. The fires seemed to be coming from the facility her team had just left. She shuddered to think about what would have happened to her team if they were still in the area. Being pinned down by a half-dozen gunmen seemed tame compared to what she was imagining was happening at the former compound.

The pop of gunfire was slowing. Raven knew where each of the attacks was coming from. She was able to see movement and heat signatures of the gunmen, hidden and protected by outcroppings of rocks. There was no way to get past them. They had the high ground.

A crackle in Raven's earpiece let Raven know the jamming signal had been cleared and radio silence was lifted. She welcomed the sound of a deep male voice calling into her ear.

"Team Alpha, Team Alpha, respond!"

Raven pushed the button on her radio. "Team Alpha leader, copy."

"Give us your Twenty!"

Raven nodded at Sandoval, turning the communication over to him. She pulled out her binoculars and trained them on where the hostiles were hiding. It only took a few seconds to zero in their location and relay that information to the voice on the other end of radio.

"Team Alpha, we have your coordinates. Prepare for retrieval in fifteen." The situation was still desperate, but Raven could feel hope. Help was on the way.

The sharp reports of the hidden rifles were coming further and further apart. Raven was tempted to peek over the top of the wall, but she knew she would be exposing the most important part of her anatomy to enemy bullets. Pulling a mirror out of the side pocket of her pack she attached it to a long, telescoping wand. It took her a few minutes to find the correct angle to see beyond the wall. At first all she could make out was empty sand and the crashed helicopter. She heard the crack of a rifle and saw a flash of light. A few seconds later an adobe brick over her head exploded, creating a shower of dust and pea-sized chunks. Raven brushed the dust from her face and refocused the mirror. She thought she caught a brief glimpse of movement just beyond the downed chopper. Drawing the twins' attention, she used gestures to describe where the man was crawling through the sand. She kept the mirror trained on the dark form slowly creeping towards the wall as the twin closest to her drew a bead on him. The rattle of the machine gun, followed by the quick twitching of the man and then stillness attested to the twins' accuracy.

Silence sang through the desert, carried on the hot wind. Raven strained to hear the sound of jet engines, but they were still too far out. There was no response from the attackers and Raven wondered if they were running low on bullets. A sudden clatter of stone on stone made Raven start. She felt something land on her leg and Sandoval screamed in her ear.

"Grenade!" he yelled. Raven grabbed his jacket and pulled him back down as he moved to jump up.

"Stay down, you fool!" She hissed it into his ear and then called a warning to the others. "It's just rocks! They're throwing rocks to try to get us to expose ourselves. Sit tight!"

The others nodded their understanding and dug into their positions. Raven pushed Sandoval away from her and grabbed the radio. She relayed the co-ordinates of the attackers just as the scream of jet engines reverberated in her ears. The others peeled off their night vision goggles just as fire lit up the sky. Raven's implant screeched in protest as the rockets exploded the rocks hiding the attackers. Two more helicopters flew out over the village. Raven pulled out a flare gun and shot the red, glowing projectile into the sky.

One of the choppers hovered over the survivors. It lowered a basket for the injured copilot while the rest of the team strapped themselves into harnesses and prepared to ascend into the belly of the beast. A sharp pain shot through Raven's hip as the winch pulled her upwards and then it settled to a strong ache all the way into the machine. Strong hands pulled her inside the cabin and started stripping rope and harness off her body. Exhaustion overtook her in waves and Raven allowed the hands to guide her to a seat and strap her body into harness and buckle.

Voices were calling all around her, raising questions, shouting orders. Raven was trying to make sense of it all, but not all the words were getting through to her brain. She closed her eyes and shook her head against the confusion. Hands were on her, patting her down, probing, searching. She was too tired to push them away.

"Lieutenant, are you injured? I can feel wetness. Is it blood?" The hand was on her hip. Raven flinched as the hand pushed against her side. "Looks like a flesh wound-not too deep. One on your hand too. Anywhere else?"

Raven knew the question was directed at her, but she didn't have the strength to answer.

The man in front of her uttered an expletive. "She needs oxygen."

She felt a mask go over her face and then a cool, tangy mist covered her nose and mouth. Taking deep breaths, Raven allowed the air to flow into her lungs and revive her. Sitting up in her seat she looked out the window and saw a second helicopter hovering just above the crashed chopper. A limp body was strapped to another soldier and they were both being reeled in. She realized the other chopper was retrieving the body of the helicopter pilot.

Drawing her eyes away from the window, Raven looked directly into the broad face of a man only inches from hers. She drew her face away and raised her hand to shield herself from his gaze.

"Welcome back, Lieutenant." His broad mouth spread into a huge grin. "It looks like we got most of you in one piece. We only lost the pilot."

Raven swallowed, trying to draw moisture into her parched throat. "The co-pilot?" She wasn't quite sure how to phrase the question she wanted to ask. The man had been so still during the entire ordeal and Raven was afraid he had suffered severe injuries.

"Unconscious, but vitals are stable."

"Any other injuries?"

The man gave a patronizing smile. "You're the only one who was hit. All the others seemed to have made it in one piece. Sandoval is pretty shaken up. He may need to spend a little extra time with psych when all this is done."

Raven didn't feel much like talking as the helicopter snaked through the mountains. Her heart beat in rhythm to the blades as they sliced the air, pushing them out of the red zone. She could see the other helicopter flying right next to them. The lights of a landing strip appeared and Raven realized there was a transport plane at the threshold preparing for takeoff. She peeled off the oxygen mask as the choppers landed on twin heli-pads and started powering down. Raven followed the rest of the crew out the door, staying low and fighting the down draft.

Her hip ached, but she double-timed it to the carrier with the rest of the team. Flager and Simmons carried the stretcher holding the co-pilot while soldiers from the other chopper carried a stretcher with, what Raven could only assume, was the body of the pilot. The slope of the ramp into the cargo carrier aggravated her hip, but she pushed herself up the ramp and into the cargo hold.

Raven moved to take a position beside the co-pilot, but the medic there waved her away.

"Let us do our job, Lieutenant." Raven moved to take a seat along the skin of the plane, but one of the medics stopped her.

"Lieutenant, you're bleeding." Raven looked down at the bright red stain growing down her leg. The blood loss was slow, but she could tell it was becoming serious. She pressed her hand against her hip, trying to find the source of the bleed. Her mind started racing, going through the treatment she would give a soldier with these injuries. She needed to get an IV started. She needed to cut off the clothes to see the injuries. A pair of trauma shears were sitting next to the medic and she reached for them. Suddenly a hand closed over hers.

"Okay, Lieutenant, we all know you are a medic, but you don't need to treat yourself." Raven could hear the laughter in the medic's voice. "Would you please just get on the gurney so we can treat you?"

It was easier to lie down than to argue. She closed her eyes and allowed the medics to administer to her wounds. The rip of fabric let her know her pants were being shredded. Cold hands against her hip let her know they found the injury.

"It looks pretty deep. Let's pack it to stop the bleeding." The voice seemed to come from far above her head. "Lieutenant, we're going to start an IV. Do you want us to push some morphine?"

Raven opened her eyes and looked at the medic. "No, I'll let you know if it hurts too bad. Right now I'm pretty numb."

She felt the pinch of the IV go in her hand. One of the medics injected a local analgesic into the hip and started cleaning away blood and sand. Her hip burned as the medics cleaned the wound track and packed it with clean, white cotton.

"It looks like you were hit in the right hand."

Raven still had a feeling the medic was laughing at her. She lifted her hand and looked at the furrow that crossed her palm, slicing her life and laugh lines in half and stripping off a chunk of the pad under her thumb. Flexing her fingers she felt pain and blood oozed out of the wound, but the injury didn't seem to affect her range of motion. She held her hand out to the medic.

"Go ahead and clean and bandage it. I don't even think it'll need stitches."

She submitted herself to the ministrations of the medics as the plane lifted off the ground.

Chapter Fourteen

THE THUMP OF THE WHEELS hitting the tarmac jolted Raven awake. Shivering slightly, she drew a blanket close around her shoulders. She opened her eyes and blinked, clearing them of the sandy grit blurring her vision. A glowing, yellow light shone in her face, causing slight double vision. Raven turned her head away from the light source and realized she was staring directly at the face of an old man who looked vaguely familiar. The man's eyes were open and staring at her, but with a glazed, uncomprehending look. A blackened, oozing lesion dominated the top of his balding head and his body was so emaciated his bare arms and legs, what she could see sticking out from under the sheets, looked as brittle as match sticks. A sickening odor emanated from him, a combination of sweat, rotting flesh and sweet lavender. Raven had spent her life working in medical facilities and she recognized the smell of cancer.

Raven had no idea who this man was, although she had the feeling she should know him. Whoever he was he obviously didn't have long to live. A few things clicked in her head. This had to have been the body in the white sack. It seemed incomprehensible to send six people in to save one dying, old man. The man blinked and his eyes focused on her. His light blue eyes were watery and filled with pain, but Raven could tell the man was studying her face. He moved and Raven could hear the clink of chains against metal. She was surprised to see both of the man's wrists were chained to his gurney by thick, heavy manacles.

Raven could hear the hiss of hydraulics and thuds as the bay door was released. Peeling the oxygen mask off her face, she prepared to sit up. Hands held her back, replacing the mask over her face.

"I hate treating medics." The man who had treated her injuries was sitting at the head of her gurney. "Lieutenant Taylor, I need you to stay still until we get you off this plane. Be patient, please. We need to get Dr. Smith off first and then it will be your turn."

Dr. Smith! It suddenly clicked in Raven's head. This was the man who had murdered her grandfather, her mother's father. A flash of anger cut through her. She had just put her life and the lives of others at risk to pull this murderer out of some terrorist rat-hole just before jets went in and blasted it to the ground. Rage filled her, tightening her chest and making her temples ache. Clutching the sheet covering her from the waist down, Raven mentally willed herself to stay on the gurney and not jump up and attack Smith as they wheeled him off the plane.

Once Raven was taken from the plane she was placed in the back of a waiting ambulance. She felt silly strapped to the gurney staring at the ceiling of the bus. Everything was upside down and backwards. The medic was sitting at her head, keeping a hand on her shoulder as if he thought she was going to try to jump out of the back of the ambulance. The trip to the hospital unit didn't take long. Raven was x-rayed, her blood was drawn and she was wheeled to the surgery suite before she was even able to orient herself to where she was. The burn of the anesthetic flowed through her veins and she drifted into oblivion.

Her whole body ached. She tried to swallow, but there was no saliva in her mouth to lubricate her throat. There were noises all around her, but they all seemed to be coming from a distance. A voice seemed to penetrate the haze and Raven thought she could hear her name being called.

"Lieutenant Taylor?" The voice was next to her and then it moved away. "She's coming around."

Raven licked her lips, trying to draw in at least a tiny bit of moisture. She tried to open her mouth to speak, but she couldn't get the words out. A straw touched the edge of her lips and she drew a grateful sip of water into her parched throat. The straw was moved away before her thirst was completely quenched, but it was enough for her to be able to find her voice.

"How bad?" she asked.

The nurse was a blurry shape in front of face. Raven blinked to clear her vision, opening her eyes to the stark whiteness of the recovery room.

"We were able to remove the shrapnel from your hip." The nurse's face was coming into focus. "The surgery only took a little over an hour. There wasn't any major damage and you should be up and around in no time. We weren't able to get all the shrapnel in your hand though. Cutting into your hand may cause nerve damage. Most of it is near the surface, so it may work its way out on its own."

It could have been worse. Raven was used to delivering much worse news. Closing her eyes, she relaxed and allowed sleep to carry her away.

The scar on her hip would be barely noticeable, Raven decided. Two stitches held a draining tube in place, just in case infection set in the wound track. Raven was on her feet and walking the halls of the hospital the day after her surgery. By the time the doctor made his afternoon rounds she was begging to go back to her unit.

Raven was cleaning the crusty, bloody discharge from the edges of her wound when the Captain walked into the room. He had a palm-sized data pad in his hand and wasn't even looking her direction as he approached the bed.

"Good afternoon, Lieutenant." He continued to scroll through the information on his pad. "I'm Captain Rivers."

Raven continued cleaning the injury, deciding there was no point in stopping. When the Captain did look up his brow wrinkled.

"Why are you cleaning your own wound?"

The man sounded more tired than angry. Raven shrugged her shoulders as she covered the wound with a fresh gauze pad.

"I'm just as capable of treating my injuries as your nurses." Raven covered her hips with her gown and pulled the sheet to her waist. "I'm going to be tending to it myself when I go back to my unit. I'm the best medic they have."

The Captain cocked his brow at her. "Well at least your hubris wasn't damaged by your injury."

It took Raven a moment to realize just how arrogant she sounded. She almost laughed at the look on the Captain's face. Sitting up, she tried to put herself at eye-level with the man.

"I am not trying to be arrogant." Raven realized she wasn't making a very coherent argument. "I just have a lot of experience in the medical field. My home was one big hospital and I trained there from the time I can remember. The only reason I didn't go to medical school was because I wanted to fight and protect my country and medical school would take too long."

"I know your background." He pulled a stool next to Raven's bed and sat down. "In fact, part of the package your team retrieved from that lab is on its way to the lab at Haven. Doctor Taylor's lab is one of the best in the world. She's about the only researcher capable of discovering all the mutations Doctor Smith developed with these bugs."

Raven shuddered, realizing just exactly what could be in the metal box they had carried out of the desert. "What about Smith? Why did we drag him out of that hole?" Raven couldn't keep the anger out of her voice.

Rivers studied the data pad in his hands. At first Raven thought he wasn't going to answer, but after a moment her looked up and held her gaze.

"Doctor Smith is an accused war criminal." Rivers' lips tightened. "He'll be brought back to the United States to stand trial for his crimes. As for you, it'll be a few days before we send you back to your unit. Don't worry, I'll find something for you to do here."

Raven relaxed onto the bed and closed her eyes. She could hear Rivers breathing as he checked her chart. His cold fingers brushed her hip as he explored her wound. Raven opened her eyes again as he took her hand to inspect the wound there.

"Where am I, by the way?" she asked. "We weren't told where this lab was we were going to and it's impossible to tell where we ended up. Can you at least tell me if I'm still in Afghanistan?"

"You're at Dalbandin Air Force Base in Pakistan." He finished his exam and helped her pull her gown down and the sheet back up over her hips. "We needed to get your delivery out of Afghanistan as quickly as possible. In fact, half of the package is already on a plane headed out to sea. Six pilots scrambled out of here almost as soon as you guys landed. I wish I could have seen what you guys brought. Did you get a chance to look inside?"

Raven knew better than to answer that question. She was sure Rivers was just asking to assuage his own curiosity, but Raven didn't want to be the one responsible for unfounded rumors spreading through the desert.

"I was more concerned about what was happening with my men." She studied Rivers' face to see if he believed her. "I don't know if you heard, but we were kind-of in a helicopter crash."

"It's amazing no one else was hurt. We lost a good man in that pilot. I don't know anyone who could have brought the chopper down as well as he did." Rivers put the data pad in his pocket. "We have the rest of your men set up in temporary quarters. You'll be able to join them in a few days. As long as you take it easy."

Raven sighed and relaxed back onto the bed. A few more days and she would be back where she belonged. She heard Rivers leave the room as she drifted off to sleep.

Raven must have been an annoying enough patient, because Dr. Rivers released her the next afternoon. Her hip ached as she pulled on her newly issued uniform. She had to pull her belt a little tighter since the pants were a size too big, but at least the clothes were new and clean. Her hip twinged a little as she leaned over to pull on her boots, but nothing beyond what she could handle. The burned edges of the wound on her hand hurt worse. Raven knew it would take a while for her palm to heal, especially since she was right-handed. Once she got back to her unit she would use some of the balm her mother sent her to clean and cover the wound. The natural healing properties of the herbal antibiotic would probably be more effective than what they were treating her with here.

When she left her room she walked down the hall to the nurse's station. She wanted to get a supply of gauze and cleaning solution so she could treat her wounds herself. The nurse at the desk smiled as Raven approached.

"Lieutenant Taylor, Doctor Rivers asked me to give you a couple of wound treatment packages before you left." She handed her a red, plastic box about the size of an old-fashioned lunch box. "There should be enough supplies in there to last you a couple of days. I'll make sure the medic in your unit has plenty of supplies before you go back to your base."

Raven felt her lips curl into a sardonic smile. "I am the medic in my unit."

The nurse's eyes widened in surprise. "Oh, usually the medic isn't in command."

"I think this is a special case." Raven took the container from the nurse. "Can you direct me to the exit? I have a map of the base, but I have no idea where I am in this building."

The nurse laughed and directed her towards the double doors. The hospital was fairly small, so Raven only had to go through two doors and down one long hall to get to the exit. Unlike the base in the states, there was no detention ward in this building, so Raven had an unobstructed path to the exit.

An orderly pushed a bed out of a room right in front of Raven, just before she made it to the end of the hall. Pulling up short to keep from crashing into the bed, Raven looked down at the swaddled form huddled under sheets and blankets. Doctor Smith's rheumy blue eyes looked back up at her. He reached up and grasped her wrist. There was a strength in his cold fingers that belied the wasted look to his form.

"You're Raven Taylor?" Although posed as a question, Raven heard the underlying statement in his tone. "You're even more perfect than I imagined. Did you know I helped create your mother?" He didn't wait for a response. "She was such a beautiful little girl. How much of her is in you?"

Raven jerked her wrist out of his grasp, not dignifying his statement with a response. She shuddered as the medic pushed him past her. It took him a moment to swing the bed around the corner and aim it down the hall.

"Where are you taking him?" Raven couldn't control her curiosity.

"He is going to surgery to remove the cancerous cells from his head and arms." The medic strained under the weight of the bed. "Then we're going to start his treatment. There's a possibility they caught the cancer in time."

Raven studied the wizened man curled up on the bed. This man, this murderer, was receiving life-saving medical treatment, but why? She wondered if his life was even worth saving, questioning what contributions he could give to society that would make up for his crimes. The medic was finally able to put enough weight behind the bed to get it moving down the hall. Smith gave her a wan smile as he was carted down the hall. As the medic disappeared around the corner Raven attempted to rub the warmth back into her wrist.

She swallowed, trying to stop the roiling in her stomach before she stepped out of the antiseptic-swathed halls of the hospital into the heat of the desert sun.

Her crew was holed up in converted shipping containers. The big, rectangular boxes were the size of boxcars. The aroma of stale sweat and hot metal assaulted Raven's senses as she entered the temporary shelter. Heat radiated from every corner making her feel like she was being roasted like a turkey. As Raven breached the threshold she could feel the moisture bead on her upper lip. She worked her way to the back of the temporary shelter and lowered herself onto the canvas and wood frame of one of the six cots. Sandoval was lying on his bed, tossing a baseball in the air and catching it with his left hand. Raven watched him out of the corner of her eye as she sorted through the few belongings that had been issued to her since her belongings were still at her other base. She put the clean uniform and sleepwear in a shelf above the cot and lined up her toiletries beside it. There wasn't much there, but at least she had enough to get by until they were all sent back to base.

Chapter Fifteen

THE HEAT IN THE BOX was stifling despite the constant thump of a fan circulating the air. Raven knew she wouldn't be able to stand staying inside during the high point of the day and decided she needed to get out and explore. She pounded Sandoval's knee as she past by his cot.

"Hey, do you want to go get some grub and check out the KP?" she asked.

Sandoval gave her a blank stare, barely interrupting the flow of tossing the ball into the air. Raven could sense his frustration and knew if she didn't say anything he would continue on his downward spiral. She sat on the end of his cot, forcing him to pull his legs up. The ball stopped its continuous journey into the air and back into his palm.

"Hey, you can't sit in this hot box forever." She tried to bring a jovial tone to her voice. "You're going to fry your brain and we need all the translators we can get out here."

Sandoval sat up, his eyes boring into Raven's. "Yeah, it's nice to know I was born for a reason, huh?"

"What do you mean by that?" Raven asked. "Weren't you designed to be a soldier?" Raven wasn't quite sure she understood the derision in his voice. Growing up in Haven it wasn't unusual to hear women speak with such a heightened sense of self-loathing, but this was usually brought on by years of abuse or neglect, most of the time stemming from early childhood. Raven knew Sandoval was part of the surrogate program and most of the soldiers coming from that program had an inherent sense of self-confidence-either it was bred into them or it was developed through extensive training. The children in the program never lacked for anything either physically or emotionally, and the care given to them was usually evident in their self-confident nature.

Sandoval tossed the ball to the foot of the bed and pulled his legs into a crossed position. He clutched the sides of his head with his hands, squeezing as if he had a headache. When he started to speak his voice was so low Raven had to lean in closer to hear.

"Look at me," his voice dripped with self-loathing. "Look at what they created."

Raven studied the man sitting before her. He was tall and wiry, his long, lanky limbs greatly outstretching his body. His nose was too big for his small face and his eyes, although large, liquid pools of brown, were set too far apart on his face to ever be considered attractive. Sandoval put his hands in his lap and stared at them.

"When they design us they mix and match DNA, meld us with stem cells from both human and animals." His voice was low, but Raven couldn't mistake the building intensity behind his words. "They want someone with stamina and strength so they give us horse DNA. They want determination and loyalty so they turn us into a canine. They want us to be good soldiers for our country with loyalty for no others so they take away mother, father, husband, and wife and tell us our unit is our family. We were designed for a purpose. To fight and protect a country where we don't even benefit from its freedoms. Born and bred to be soldiers. Born to die for our country when our country is falling apart all around us. Why are we fighting wars on foreign soil when homegrown insurgents are ruling in fear and terror at home?"

Raven listened to his mantra, wondering why he sounded so bitter. The military had given her everything she needed to live and had given her the training she needed to survive in an ever-increasing violent world. She felt safer in the unit than she did living at Haven.

"Do you even realize how much better your life is in the Army than it ever could be on the outside?" Raven couldn't keep the derision out of her own voice. "Here you are fed, clothed, taught to survive. You don't need to worry about where your next meal is coming from. You have a purpose. No one can hurt you here, unless you let them."

Sandoval looked at Raven's hand. White gauze covered the angry, red slash across her palm.

"No one can hurt us? What do you call the bullet wounds on your body?" he asked. "I don't see how we can avoid being hurt when we are shot at every day."

Raven swung her legs down and stood up. She had to move away from all the anger he was exuding from his body. Her skin felt dirty even though she had just taken a shower and she had to move out of the box.

"I joined the military to bring freedom and choice where people are held in subjugation." She couldn't managed to keep her voice even. "The governments here rule with hatred and fear. At least at home we are still allowed our freedoms. The insurgents at home will be brought down. It's just a matter of time. There are only a few rebel groups anyway and you can leave the military any time you want to anyway. You always have a choice."

Sandoval rose to his feet, matching Raven in height. "I don't know what rock you live under, Lieutenant, but life doesn't work that way. I was born as a soldier, bred to learn and assimilate into foreign cultures. I don't have any skills beyond speaking and translating about two hundred Middle Eastern languages. What am I supposed to do in the world outside of the military? No, I was bred for one purpose and I will fulfill that purpose until the day I die. Which should be soon, considering the world we live in."

"Everyone has a choice, Sandoval." Raven was so angry she wasn't even sure she could make coherent sentences. "You are not a slave to destiny. Make your own path, like the rest of us."

Raven spun on her heel and marched out of the box. She didn't even notice the twins as she blew by them. Nor did she notice when they turned and followed her as she marched toward the mess hall. As she reached for the plastic tray to collect her grub two arms reached around on either side, grabbing the trays from the top of the stack. Startled, Raven leapt back and swung around. The twins' matching grins defeated her sour mood and she turned and picked up the next tray. She walked down the chow line with them on either side of her, allowing her tray to be filled with rich, protein-filled food. She had developed an affinity for the richly spiced food of the region and was glad to see the yellow curry stew that was quickly becoming her favorite.

The twins led her to a table at the far end of the cafeteria, where they would be able to sit and enjoy their meal in relative privacy. As soon as the trio sat down they leaned close to each other. The twins mirrored each other in their movements as if they were one person. Raven hadn't spent much time with the siblings, but she always enjoyed watching their antics around the base. Despite the fact they were brother and sister, the two looked and acted so much alike it was difficult to tell which one was which. They both had dark red hair, cropped short, a small, wiry frame, blue eyes and symmetrical features. Unlike most red heads, these two were actually able to develop a slight tan with a sprinkle of freckles across their noses. Their facial features were completely gender neutral so you couldn't say the sister looked masculine nor the brother looked feminine. They were just the male and female version of the same person.

Raven concentrated on eating for a few minutes. She didn't realize how hungry she was until she smelled the richness of the food on her tray. The twins were talking in low tones between bites of food. Raven studied the two out of the corner of her eye. It took her a few seconds to be able to distinguish one twin from the other. She realized the girl, Audrey, was right-handed and her brother, Jesse, was left-handed.

"Lieutenant, you looked pretty mad coming out of the box." Jesse was using a piece of flat bread to soak up the sauce in the bottom of his bowl as he spoke. "What had you all bent out of shape?"

Raven pushed her bowl away, having eaten her fill. "Sandoval just got under my skin. He doesn't realize how good he has it here. I'd like to see him try to survive outside of the unit. He wouldn't make it two weeks."

Audrey snorted. "He's been like that since we were kids. He hates being part of the unit. They need to give him some sort of civilian training and get him out."

It suddenly dawned on Raven that she was the only member of the team who did not grow up as part of a surrogate unit. She had always felt she had so much in common with the members of her team she didn't realize they had all grown up together and knew one another since birth. Raven studied the twins, trying to decide what genetic manipulations were done to their DNA to create them.

"Doesn't genetic screening filter out problem personality traits?" Raven was thinking about the negative energy she felt oozing out of Sandoval. His personal angst seemed to permeate the quarters in the brief time she spent there.

"The genetic alterations enhance physical traits, but the scientists can only work with the DNA they have access to." Audrey finished her food and pushed the tray away. "During training they loved to tell us they created the vessel, but it was up to us to fill it. The genetics give us the ability to develop certain character traits, but without training those traits never develop."

The mess hall was filling up and Raven didn't feel like continuing this conversation where others could overhear. She motioned for the others to follow and they headed back to the box. It was empty when they got there, but none of them felt much like going inside. They pulled out canvas and wood camp chairs and set them in a close circle. Raven grabbed bottles of water from a box just inside the opening and gave them to the twins. The box was empty, Sandoval must have left to find relief from the heat. Someone had set up a canvas canopy and Raven and the twins sat underneath, trying to find some element of relief from the blazing sun. Raven poured water onto a bandana and tied it to her head. It helped, for a while.

"Where do you think Sandoval went?" Raven asked.

"He might've got called to Command." Jesse poured the lukewarm water over his head, sprinkling his tee-shirt with moisture. "His behavior wasn't very exemplary on the mission. He froze when the helicopter crashed. I could barely get him out of his seat and then, once we were out, he just hunkered down in the sand and refused to move."

Raven was completely exhausted. Her limbs felt heavy and useless as the heat pressed down all around her. She stood and stretched, trying to get blood flowing into her extremities.

"I thought your training in the Surrogate units would drill you in live fire situations. Didn't Sandoval go through the training?" Raven tried to ask the questions without allowing judgment to creep into her voice, but it was difficult when she was so frustrated with the man's behavior.

"Sandoval just never had much of a backbone. That's why he wasn't placed in close combat situations before." Audrey was doing everything she could to keep herself cool, just like the other two. "I hope he gets sent back to the States. I hate having people like that defending my back. I can't trust him."

Raven heard the crunch of boots on sand and turned to the source of the sound. Sandoval was marching across the sand, his boots kicking up clouds of gritty dust. The scowl on his face made Raven shudder. He glanced at the group under the awning, but made no move to join them. He disappeared into the box without a word.

Raven sat in silence, her companions' faces reflected concern and frustration. Sandoval was a member of their team and had been since birth. The companionship developed in the surrogate units was stronger than any of the units Raven had seen in her experience as a soldier. Despite the comments the twins had just been making about their team member Raven knew they were concerned about their friend. A loud ringing thump came from inside the crate. Raven pulled herself from her camp chair and moved to the entrance of the metal container.

Sandoval was standing in the middle of the container. His cot had been flung across the room and his belongings were scattered throughout the space. Raven glanced at the twins who were standing at her back. Their identical faces wore matching expressions of concern. She signaled the two to stand back and entered the temporary shelter. Sandoval kicked a knapsack. It landed across the room with a clank and came to rest against the metal wall. Raven knew she needed to reign the man in before he caused any major damage. She drew a deep breath, filling her lungs, so her voice would be at full volume.

"Soldier, cease and desist." Raven's voice sang off the metal walls and vibrated with sharp tones.

Sandoval stopped short and swung around to face her. His face was contorted into a mask of rage. This was a key moment for Raven; she knew if she backed down she would never gain control of the situation.

"Sandoval, get this mess cleaned up now!" The tone in Raven's voice didn't leave room for any argument. Sandoval straightened his shoulders and stared her down.

"You are not my commanding officer." His voice cracked with suppressed rage. "It's bad enough they are making me stay in this God-forsaken land, I am not going to take orders from some wanna-be officer who has no authority over me."

Raven pulled herself to her full height, taking advantage of her nearly six feet, and stepped into Sandoval's personal space. He didn't back down and she found herself standing inches from his face. His eyes were rimmed in red and thick spittle was forming at the corners of his mouth. Raven narrowed her eyes and stared him down, noting the tensing of his muscles as his hand curled around the baseball in his grasp.

Raven heard footsteps coming up behind her. She didn't want to take her eyes off the man, but Sandoval's facial expression changed drastically as fear washed over his eyes and all color disappeared, leaving his cheeks pale and wan. Raven turned and immediately pulled herself into attention, offering a smart salute as she saw the wings on the colonel's lapel.

"At ease, Lieutenant."

Raven relaxed into the at ease position, feet apart and arms behind her back, but didn't allow her mind to relax, knowing the colonel wouldn't search her out if there wasn't something important happening. She had never met this man before, but had heard a lot about him and the high expectations he had for his soldiers. It was apparent from the silence behind her Sandoval had heard of his reputation as well. All it took was a look from the man for her to hear sudden movement behind her. She knew the mess Sandoval had made was being straightened up.

"Taylor, report to my office in ten minutes." The colonel looked her up and down. "I heard a lot of good things about you and what you did out there. I wanted to get a good look at you to see if the rumors could be true." He turned and walked out of the box, leaving Raven standing in a state of confusion and amidst a flurry of activity as Sandoval cleaned around her.

Chapter Sixteen

RAVEN MADE SURE SANDOVAL WAS well on his way to getting the box cleaned up before she reported to the Colonel's office. She made her way to the command center well within the ten minutes the man had given her. The undulating waves of heat sucked the air from her body and made her feel lethargic. It was a relief to enter the air-conditioned halls of the command center, even though the ancient machines barely stirred the air. It was enough to create the illusion of a cool breeze flowing through the halls. Support staff buzzed around her like members of a well-structured hive. Raven was directed to an office on the second floor. She was shown into the large room by a tall, stocky soldier whose spreading waist-line showed he was obviously more familiar with desk work than weaponry.

The colonel was working on something on his data pad and barely looked up long enough to motion Raven to a chair when she walked into the room. He finished what he was doing and placed the data pad on his desk.

"Welcome, Lieutenant," he said. "I'm Colonel Jackson. It's nice of you to come back with your feet on the ground and more bodies than you left with."

"I was just doing my job, sir." Raven tried to keep her tone level, pushing away the images of the chopper and the limp body of the pilot spinning through the air.

A smile spread across the Colonel's face as he leaned back in his chair. "Well, that's one of the great things about field heroics, they usually earn you your own command."

Her own command? Raven stared in stunned silence as she processed this information. It wasn't like she wasn't used to giving orders. She did it all the time during medical emergencies. When she was in the zone, her entire focus was on her patient and the lifesaving measures necessary to do her job. Giving orders, expecting quick unwavering response and immediate reaction from subordinates was all part of the symphony of medicine. Her own command was different, though. Her own command meant she would be in charge of every aspect of her subordinates' well-being and she may actually be the one responsible for ordering them to their death.

A new command usually meant a transfer and an extension in service. She had already been in Afghanistan for over a year and even though she had resigned herself to leaving Haven, she still missed her home and family. It would have been nice to have leave to see her child. According to her mother's letters, Lakota was already walking, talking, making all the benchmarks he should be hitting as he grew and she wasn't be able to see him. It felt strange to have these strong feelings for the child when she didn't feel very connected to him at his birth. She had seen the attachment many of the surrogates had felt with the children they were carrying, even though they knew the children weren't theirs and were going to be raised in the units. Many times the women would spiral into a deep, dark depression and were unable to cope with the loss of the child. Some of the women attempted to run away before the child was born. They were always caught and brought back.

Raven shrugged, allowing her thoughts and her emotions to roll off her shoulders. She knew when she lifted her face to eye the man at the head of the table her face was a mask, unreadable and strong. "What are my new duties?"

"We're putting you in charge of a new security detail." Jackson handed her a data pad. "Dr. Smith has some high powered connections and there's always the danger some of them will try to get him back. We need to transport him stateside as soon as possible. We're sending you back with him."

"What?" Raven could feel the octave jump in her voice. "Don't you know the history this man has with my family?" She was incredulous. Defending the man who was responsible for the death of her grandfather and causing her mother sorrow and pain was not her idea of a prime mission.

"Of course I do." Colonel Jackson stood and walked around his desk to stand in front of her. "That is why I think you'll be uniquely qualified for this job. You're going to make sure Smith makes it back to the states to stand trial for his crimes. He's not stable enough to move now, so it's going to be up to you to protect him until we can get him out of the country."

Raven looked down at the data pad in her hand. It seemed every time she turned around she was receiving a new device. Her own personal data pad was still at her other base buried in the bottom of her footlocker. She hadn't written to Billy in a long time, but she knew she had to tell him about this. Opening the first file, she scrolled through the names of the members of her unit.

"You know everyone in your unit, except for Anderson." The colonel stood and stretched a kink out of his back. "He was part of the retrieval unit. We had him embedded in the research facility as a native. Without him we would never have been able to get Smith and the samples out. I want you to meet him and get his debriefing. Take his statement. We need to know everything that happened while he was there. I think you'll be impressed with this young man."

Colonel Jackson led Raven from the conference room and handed her over to his aide. The man led Raven to a debriefing room a few feet down the hall. She sat behind the desk as the computer lit up beside her. The screen prompted her to input her microchip information. Raven waved her bandaged palm over the reader. Nothing happened. The screen didn't even flicker.

"Oh, I forgot," the aide handed her a set of dog tags. "When your hand was injured it took out the chunk of skin containing your microchip. Those tags contain a new chip with all your information. It's going to take awhile for your hand to heal enough to replace your chip."

He dropped the shiny, silver tags into her white-gauzed palm. As she closed her hand around the cold metal of the tags she felt the sting of her wound, but more than that, she felt the weight of her missing chip. The tiny, microscopic chip had been a part of her since she was an infant. Without the chip there was no record of who she was and to whom she belonged. An image of her mother flashed in her mind. The blonde hair, blue eyes set in the scarred, but still beautiful, face looked nothing like her own. An unwanted image of her genetic mother suddenly forced its way to the forefront of her mind. She remembered the ugliness of her scarred face, but more than the scars distorting her features, it was the hatred-filled eyes showing Raven haunting pain that made Kai so ugly. Raven suppressed a shudder and forced the image of the woman out of her mind.

The aide exited the room, leaving Raven to her duty. Holding the tags in front of the screen she watched as it lit up, displaying a start menu. A message 'say begin when ready to record' flashed across the screen. The door slid open to reveal Anderson standing on the other side. He grinned and saluted as he stepped through the door.

"So, we meet again." He sat down where Raven motioned him to a chair. "Before we get started, Lieutenant, I just want to let you know I heard about your actions during the crash. I'm excited I'm going to be joining your team."

Raven could feel her cheeks heat up. She was glad her skin tone didn't show a red face like her mother's did when she blushed.

"I'm sure you've been told why we're here." At his affirmative nod, Raven continued. "We need to make an official record of your experiences at the research facility." Raven looked towards the computer screen, a completely unnecessary movement.

The computer could pick up sound from anywhere in the room. "Begin recording."

A light flashed letting her know the computer picked up her voice command. She turned back to the young man sitting in front of her. He was young, very young. His lanky legs stretched out in front of him. Raven studied his facial features. His narrow face was almost an exact replica of Sandoval's, the same nose and mouth, but his eyes were closer together and bigger. All together the effect was much more aesthetically pleasing on him than it was on Sandoval. The perusal only took the few moments it took Anderson to find a comfortable position and start talking.

"I was embedded in the facility for nearly six months." Anderson's voice had a low-toned, bell-like quality to it. "I was able to infiltrate by joining a group of refugees in a camp. We were hired by the facility to work as cleaning staff. It didn't take long to learn they were experimenting with some pretty nasty diseases. Most of the refugees I came in with were dead within two months. They were using the refugees as guinea pigs to test the veracity of the diseases."

Anderson took a deep breath and a quick drink of water before he continued. Raven allowed him a moment to collect his thoughts. She leaned forward to prompt him to continue, but he continued before she spoke.

"When it was discovered I had an immunity to most of the diseases they put me in charge of disposing of the bodies. Once I was able to establish trust with the guards they left us alone. Zaahid and I were the last of the survivors from the refugee camp, but they always seem to find more research subjects. We were so close to the border up there they were able to bring in tribes from all over to run their experiments. It was easy to ingratiate myself with the members of the facility and become invisible. No one expects a refugee to know anything about labs. I was able to collect samples of the experiments and keep them at the crematory. Everyone stayed away from us and the crematory. We were called unclean and even had quarters away from anyone else. Dr. Smith was the only one who would have any contact with us. It didn't take long to come up with a plan to smuggle Smith out of the facility with the samples I collected."

A smile flirted across his face as he told the next part of the story. "I was able to make contact with my CO and share my findings with him. Together we developed a plan. Smith always had me deliver coffee at 0030 hours. No one else was willing to go into his lab. It wasn't difficult to slip a paralytic into the drink. It didn't take long to get him in the body bag and out of the facility. No one stopped me. Everyone was used to seeing body bags rolling out of his lab and I'm used to putting bodies in them by myself. Zaahid met me at the gate with the truck and we made our way to the rendezvous point. I didn't tell him what was happening. He'd been talking about trying to escape, but he was terrified. He didn't think there was anywhere to go. I couldn't leave him there when the bombers came in, so when I made my escape I decided to bring him along. I think he is so shell-shocked right now he doesn't even know where he is."

He stopped talking and Raven realized he had finished his report. She tapped the computer screen, ending the recording. "I'll get this report to the Colonel. Welcome to the team."

Anderson saluted as he stood up and then stepped out of the room. Raven saved his testimony to a file and sent it to the colonel. She logged off the computer and leaned back in the chair, contemplating the ramifications of her first command. She allowed a smile to spread across her face. For the first time in months she felt completely relaxed, completely in control.

Over the next six months Raven and her crew shared guard duty, both in Smith's room, and around the hospital. Smith's cancer had metastasized throughout his body and he was too weak to move due to his treatments. Raven hated spending time in his room, but she wouldn't shuffle the duty to another member of her team. The sweet, slightly cloying smell of dying flesh assaulted Raven's sense of smell as she entered Smith's room. He was sitting up in the bed, eating the soupy gruel that was the standard hospital breakfast. White gauze swathed his head, hiding the red slash marks where the tumors had been removed from his scalp. His cheeks had lost their faded, wasted look and he had actually put on a bit of weight. Raven felt it was extremely ironic that the treatments for Smith's cancer had been developed decades ago by the very man whose life he had taken nearly twenty years before.

Smith was stable enough to transport, finally. Raven was looking forward to loading him on the plane with her team and beginning the long journey home. Two nurses entered the room to tend to Smith. Raven moved to a corner of the room to be out of the way while the nurses performed their duties but could still observe and guard the women in their work. She could feel Smith's eyes follow her around the room even as the nurses tended to his linens and the medications dripping from tubes into his veins. His focus never wavered from her. They finished their work in silence, gathered soiled linens and left the room.

Raven moved to follow them, but she froze when she heard Smith's voice calling her name. Dropping her hand from the door latch she turned to face the man.

"Raven, do you really think they will put me in prison when we get back to the states?" Smith asked.

"I think they'll put a needle in your arm." Raven bit the inside of her cheek. She knew better than to respond to this man's goading.

"I think they'll give me my own lab." Smith's choking laughter followed her from the room.

The air was hot and layered with grit, but Raven took great gulps of it as she tried to clear the bile taste from her mouth. Being in the same room with Smith made her sick, but she wouldn't send anyone else in to do her job. Walking to the gates she debated on going to the refugee camp near the far side of the village to check one more time, but instead she turned towards the tarmac and looked at the massive cargo plane sitting with its back open, ready to be loaded. It would be taking off in the morning and she was scheduled to be on board, with Smith and her crew.

She wasn't going to go to the camp. It was a long-shot anyway. Even though this camp was one of the closest to the border where the children would have crossed, there were hundreds of such camps scattered across the border lands. Raven turned to go back to the main compound, but movement near the camp caught her eye. She waited while Molly ran towards the main gate, her short blond curls quivering as she was stopped by the guards. Raven heard her name mentioned and could hear the urgency in the woman's voice, despite the distance between them. The guards were familiar with Molly and her many visits to the base as she sought out supplies and help for the many refugees at her camp. Even here, in the far corner of the world, her mother's influence affected the lives of many. The first time Raven visited the camp to see if she could find any news of the children she was surprised to find Molly working there as the director. Over the months she was just grateful to find someone who was so willing to help her.

Molly rushed towards her, a grin spread across her face. "Raven, we found them."

The simple declaration, and said with such joy, Raven felt a great weight lift off her shoulders, a weight she didn't even know she had been carrying around.

"They showed up at a refugee camp south of here." Molly was talking so fast Raven was having difficulty understanding what she was saying. "Your mother already set the paperwork in place to get them stateside. They're going on a medical visa. None of the refugee camps will allow the children to enter since they're testing positive for TB antibodies. The children aren't contagious, but the camps aren't taking any chances. Right now they're in a hospital on the edge of the city. It doesn't matter though, the children will be in the states in two weeks.

Chapter Seventeen

ALARMS SINGING THROUGH THE COMPOUND woke Raven from her deep sleep. Grabbing the data pad from the head of her cot, she jumped out of the bed and pulled on a pair of pants over her underclothes. The off-duty members of her team were stumbling around in the darkened box seeking clothes, weapons and packs. Raven was the first to find a light and she turned it on, flooding the metal container with a bright yellow glow. The data pad in her hand flashed red alert as she grabbed her pack and slung it over her shoulder.

Orders were being shouted from all quarters as she raced across the grounds towards the hospital. A bright red glow lit up the sky as the whistle of a rocket filled the air and landed with concussive force in the courtyard of the command center. Raven was at the door of the hospital when a second rocket hit with targeted precision in the center of command compound. An ambulance pulled up behind her as the door of the hospital opened and two aides pushed Smith out in a wheelchair. Raven helped load him onto the back of the ambulance and then ordered it to the cargo plane.

Her unit joined her as she double-timed it after the ambulance. The sky was a fiery red and the scent of burning sulfur clouded the air, assaulting Raven's nostrils. Another rocket whistled through the air, exploding the barracks to her left. Despite the explosions and flames, the hospital stood stark and bright against the night. Shadows were springing up at the edges of her peripheral vision. Another rocket sang through the air, landing in the middle of the courtyard. Bodies flew through the air, fragments raining down on her and her men. A flaming figure ran past, arms flailing, leaving the smell of charred flesh behind. Her team picked up the pace and she ran beside them. A sudden force pushed at her from behind, knocking her to the ground. The smell of burnt flesh smothered her and she couldn't breathe. A rattling grunting emanated from the form pinning her to the ground. Raven could feel flesh slipping under her hands as she tried to push the weight off her chest. As suddenly as the weight appeared, it was lifted and she could feel her arms being pulled as she was pulled from the ground.

"Let's go!" Anderson's voice was loud in her ears.

They were near the tarmac. Raven could see the ambulance on the cusp of entering the plane. She could hear truck engines in the distance. The roar of the jet engines split the night open as the ambulance rolled up the ramp and disappeared inside.

Raven paused at the bottom of the ramp and turned to make sure her team made it into the cargo bay. Her eyes were drawn to the refugee camp, only a few meters away. There wasn't enough time- even now the lights of the invaders were broaching the hill. Her team was on board, waiting for her so they could take off. She turned away from the orange and red glow of the firefight and climbed up the ramp. A sudden sharp pain shook her body and pushed her to the metal grate of the ramp. She heard her voice being called and a hand closed over her arm, pulling her forward. Her body felt like it was being pulled into forty different pieces as she felt the lift of the airplane coupled with being pulled into the bay. Warm wetness filled her ear and dripped down her cheeck. A bitter, metallic taste filled her mouth and she realized she was tasting her own blood. The discordant sounds around her became an out-of-tune symphony and it was too much for her brain to handle. She let the darkness take her.

It sucked. She was being heralded as a hero and she couldn't even remember the journey home. Two weeks after the evacuation of Smith, Raven woke up in a hospital in Virginia. Her head felt like there were nails drilling into her skull and every time she moved her head felt like a block of wood, weighing down the pillows. The pain was overwhelming and it didn't take long for her to lose herself in oblivion again. Over the next weeks her friends were able to explain what happened, she could only take in bits of information flashes at a time. Jorgenson explained how just as she was entering the aircraft a flying piece of shrapnel had flown through the air, sliced into her backpack and shoulder and finally rebounded off her head. Her unit had grabbed her as she started to roll back down the ramp and pulled her into the cargo bay just as the doors were closing and the plane started its journey down the runway. If the medics hadn't been on board with the ambulance and all their gear, she would have bled out somewhere over the Baltic Sea.

Raven never saw Smith again. He had been sent on to Washington, to stand trial for treason. Raven spent three weeks in Virginia before her mother's clout brought her back to Haven. For the first time in her life Raven was able to experience her mother's power and influence first hand. Raven wanted to go to the base at Mountain Home for her recovery, but Savanna wouldn't release her from Haven. For the first six months of her rehab Raven stayed in the hospital wing of Haven, where doctors and nurses worked diligently to repair damaged nerve bundles, muscles and tissue. Her physical therapy was grueling and she would often suffer from blinding headaches. When she did finally move back to the main campus, she was placed in her old apartment and Lakota and Marwa were moved in to occupy the bunks built into the wall.

It was difficult to assimilate back into the community after being on the outside so long, especially since all Raven wanted to do was get back to her unit. Friction was arising between state borders and her unit had been moved to the border between Arizona and Nevada to give extra support to the guards stationed there. The range of motion in her shoulder was still limited and her occasional blinding headaches made it almost impossible to do much work beyond the ten hours of labor required of all Haven residents. After a time she started working in the surrogate hospital again, just as a way to keep herself tied to the Guard.

Raven reached up to brushed her hair out of her face and allow it to fall down her back. It had been nearly a year since her injury and the range of motion was almost completely back in her shoulder and her headaches had nearly subsided. She was still listed as disabled, but at least she was allowed to go back to training with the surrogate units. Grey had put her in charge of drilling the fourteen and fifteen year-old group and she found she was actually enjoying the work. She would spend a part of each day drilling and training the surrogates and then return to Haven for dinner and time with her family.

Raven finished getting ready for bed and left the bathroom. Her eyes were drawn to the two tiny forms huddled in the center of her bed. Lakota's bright eyes still shone with a tiny bit of fear despite the months he had lived with her in her apartment. A grin split Marwa's face and she reached up so Raven could pick her up and give kisses. Raven crawled onto the bed and gathered both children into her arms. She noticed Lakota resisted a little before he relaxed into her embrace.

When the children were moved into her quarters, Lakota didn't adapt well to the change. For the first few weeks he cried out for his "Nanna" all through the night. Raven tried to comfort him the best she could, but she was struggling with her own nightmares. Many nights she would toss and turn, startling awake and crying out into the darkness. Her screams would wake the children and they added their sobs to her own. They would all end up huddled in the bed trying to assuage each others' fears as Raven tried to soothe them back to sleep. After a few weeks Raven gave up on keeping the children in their own beds at night and allowed them to crawl into the bed with her. The children would press against her in the darkness. Their deep breathing would calm her when she woke and help temper her racing heartbeat. She would allow the gentle rhythm of the children's breathing and the soft flutter of their heartbeats to guide her back to sleep. Raven pulled the children close and settled into her cocoon of warmth and safety, pulling the blankets over all three of them.

Haven hadn't changed much in the past five years. The main facility was still a shelter for women, but instead of just sheltering victims of abuse, the walls housed women fleeing from battle-ravaged towns, their children in tow. Raven spent many hours working with her mother in Haven's offices. It always amazed Raven to see her mother control so many different programs and keep them running smoothly. Savanna received daily reports from all her facilities and she had to filter through the information and make decisions affecting the lives of thousands. Raven could see the weight of the decisions in the stress of her mother's face, drawing lines around the deep blue eyes.

In addition to the main campus, Haven had a number of sub-facilities scattered throughout Idaho, Oregon, California and Washington. These tiny, self-sufficient towns did everything from producing food products, clothing, medical supplies, building materials and many other supplies needed to keep Haven running. With the surrogate program in place around Haven, the facility was secure, but the other facilities were always in danger of invasion from marauders. Travis' security personnel were pivotal in securing these outlying communities.

Raven knew the stress was telling on her mother and wished there was more she could do to take on some of the responsibility. It wasn't difficult for Raven to figure out where Savanna's insecurities stemmed. Ever since Emily's betrayal, Savanna had a hard time relinquishing control and trust to other people and was always double checking records and reports. Raven wanted to take over some of her mother's responsibilities, but she had no idea where to begin.

She started studying the reports crossing her mother's desks, trying to see where she could help.

The dark circles under her mother's eyes concerned Raven deeply. Yet, despite her concerns for her mother, Raven still didn't feel she fit into Haven. She felt safe and protected within the stone confines of the building, but it didn't take her long to become bored and dissatisfied with the activities at the facility. Her head injury put her on light duty with the Guard and she was expected to try to rebuild some of her lost reflexes, but she was left with a sense of restlessness she couldn't shake. She found herself spending more time in the clinic and in the surrogate facilities and, since she had little else to do, found herself working with Travis, training members of the Haven community in defense. The hard work combined with the responsibilities associated with being a resident of Haven brought on physical exhaustion and allowed her to fall into bed and drop into a deep, dreamless sleep.

Raven was bristling with the confines of living in Haven, so when Travis offered her a position as part of the security force working in Boise she jumped at the chance. Travis brought her, Lakota and Marwa to the house on Warm Springs where they would be living while she was working for the agency. She also thought about bringing Hamasa and Asal with her, but they were adapting so well to the Haven programs and had developed an attachment to Travis and Savanna, she decided they were better off at the facility. Despite her many protests, Travis insisted on bringing Joseph with them. Joseph and Caleb had both entered the Marine Corps as soon as they turned nineteen. After the required two years service Caleb signed up for an additional four. Joseph returned to Haven and joined Travis's security force. This decision was particularly hard on Raven. She never told Joseph the DNA tests had come back on the remains from the hill where she had sent her rocket that day five years ago. She just couldn't find the words to tell him his father was on that hill.

Tracy always had dinner waiting when Raven returned from her patrol duties. Rose had passed away the last year of Raven's deployment and Tracy had taken her place as the caretaker of the Warm Springs house, but it was still strange to see a new face hovering over the appliances in the kitchen. Tracy was taking care of the old family home as if it was her own, but Raven still missed Rose's sweet face.

It was easy to establish a routine, with Tracy taking care of the house and the children while Raven worked. Everyone fell into a comfortable pattern centered around Raven and Joseph's work schedule. Raven and Joseph took alternating shifts so one of them would always be at the house. Both children kept the on-line education program they had started at Haven since they were so far ahead of the other children in the local school. Raven would check their work after school and spend a few hours with them every night. The children never left the gated yard unless Joseph or Raven were with them. It was supposed to be safe in this area of town, since no one was allowed past the security gates into the city without a microchip or a health card, but every once in a while some desperate soul would try to sneak over the wall and try to raid a supply depot. Those who were good at it were rarely caught and made it in and out with barely a ripple disturbing the quiet sanctity of the city, while those who weren't were inevitably caught and sent to an internment camp.

Travis made regular visits to the house and, every once in a while, Savanna and the other children would come with him. It was always a treat to have the entire family at the house, enjoying dinner, discussing the challenges of the day and Raven found simple joy in those moments.

Life was simple, and busy. Within six months of moving to the city Travis put Raven in charge of training his new employees in use of non-lethal force. Despite her busy schedule, Raven did miss working in the fields and the open air and when spring came she asked her mother to send seeds and supplies so she could plant a garden in the yard. The first harvest was pretty sketchy. Although Raven had worked the fields at Haven most of her life, she never really paid attention to how and why things were planted. The most she was able to pull out of the raised beds was a few zucchini and one very sad little cucumber. During the winter she introduced a gardening unit to the children's studies and they planned a new garden together. By the end of the next summer she was able to supplement the food sent from Haven with fresh foods from her own garden.

It seemed Raven was continuously busy, but a sense of frustration and boredom hovered over her like a shroud, keeping her from truly enjoying her work. Boise was relatively safe, unlike cities and towns in other areas. Daily reports of riots and atrocities flooded the news and Raven wanted to join the unit in defending the state's borders. It seemed there was always a need for new soldiers. Between the growing unrest in the states and continued conflict in the Middle East and Asia there always seemed to be troops either deploying or returning from some war somewhere.

It was late summer of Raven's third year in the house. The table felt crowded with the residents of the Warm Springs house and Travis, but it still lacked the boisterousness of dinner at Haven. It was actually fairly easy to carry on a civilized conversation without having to yell over the top of hundreds of other voices. Travis was telling Raven about the first time he and her mother had dinner alone in the house. His worst fear was that Emily would come bursting in on them while they were in the middle of dinner. Just as he was explaining to Joseph just how overprotective Emily could get over Savanna the chime chirped on his pad.

"It's Savanna." The concern in his voice gave it a fine edge.

Raven leaned over so she could see her mother as Travis pushed the answer icon. Savanna's face appeared on the screen. Dark circles surrounded her eyes and deep furrows sliced into her brow.

"Travis," Savanna's voice was low and throbbed with emotion. "There's been another attack on a truck carrying supplies to Surrogate House."

Raven drew in a breath. Despite Savanna and Travis' best security efforts, transport trucks between Haven facilities were still being attacked by insurgents. Nearly a third of the supplies meant for Haven residents never made it to their destinations. Raven knew compared to other transport companies this number was low. Some companies lost up to two-thirds of their inventories due to theft and militia attacks.

"Was anyone hurt?" Travis asked.

Her stepfather's overwhelming concern for the human factor of these attacks always impressed Raven. She saw her mother's forehead relax slightly. Always a good sign.

"No," Savanna shook her head slightly and then shrugged. "Whoever did this obviously didn't want any loss of life. They used spike strips on the tires and brought the guards down with tasers. You know we teach our drivers nothing in the truck is worth losing your life over. The insurgents absconded away with about five-hundred pounds of food and some fertility drugs. They knew what they were after and were very systematic in what they took. General Grey thinks they might have an insider working with them. The thing is, I can't figure out exactly who would be doing this and why would they take fertility drugs and leave some high tech equipment behind?"

The furrows were back on Savanna's forehead. They were there so often, Raven knew they would soon be permanently etched in her mother's smooth brow. This time the furrows were accompanied by a slight tic in the corner of her mouth, drawing up the faded scar on the right side of the face.

"I'm sending a report to your data pad. General Grey will be there in less than an hour. He's going to go over the details with you." Savanna buried her head in her hands and then ran her fingers over her hair, smoothing down fly-away strands. "Travis, watch over the children. Bring them back here if there are any problems."

Raven knew her mother was including her and Joseph in the mention of the children. Sometimes it was frustrating being a twenty-eight year-old woman and having a mother who wanted to draw you in like a chick under her wing. Despite her annoyance, a sense of warmth formed just under her heart at the thought of being back at Haven, under her mother's care. Raven looked across the table to Joseph and saw a faint flush and a smile flirt at the corner of his mouth. Obviously he had caught the "children" remark and knew it included him as well.

Raven sent Marwa and Lakota to get ready for bed while she helped the others clean the kitchen. Once teeth were brushed, faces were washed and prayers were said, she tucked each of them in and kissed the top of their foreheads. It was amazing how fast they were growing up. Although there was no way to know exactly how old Marwa was, she and Lakota were close enough in age they acted almost like twins and rarely did anything unless the other was involved. They were closer than natural born brother and sister and, even though she was unable to legally adopt Marwa due to restrictions about adoption from the Middle East, Raven still considered Marwa her child. Raven stepped into the hallway and stood for a minute, halfway between each room just listening to the hum of her children's soft breathing.

Chapter Eighteen

GENERAL GREY WAS SITTING AT the kitchen table talking to Travis and Joseph by the time Raven returned. He hadn't come in alone, though. Sitting next to him, a bundle of nervous energy, was the director of Surrogate House. Raven felt a grin split her face as her eyes met her childhood friend. Aida's smile eased the worried expression from her face and she sprang from her seat.

Raven rushed forward and embraced her friend. As her arms went around Aida's waist she could feel the thickening and as they parted Raven put her hands on the woman's belly.

"What is this, three or four?"

Aida grinned and put her hands over Raven's. "Well, since it's twins, it's three and four."

Raven couldn't help smiling at Aida's exuberance. "You and Zach are very lucky."

Aida had met her husband when he joined the security force guarding Surrogate House. Raven was in Afghanistan when the two signed the commitment contract, but she heard all the details through the many letters and e-mails her friend had sent her. Aida followed Raven's lead and signed a lifetime contract with Zach, wanting as much protection for her children and family as possible. Aida was glowing with the first stages of her pregnancy, being one of those few women who did not suffer excessively with morning sickness.

"You should consider marrying again and having more children, Raven." Aida had led the way to the table and took a seat beside General Grey. "Those of us who can have children have a responsibility to bring life to this world."

Aida smoothed her hand over the slight bulge of her belly. Raven tightened her mouth against a sharp retort. Any time she thought of marrying someone else, Billy's face would flash through her mind and her throat would tighten with unshed tears. Raven swallowed and offered a smile she hoped hid her pain.

"Every birth is necessary." Aida's grip on Raven's arm belied her small frame. "The negative population growth is spiraling out of control. We need as many children as possible if the human race is to survive."

Aida released Raven's hands allowing her to turn her attention to the men sitting around the table. Grey had a number of charts and files pulled up on a data pad and was scrolling through them, comparing the information to files on Travis' handheld.

"I know Joseph has never had a chip implanted." Grey flashed a glance to the young man sitting across the table. "The problem is going to be finding an unmarked woman to play the part. Most of our unmarked, embedded units are of Middle Eastern descent."

Raven rubbed the palm of her hand. Her fingers brushed against the faded scar dividing the pad beneath her thumb. The chip embedded in the soft flesh had been excised when the bullet hit her palm and she hadn't ever had it replaced. At first, there was too much damage to the hand and then, by the time her palm had healed enough to take the chip, she was used to using her dog tags for identification. Reaching up, Raven removed the tags from around her neck and placed them on the table.

"I don't carry the mark." she said. "I can do the job."

Thus it was in the early morning hours, the moon still hanging low in the sky, Raven and Joseph left the city limits of Boise in the back of an unmarked van. Travis was driving, his knuckles showing pale as they gripped the steering wheel. Both he and Aida had tried to argue against this course of action. Travis pleading for Savanna's sake, Aida for Lakota and the other children. Raven refused to be swayed from her course once her decision was made. She wouldn't allow Travis to call her mother and tell her what was happening, stubbornly stating she was a grown woman and could make her own choices. Charging Aida with the care of her children, telling her to bring them to Haven where they would be safe and cared for, Raven again left her son behind. She assuaged her guilt by convincing herself this mission was for the greater good. Her mother could give Lakota and Marwa stability and safety at Haven. Despite her misgivings of leaving the children behind, Raven couldn't tamp down the rising excitement bubbling in her chest. She was actually going to be able to do something to help defend innocents from being attacked.

As the van wound down back roads and past small encampments, Raven reviewed the mission parameters in her mind. Joseph and Raven were to pose as a married couple, trying to survive under the radar of the government. They were to embed themselves in one of the migrant groups travelling from farm community to farm community, laboring and working in the fields.

Raven was dressed in a tattered, pull-over, ill-fitting blouse and a loose, multi-layered wrap-around skirt draped almost to her ankles. A scarf was tied around her head, hiding her hair, now pinned in a tight bun on the crown of her head. She had studied the effect it gave in the long mirror in the bathroom before they left Boise. The clothing didn't have the same effect on her as it did the women she had met in the Little Haven communities. Maybe it was because of the way she carried herself. The clothing couldn't disguise the military bearing ingrained into her form.

Joseph was grinning at her from the other side of the van. His shirt was similar to hers, but he was wearing loose fitting pants and a wide-brimmed hat.

He and Raven both had work cards tucked in a pouch tied around their necks with cords. The cards entitled them to work, stating they had their most recent health-check and were up to date on their vaccinations. Even with these papers there was no guarantee they would be able to find jobs or be accepted into a community.

Raven wasn't sure if she could pull off the devoted wife role. She liked Joseph. He was a good kid, but he was six years her junior. He had never gotten over his hero worship of her and every time they were together his eyes would follow her. She would catch him glancing away quickly whenever she looked at him, but she could still feel his eyes trailing after her when she looked away. Raven had a feeling he was going to throw himself wholeheartedly into the role of a devoted husband.

Travis pulled over at the edge of a mountain road. The sun was just sending fingers of light over the horizon as Travis helped Raven climb down from the back of the van. She wasn't quite used to moving around in long skirts and there just seemed to be a lot of extra cloth grabbing at her legs. Travis embraced her, holding her tight and rocking back and forth slightly before he released her and held her at arm's length.

"This is going to kill your mother, you know." Travis seemed to understand her reasoning behind her decision to volunteer for this mission, but he said he didn't relish being the one to tell Savanna her children would be deliberately putting themselves in harm's way. "She worries so much about Caleb doing border duty in Southern Mexico, now both you and Joseph are running away into the wild and I'm not even going to be able to tell her where you'll be."

Raven ducked her head to hide the tiny smile creeping up her face. The thought of being able to be actively involved in finding the insurgents harassing supply trucks and established communities gave her a sense of purpose and she couldn't tamp down the excitement bubbling up in her chest. Her heartbeat throbbed and the blood hummed through her veins as her anticipation built. She turned towards the campsite as Travis climbed into the van and drove away.

A white canvas tent was erected in the center of a clearing. Raven could hear the playful gurgle of a stream nearby. The campsite had an ethereal quality as mist flirted around the tent and the grounds. Logs were laid out in the fire-pit, just waiting to be lit. Raven walked the perimeter of the campsite, assessing the defensible space and taking stock of the inventory.

Two bucket-style bicycles were stationed next to the tent, both stocked full of provisions. It looked like she and Joseph were supplied with enough food to last a couple of months. A couple of fishing poles were attached to the side of one of the deep-welled buckets on the back of the bikes. Raven crouched down by the bicycles to check out their construction. She had seen these bikes before. They were popular in many of the Little Haven communities. The solid steel frames were designed to carry heavy loads. A deep-welled plastic bucket straddled the rear of the bike, like overgrown saddlebags for horses. These bikes were capable of carrying up to five-hundred pounds of equipment and were balanced enough for anyone to be able to ride comfortably. The larger of the two bikes had a cargo trailer attached to it. The trailer was empty and Raven assumed this was where they would be loading the tent and the other camping supplies. At least they weren't being dropped off in the middle of nowhere with nothing to survive on and no resources except a field knife.

She could hear Joseph moving around the camp behind her and she stood up to get started on breakfast. He already had a fire going and was sorting through items on a picnic table near the tent. After placing an empty five-gallon bucket at the edge of the table, he started taking items out of a cooler. Raven took the bucket and headed down to the stream to get water. As she walked to the rocky shore she rehearsed her role over and over in her head. It was going to be hard to get used to the division of labor in this new situation and she couldn't afford any slip-ups.

The society she was trying to infiltrate had definitive roles dividing men and women. It wouldn't look good for other communities to stumble upon their campsite and find Joseph cooking and cleaning and, although Raven would be allowed to carry weapons to defend herself, Joseph would be the one responsible for hunting any big game, a staple food for these communities. Fortunately, Raven was familiar with camping and cooking over a campfire. Between camping trips with her grandfather and her survival training in the guard, she was a fairly good camp cook.

The handle of the bucket was biting into her hand as she walked back to camp. Joseph had the filter set up by the time she returned. He took the bucket from her and poured the water into the system. Raven moved to the table and started to gather the supplies for breakfast. It wasn't long until she had eggs and bacon frying in a pan and water boiling for tea over a bed of coals. Joseph sat across the fire, his boots were off and was scrubbing the black leather with handfuls of gritty dirt. Raven served up a plate of food and he wiped his hands on his shirt before taking it.

"What are you doing?" Raven was looking at his scuffed boots and his now grubby shirt.

"Our clothes are too new." Joseph explained. "We're never going to be able to pass ourselves off as members of the travelling communities if we appear too well-kempt.

Raven studied her own shoes. The dark brown leather had a few scuff marks, but didn't look the worse for wear. She put one foot on top of the other and used the sole of her shoe to scuff the leather. The look bothered her and she wanted to immediately find some polish and a brush and go to work on the shoe.

"You're going to have to do better than that, wife of mine." Joseph grinned as he spoke. "You need to look travel-worn and poverty stricken."

Raven looked at the richness of supplies all around her. "We're going to have a hard time pulling off the poverty-stricken act with all this equipment. I've seen entire families with fewer supplies than this."

Joseph stood up and removed his belt. "I'm going to distress the clothes they packed for us a little bit and go for a swim in the creek." He pulled his shirt off over his head, muscles rippling as he wadded it in his hands. The faint, white line of the scar on his arm showed stark against the paleness of his skin. Raven had to stifle a smile.

"I think your white skin is going to be a beacon to anyone for miles around," she said.

Joseph shrugged his broad shoulders, allowing the thick muscle to ripple again. "I'm weather-beaten enough where it counts. You need to work on distressing your clothes. The communities keep themselves clean, but it is difficult to avoid stains and damage."

Raven cleaned up the breakfast mess, using boiling water to scrub plates and pans. By the time she was finished working, her shirt had a few black streaks and she had snagged her skirt a few times, causing loose threads to appear in the worn fabric. She dragged her feet in the dirt, causing dust to fly and scuff marks to appear. Once dishes were done Raven moved down to the stream to help Joseph distress the spare clothing they had been given. Soon colorful scraps of clothing fluttered from a line tied between two trees. Raven shook her head at the newly stained clothing, now gathering wrinkles in the warm summer sun. The new clothes looked worn and used and Joseph seemed satisfied enough to relax in one of the camp chairs.

Camp was so well organized there wasn't much work left to put things away. The site was a well-travelled route for Communities so there was nothing more for Raven and Joseph to do but wait for one group or another to make camp. They would give the community members their cover story and hope the group would invite them to become one of them. Hopefully they could be convincing enough and would have enough to offer for some group to adopt them.

With nothing left to do but wait, Raven decided she would try her hand at fishing. She set up a camp chair beside the stream, assembled her pole and speared the bait on the barbed hook. The sun was warm on her back, but the heat wasn't overwhelming. Dropping her chin to her chest, she almost dozed off, but a tug on her line brought her back awake. Whatever was nibbling got away, but the thrill gave her enough energy to stay awake for a while. Joseph placed a chair beside her, setting his own pole for fishing. They sat in silence for a while, trying to tempt fish with tiny bits of worm.

The sun was approaching its zenith when Raven reeled in her line for the last time. After about an hour of fishing they had each caught two nice sized trout. Raven pulled the line of vigorously flopping fish from the tiny pool at the bank of the creek. She brought the fish back to camp, cleaned them and had them frying with onions and garlic in a cast iron skillet within ten minutes. Lunch was a quiet affair and afterwards Raven again had cleaning duty as Joseph ran the perimeter of the camp. By the time she was finished with the cooking and cleaning, her clothes were liberally streaked with dust and grease. There was no way Joseph could complain about her being too well groomed now.

Raven spent the afternoon folding the now dry clothes and making sure everything in the camp was orderly. Joseph explained to her the code of the communities they were attempting to infiltrate.

When travelling in the communities, possession left lying around had a tendency to disappear. The communities had set rules about personal possessions and laws governing behavior and those laws were obeyed on threat of being expelled from the group. As long as your belongings were within the circumference of your own camp, they were safe. Outside the boundaries, belongings were considered community property. Joseph had been teaching Raven the many signs set up around the camp and what each one of them meant. Stones inscribed a circle around the tent and their belongings. The stones alternated, large then small, all the way around, designating their encampment as one for outsiders. Raven made sure everything was in order and all their possessions were well within the camp boundary markers.

Chapter Nineteen

RAVEN COULD HEAR THE RHYTHMIC chopping of a hatchet in the little copse of trees near camp. Joseph had headed into the trees with the little trailer to fill it with firewood an hour before. He ambled back to the camp, pulling the fully loaded cart behind him.

"Come look what I found." He gestured Raven over.

Raven looked in the bucket Joseph pulled out from among the dry twigs and branches. It was half-full of gleaming blackberries. Her mouth started watering and she grinned up at Joseph.

"I know blackberries are your favorites." He reached in, pulling one of them out. When he brought the berry to her lips Raven opened her mouth and allowed him to place it inside. His fingers brushed her face and she pulled away slightly. Joseph put the blackberries down and took her face in his hands. The warmth of his fingers tingled against her face. She wanted to pull away, but his eyes caught hold of hers and she couldn't move.

"Raven, I love you," he said. "I've loved you since that first day when you gunned me down on the road." Joseph's voice was low and husky. "Please don't draw away from me."

"Joseph, you're just a kid." Raven's voice lacked conviction. She stared into his blue eyes, mesmerized by the pools of liquid ice.

"I'm older than you were when you married Billy."

Raven stiffened and started to pull away, but Joseph's arm dropped and caught her around the waist, pulling her close.

"No, Raven. Don't pull away." Joseph's voice quivered with emotion. "I didn't mean to hurt you. I just wanted to point out that I am old enough to take care of you. I know you love Billy. I don't want to take that away from you. Just, see if you have enough room in your heart to love me, too."

Joseph brought his face down to hers and gently brushed his lips against hers. Raven's lips tingled at the caress and her heart tapped a quick beat. Blood was throbbing through her body making her light-headed. She had to stop this before Joseph got the wrong idea. Stiffening her body, she prepared to pull away, but before she could move a voice calling from outside the camp made Joseph jump back.

"Ho, the camp!" Someone was calling from far outside the camp.

A man was approaching the camp from the same road Travis had brought them in on early that morning. He was dressed in clothes similar to what Joseph was currently wearing and pulling a small cart behind him. It looked like it was time to test their cover story. Raven ducked her head and stepped behind Joseph. Making sure her head covering was in place, she adjusted the belt slung low around her waist, subtly loosening the snap holding her knife in place. She backed away until she was close to the entrance of the tent. Glancing one more time at Joseph to make sure he was in a defensible position, she ducked inside.

The voice of the man carried through the canvas walls of the tent as he spoke to Joseph. The stranger seemed amiable enough as he gave Joseph a traditional greeting and asked to be invited inside the stones of the campsite.

Raven realized this was the first time she entered the tent. Looking around, she took in the details of the temporary shelter that would function as her home during this mission. The walls of the canvas structure had vinyl bonded to the inside, strengthening the fibers and giving it a waterproof seal. A low bed, piled with pillows and blankets, dominated the space. The only other furniture in the tent was a long, low table near the back. Wires descended from the peak of the tent and were attached to a black charging pad laid out on the table surface. A data pad was resting on the pad. This was to be their only contact with the outside world. Access to technology was a luxury for many of the travelling communities, but it wasn't unheard of for tribes to have at least a few devices for communication. Raven was aware the wires connected to a solar panel stretched across the top of the tent. The wealth reflected in the few possessions scattered around the tent and the camp was well beyond what most travelling communities could gather on their own. She just hoped their cover story was strong enough to explain away the possessions. From the conversation she was hearing, it was apparent the story was about to be tested. Joseph and the man were standing close to the tent opening and Raven leaned over to hear what they were saying.

"I'm called Bear," the man said. "I'm the scout for the travelling community known as the West Mountain Trekkers. This is our territory, although we do welcome visitors and other families to join us in our work."

"We're not here to take work from other communities." Raven could hear strength and confidence in Joseph's voice as he spoke. He obviously knew the vernacular of these people and was able to speak to them with ease. "My wife and I are from a tribe in Northeast Montana. We found it necessary to leave the tribe and are seeking another family to join. I heard there are tribes in Idaho who are seeking healthy, young workers and we decided to try our luck here."

"You are welcome to camp here," Bear's voice carried a deep bravado. "I'll bring your request to the elders of our tribe. You'll be able to tell your story to them." There was a pause and Raven realized the men were walking around the circumference of the camp. "May I meet your wife?"

Raven knew it was time. She took a veil and placed it over her face. The thin, dark fabric disguised her face making it difficult for anyone to discern any distinguishing features. Women in the communities wore veils in public to hide their age. It wasn't unheard of for women to be stolen from communities to be kept as slaves. Most were stolen for the sole purpose of having children. Raiders didn't want to steal women who were too old to have children so, to protect themselves, the women of the tribe wore veils to hide their faces.

Raven affected a slightly stooped posture as she stepped out of the tent and approached the men. She kept her eyes turned down to avoid looking directly at the stranger. It rankled her to have to act so submissive, but she knew she couldn't break character. She came to a halt right behind Joseph, taking her place behind his right shoulder; the position showing her role as a first wife. Glancing up briefly, she assessed the man standing in front of Joseph. He was huge. His body seemed to sprout reddish-brown hair from his full beard to the little bit of chest and arms uncovered by his linen shirt.

"This is my wife, Bly." Joseph didn't move from in front of Raven. His subtle posture let Bear know he would do everything in his power to protect Raven in case the man had any untoward intentions.

"I'll set my camp on the other side of the glen." Bear pointed to a section of the meadow. "If you're interested in sharing a meal, I brought the meat." He brought a brace of rabbits off his shoulder and placed them on the table.

"Well, we can hardly turn down the offer of free meat." Joseph extended his hand and the two men grasped forearms. "I'll help you set your camp while my wife prepares dinner."

Raven had a hard time preventing her eyes from rolling. She picked the rabbits up and carried them towards the stream as the two men walked across the meadow to set up camp. Fortunately, the rabbits were already field-dressed and required very little cleaning. Most of Raven's experience with cooking wild meat stemmed from her survival training. The only problem with this training was she was taught to cook food to the point it could be eaten safely; she wasn't sure if she could make the rabbit taste good. The meat was so lean it could easily become tough and stringy if not cooked properly. This was going to be a true test of her ability to fit into the community. The meal would take time if she was going to do it right. As soon as she returned to the camp she stoked the fire and started the cast iron pans heating. Using every lesson she learned about seasoning from her aunt Emily and working in the kitchen at Haven, she prepared each ingredient carefully and soon had a savory rabbit stew simmering over the low coals.

The stew and dumplings couldn't have turned out more perfect. The sun was just beginning to set as the men cleaned their plates of the last scrap of food and drop of gravy. Raven had eaten her own dinner in the seclusion of the tent and, when she was finished, covered her face and brought her dishes out to the table. Joseph had placed a lantern on the table next to the dishpan before he moved to stoke the fire. A second lantern rested on a flat rock between the two men. Raven boiled water and scrubbed the dishes while the men sat and talked by the fire. She made sure to put everything in its place, double checking the food stores and the locks on the bicycles and supply bins. Although there were rules established in the communities, not all travelers abided by these rules.

Joseph walked the perimeter of the camp, setting trip wires attached to a bell system. The low tech device was the only alarm system they had to protect the camp from unwanted visitors. Raven carried the lantern into the tent and set it on the low table near the back. She wasn't sure how long she would have until Joseph entered, so she hurried to undressed and put on a nightgown. She was tempted to throw a shirt over the gown, but she knew if they were called out of bed in the middle of the night it would look odd to have a shirt over the already voluminous gown. She stood at the edge of the bed for a moment, staring at the linen covered pad. Despite taking up nearly a third of the tent, the bed looked way too small to accommodate two people. Lakota and Marwa had both been sleeping in their own bed since they were six so it had been a couple of years since she had to share with someone else. She just hoped Joseph wasn't too much of a bed hog.

Raven flipped the switch on the lantern, plunging the tent into darkness. She blinked her eyes once, to allow them to adjust to the lack of light. The confines of the tent took on a shimmering quality as her feline vision took over. Sighing, she pulled back the blankets and crawled into the bed. The pad was a dense polymer, offering little more than a miniscule buffer between the ground and her body. Raven counted no less than three stones jabbing into her back and what felt like a tree root under her knee. She decided the next time they set up camp she was going to chose where to place the tent. There had to be a better site in the visitor section than where they were now.

Light from Joseph's lantern illuminated the sides of the tent, allowing Raven to watch his progress as he made his final rounds. She saw the light pause as he approached the opening of the tent. She wondered if he was nervous to enter considering his revelation and behavior from earlier. The opening parted and he stepped inside. His posture didn't reflect any tension or nervousness and the broad grin on his face belied any contrition for his behavior. His whole demeanor projected an aura of the cat that ate the canary. Raven couldn't help but scoff at him.

"You caught me off guard earlier." Raven kept her voice low but there was no way he could have missed the anger reverberating in her tone. "Next time you try a stunt like that, I'll put a knee in your kidney."

Joseph chuckled. His face didn't lose any of its pleased look. In fact his grin just got bigger. "Don't worry Raven," he whispered, "I plan on slowly working you over. I just wanted to let you know

155

my intentions. I am a very patient man; I'll wait until you fall hopelessly in love with me before I try to kiss you again."

Raven snorted and rolled on her side, giving him her back. The noises of him changing and shuffling around the tent preparing for bed kept her on edge and she could feel her muscles stiffening. She heard, rather than felt, him slip into bed beside her. The pad was so low to the ground there was nowhere for it to go as Joseph settled in beside her.

"Relax, Raven," Joseph's voice carried a trace of laughter. "You're safe with me. I love you and won't let any harm come to you."

Despite these reassurances, Raven had a hard time relaxing enough to close her eyes and go to sleep. Perhaps it was because of the tension she felt as she drifted off that her nightmares were extremely vivid. Her nightmares were usually a confusing jumble of images, one coming right after the other and tonight was no exception. The dream started with the overwhelming sense of being trapped in some sort of container. Outside there was a constant throbbing sound, like the steady beat of helicopter blades. Tiny sand particles drummed against the outside of the container, their steady patter forming a constant beat. The beat came louder and steadier, increasing in tempo. A reverberating boom, followed by a staccato beat, startled her awake.

Raven sat up in the bed, barely managing to stifle a scream. The process of sitting up had pulled the covers off Joseph and he rolled over in the bed. Raven could see his eyes peering up at her in the darkness of the tent. His gaze was piercing as she tried to get her breathing under control. Another crashing sound caused her to jump. She was very aware of Joseph studying her as the thunder rolled across the campground. The lightning strike had to have happened close-by. She could taste the tang of ozone and her skin tingled.

Joseph placed his arm around her shoulders and pulled her body towards his. At first she tried to pull away, but the warmth of his body drew her in and eased her breathing. She relaxed into his body, listening to his heartbeat and breathing, allowing his natural body rhythms to assuage her own racing heart.

"It's just a little thunderstorm, Raven." Joseph's voice was tender and his hands were gently massaging her back and shoulders. "It's okay Raven, I'm here."

His voice was so soothing, it was easy to believe he was there to take care of her. Raven's breathing slowed and she closed her eyes, savoring his masculine scent. It was a feeling she hadn't had in a long time. It was a feeling she didn't think she needed to feel until now. If this is what married life was going to be like with Joseph, it was something she could easily get used to. The thought flashed through her mind that, although they hadn't stood before witnesses and swore vows before God, on paper, their marriage was as legal as any other performed in the country. She squashed the thought before it could get very far, but the germ of the idea was there.

Chapter Twenty

DESPITE THE STORM AND THE hard ground and rocks, Raven finally managed to relax enough to go back to sleep. There wasn't an alarm clock to wake her up in the morning, but the birds chirping as the sun crested the mountains was enough to do the job. Joseph was already up and moving around the tent, pulling on his clothes and checking the messages on the data pad. The device definitely lacked the sleek qualities of the pads Raven had used, both during her time in the service and at Haven. She missed her own data pad, the one containing all the letters to Billy. It had been shattered when the shrapnel had hit her backpack all those years ago and she was afraid to try to get it repaired, afraid someone would discover her secret stash of letters. She kept the pieces of her pad in a storage bin at Haven. Joseph's pad looked like it had been pieced together from multiple devices. The frame was beaten up and the screen contained multiple scratches across its surface. Joseph used a stylus to move through a few files then pocketed the device before leaving the tent. He was going to be in charge of keeping track of the device and embedding code words in e-mails and messages. The code was complicated. Joseph had spent some time explaining some of it to Raven, but it was more complex than he had time to explain in the few hours they were alone the day before.

Raven dressed quickly and stepped out of the tent, silently assessed the situation. Bear was standing at the edge of the camp, just beyond the border stones as Joseph moved around the perimeter, removing the alarm system. Raven made sure her veil was securely in place as she picked up the water bucket and walked to the stream. Out of the corner of her eye she saw Bear hold up a hunk of what looked like a slab of bacon and Joseph motioned him inside the boundary of the camp.

Raven fried up the bacon with reconstituted onions, potatoes and eggs for breakfast, serving it with biscuits baked in a cast iron kettle, washed down with hot tea. It was a good breakfast. The camp routine was obviously becoming well-established as Raven cleaned while the men sat and talked. She made sure to stay close enough she could hear their conversation as she cleaned the dishes and sat down near them to sort beans before setting them to soak in a pan of water.

"The rest of the community should be here about noon." Bear was running his fingers through his beard as he spoke. "We're following the harvest right now. Nearly two-thirds of our family is traveling to local farms and offering their services for the harvest. The remainder of our people are at our winter quarters. It's always a risk and a sacrifice to leave our families behind, but we need to be able to work to feed them."

Joseph was nodding in agreement. A thought flitted through Raven's mind as she watched the two of them together. Joseph looked extremely comfortable sitting next to Bear, discussing the roles of life on the road. This was the environment in which Joseph grew up. One filled with fear and danger, lost in wondering how and when he would be able to feed his family or himself. Raven had never gone hungry a day in her life. There was always an abundance of food around, no matter where she was. Even here, in this tiny little camp in the woods, there was plenty of food. But, what was going to happen when the food ran out? Unless they were adopted by a community they would have to scrounge and beg for work and food, living on the fringes of society. Calling for back-up or food drops was out of the question. She couldn't send a letter to her mother requesting a Haven care package. They were on their own. The only people they could count on for survival were each other. Raven glanced at Joseph and found him looking at her out of the corner of his eye. Bear had stepped out of the boundary stones and was walking towards his own tent. Joseph gave her a small grin and motioned her over.

"I'm going to go get some more wood. Whistle if you need anything." Joseph nodded in Bear's direction. "I'm going to stay well in sight of camp. You know what to watch for."

Raven nodded as she placed her hand on the hilt of the knife. Not that it did much good to bring a knife to a gun fight, as most of the men in the community were known to carry firearms, but it was comforting to know she had the weapon at her disposal. Besides, if Bear was being deceitful and was just trying to lull them into a sense of complacency before he attacked, he would be more interested in capturing her alive and wouldn't shoot her if he could help it. Joseph embraced her and kissed her gently on the forehead, a perfectly acceptable gesture between a man and his wife in the community. Raven accepted the kiss with grace and dignity. She was starting to see Joseph in a different light. Not that she was going to fall in love with him, but if they were going to pull off the happily married couple routine she was going to have to accept his small gestures of affection. He grabbed the handle of the ax and headed to the trees.

The camp had an orderly, homey feel about it by the time Raven was finished cleaning and organizing everything. Joseph returned to camp with another load of wood and stacked it near the fireplace. Raven helped him clean out the cart, making sure there wasn't any dirt or dust left in the bottom. It seemed a little obsessive, but when survival was dependent on the condition of camp supplies, everything had to be maintained with the utmost care.

Once the main camp was orderly, Raven and Joseph ducked under the awning where the bikes and the food supplies were stored. Together they searched through the supplies, assessing the effects of the storm. A little water had evaded the awning and the tarp covering the supplies and had settled in the bottom of the buckets, but the food containers had held up under the storm. Raven wiped everything down and packed the supplies back in their containers.

A sharp whistle drew her attention to the road. A line of figures were approaching the camp, spread out across the length and breadth of the road. Some were riding bicycles, others were walking and pulling carts. Sheep and goats were being herded and chased by children of all ages, intermingled with the crowd. Raven could hear the bark of a dog and the occasional cluck of a chicken. It took her a moment to spot the cages suspended at odd angles from the carts. She started mentally going through her supplies, trying to figure out what she could use for trade for fresh eggs. The dehydrated, powdered eggs she used that morning weren't very appetizing.

As the crowd filtered into camp they dispersed into different campsites and began to establish boundary lines. Raven noticed Bear in one of the campsites. He was talking to some of the men as everyone moved around the open field. It was obvious the conversation involved her and Joseph since many of the arm gestures involved pointing in their direction. Raven tried to make herself as unobtrusive as possible. Slipping under the awning she put together a quick lunch. The small, battery powered cooler held a supply of cheeses and meats she used to create sandwiches. Bringing Joseph his, she slipped into the tent so she could remove her veil to eat her meal.

Voices carried through the walls of the tent, muffled by the still damp canvas. Raven had the overwhelming impulse to go out and offer her assistance to the campers, but she knew it would be out of character for a woman to put herself forward to be noticed. She had to resign herself to sitting in the stifling humidity of the tent, waiting to be called forth and be introduced to the others in the camp. Her arms were dusty and streaked with black marks from cooking over the camp fire. She realized her face and clothing were just as filthy. The clothes she washed yesterday were sitting on the low table at the back of the tent. She had time so she took the opportunity to change clothes and scrubbed as much of the dust off her face and arms as she could. The greasy black marks didn't come off; she would need hot water and soap to get completely clean. After she washed her face she replaced her veil.

The flap of the tent lifted and Raven could see Bear and another man standing at the edge of the campsite. Joseph motioned for her to come out of the tent. Raven ducked her head and followed him to the edge of camp. Keeping her eyes downcast she took short, shifting steps to avoid stumbling. When Joseph stopped she took her place behind him. Barely lifting her eyes above the edges of her veil, she studied the two men standing outside the boundary line. Bear's wide stance and broad shoulders denoted his power and confidence. The stooped, elderly man was a stark contrast to the huge man beside him. Despite the short gray hair, stooped posture and slack, wrinkled skin, his bright blue eyes shone with wisdom and alertness.

Joseph removed his hat and bowed his head, a gesture of respect to Elders in the community. Placing her right hand over her heart and lowered her head, Raven kept her eyes glued to the ground. It rankled everything in her soul to show such a submissive posture, but her wellbeing and the success of the mission depended on her ability to adapt and that was what she was going to do.

"This is Elder Elias," Bear pointed to the man as he talked directly to Joseph. "He's in charge of this camp. He would like to speak to you."

"Would you like to come into our camp and sit down?" Joseph gestured for the men to step into the camp. "My wife can make us some tea and we can talk."

"Thank you, Joseph," Elder Elias said, "but I'm afraid I must decline your offer. There is still much work to do to set up camp so I only have a few moments. I just wanted to inform you that Bear has told us of your desire to join a community. We are a small family and desire to increase our group. We will hold counsel after supper tonight and you will be able to put your request before us for consideration. In the meantime, we would like to extend the offer for you and your wife to join us in our evening meal. Bear tells us your wife is a fine cook. If she would like to join the women in preparing the evening meal they are all in the main campsite." He pointed to an area in the center of the encampment. A group of women were gathering, all of them carrying some sort of kitchen implement or food item.

"My wife is very knowledgeable in herbal remedies and healing." This was going to be part of their cover story. Raven knew if someone was sick or injured she wouldn't be able to control her natural instincts to help. Explaining she was trained in the medical arts might give them a better chance of being accepted and it would explain her desire to help. "If there are any sick or injured among you she may be able to help."

For the first time Elias looked at Raven. His eyes assessed her from top to bottom, seeming to peer through the thick veil covering everything but her eyes.

"I would be happy to help set up camp." Raven knew Joseph's offer wasn't done out of generosity. It was important to establish a strong work ethic and a willingness to help from the beginning. The community wouldn't accept any shirking of duty and it was important to work from sunrise to sunset if you wanted to eat.

"Yes." Obviously Joseph's offer was well received. Elias was smiling as he spoke. "Bear and a few other men are gathering firewood. You can join them since you have a cart."

Joseph patted Raven's cheek as he moved across the camp to get the cart, and then chuckled as she flashed him a glare from under her eyelashes. She had a feeling he was going to take a number of liberties in these small gestures of affection. Before Raven left the campsite to join the other women she made sure her veil was securely in place. Although she had managed to keep a low profile for most of her life, due to her mother's diligence in keeping her children out of the media's eyes, there was still the off chance that there was a member of the community who might recognize her.

All the women stopped their work and stared at her as she walked to the center of the camp. Children stopped their play and hid behind their mothers or moved to the far side of the meadow. Raven stopped at the edge of ring of stones signifying the new cooking hearth. A woman sitting in a camp chair at the edge of the activity motioned to one of the women working near the fire. The hand gesture was subtle, but effective. The woman at the fire put down the spoon she was using to stir the pot and walked over to Raven.

"Have you come to help?" She asked.

Raven nodded, unsure of what to say to the woman.

"My name is Samantha." The woman opened her arms in a gesture of welcome, but her body was stiff and Raven could see anxiousness in the lines of her frame. "You have already met my husband, Bear. I'm his second wife. The woman in the chair at the edge of camp is his mother. She is the Matriarch of the community."

Raven glanced at the woman who was apparently holding court over the site. Children climbed over her lap and played at her feet. Older children and young adults were bringing her tidbits of food or interesting items they found in the woods. Despite being outdoors the camp had a homey, familial feeling about it. The Matriarch's slightest gesture or word was immediately interpreted and the order was fulfilled.

"You're welcome to join us in preparing an evening meal." Samantha turned and gestured for Raven to enter the camp. From the angle of her stance Raven could see the woman was about five months pregnant. "My husband says you're a fair cook and a good worker. He was grateful you and your husband welcomed him into your campsite these past two days."

Samantha led her to where the old woman was holding court. Her face was as wrinkled as Elder Elias' had been. Blue-grey eyes assessed Raven shrewdly and the woman even reached forward and grasped Raven's hips with a surprisingly strong grip. The woman smiled as her fingers bit into the flesh covering Raven's hip bones.

"You are young and strong." The woman's voice had a slight quiver and the flesh under her chin wobbled like a turkey's dewlap as she talked. "We will be interested in hearing what you have to offer."

Raven had to bite the inside of her check to keep a retort from spewing forth. She wanted to ask if the woman thought she had good, strong, child-bearing hips, but knew it wouldn't be couth to be sarcastic to the woman who could determine her destiny in the community. A slight gesture brought Samantha to Raven's side.

"Have her gather dry wood and kindling." The Matriarch spoke through Raven as if she wasn't even there. "We won't have her handling any food until we know they can be trusted. She can tend the fire and help clean until then."

Raven knew she had just been dismissed and was now expected to work as hard as anyone for the good of the community. All her hard work would be for naught if she couldn't gain the trust of the members of the community. She returned to her campsite for the bucket and started gathering the dry branches and twigs used to start fires. The work was laborious, but each bucketful she added to the growing pile was one more step towards gaining trust. By the time the men returned with their haul she had gathered enough small wood to start several fires. Joseph had shown Bear where he had found the blackberry bushes and when Samantha asked the matriarch for permission to organize a gathering party, the old woman told her to take Raven with her. The "keep an eye on her" was implied, if never spoken.

Chapter Twenty-One

IT WAS LATE IN THE evening when the women started setting tables for dinner. It seemed there was a lot more food than could be eaten by the group currently in the camp. Raven counted the members of the camp, being careful not to appear to be studying the group. She counted six men, eleven women and about eight children of various ages. Raven brought her prepared beans to the table and the community added the pot to the growing pile of food. She noticed the pan was placed near the edge of the table, away from the main courses. The food being laid out on the table looked like it would feed at least forty. Just as she was about to ask why they were preparing so much food, she heard the roar of a diesel engine from the direction of the road. An ancient bus pulled into the campground, followed by a van and a couple of people on motorcycles. By the time the occupants off-loaded from the vehicles Raven counted twelve more men, five women and ten children, most of them teenage boys.

Raven had nearly forgotten most of the community's group didn't spend the day in the camps. Most of the able-bodied workers would fan out into the surrounding farm lands, seeking work in the fields as laborers. The work was tedious and often times backbreaking, but the earnings from this labor were the only means of sustaining the communities during long, dark winters.

Once the workers washed the layer of field off their hands, arms and faces everyone gathered around the food tables. Each person grasped their own plate and silverware as they took their place in line. Elder Elias took his place at the head of the line and turned to the crowd.

"My family," despite his age the man's voice was clear and strong. "We have visitors with us here today. Please welcome them.

They have worked hard today, so we have invited them to join us for our evening meal. We will hear their story and news after our meal. Now, let's everyone bow our heads so we can say grace."

There was a desperate shushing of children as arms were folded and heads bowed.

"*Our Dearest Father*," Elder Elias' voice sang into the night. "*We bow our heads before you to give thanks for this bounteous meal. We thank you for the many hands who prepared this meal for us and the work our family has put into providing the food. Please bless all members of our family and our guests as we take the nourishment you have provided for us into our bodies. In the name of your Son, Amen.*"

A chorus of amen's was followed by shuffling as the family formed two lines, one of men and one of women and children. Samantha led Raven to a spot near the back of the line of women. A group of half-grown children shifted, allowing Raven to take a place in front of them. This was a good sign. It showed the community valued the work she did today and would allow her to eat before the teenagers in the group.

Although the community shared the work and the food there was a definite hierarchy among the members. Joseph had explained the system to Raven the day before. No one was to starve, but able-bodied workers, leaders of the community and women who were pregnant or could get pregnant always ate first. They were allowed the most nutrient-rich, high-quality food. Mothers were expected to ensure their young children had their share and often times nursed the infants until their third birthday to provide needed nutrition. Children too young to work, but not relying on their mothers for food, were next. At the end of the line came those who, for some reason, were unable to perform physical labor. They would eat whatever was left over. Members of the community were taught portion control from a very young age and severe penalties were issued for anyone caught stealing or hoarding food. One of the tenets of the community was everyone works and everyone eats.

Raven watched each member of the community to see how they portioned out their food. She carefully filled her plate with the protein rich stew, fresh vegetables, a chunk of yellow cheese and a slice of bread. Her pot of beans were nearly untouched and she scooped up a large ladle full to put on her plate. A few other community members followed suit, but Raven knew she would have leftover beans tomorrow. The end of the table contained bowls of blackberries and pitchers of goat's milk. She put a scoop of berries in her cup and poured the milk over the top. The problem with goat's milk was it tasted like what the goats were eating. Raven developed a dislike for the milk when she was visiting her grandfather in Arizona as a child and the family goat had gotten into the mustard seed grass, but she had gotten used to the taste during her service in Afghanistan and sweetening it with the berries actually made it tolerable.

Joseph caught her eye and motioned to their campsite. They took their food into their space to eat. Raven moved into the tent so she could remove her veil. Joseph followed her, sitting on the floor and putting his plate on the ground.

"How are you holding up, Raven?" His voice was low and Raven knew it wouldn't carry past the walls of the tent.

"I'm fine." Her voice was barely above a whisper. "There's not much difference between the work here and the work at Haven."

"Do you see anyone you recognize?" Raven shook her head. Once the women of the camp got used to her being there she was able to observe them unobtrusively. The women had all been told to remove their veils while they worked by the Matriarch, although Raven wouldn't be allowed to until Joseph gave her the official okay and publicly acknowledged her complete freedom around the camp. The strictures were actually working in their favor. Joseph reached over to touch her face but Raven pulled away before he could make contact. His blue eyes flashed disappointment and he gave her a slightly uncomfortable smile.

"You need to stop pulling away from me, Bly," he said.

Raven realized Joseph deliberately used her real name as a reminder of their mission. She was going to be called Bly Baker, first wife of Joseph Baker. It was the first time in her life when she was going to be known by a last name other than Taylor. She had never changed her name when she married Billy, deciding she wanted to keep a small piece of her mother with her. It was why she gave her son the last name of Taylor; she wanted her mother's name to be past down to future generations. So many details to get used to almost overwhelmed her mind. She ate in silence, enjoying the rich, slightly smoky flavor of the food. She affixed her veil in place before leaving the tent to help clean.

The fire was shooting bright sparks into the darkness, illuminating the faces of the community members as they gathered in the shadows. Raven could see the glow of eyes in the firelight and she kept her face carefully averted so no one would she the sheen of her cat's eyes against the light. Elder Elias stood in the center of the light and called everyone to order.

"My children." All whispering hushed and eyes turned to him as he spoke. "Before we adjourn tonight, our guests would like to plead a case before us. I have agreed to hear them out. This is Joseph Baker and his wife. Let's hear what they have to say."

Joseph squeezed Raven's hand before he stood and took the place Elias had just vacated. "My friends," he began. "My wife and I have traveled from our family in Montana to Idaho, seeking work. We could have stayed in Montana, but the situation there is so volatile it is impossible to safely raise a family. In fact, my older brother was killed six weeks ago when a militia group attacked a food warehouse where he was working as a guard. My wife, Bly, was his second wife. When he died another brother said he would take my brother's first wife as his second and take custody of my brother's two children, but he was not able to afford to take a third wife. I was yet unmarried so it became my responsibility to take Bly as my wife and care for her and any children she may have. We decided to leave and come somewhere safe so we could raise a family of our own. My wife and I are good workers and we carried away many gifts from our family and friends to offer any community who would take us in and allow us to join them."

The whispers and shuffling started up again as Joseph finished speaking. Members of the community were staring at him as if they were expecting him to say more. Raven kept her eyes downcast, waiting for the inevitable questions. They weren't long in coming.

"What are your backgrounds?" The question was asked by a middle aged man.

"I was raised in the community." Joseph didn't even hesitate in his answers. "When I was nineteen I served my required two years in the service, although I refused to allow them to mark me with an implant. I mostly worked border duty down in Old Mexico." It was easier to keep track of information by telling half truths and there was always an off-chance they would run into someone they served with in the military, so Raven's and Joseph's stories needed to incorporate truths about their past. "As soon as I was released from duty I returned home and started working on our family land. That was six months ago."

Joseph waved Raven forward. "My wife Bly was born in Arizona. Her mother was a Navajo tribe member and her father was one of the National Guard soldiers sent there when the first pandemics started. Her father developed some strong anti-government sentiments while in the service and was dishonorably discharged when Bly was three years old. His wife died when a second outbreak of small pox broke out not long after. Bly's father cut the microchip out of her hand and took her with him to Montana. He was working for our community as a guard, but he was killed when Bly was thirteen. My family took her in and raised her. She joined the service when she was eighteen and served three years in the military as a medic, but when she returned home she took her place back in the community. Not long after her return she became my brother's second wife. Bly's father was actually a Gen and she has some characteristics of the genetically altered soldiers. I'm not going to lie to you, my wife is very afraid we won't be accepted because of her DNA, although she has proven her own fertility."

The Matriarch stood, drawing all eyes to her. "Why aren't her children with her?"

"She gave birth to twins four years ago, a boy and a girl." The image of Lakota and Marwa flashed through Raven's mind at the mention of the children. "The boy was given to my brother's first wife since he was my brother's first born. But like many children born together, the girl could not bear to be parted from her brother when it came time for us to leave. Our community promised to care for them both and gave us many gifts in exchange for leaving the children there. Between their gifts and the reserves we both have from the military, we could easily find a place and establish our own life, but we don't want to rely on the government for our livelihood and we want the protection of living in a community."

Silence followed Joseph's speech. Raven saw Samantha rubbing her belly, a concerned look on her face. She wondered if Samantha's child was destined to be given over to Bear's first wife. Perhaps this would give her a chance to build a bond with the woman. The common ground of the loss of a child had the potential for binding women together, no matter the circumstances. Raven knew her children were safe with her mother, but she was starting to wonder if leaving them was the best decision to make.

"What Gen traits does your wife have?" Elias' question drew all eyes to Raven. She paused for a moment then raised her head, staring directly into the firelight. From the gasps she knew she had turned her face just right and her eyes caught the glow of the light. She couldn't suppress a smile and was thankful she had the veil to cover her face.

"We don't know all the genetic modifications her father had. My wife's vision is about forty percent better than the average human's and she can see in the dark as if it's as bright as day." Raven lowered her eyes again, feeling the discomfort of the people around her. She didn't want to push them past their limits. "She also received a cochlear implant when she was a child for a hearing impairment and it was upgraded when she joined the service. We both learned to be good soldiers and can fight and defend with the best of them but we hated what the government was doing. We think the military was being used to police other countries and very little was being done to defend the people at home. We want to integrate back into the community, where our skills we learned in the military can be put to use."

A man stepped forward, standing near Elias. "How do we know you aren't spies sent from the government?" His voice carried a tone of confrontation. "And what do you have to offer us if we did accept you?"

A few heads nodded in agreement and the murmuring rolled through the crowd. Elias held up his hand and silence fell over the group. He turned to Joseph and gestured for him to continue.

"In addition to our strength and ability to work, we bring knowledge in defense." Joseph gestured in the general direction of the encampment, now only vague shadows outlining the tent and smaller elements of the camp. "I was trained as an engineer in the Guard and can rebuild almost anything from the ground up. My wife was in the medical corps as a nurse practitioner and can bring those skills to any family we join. We also have many supplies we are willing to share with our new family. We have seeds and technology we can bring to the permanent settlement to share with everyone. If it will help you make your decision I would be willing to show the supplies we have to offer to the leaders of the community at first light tomorrow."

After Joseph's promise to share the wealth of their camp and plans were made to survey their belongings in the morning, the meeting broke up and everyone separated to go to their tents. Raven saw a small group of men gathered near the fire, each of them armed with a rifle or bow. Morning was going to be interesting.

Chapter Twenty-Two

RAVEN WAS UP AND DRESSED before sunrise. She could hear the stirrings of the other members of the camp. Reaching up, she made sure her veil was securely in place before leaving the tent. Joseph was already outside, talking with Elder Elias and three other men from the camp. Raven overheard Elias introduce the men as workers in the community, Steven, Marcus and Derek. Raven recognized Derek as the man who was so confrontational at the meeting the night before. He nodded to her as she walked around the corner to get breakfast supplies. She pulled out some parched grain, buttermilk and dried fruit.

The camp was illuminated by the first rays of the rising sun as she prepared flapjacks and soaked the fruit in water. She could hear the men talking about the supplies Joseph was showing them. The men were exclaiming over the plethora of seeds sealed in moisture-proof bins. Joseph showed them the solar panels and the power generators attached to the bicycles. The wealth he was showing the men was more than two people living on their own should have.

Raven watched out of the corner of her eye as Joseph led the men to the edge of the camp. He shook their hands, promising to join them and do whatever work they needed him to do. Elder Elias paused and turned to face Joseph, putting his foot on one of the boundary rocks.

"I will talk to the council tonight." He extended his hand for Joseph to grasp. "If they are agreeable, and I think they will be, you can remove these boundary stones and you can join us in our labor during the harvest. If you show you will become an integral part of this community we will invite you to winter with us. If you are not a good fit we will make sure you have enough supplies to get you through winter and bring you to a place where you can find shelter. When spring planting starts we can guide you to a number of families who may be looking for others to join them."

The comment about removing the boundary stones was a good sign. Even though Elias hadn't made a direct offer for Raven and Joseph to join the camp, he was making it apparent he would be considering allowing them to become part of the community. Raven and Joseph finished their breakfast quickly and straightened up the camp. Together they approached the center of the encampment. It was time to find out what they got themselves into.

Joseph and Raven insinuated themselves into the community and, within a few days, they had had moved the boundary stones from their camp completely. Joseph had made many necessary repairs to the equipment the community had in their possession. Raven stood by and watched as he repaired motors, wheels and a variety of electronic devices. She was impressed with the range of skills he displayed as he deftly worked on the community's equipment. Both of them joined the harvesting crews spreading out among the farmlands, offering their services to farmers and ranchers needing help with harvest.

There were many large corporate farms taking hundreds if not thousands of acres of land. These farms were run with expensive, powerful equipment, not needing much more than a handful of people to operate. The food produced on these farms was destined for towns and cities populated by registered citizens of the United States. Unless a citizen had an embedded microchip or a card with a code marked on it, this food could not be purchased. The chip and code contained the work, medical, financial and citizenship status of the individual. Without this link to civilization individuals were not allowed to reside with the general public or shop in stores where members of the general populace also shopped. The risk for spreading disease from the great unwashed, as they were referred to in many circles, was too great.

The community worked the small farms tucked away in hilly areas, between populated regions. These farms were usually owned by families with limited resources. The owners couldn't afford the high-powered farm equipment available to the larger corporations and had to rely on older tractors and manual labor to produce crops. The Communities and the farmers created a symbiotic relationship, necessary for the survival of both units.

Raven and Joseph both volunteered to work with the harvesters, leaving their personal belongings in camp to show their trust for the community. The entire camp would arise before the sun peeked over the mountain. The women would prepare breakfast for the entire camp, Raven joining the women in their work. The Matriarch would give daily assignments, ordering the members of the camp around like an old hen in the barnyard. No matter what task was thrown Raven's way, she worked hard to prove herself with the community. The ease with which she fit into the community was due more to her work and the skills she learned in Haven than what she learned in her service in the Guard. The community was a self-sufficient agrarian society, much like Haven.

Surprisingly, Raven was actually enjoying her time with the community and started developing bonds with some of the women in the camp. By the third day in camp Raven had exchanged her veil for a simple headscarf covering her hair. She kept the veil tucked in a pouch attached to her belt, like all the women in the community. If the women needed to appear in public they pulled out the veil and quickly and deftly wrapped it around their heads and faces. Raven wore a lightweight veil when she went with the work crews to work the harvest very similar in style as the other women.

The harvesters developed a rhythm and pattern to their work. No matter what was being harvested the system was the same. This day the community was going to be working in the early fruit harvest. Right after breakfast the harvesters would pile into the vehicles and head to the field. Those left behind were charged with keeping the camp safe and searching the surrounding land for wild food and firewood. There were always able bodied men left behind to protect the women and children from raids.

Raven joined the other harvesters on the bus for the journey to the cherry orchard. As she disembarked she followed Joseph and the others to the check-in desk. Joseph was pulling the cart by its handle. Raven presented her work card to the woman behind the counter; the first step in getting to the orchards. Raven lowered her veil briefly so the woman could check her face against the picture on the card. She entered Raven's statistics into the data pad on her desk and handed her back the card and pointed to a stack of buckets and ladders.

"You get a dollar for every ten pounds you pick." The woman didn't make eye contact with Raven as she spoke. "You can take one ladder and three buckets. Here is your work ticket. It's your responsibility to present it at the weigh-in at the end of the day. We will either credit your account at the end of the day or exchange your pay for work tokens to be used in the company store."

Raven presented her work ticket to the bucket distributor. The woman scanned the card and printed out three bar codes, attached the printed form to the handle of three buckets and handed them to her. Raven placed the buckets in the cart, along with the others from the community. It was hot in the orchard, but the trees provided shade as Raven climbed into the sweet, green canopy. Her fingers reached for the tiny red globes, plucking the juice-filled cherries from their hiding places among the leaves. The fruits made a satisfying plunk as she dropped them in the buckets balanced among the branches. When a bucket would get full she would hand it down to the community member in charge of running it to the scale, usually a younger teenager who wasn't as fast as the others at picking. The runner would place the buckets in the cart, take the pickers card and bring the buckets to the scale. All in all the system was very efficient, allowing the pickers to stay in the trees and pick more fruit. By the end of the day Raven had earned just over forty dollars and was filled to the top with cherries. There was something about sitting in the top of the trees and eating sweet, juicy fruit warmed by the sun.

It was nearing sunset when everyone piled back on the bus to return to the campsite. Each person had ten pounds of cherries, purchased with a portion of wages from their labor. Most of the workers wages were taken in the form of credits on their work cards. A few individuals had used the coin shaped work tokens to purchase a few staples from the company store. Raven spent a few minutes looking at the items in the company store, but the prices were so inflated and supplies limited that in order for her to get anything of quality she would have had to spend more money than she earned during the day's work. She was satisfied with her ten pounds of cherries overflowing the top of her box. Raven had a secret tucked in the corner of her cardboard box. A tiny gift she would present to the camp after supper.

The evening meal was prepared and waiting for them when they returned to the camp. Raven washed her hands and joined the queue to get her share of the food. Obviously one of the old brooding hens had been sacrificed for the chicken and dumplings dominating the center of the table. Raven could feel her mouth salivating in anticipation as the smell of the meal wafted over the camp.

After the meal and the clean-up, each of the harvesters brought out their boxes of cherries. Raven dug around in her box, pulling a tiny can with a tree standing about twelve inches high from among the red fruits. She carried it to the Matriarch and placed it at her feet.

"The owners of the orchard were down by the stream pulling seedlings from the mud when I went down to wash my hands before lunch." Raven smiled down at the tiny seedling. "They were throwing them on the bank and complaining about how they choke out the water supply. There were about a dozen seedlings up and down the banks. I told them I would dig them if I could keep three of them. Since you were planning on sending this week's load of goods up tomorrow I figured these could go to Winter Quarters, along with mine and my husband's share of the harvest. The trees need to be transplanted right away if they have any chance of survival."

The old woman's face split into a toothless grin. "You are not even part of this community yet and you are already making great contributions." She gestured to one of the young teens standing by the bus. "Take these trees from your new sister and transplant them into better containers. They will go with our other contributions to Winter Quarters."

The acceptance of the fruit and the trees sealed the deal with the community. There was no longer any question where Raven and Joseph were going to be spending the winter. Even their tent location evolved as the community transitioned to new campsites, moving closer to the center of camp. All of the food in their camp was transferred to the communal kitchens and they were preparing and eating their meals with the family.

The hot days of late summer and the harvest of cherries, peaches and apricots and so many other early fruits and vegetables gave way to the nip of early autumn mornings and the harvest of apples, potatoes, onions and other fall crops. The days were still warm enough to easily break into a sweat as Raven worked the rows of crops, bending low over the ground crops, or reaching above her head to pluck fruit from the trees. Each crop brought a different ache to an area of her body, but it was a good ache, one that ensured the security and well-being of the community. Samantha would often work side by side with Raven, especially when Raven stayed to help out in camp. The woman asked Raven about her children and if she ever thought about them being so far away. Raven had the feeling Samantha didn't have very many female friends and the blossoming woman opened herself to Raven in the hopes of having someone with whom she could share her concerns and fears.

The work kept coming all through the summer and into fall. Postings on the chat rooms and blogs would let the community know who was hiring and what was being paid for the services. The members of the camp would gather around the fire in the evening and discuss and decide where they would be working the next day. There were enough small farms in the region to keep everyone working for the entire season. Raven and Joseph's new family consisted of fifty or so individuals, but they weren't the only family group seeking work. Thousands of migrant workers were traveling through the region looking for work. It took dedication to arrive at the work site early in the morning and fight for a spot on the work crew. Joseph and Raven both listened attentively to conversations taking place in the fields, trying to find any hints of revolt among the workers but, other than a few grumblings about the hard work, very little was said about revolution.

Once a month Raven reported with the others to a local health clinic for a wellness check. She would submit to the tests, giving samples of blood, urine, sweat, and saliva. The workers grumbled about the lost work day, but unless they received a clean bill of health from the tests their work card would not be reactivated. The clinic offered free health screenings and checkups for the workers, enforcing the still rigorous standards set in motion over thirty years before. Despite massive inoculations and widespread healthcare the terrorist plagues were still cropping up, especially in the agrarian population.

It was near the end of her second month working with the members of the community. Raven was sitting in the waiting room of the clinic waiting for the nurse to return her work card, trying to breathe the hot air through her heavy cloth covering her face, when Samantha came from the exam room. Her head was bowed and her shoulders were shaking as soft sobs escaped from beneath her veil. Everyone was shifting uncomfortably in their seats and Raven could feel eyes peering at her. Even Bear was staring at her, pleading with his eyes for her to do something.

Raven stood and approached Samantha, wrapping her arms around the sobbing woman and leading her to a chair. Other members of the community gathered around, some kneeling on the floor, others pacing and crowding, bringing more heat to the small waiting room. Samantha was turning paler by the second, her breathing becoming more ragged. The crowd was becoming overwhelming and Raven wanted to focus on Samantha. A nursing assistant forced her way through the crowd and handed Raven her work card. Raven stood and pulled the nursing assistant aside.

"Is there somewhere private where my sister and I could talk?" she asked.

The aide looked from Raven to the sobbing woman sitting in the chairs. Nodding, the woman led both of them down a hall along with Bear. Samantha was clutching a square of paper in her trembling hand. Raven directed her to the exam table and helped her sit down.

"The doctor says I have preeclampsia." Samantha's voice was trembling and barely audible. "He said I need to go on bed rest and they may need to deliver the baby early."

Raven pried the slip of paper from Samantha's hand and studied the medication printed on the sheet. It wouldn't be too hard to get the medicine from the clinic pharmacy, but keeping the woman on bed rest and on a restricted diet would be difficult if she stayed with the camp. She needed to be in a house in a bed with her feet elevated. Raven's first instinct was to call her mother, but she knew that doors to Haven were closed to her right now. She couldn't break cover, even for the life of Samantha and her child.

The door opened and the Matriarch slipped into the room, followed closely by Joseph. She carried a sense of authority and Samantha actually stilled her tremors when the old woman approached. Raven sat beside Samantha and took the emotionally charged woman's hand. The Matriarch approached Samantha, taking the young woman's other hand and looking deep in her eyes.

"You will return to Winter Quarters until the child is born." It seemed the Matriarch knew the problem even before anyone spoke. "Bly will return with you, if her husband agrees to be parted with her while we finish harvest. We need his strength during this last month."

Joseph pulled Raven off the table and wrapped his arms around her. She relaxed into the embrace, knowing he was taking advantage of the moment and if she tried to fight him it would look odd to the others in the room.

"I will let her go, briefly." Raven could feel the rumble of his voice from where her cheek rested against the warmth of his chest. "Harvest is almost over and if my wife can help Samantha have a strong, healthy baby then my sacrifice will be worth it."

Chapter Twenty-Three

SO, THE NEXT MORNING, RAVEN and Samantha climbed on board the bus to take the trip to Winter Quarters. In addition to the women, the bus was loaded to the top with potatoes, onions and other fall produce. Raven had no idea where they were headed. She just knew the trip was going to take at least four hours. It was rest day for the camp. The one day a week when the workers took a break, spent time worshipping together and re-energize for the work week ahead. The community bus would make its odyssey to Winter Quarters, bringing the supplies purchased with the earnings from the week's labors loaded in the back.

Usually the bus only transported a driver and a guard back to the settlement established as a permanent residence for the transient society. Despite a bad case of nerves, Raven was actually looking forward to seeing her new home. They were going to be making frequent stops, both for fuel and for patrol checkpoints and there was no way of telling who would be visiting Winter Quarters and since neither woman could risk exposing her features to strangers, both women were heavily veiled.

Samantha was resting on a stack of cushions piled on twenty pound bags of beans and wheat. Raven had piled so many bags around the pregnant woman there was no danger of movement and harm coming to her and the baby. The wealth of food was the lifeblood of the community. Already Raven was thinking of ways she could help to preserve the variety of food piled into every quarter of the bus.

The driver pulled the bus in to a check point, rolling to a stop next to a guard shack. Two soldiers sauntered over to the bus, motioning for the driver to open the door. The young man entered the bus, nodded to the driver and walked down the aisle to the two women. Raven ducked her head and turned her face away from the man. She recognized him as a soldier she had worked with briefly when she was stationed at Mountain Home. The man stopped and crouched down beside Samantha.

"Ladies," he said. "Can I see your ID."

Raven pulled out her work card and handed it to the man. Samantha fumbled briefly, finally pulling her wallet from where it was tucked between two sacks. The soldier scanned the bar code on the cards and returned them to the women.

"Thank you," he said.

Raven was still keeping her head down, not allowing the man to look into her eyes. The soldier finally stood and walked back down the aisle. His partner was handing back the ID cards he had scanned from the men and they both exited the vehicle allowing the bus to continue on its way. The rest of the trip was fairly uneventful. Raven was concerned about the condition of the roads. Once the bus left the main highway the roads were riddled with cracks and potholes. It was indicative of the times. The main transportation thoroughfares were usually well-maintained, but once the bus left the main artery the disrepair of the roads caused the bus to twist and jerk uncomfortably. Raven kept a close eye on Samantha, but the ultra-padded bed that had been created for her kept her cushioned from everything but the worst of the jolts.

The dirt road leading to the complex was well-maintained; much like the road to Haven was, before it was paved by the military. A small cloud of dust followed them from the gated entrance to the wooden structures on either side of the small stream. The bus pulled up to the front door of one of the many structures. A group of women and children crowded around the bus, chattering excitedly as the door opened. Raven gasped as the first woman led the way onto the bus. Fortunately, the woman wasn't looking her direction and was talking to the driver when the emergency exit door was opened by another woman. Raven helped Samantha to her feet and held her as she stepped down from the bus. She was very careful to keep her back turned to the woman at the front of the bus. It would blow her cover if her Aunt Emily saw her now.

Raven stepped out of the back of the bus and moved to the side so the women and children gathered around could easily unload supplies. Emily's voice carried around the side of the bus, approaching the rear bumper. A slew of women and children moved away from the bus, each loaded down with bags, boxes and crates bulging with food. One of the last things to come off the bus was Raven's bicycle. There was quite a stir as the women ran their hands over the smooth metal and peered in the basket. Raven reached over and put her hand on the handlebars, subtly letting the women know the bicycle belonged to her. The women stepped back and returned to unloading the bus. None of them seemed prepared to confront the new woman in their midst.

"What is going on with Samantha?" Emily's voice rang out behind her. "I understand you have a medical background and have been helping her out."

Leaning the bike on its kickstand, Raven slowly turned to confront her aunt. Her face was still covered by the veil, but she knew it wouldn't take the woman too long to figure out who she was. No one was around to watch so Raven brought her hands up in front of her and made the sign for her aunt's name. Emily's eyes widened with shock and she opened her mouth to speak. Raven gestured her into silence.

"I want to make sure Samantha is comfortable." As Raven spoke she signed continuously to her aunt, offering reassurance that she would explain everything when they were alone. "I will give you all the details once I have checked on my patient."

Emily closed her mouth and nodded as if making a quick decision. She motioned for Raven to follow her. "Bring your bicycle. We'll put it in the visitors' storage. It'll be safe there."

Samantha had been placed in a bed located in a long, wooden structure. When Raven stepped through the door she was reminded immediately of barracks. Narrow beds lined either side of a long aisle. Each bed had a trunk resting at its foot and a shelf at its head. The beds were made with perfect military precision with squared hospital corners. There wasn't a speck of dirt or item out of place. Emily led Raven down the aisle to where Samantha was laying on one of the beds. Light was streaming in from skylights on the roof causing everything to take on an ethereal glow. Raven blinked and shook her head trying to clear her vision.

As her boots hit the hardwood floor they made a hollow, drumming noise. She tried to step lightly as she walked down the aisle, but the tapping rhythm tracked her as she paced the long walkway. Samantha's veil was off and she was smiling as Raven and Emily approached the bed. Raven reached up and slipped her own veil off her head, leaving only the triangular head scarf covering her bound hair. Samantha was laying flat on the bed, her skirt twisted beneath her and the blanket bunched and wrinkled under her body. There was no way Raven was going to allow the woman to stay in that condition. Other women were strategically placed around the room, all with a clear view of the bed. Theoretically, it looked like they were busy with small tasks, but Raven could feel all of their energy focused on the woman in the bed and the two women standing over her. She motioned one of the women over and asked her to get a basin of warm water.

Raven turned to the other women and made a few short, crisp orders. Although the women had no idea who she was, the authority in her voice caused them to scramble to obey. It wasn't long before Raven had Samantha scrubbed and in a clean nightgown, her head and knees propped up by pillows and a sheet and thin blanket covering her to her chest. Emily helped maneuver the pregnant woman into a comfortable position, smoothing the blanket and brushing her hair back. The entire time both women were whispering words of comfort and reassurance to Samantha.

Raven leaned over the bed as she smoothed the sheet. Samantha's warm fingers grasped Raven's hand. "Thank you, my sister." She brushed her lips against Raven's cheek before releasing her hand.

Emily took Raven's hand in hers and pulled her towards the door of the long-house. "Come," her voice was ripe with lingering questions. "I'll show you around your new home, sister."

Raven bowed her head and followed submissively. Her heart's rhythm was beating an allegro in her chest. This was going to be the final test. She rehearsed what she was going to say in her mind as Emily showed her around the facilities. Raven could tell Emily was chomping at the bit to talk to her, but there was a sense of pride in the woman's carriage as she pointed out the buildings in the compound. Emily pointed out the living structures. The long-house was a structure for women without children. There was another, larger structure for families; this one divided into separate, smaller apartments. Another one for single men, although this one was tiny compared to the others. Food supplies were stored in a building in the center of the complex, much like the kitchens of Haven. In fact, much of the structure of Winter Quarters was reminiscent of the powerful structure of Haven.

Emily was moving Raven quickly through the complex, barely allowing her the opportunity to take in the details of the buildings. The structures looked strong and well-maintained. Raven spotted solar panels and windmills throughout the property but there were no incoming wires from an outside power source. The buildings were flooded with natural light from skylights and the walls had a number of sconces, each with a pale, white bulb ready to illuminate the interiors once the sun set. Emily pointed out a building separated from the others. Raven could see steam lying low around the ground surrounding the flat-roofed structure.

"That's our hot springs." Emily turned away from the building. "We pipe the water to the buildings to use for heat and to generate electricity. I can't bring you inside. Only our engineers are allowed in the building. Follow me. I have something more important to show you."

Emily led Raven to a square, squat building surrounded by a thick stand of trees and shrubs. The building blended with the environment so well it took Raven a few minutes to make out the dimensions blurred by the trees. Emily was smiling as Raven studied the unobtrusive building.

"This is my contribution to the community." Emily unlocked a metal door and pushed it open. "I've been able to use my contacts to get medical supplies and equipment. We've set up hundreds of these clinics in communities like these all over the country."

The only person in the room, and from what she could see through the open doorways, the only person in the building was sitting at a desk in the middle of the room. She was working at a computer and only glanced up briefly as Emily walked into the building.

"Sarah," Emily addressed the woman sitting at the computer. "I'm showing our new community member around the clinic. She has a medical background and may be able to help us in our mission."

Raven could feel Sarah's eyes follow them as Emily escorted her past the desk and into one of the empty rooms. An exam table dominated the tiny room. All the cabinets and drawers had shiny, metal locks securing the contents. The only other piece of furniture in the room was a metal rolling chair padded and covered with black vinyl. Emily pushed the chair towards Raven and motioned for her to take a seat. Raven recognized what Emily was doing. It was a psychological technique employed by interrogators. Emily was taking the dominant position, keeping her body above Raven and forcing Raven to look up at her. Emily leaned against the table and crossed her arms. Raven sat on the stool. As long as she was aware of what Emily was doing the older woman couldn't intimidate her.

"Raven." There was a direct challenge in Emily's voice. "What are you doing here? Why aren't you at Haven, where you belong?"

Raven almost laughed out loud. Emily didn't have any right to lecture her about abandoning Haven. Her mother never went into detail about why Emily left the shelter, but Raven remembered well the horrible stress and strain her mother had felt at the loss of her friend and helpmate and the sense of betrayal Savanna felt at the loss of her embryos. Raven wanted to be angry at the woman, but there were so many other reasons to be angry, so many other injustices in the world, she just couldn't muster the strength.

"I'm here with my husband, Aunt Emily," she responded.

"Your husband?" The disbelief was apparent in Emily's voice. "What's going on, Raven? Getting married is no reason to leave Haven. Even out here we've heard how unassailable Haven is now. Every few months there's talk of trying to get up a raid on the compound, but it's too well protected. Why are you really here?"

"I met my first husband when we were both serving in the military." Raven had to be careful to keep as much of her cover story present without contradicting what her aunt knew of her personality. "He wanted to live in Montana, with his family. I did the best I could to fit in there, but they never trusted me. They knew I was an outsider. My husband died not long after I became pregnant. I didn't have a way to get back to Haven and the pregnancy was really rough on me. Joseph stepped in to take care of me and the twins when they were born, but things just never got any better. I wanted to go home to Haven, but since I had been living with the community, I no longer had the security clearance to return. Haven is nothing more than a glorified military base now. Joseph and I decided to get married. I couldn't stay with the community in Montana any longer. No one there trusted me. Mom helped us get state line passes. She really wants me back at Haven and is still trying to work on getting me clearance."

Emily stared deep into Raven's eyes. Raven met her eyes, unwavering in her own intensity. There could be no appearance of subterfuge here.

"Where are your children?" Emily dropped her hands to her side and leaned forward, a sure sign of acceptance.

"They're at Haven." Raven made a strategic decision at this point. She allowed her body to collapse a little and she chewed on her bottom lip giving the impression of nervousness. "We told the community we left the children with my late husband's first wife. I'm afraid if they find out I'm from Haven they'll reject me. Please don't tell anyone. I go by Bly now and I accept the fact that this is my life. Please don't make it harder for me."

The final plea must have convinced her aunt because Emily pulled Raven from the stool and embraced her. "I missed you more than you can know, Little One. Welcome home."

Chapter Twenty-Four

EVEN THOUGH RAVEN WAS NO longer working on the migrant harvest she was, by no means, off the hook for hard labor. The community had their own acreage as part of their Winter Quarters. The grounds had extensive gardens, fields and orchards and Raven was expected to help harvest and process the food for storage. Winter Quarters was a working farm, hosting chickens, turkeys, pigs, sheep, goats and even a few cows. Raven learned how to milk cows and goats and how to pasteurize and process the milk into products like butter and cheese, one skill she never did pick up while growing up at Haven.

The clinic drew her like a bee to honey. It was obvious Emily didn't trust Raven completely. Her aunt kept her away from the computer and the complicated system used to get supplies for the clinic. There was a secretive air surrounding her aunt, despite the shared responsibility they both had in caring for Samantha. Raven was able to keep close to Samantha and monitored her blood pressure religiously. Keeping her on bed rest was helping, but Raven didn't like the edema swelling the pregnant woman's legs and ankles. Although the clinic didn't have everything a fully functional hospital kept on hand, there was enough equipment to closely monitor Samantha's condition. Raven knew the pregnancy couldn't go on much longer. She would have to induce Samantha and hope the baby was strong enough to survive. Fortunately Emily had been able to obtain the steroids necessary to make sure the baby's lungs were fully developed. Even if they had to deliver early, the medication gave the baby a fighting chance for survival.

The storage sheds were bursting at the seams with food. Raven helped those who had been left to care for Winter's Quarters store away the last of the root vegetables coming in from both the fields surrounding the quarters' buildings and being bused in from the migrant workers. Food was canned, dried, processed and stored in cool, dry storage sheds. As the last of the fields were cleared and the food was stored away a buzz started to sing through the miniature town. Women and children started talking about the family returning. If children acted up they were warned their parents would be home soon and discipline would rain down on their heads like fire and brimstone from the heavens. Raven was trying to convince Samantha it was time to induce. Samantha adamantly refused to allow either Raven or Emily to bring her to the clinic and start her labor.

The buzz in the air had become palatable. The weekly delivery of supplies had brought news the Family was going to be returning that week. The excitement was contagious and even Raven started to look forward to the return of the community. Joseph's earnest face kept coming, unbidden, to her mind. She realized she actually missed him and was looking forward to seeing him again.

One of the benefits of living in Winter Quarters was the access to hot showers. Hot water from the springs was piped to a shower room near the springs and Raven loved to soak in the hot water despite its slightly sulfuric smell, scrubbing every inch of her skin and washing her long dark hair. It had been a long day working the potato fields and Raven decided to take a shower and soak away part of the day. Afterwards she braided her hair, leaving the dark length to fall down her back before she tied on her head covering. Her skin tingled in the cold air as she left the shelter of the warm building and walked up the path towards the main complex. A young girl was running down the path, a sense of desperation in her stride. Raven recognized her as a young thirteen year-old called Senya.

"Bly! Bly!" Senya called, her blue eyes flashing concern. "Bly, Emily needs you at the clinic! Something's wrong with Samantha."

Raven thrust her damp towel and soaps into Senya's arms and rushed up the path leading to the clinic. Emily was waiting for her at the entrance. Together they walked into the exam room, where Samantha was laying on the exam table.

"Her blood pressure spiked." Emily pointed to the readout on the monitor. "The baby is showing signs of distress. I'm afraid if we don't deliver now we are going to lose both of them."

Raven studied the frightened face of the woman lying on the bed. Tears were streaming down her cheeks and her breath was coming in short, quivering gasps. Emily's assistant came clamoring into the room. She placed a tray of medical implements on the tray table and started to string an IV bag. Samantha's eyes got even wider and the tears streamed more vigorously. When Sarah approached the bed with the IV needle Samantha jerked her arm away.

"No," she sobbed. "I can't have this baby yet."

Emily's lipped narrowed into an expression with which Raven was very familiar. Her aunt wasn't a very patient person and Samantha was obviously testing the edges of her patience. Raven held out her hand to Sarah.

"Give me the needle," she said. "I'll take over from here."

Sarah and Emily both stepped back as Raven pulled the stool next to the bed. She took the sobbing woman's hand in hers, leaving the needle on the implement tray. "Samantha, if we're going to save your baby we need to induce now."

Samantha's gripped tightened on Raven's as she shook her head vigorously. "No, you don't understand." Samantha's voice was barely audible. "Once this baby is born she will no longer be mine. She will belong to her. If I'm sick with this baby I won't be able to have one of my own."

The full impact of Samantha's statement struck Raven. Obviously the woman had made a contract with Bear's first wife. Raven knew the details of these types of contracts because it was one she had to study as part of her cover. A woman would offer to give her first born child to an infertile couple and in return the woman would be offered the safety and protection of the family. She would have the option to have other children with her husband or to just stay in the marriage and be assured of being supported for her entire life. The woman was expected to contribute to the community, just as Raven and Joseph were expected to do if they expected to live with these people.

"Samantha," Raven kept her voice low and soothing. "We need to get this baby out. That is the only thing that matters right now."

Raven kept a steady gaze on Samantha, looking for any signs of wavering. Finally, Samantha lowered her eyes and, with a tiny nod, capitulated. Raven had Sarah help Samantha undress and put on a gown and then sent the young nursing assistant out of the room. She started the IV and hooked up the lactated ringers. Delivering babies wasn't a complicated process and Raven had faith that between Emily and herself they could handle any problems that came up. Once the fetal monitor was hooked up and Samantha was ensconced in blankets and pillows Raven started the process of inducing her. Now it was going to be a carefully balanced waiting game.

Samantha progressed well in her labor. After about eight hours the baby dropped and she started having strong contractions. An hour later she gave birth to a tiny baby girl. The infant's cries filled the delivery room attesting to her fully developed lungs. Raven quickly weighed and measured the wrinkly, squirming infant. Five pound, nine ounces, nineteen inches made her a little small but, since she was four weeks early, Raven wasn't too concerned. She cleaned the baby and swaddled her in a bundle of blankets before carrying her over to Samantha.

"It's a little red-headed girl." Samantha pulled away when Raven tried to deposit the baby in the woman's arms. Emily reached over and took the infant.

"You take care of Samantha," Emily kept her voice low. "I'll make sure the baby is taken care of. It's better this way."

Emily disappeared and Raven turned to her patient. The woman was curled up in the bed with her face buried in the pillow. Her body was shaking and Raven could hear the sobs issuing from deep within the woman's chest. Raven called Sarah in to help her change Samantha's gown and bed sheets. She did her best to make sure her patient was warm and comfortable, but she couldn't do anything to stop the woman from crying. Not knowing what else to do, she gave Samantha a sleep aid. It took about twenty minutes for Samantha's breathing to ease, allowing the woman to drift to sleep.

Raven finally left the room and went searching for her aunt. She found her at the far end of the building, in the nursery. There was another woman sitting in a rocking chair holding the infant and feeding her with a bottle. Emily gave her head a slight shake. Raven knew she was warning her not to say anything. The woman looked up at Raven and smiled.

"Thank you for saving my baby." The woman held the child closer to her chest, humming a wordless tune.

Raven tightened her jaw against the words she wanted to say. She wanted to rail against the woman for the emotional strain she was putting on Samantha, but she had to keep her mission in the forefront of her mind. There would be no way to regain the trust of the community if she expressed her opinion about the practices of its members, especially when she was supposed to believe those opinions.

Emily took the infant from the woman's arms and bathed her, giving her all the immunizations required of a newborn. Where she had gotten the medicine was a mystery. There was a deep, sinking feeling in Raven's gut; a feeling that the answer to where the medicine was coming from was deeply connected to those involved in attacks and raids outside the community. Raven didn't have any physical evidence against her aunt and, even if she did, Emily was just one hub in the wheel. The entire scope of the investigation was starting to form in Raven's mind. This wasn't going to be a quick, in and out, flash in the pan job. In order to succeed in this mission she was going to have to spend years as a member of the community.

The baby was healthy and strong. Samantha was resting quietly. There wasn't anything else for Raven to do at the moment. She left the nursery and removed her gown and surgical cap. For a moment her hair was free and the strictures of the society she was living in were far from her mind, but voices in the hall brought her back to herself. She stepped into the washroom to scrub her hands and arms and fix her hair. The clock told her she had been summoned a mere twelve hours ago. It had been late evening when she had finished her shower, now it was late in the morning. Her stomach rolled, reminding she hadn't eaten breakfast. Meals in the community were tightly regulated and she doubted she would be able to get any food from the kitchen. She would have to wait the two hours until lunch service.

When Raven walked out of the scrub room Emily was waiting for her with a tray. The glass of apple juice and the chicken salad sandwich wasn't a big breakfast, but it would be enough to hold her over until lunch. Emily led her into a cramped office and set the tray on the desk. For a few minutes the two ate in silence, but then Raven couldn't hold back any more. The questions bubbled up and spilled out of Raven's mouth.

"How can you stand here and allow these women to go through this, Emily?" Raven kept her voice low so anyone who might be beyond the door couldn't hear. "I know you and mom argued about a lot of things, but you always supported her work against the exploitation of women. Now you're providing medical care for these people who are using women as breeding factories. It isn't right. Samantha shouldn't be forced to give up her child if she doesn't want to."

"I would agree with you if the baby really was Samantha's." Emily's smile was patient and slightly condescending. "I've helped eliminate many of the injustices done to these women using the skills I learned in your mother's labs. I've been able to get some equipment through my connections and we have built a complete lab. We use in-vitro just like your mother's programs. Samantha volunteered as a surrogate. She's just upset because we won't do another in-vitro for her since she had preeclampsia."

Raven took a few minutes to wrap her head around this new information. "Why would you need to do in-vitro? Is Samantha having problems with fertility?"

"It wouldn't matter in her case." Emily was finishing the last bites of her sandwich. "I've managed to change a few things in this community. It's a small change, but I'm pretty happy with it." Emily pushed her tray aside and stretched. "You know infertility in the general population is now close to sixty percent for both men and women. And it doesn't help that females greatly outnumber males."

Raven knew all too well the cost of war. Her first husband was one of the many casualties of the multiple wars spreading over the face of the Earth. Casualties numbered in the thousands. Every day, lists of young men killed-in-action where sent home to be read over the news broadcasts. Boys dying in the sands of the Middle East, the jungle swamps of Asia, and the newest bloody conflict with the inclusion of Old Mexico as a protectorate of the Union. The war on drugs pushed American soldiers across the broad peninsula to the narrow neck of land and the Panama Canal. Drug lords were well-armed and knew the territory better than the controlling armies. Their soldiers would slip out of camps hidden deep in the wilderness, carry out a blitz attack with impunity and slip back into the depths of the untamed wild. Her brother, Caleb, was stationed in Texas right now working border patrol. Joseph's last stint before being assigned to this reconnaissance mission was deep in the combat zone. He was lucky he avoided any serious injury.

Raven shook her head, trying to dislodge the thought of Joseph flitting through her head. "What does this have to do with the community?" she asked. "They're not required to join the military. Their population should be fairly equal."

"It should be, but it's not." Emily's lips tightened as stress flowed back into her face. "The boys are joining the military for the benefits and suffering the same casualties as the registered population. Fighting within communities and raids from other unregistered groups are taking their toll as well. Women outnumber men three to one, at least, and there is no way to protect ourselves unless we band together."

"How is what you're doing helping?" Raven knew she was taking a chance in asking these questions. She didn't want to blow her cover and she was already walking on thin ice with her questions. "I mean, I only agreed to marry Joseph because he promised he wouldn't take another wife, even if we lived in the community."

"That's where this community is different, Raven." Emily's smile was back. "Any marriage after the first one is in name only. The woman is guaranteed the protection of the family and we give them children. My group is using artificial insemination and in-vitro to create children. It has eliminated the need for the indignity of the second marriage. We need to ensure the next generation. Left to its own devices the human population is going to drive itself to extinction."

Raven stared at her aunt, silently trying to process what the woman was trying to communicate. She knew the world population was steadily declining, but she didn't think it was as desperate as her aunt was making it out to be. Children were still being born and, the last time she saw the numbers, the population was still over three billion. Knowing she had already said too much, Raven decided it was time to do damage control.

"I know it's going to be hard to fit into the community." Raven stood and stretched. "Please don't tell anyone about what I said here. I'm trying really hard to fit in, for my husband's sake."

Emily smiled indulgently as she picked up the food trays. "Don't worry. As long as you don't do anything to interfere with my work I won't tell anyone about where you came from."

Emily left the room, leaving Raven to contemplate their conversation. Despite her mother's work and the surrogate program the population was still declining. It didn't seem so desperate when looking at the billions of people in the world, but when the population dropped from over five billion fifteen years ago to three and a half billion now and was still declining, the numbers took on a whole new connotation. Raven sighed and stood up from the desk. She had a job to do and couldn't get caught up in her aunt's problems.

Chapter Twenty-Five

THE BRIGHT SUNLIGHT SLASHED ACROSS her eyes as Raven exited the clinic. Her hair was tightly bound under her head scarf, hiding the dark braids. There was a slight nip in the air as she drew in deep breaths. It was time to harvest any leftover vegetables from the gardens.

The compound was built on the juncture of three claims of forty acres each. A hundred and twenty acres of land, all granted to three former soldiers. The land was given to the soldiers as a grant after five years of service. In order for the land to be proved up the former soldiers needed to build living quarters and keep a productive farm for three years. Although the majority of community members were traveling and working the fields away from the facility, the farm still teemed with life. Those too young or too old to travel to the far away farms and work the fields would stay and tend Winter Quarters. The fields and animals needed to be tended through the summer. More importantly, the compound needed to be tended and protected from the elements and attacks. The grounds hosted a minimum of ten guards. Raven learned these guards rotated in and out during the harvest months, each man taking their turn in offering protection to the women, children and older men of the community.

Raven was halfway up the trail from the clinic when the alarm sounded. The outlying alarms had been triggered and the intruder warning blared, its loud klaxon reverberated across the fields, giving warning. She took off at a sprint, making a bee-line for the dining hall.

Raven made it to the stone building with the bulk of the other residents of the farm. As she stepped through the door she peeled a badge from where it was velcroed to her belt and posted it on the railing leading to the cafeteria. Three rows of ten badges and Raven's made a third on the fourth row. Thirty-three people, mostly women and children, were going to be locked in the dining hall. Guards would take their place on the roofs and in tree blinds, weapons aimed to take out invaders, or be taken out themselves. The stone walls would protect the women from anything short of a rocket blast and the provisions in the pantry could keep them fed for months, if not years.

Raven could feel her shoulders tighten as the door slammed shut, locking the women in the building. She wasn't afraid. If anything, she wanted to be out on the roof with one of the guns. It rankled her to have to rely on someone else for protection. She hadn't needed to rely on anyone else for protection since she was twelve years old and Travis had trained her in weapons handling and hand-to-hand combat.

The residents of the community were all huddled in the far corner of the dining hall. Children were sitting on the floor playing games on spread out blankets. Women were milling around performing small tasks, apparently trying to keep their hands busy. The tension in the air was almost palpable. Raven moved over to where her aunt was sitting with a group of women. She needed to find a task to take her mind off of what could be happening outside. A woman Raven barely recognized was sitting near Emily. She was holding a baby in her arms as she rocked back and forth humming a wordless tune. The baby was hiccupping slightly as if it was about to start crying, but it seemed the woman didn't notice. Her eyes were glazed and she was pale and trembling.

Emily was busy with a crying child when Raven approached. Her aunt was just too busy to deal with her. Raven looked around trying to find a task to keep herself busy, but there was nothing to do. Everyone had a job except Raven. She had only been at the compound for a few weeks and most of that time was spent tending Samantha. The children were running around the length of the mess hall, darting between tables and laughing as they played. None of the women made eye contact with Raven as she sat at a table.

Senya approached Raven and thrust a length of cloth in her hands. Raven looked at the pale blue veil the girl brought her. She realized when she had thrust her belongings into the girl's arms her veil must have been entangled in the mass of towels. All around her women were pulling veils out of pouches on their belts and wrapping them around their heads. Raven carefully wound the length of fabric around her head, hiding her features. Senya sat on the bench next to Raven, her whole body trembling, almost causing the bench to quiver under them. She reached over and put her arm around the child, drawing her in and soothing her. Subconsciously, she started gently rocking her body and humming a simple lullaby. The girl's trembling eased and she rested her head on Raven's shoulder.

"I wish my mother was here." Senya's longing whisper struck Raven. She wondered if her own children were wishing she was close to them. Lakota and Marwa were safe with her mother, but she missed them more than she realized.

The alarm klaxon suddenly ended and all activity stopped. As loud as the alarm was, the silence was almost deafening. A man's voice came through the speaker placed high on the wall.

"All clear, all clear!" he sang out. "Our community has returned. Come out and greet your family."

The announcement was followed by a roaring cheer reverberating from the mouth of every woman and child in the room. The sudden thrust of bodies pushed towards the entrance of the building was overwhelming for a moment; even Senya stood and pushed her way towards the door. Raven waited until the queue at the door cleared before she stood up and made her way outside. Barely any time had passed since she had left the clinic and the sun was still brightly shining. She blinked to clear her vision and turned to follow the crowd.

There were a lot more people than Raven was expecting. The yard between the two buildings was teeming with bodies. Children were running through the crowd and throwing themselves into the arms of parents and spouses were greeting each other with embraces. A feeling of peace and rightness filled Raven as she searched through the crowd.

She turned when a hand on her arm drew her attention. Suddenly she was looking into Joseph's bright blue eyes. His smile was so wide it crinkled the corners of his eyes. Raven allowed him to draw her into his arms and kiss her between her eyebrows, the only exposed skin on her face. She lingered in the warmth of his arms, resting her cheek against his chest. This wasn't too bad. She could hear the drumming of his heart against her cheek and felt it speed up as he held her close.

A sharp whistle drew her attention to where Bear was standing on a bench, his head and shoulders rising above the crowd. The residents of the community turned to face him; all chattering stinted.

"We have a lot of work to do now that we are back in the community." A roar from the crowd forced him to pause for a moment. When everyone quieted Bear started again. "We need help unloading supplies and getting everything put away. It's time to get settled for the winter. Report to your section leaders for your assignments."

Joseph kept his arm around Raven's shoulders as they walked over to Bear. The huge man jumped off the bench and strode over to the two of them.

"I see you found your woman." Bear grinned as he pounded Joseph's shoulder with such force Raven almost felt her knees buckle. "We don't have any strangers here Bly. You can remove your veil. It'll do good for Joseph to see the face of his bride. He's been moping around camp for weeks."

"I've missed my husband, too." Raven spoke softly as she unwound the length of cloth from her head and tucked it in a pocket on her belt. She realized her words weren't just empty platitudes. She really had missed Joseph. There was a closeness she was starting to feel for the young man. It wasn't quite the same feeling she had from the first day she had met Billy, but the peace she was feeling when Joseph was near was worth exploring.

"The council wants to speak to both of you as soon as we get everything packed away." It was obvious Bear's smile was an attempt to be reassuring. It didn't help the tension in Raven's stomach.

Joseph had ridden his bicycle for the journey back to Winter Quarters. The buckets were loaded down with bags of wheat and beans. The trailer was packed with boxes filled with potatoes and other root vegetables. Raven helped unload the food supplies and transfer them to the kitchens. The fruits of the fall harvest were being carried into the dining hall. Emily was directing traffic. The bags and boxes were piling up in all corners of the room.

Unlike earlier harvests, late fall harvest was bringing in more staple products. The delicate fruits and vegetables from summer and early fall had all been dehydrated or canned and stored in the food cellars. The root vegetables, grains and winter squash could easily be stored in their current condition as long as the storage area was cool and dry with minimum light. Raven wondered if she was going to spend the next few days processing this newest shipment of food or if the newcomers were going to become part of the work crews. Many hands would make light work of it and Raven knew the easy friendship she had been developing with the women of the camp would make the work easier as well.

After the food was moved to the kitchens, all attention turned to the camping supplies and the animals. The older children herded the goats and sheep into the fenced pasture and carried cages of chickens to the coop. Joseph pulled their tent from the storage bins on the bus and Raven found all their camping equipment in boxes right next to it. They carried everything to where Joseph had left his bicycle.

Raven looked over the pile of belongings allotted to her and Joseph. It wasn't much, especially if it was all they had to live on through the winter. Of course they had the money they had earned during the harvest, but they had come into the harvest late and her work had been cut short when she returned to the compound with Samantha. There wouldn't be enough money to make it through the winter unless this community accepted them. On the other hand, Raven hadn't seen any evidence the members of this community were involved in any subversive behavior. It might be more advantageous to leave this group while it was still warm enough to camp.

They were still standing by the camping equipment when Bear found them. He took her arm and led them both towards the dining hall.

"They want to talk to you." Was the only explanation he would give.

Raven followed Joseph into the dining hall. She kept her head down as they walked through the doors. Twelve men sat at a table at the far side of the cafeteria. Behind each man sat a woman. Raven recognized Emily and the Matriarch sitting with the women. Bear took his seat next to Elias and the other men, but Raven didn't recognize any other person sitting there.

Joseph came to a halt, facing the group of men and women while Raven stood behind his right shoulder. Bear gestured and two of the women brought chairs forward forcing Raven and Joseph to sit side by side in front of the tribunal. Raven's mind was spinning, making it difficult to complete a thought. She wondered what the end result of this meeting was going to be. Bear was obviously facilitating the meeting. He stood to address the group.

"We're here to decide whether or not to allow Joseph and Bly to join our community." Bear's face was an open book. He gave her a very soothing, open smile. The rest of the council was more difficult to read. Their stoic expressions gave nothing away. "I would like to start this meeting by saying we have only known Bly and Joseph for twelve short weeks and it's hard to make a decision based on the short amount of time we have known them, but I have to say I am completely impressed by these two. Both Joseph and Bly worked as hard as any member of this community. Joseph has promised us the money both he and his wife earned during this harvest if we allow them to join. Bly's skills as a medical professional have been proven in the care she gave Samantha and the successful birth of the child she was carrying. Both of them have served in the military and can bring the skills they learned to defend our community. I, for one, would be happy to welcome them into our group."

Some of the tension Raven was feeling between her shoulder blades seemed to melt away. They were over the first hurdle. She glanced up, trying to assess the feelings of the other community members. None of their expressions had changed. A man at the end of the table leaned forward and raised his hand. Bear nodded and gestured for the man to speak. The man looked fairly young. His skin was weather-beaten and darkened by the sun, but his black hair was free of grey and his face was unlined.

"I want to know why Bly wants to join this community." His voice had a slightly challenging tone. "Most of the women who join us are looking for protection because they don't have the skills to defend themselves from the threats of the world. From what we have seen, Bly could easily get a job and stay well within the protection of the government-run cities."

Raven looked at Joseph and then Bear. She realized she was on her own for this answer. Ducking her head, she studied the blue and white tiles on the floor for a moment to gather her thoughts. She had to make this good if she was going to inject herself into the community. Looking up she stared directly at the man. Eye contact was key to pulling off a successful lie.

"I joined the army when I was nineteen," she said. "I wanted stability in my life. When my father died I had nothing, no stability, no way to take care of myself. Despite my father's absolute hatred of government control, he had talked about all the skills the military had given him. I joined because I wanted to have a career in medicine and the army promised to give it to me. I spent three years in Central Asia and saw more action than I ever wanted to. I saw our men and women torn apart and destroyed and I had to put them back together again. I hated being one of the king's men. Then, when I came back they had me working the surrogate unit. I was there, creating children I knew would be sent to be torn apart by war as adults. It was a vicious cycle and it was making me sick. I decided to return to my family, where I belonged. I didn't see how my skills would do anything more than perpetuate death and destruction if I stayed under government control."

Bear was nodding. Many of the council's expressions had changed, becoming less stoic and more accepting.

"We need to deliberate and formulate a plan before we make a decision." The council stood as Bear spoke. "In the meantime, we have limited room in the compound. It's going to take a while to get everyone situated in their rooms and find a place for you. It might be a good idea to set up your tent and stay there for a few days."

Raven and Joseph both stood and walked out of the room. Joseph put his arm around Raven's shoulders as he led her out of the room.

Chapter Twenty-Six

RAVEN AND JOSEPH SET UP the tent in a fallow field a few yards from the main compound. The days were still warm enough to keep comfortable and, even though there was a slight nip in the air during the night, their shared body heat kept them from noticing. Raven expected to be uncomfortable with Joseph's awkward advances, but instead she started to feel closer and a real warmth grew between them. Joseph was so attentive and understanding without asking for anything in return it wasn't hard to pretend they were newlyweds as they worked side by side with other members of the community. Despite living in the tent, Raven and Joseph spent all their waking hours working with the members of the community.

The sun was setting at the end of the third day in the encampment. Raven was relaxing on the bed, a blanket pulled up to her shoulders to ward off the chill of the night. The front panel of the tent was rolled up, exposing the night sky and Joseph was standing in front of the tent, staring at the moon. The bright, white orb illuminated the landscape, giving it an eerie, iridescent glow.

Joseph turned and stepped into the tent. He reached up to loosen the ties holding the front panels open. "I almost hate to close off the view," he said as the curtain came down. "On nights like this I think I can almost see the colony on the moon."

Raven smiled as he approached the bed. "It's hard to believe the colony has been able to hold on for so long with everything that has been happening here. They were fortunate they were well supplied and were able to hold out until the plagues were under control. I wouldn't mind going into space, but there's so much work to do here; it's hard to think about going to work for the space program."

Joseph lowered himself onto the mattress, resting on his side to face her. "I'm satisfied keeping my feet here on solid earth." He adjusted his body in the bed so he was facing Raven, but wasn't touching her. "Bear brought an interesting proposition to me today." Raven raised her eyebrows but didn't say anything, allowing Joseph to speak his piece. "The community has decided to allow us to stay with them, as long as we continue to work. They also want to know if we can still apply for the land grant we are eligible for as veterans. There are two forty-acre plots connected to this compound and they want us to file claims on them. There are enough new people in the community to build some more living structures and they want to have more room to spread out. Eighty acres will allow them to grow some alfalfa and put up beehives. They want to become more self-sufficient."

Raven studied Joseph's face as he spoke. Warning signs flashed through her mind. "Is this the best place to gather intel?" Raven kept her voice low and steady. "This group seems fairly benign. I don't think we are going to get what we need by staying here."

Joseph didn't speak for a long time. At first Raven thought he was dozing off. The faint light seeping in through the seams of the tent made it difficult to make out his facial features, despite her enhanced vision. His pale skin seemed to take on a shimmering glow. When he finally spoke the low whisper almost startled her.

"There are a lot of secrets still floating around this compound," he said "Everything isn't as tame as it appears on the surface." Joseph wrapped his arms around Raven and pulled her close. "The Elders weren't asking about your service in the military because they were confused, they were asking because they want to know exactly what tactical skills you have. Bear has been probing me for information for a while now. I've relayed my findings to my contact and he thinks this would be a perfect way to gain the trust of this group." Joseph kissed the top of Raven's head. "The militia groups are a web-work of individuals buried within these communities. Their ties are strong, but very subtle. It may take years to gather all the intel we need to find the leaders of this particular militia, and this militia may only be the tip of the iceberg. Do you think you can pretend to be my loving wife for a couple of years?"

"I know you want more than just a pretend marriage, Joseph." Raven had a hard time keeping her voice flat and emotionless. "I can't say that I didn't miss you, but I want to be careful. You're so much younger than me and I don't want to rush in with my eyes closed like I did my first marriage." And for a moment Raven realized how quickly she had fallen in love with Billy and how drastically her life had changed with him. Her love for him had burned hot and quick and she had never forgotten. It still burned deep inside her and occasionally flared up with an unexpected intensity. Tears burned at the corner of her eyes and she tried to blink them away before Joseph could see them.

"Raven, did you really mean those things you said in the meeting?" Joseph's voice was filled with concern. "Do you really hate the surrogate program that much?"

Joseph's questions managed to tamp down the emotions she was feeling for her lost husband. She thought about her work with the surrogate unit and the genetically altered infants being born and raised in military units. The surrogate unit had been developed in secret more than fifty years ago with genetically altered soldiers being integrated into the ranks. Most of the children seemed to be well-adapted to the structured life of military training. Those who weren't were directed to other careers, still receiving their education within the unit. Every child born was given a chance to make a life for themselves. Raven wondered if the children of this community would have the same chance.

Joseph wrapped his arm around Raven and pulled her close. "Penny for your thoughts?"

"Good luck finding a real penny. You know they're all collectors' items now." Raven couldn't help laughing at him. Settling down into Joseph's warmth, Raven turned her face so her words wouldn't be lost in his chest. "I just can't get Sandoval out of my head. He hated himself so much. I've served with some of the most amazing people and they all came from the surrogate program, but there was something really wrong with Sandoval."

She could feel Joseph's arms tighten around her. "Was Sandoval in your unit when you extracted Smith?"

Raven trusted he could feel her nod against his chest. "I can't believe we made it out of that one alive. I think the only reason we made it out is because the Taliban wanted Smith alive. If they would have been more aggressive we would have all been killed. I still get headaches sometimes from my injuries."

"Pain only lasts for a few minutes, Raven. Glory lasts forever." Joseph's voice sounded drowsy. "Smith is in prison, now. He isn't going to be building any more killer viruses or Über children in the near future. Go to sleep, Raven. We'll be back to work tomorrow. Every day we are here we gain a little stronger toehold in the community."

Raven rolled to her side and then flopped back to her back. The padded mat was sitting on a slight slope and her body kept slipping toward the foot of the bed. No matter what position she tried, she just couldn't get comfortable.

"Can't sleep, Raven?" Joseph asked.

Raven rolled over to face Joseph and found her face only inches from his. "I wish I had some music to listen to. I used to be able to find music in my mind to help me to sleep, but there's nothing there now."

Joseph reached across the bed and picked up his data pad from where it was resting on the charging pad. "The sound isn't the best quality, but---" He tapped a few icons on the screen. "What do you want to hear?"

"Put on something classical, like Bach." Joseph tapped an icon and soft music filled the tent. The symphony was beautiful. The music flowed into Raven and relaxed her. She felt herself drifting off and allowed Joseph to wrap his arms around her and draw her into his warmth.

The next morning Bear drove Joseph and Raven into the small town about a forty-five minute drive outside of the community compound. They went to the small, county seat offices and filled out paperwork. Raven questioned how legal the claims were since the paperwork was filed in their undercover names. She hoped the residents of the community wouldn't be adversely harmed when Joseph and Raven left.

Once the claims were filed, plans to build living structures were put into place. The land needed to be proved up in order to establish ownership. It seemed like a lot of work just to establish trust with a group who may or may not be planning an attack on the government. Each forty acre plot needed to have a habitable structure built within a year of the claim being filed. The land needed to fenced and cultivated to prove the claim within the first three years of filing.

Raven and Joseph went with Bear to tour the land and decide what to do with it. Raven let Joseph take the lead in the discussions. She just didn't feel like making plans for establishing a future with a group of people she was spying on and who could possibly be causing harm to countless people.

Late fall progressed into the cold days of early winter. It was starting to get too cold to stay in the tent but there weren't any empty rooms in the family unit. However, there were extra beds in the women's dorm and in the bachelor lodge. The tent was rolled up and put away in storage and Raven and Joseph moved into separate living quarters.

The construction of the buildings on the newly staked claims progressed at a steady pace. Raven was surprised by the skill level of the residents of the community. The community's acreage encompassed an entire valley, resting between two mountains with Joseph's claim completing a grid bordered on two sides by current community lands. Raven's claim rested just behind his and was surrounded by federal lands. Each parcel of land was fenced off and foundations were laid for buildings on each property. The building on Joseph's property was going to be another family complex, built close to the main community structure. Once the pipes for the water and sewer were laid and the cement foundation poured, work went fairly quick. The external structure was actually completed within three weeks and the workers moved on to the construction of the interior of the structure.

Raven's property proved to be more troublesome. Any house built on her claim was susceptible to raids. The property boundaries were so far from the other structures that any living quarters on the grounds would put those residing in it at risk. It needed to be built though, for the claim on Raven's lot to be legal. The structure didn't need to be beautiful; it just needed to be habitable. The community decided to build a simple, straightforward cinder-block bunkhouse. It was a long, narrow structure with a bath and shower room at one end and a kitchen at the other, with room for bunks in between and a cellar beneath. A metal door in the center of the building was the only visible entrance while a trap door to the roof allowed access to the armaments on the four corners of the building. Raven couldn't shake the feeling that the building was a miniature fortress.

The external components of the buildings were completed before the first snowfall and once they were done the workers moved to the interior. Despite taking longer to build the outside of the house on Raven's claim, her building was actually completed first. There were fewer interior structures to contend with and the building was much smaller. Raven had the thought that she and Joseph could actually move into the building by themselves to keep up the illusion they were a happily married couple, but the Elders in the community wouldn't allow it. The building was just too far out to allow two people to live there alone. Instead the elders moved a group of young men from the crowded bachelor lodge to the building. The men carried a surprising number of weapons with them when they moved. Raven watched as Bear and some of the other men in the community pulled a number of containers from a bunker behind the family lodge, each with automatic rifles, pistols and some military grade equipment. These weapons were loaded in a truck and brought to the new bachelor residence.

Bear was excited about the new buildings being added to the property. He couldn't stop talking about how many more people could come into the community and be saved from the terrors of the world. Raven couldn't help noticing the zeal in his eyes was similar to what she saw in her mother's when Savanna talked about the work she was doing at Haven. Raven really liked Bear and his exuberant personality. She sincerely hoped he wasn't part of one of the militia groups the government was targeting, but the stockpile of guns hidden in catches and cellars were beginning to give her doubts.

Winter was a time for planning and preparing for the transient nature of spring and summer. The community members were restless and always trying to find work. The new family residence was completed mid-January and was cause for celebration. The women created a spectacular meal and served it in the main dining hall. Once everyone had eaten their fill, the tables were pushed to the side of the room, clearing the floor for dancing.

Raven smiled when she saw the guitars and the fiddles. The first twang of the fiddle made her heart race and her feet start tapping. It wasn't long before Joseph had her in his arms and they were dancing with the other couples in the middle of the floor. Women and the unmarried men circled the dance floor and danced in lines, twirling in and out between couples. Children flew through the crowd, hands and eyes into everything. Sweet treats and drinks filled tables at the edges of the floor. The party lasted far into the night the residents needed flashlights to find their way to the living quarters. Raven could hear friends calling good night and children singing in the night. She followed Joseph to the new family dwelling. He opened the door and led her into the long hallway.

The building smelled of fresh plaster and paint. It had a clean, warm, snug feeling. The concept of the building was similar to the women's unit, but instead of rows of beds, the structure was divided into tiny rooms barely big enough for a bed, a crib and a dresser. Like the other buildings, this one had a bathroom and shower room at the end of the hall. It didn't have a kitchen at the other end, though. Instead the hall ended in a huge, circular addition separated into two rooms. This was the children's room. In the community, infants would stay with the parents for the first three years. Once the children reached three years they would move into one of the rooms in the circular addition until they turned twelve. At twelve they moved to either the women's dorm or the bachelor lodge.

The building reminded Raven of the facilities of Haven. There was a strong feeling of Emily's hand being all over the construction. The whole community was structured similar to the Little Haven communities that were extensions of her mother's outreach programs. Raven was starting to have serious doubts about the dangers this community was posing to the government and to the general population. Everything she saw was indicative of a group of people just trying to protect their families and work their land.

Chapter Twenty-Seven

ALL THROUGH THE REMAINDER OF winter Raven and Joseph would secret themselves in their room and discuss options in whispered tones. Joseph was convinced if they stayed with this group they would eventually be led to the leaders of the insurgent groups. He kept telling Raven to be patient. Finding the rebels was going to be a marathon, not a sprint.

The new family barracks remained mostly empty through the remainder of the winter with only Joseph, Raven and a few of women with young children staying in the rooms. Spring came with the rush of plowing and planting. The goats, sheep and cows all dropped their young in the first weeks of March. Raven loved seeing the younglings staggering around the pasture on wobbly legs. She didn't see the piglets very often. The sows' pens were located below the bachelor lodge and were cared for by the young men. Bear seemed more exhausted and happy than Raven had ever seen him. It was obvious he was the person in charge of the community. At least that was the impression Raven had, until one day he was walking around the pasture with the Matriarch. The older woman tottered around with a cane and was as unsteady on her feet as the newborn lambs. Bear was talking about the plans for the harvest season and pointing out all the animals still in their pens.

"Mother," Bear was saying, "I think we have everything we need here. We have enough animals to sell to make the taxes on the property. Our seed reserves can last us through three growing seasons. I really don't think we need to follow the harvest this year."

"No!" The Matriarch's words were punctuated with thrusts from her cane into the dirt. "We need to make sure we have enough put away for emergency. Crops fail, animals get sick, raids can come at any time. We're not safe!"

Every word proved exactly who was in charge of the community. The council gathered to plan for the harvest. The twelve men and twelve women gathered behind closed doors to discuss and make decisions. Each head of household would meet with the council to discuss their role in the coming season.

Raven worked with Emily in the clinic. In addition to the hundred and thirty residents of the community, Emily also cared for the animals that were the heart's blood of the farm. Raven still had no idea where all the medical supplies were coming from, but Emily had all the immunizations, antibiotics and anti-virals she ever needed. Raven helped give all the newborns their immunizations, human and animal.

The bright spring morning promised to be gloriously warm and Raven was helping the young boys and girls herd the sheep into the lower pasture. There were about three hundred sheep all together, ewes, young bucks and dew drops. Raven couldn't help smiling at the antics of the youngest of the sheep. The fresh clover field did something to the sheep and even the oldest, most dignified of the herd were kicking up their heels. It even made Raven feel young to see the children and sheepdogs run among the herd and keep the more adventurous ones from wandering too far. It was hard to believe she had just celebrated her twenty-ninth birthday during the winter.

The proximity alarms suddenly blared across the meadow. Everyone froze for a moment before bursting into action. One of the boys whistled sharply and the dogs whipped around and started nipping at the heels of the sheep, bunching them together. The young girls ran to the front of the herd and the boys ran behind. A few of the larger boys scooped up the smallest of the sheep and hoisted them up to their shoulders. Raven waited until the last of the sheep and children past before she turned and headed towards the main compound.

Catching movement out of the corner of her eye, Raven turned and braced to see what was coming up the field. A half a dozen figures were emerging from among the trees at the edges of the pasture. Raven could make out the men on all-terrain cycles as they approached the fence line. Her vision allowed her to see further than her companions and she knew the invaders would be on them before the herd made it to safety. A simple barbed wire fence separated the raiders from the sheep and the children herding them to safety. The herd was too far away from the main compound. Any help coming from the main structures would be too late.

Raven braced herself, positioning her body between the herd and the unknown figures. She was standing on a hillock that was covered with outcrops of stones. If the invaders made a bee-line for the receding sheep they would have to cross the hill and go right past where Raven was standing. A stone rolled beneath her foot. She reached down and picked it up, feeling the weight. The rock was about the size of a baseball and fit her hand nicely. Pressure against her knee caused her to glance down. One of the dogs, a broad-headed Akita, was leaning against her leg. Two boys had taken up positions to the right and left of her. The four of them were the only defense between the herd and the invaders.

Raven motioned the boys to take up positions behind two rock formations. Her sharp eyes could make out the men as they cut the wire fence and pointed their bikes up the hill. She could see her instincts where correct; the trespassers were headed straight for the herd. Raven wished she had more than her knife and rocks to defend herself and the children caring for the sheep. Whatever happened, her main goal was to slow down the attackers. Raven dropped behind the same outcropping as one of the boys. The dog followed her. Signaling the boy to keep the dog from lunging, Raven crept to the top of the rock. She crouched as low as she could, hoping the muted colors of her skirt and top would allow her to blend into the grey rock. The second boy was creeping around the side of his rock. Raven motioned to him and signaled him to wait. He nodded and ducked behind his rock. After a moment Raven saw his head on the top of his rock. He had climbed up and taken the same position as Raven.

Raven could feel her heart pound and her pulse sang in her ears. She could feel the drumming of the bikes' motors through the vibration in the rocks. All she wanted to do was buy some time for the children to make it to the shelter of the community. The bikes crested the hill and Raven caught a glimpse of the invaders. Twelve men, all masked, all armed with rifles and knives. The men had to drive cautiously around the rocky protuberances dotting the hillside. One of them came too close to the rock where Raven was crouched. Timing her movements carefully, Raven dropped from her hiding place directly on the back of the man. She peeled him off his four-wheeled ATV and slammed him to the ground, landing on top of him. Raven punched him with her fist holding the rock and released his limp body, kicking it down the hill. One of the bikes swerved to go around the body and the rider lost control, spilling to the ground. Both boys jumped on the rider and one of them clocked him with his shepherd's staff.

The four wheeler Raven had stripped of its rider had come to a standstill only a few feet away. Its motor still throbbed as Raven ran to it and jumped on, hitting the throttle. She could feel the cool breeze brushing her thighs as her skirt flapped in the wind. Modesty was the furthest thing from her mind as she raced after the other cycles.

She past the Akita, who had pulled one of the riders to the ground and was biting at his victim's arms. The man was trying to roll over to his back but the dog wouldn't let him move. Raven heard the man scream as she rolled past, but she ignored him as she headed towards the leader of the invaders. The remaining attackers had almost reached the sheep and the children herding them. The cries of fear from the younger children assaulted Raven's ears and she turned the throttle to maximum. Her tires hit the bike in front of her, causing the rider to be thrown and the bike to spin.

The leader turned his bike and stared down at Raven. His dark eyes bore into her as she eased back of the throttle. She knew exactly when he made his decision to attack. The tendons in his wrists twisted as he gunned the motor of his bike. Raven could feel the smile creep on her face as he raced towards her. Standing on the foot pegs she gunned her own engine. The man was on a two-wheeled cycle and had difficulty controlling the bike over the rough ground. Raven kept a steady pace until she was inches from her aggressor. At the last moment she turned her bike, allowing the man to pass by her. A stiff arm to the chest forced the man off his bike and Raven felt, rather than heard, the thud as he hit the ground. She spun around and parked her bike inches from the man's head. His eyes were rolled back in his head and he was making grunting noises from deep within his throat.

The other bikes had pulled up near where Raven was hovering over their leader. She pulled her knife and leapt from her ride. Her knife was at the throat of the man, forcing the others to stop. The man groaned and tried to sit up. Raven backhanded him, forcing him to the ground. One of the men reached for his rifle, but sudden movement behind Raven caused him to drop the weapon. Raven didn't remove the knife from the throat of the man until all the invaders dropped their weapons and stepped off their bikes. And as quickly as it started, the battle was over. Men from the community were bearing down on the trespassers, weapons drawn and beaded on the intruders.

Raven's heart was still throbbing, her body shaking from the surge of adrenaline. Looking down, she realized her hand was gripping the handle of her knife so tightly her knuckles were turning white. Her hand was shaking as she slid the blade back in its sheath. She really needed to get a gun if she was going to go out with the herds.

Stepping back, she allowed the men to move forward and take control of the invaders. Joseph glanced at her as he went by, an undecipherable expression on his face. The two boys who had stayed behind to help rode up on a shared cycle, matching grins spread across their faces. It was only when they came close that Raven realized the boys were twins. They obviously didn't know how to handle the bike and as they approached the crowd they were unable to hold it steady. The bike wobbled and they had to lay it on its side. The boys sprang up, unhurt and still grinning.

"That was amazing." The boy who was driving the bike ran up and grabbed Raven around the waist. He was so exuberant he actually managed to lift Raven up a few inches and they both tumbled to the ground. Raven pushed him away and jumped to her feet pushing her skirt down around her knees.

The invaders were all trussed up, the last one was being dragged up the hill by Bear and Joseph. The man was screaming and swearing, but his arms and feet were so tightly tied he was unable to struggle. A community truck pulled up next to the captives and the men from the community started picking up the trussed invaders and tossing them into the back. The leader of the pack tried to get to his feet, succeeding only to roll over and push up on one elbow.

"What are you going to do to us?" The man's voiced quivered. Raven couldn't tell if it was from anger or fear.

Bear approached and stood over the man. "We're going to take you into town and drop you off at the Guard station." Bear used his foot to push the man down to the ground. "I'm sure you and your men will have a few warrants on you. Only cowardly criminals would attack innocent children taking their flocks to field."

The man snarled and tried to squirm out from under Bear's foot. His grunt and groan attested to the force Bear used to push him back down.

"We had no intention of hurting anyone." The man had to force the words out once he caught his breath. "We just wanted some meat. Our people are starving."

Bear didn't appear to have any sympathy for the man under his foot. Once all the invaders were loaded in the back of the truck Bear turned to face Raven. His grin was as broad as the twins.

"You are one crazy woman." He wrapped his arm around her shoulders. "The council will want to meet with you and your husband. It's going to take a couple of hours to deliver this rabble to town. We'll reconvene when I get back."

Bear hoisted his lumbering frame into the back of the truck and gave a long, sharp whistle. The driver waved as he slammed the truck into gear and flipped around. Raven shook her head as the truck made its way out of the field. She turned back to see the carnage and was surprised at how calm and peaceful the field looked. Some of the men from the community actually took the invaders' bikes and rode them down to the damaged fence. Raven's sharp eyes caught every movement as they inspected the damage. She couldn't hear what they were seeing or make out the details, but they didn't look too hurried as they worked on repairing the fence. Raven turned her focus to the people around her. Joseph was staring at her with an stunned expression on his face.

"Are you okay?" he asked.

He reached up and touched her face. When he pulled back his hand there was blood on it. Raven brought her hand up to her cheek. She didn't feel any swelling or pain. The blood felt sticky against her fingers.

"I don't think it's mine." She felt a quiver in her voice as she spoke. "I'm fine. Is anyone hurt?"

"Just the bad guys." There was a hint of laughter in Joseph's voice as he spoke.

The Akita who had stood at Raven's side during the attack limped up to her. He leaned his body against her knee and whined. Raven patted the animal's head and stroked his fur. He flinched when she past her hand over his shoulder and she felt blood and the edges of a knife wound.

"We need to get the dog back to the compound." Raven held up her hand to show the blood. She hopped on a four-wheeler and had Joseph drape the dog across her lap. The animal's nose and tail almost dragged the ground on either side of the bike and its whole body quivered anxiously, but it stayed in place as she slowly drove to the clinic.

Chapter Twenty-Eight

EMILY WASN"T TOO HAPPY WHEN the dog was brought into the clinic, but Raven insisted on bringing him into the exam room and cleaning and stitching the wound. Raven allowed the nurse's aide to take the dog out and then helped Emily scrub the exam room. When it was clean Emily insisted Raven go back to her complex to shower and change clothes.

Her clothes were smeared with mud, grass and blood and she could feel tendrils of hair falling down around her shoulders. She peeled the trappings of the society from her body and stepped into the steam of the shower. The bar of homemade goat's milk soap slid with creamy smoothness through her fingers, filling her hands with a rich lather. She scrubbed until her hair squeaked and her skin tingled.

Her filthy clothes lay in a pile outside the shower door. The thought of putting them back on caused her skin to crawl. Instead, she wrapped her hair in a towel and wrapped a sheet from the linen closet around her body. No one else was in the building anyway and they wouldn't see her ghost down the hall in her bare feet. Joseph was waiting for her in the bedroom. His face was pale and he was trembling. Raven could hear wind chimes outside the window, tinkling their song to the breeze. The intensity of Joseph's expression sent a thrilling shock through Raven's body.

"Joseph, I'm fine." The words didn't seem to reassure him. "I've been through worse. You know that."

"I wasn't there for those times, Raven." He tried to approach her, but there seemed to be a barrier between them. "You just seem so indestructible and unreachable. Sometimes I don't even know if you're real."

Raven's hands felt cold. She started to shiver uncontrollably. Joseph reached for her and she fell into his arms. Holding him close, she rubbed her hands up and down his back. The motion was meant to soothe him but she could feel his warmth bleeding into her hands, so she kept up the motion.

"I'm fine, Joseph, I promise." This time she didn't resist his kiss. She allowed him to lower her body to the bed and, for the first time since Billy died, she felt the touch of a man as he made love to her.

It was late evening when the council convened. Raven had actually slept for an hour or so before supper; no one seemed to want to disturb her. After the end of the meal and the clearing of the tables, all the residents of the community were sent off to various tasks. Raven and Joseph stood in front of the twelve men and twelve women for the second time since asking to join the community. Raven had come to know many of the men and women sitting before her and wished there didn't have to have so many secrets between them. Bear was laughing with the man beside him and smiled and winked at Raven as she sat down. Joseph put his arm around her and Raven could feel their newfound intimacy rearing his protective instincts.

Bear raised his hand, calling the meeting to order. The group fell silent. Raven could feel the hair on her arms prickle as the hush seemed louder to her than the roar of a missile.

"I just wanted to report we dropped the invaders off at the Guard station." Bear said. "They all had warrants and actually there is a fairly substantial reward for their capture." His words brought on a flutter of whispers. After a few moments Bear started up again. "For some reason none of the men wanted to 'fess up to the attempted rustling and have that added to their resumes. I kind of neglected to tell the Guard about the bikes. I think we're going to consider them spoils of war. But, we're not here to belabor these points. We want to talk to you, Raven."

Raven, he called her Raven! She looked up, trying to assess Bear's mood. His smile didn't waver and he meet her eyes easily.

"Your aunt told us the name she used to call you when you were a child." Bear glanced at Emily but he directed his words to Raven. "Emily told us how she lived on the same reservation as you when you were a child and she told us she helped raise you until your father took you away. It's hard not to notice the family resemblance. We had to pry the information from her, though. She said your childhood was pretty traumatic, with your mother dying when you were young and your father being such a rabid conspiracy theorist."

Emily was protecting Raven's secret. It wasn't exactly clear if she was doing it for Raven's protection or for her own. Emily had her own secrets and reasons for keeping them. Raven wondered what the community would do if they knew Emily had a warrant for custodial interference. The question of where Emily was getting her medical supplies for her clinic still resounded in Raven's mind. She looked at her aunt, trying to get a read on the woman. The only tell was a slight tightening in her aunt's eyes. A warning to tread carefully. She was entering dangerous territory.

"I've tried to put that part of my life behind me." The steadiness of her tone surprised her a little. "Those were bad times for all of us."

Bear held up his hand, forestalling any further comment. "You don't need to explain. Those were dark days, and we still suffer the consequences. We don't want to talk to you about that. We have a request to make of you and your husband."

Raven glanced over at Joseph. His expression was stoic, but his arm was tense against her shoulders. If their cover was blown the entire mission would come tumbling down around their ears. She would just have to see what Bear had to say.

"We need your help." Bear's smile disappeared. "Raven, you have skills beyond just about any of us here. We're not using you to your full potential. Emily told us you have more medical knowledge than many of the doctors she has worked with in the past. You have combat training both from the military and from your father. We've all seen evidence of that. You sprang headfirst into danger with no concern for your own safety. You saved lives today, we all believe that. It's like they say, danger doesn't make heroes, it finds them."

Joseph shot to his feet, leaving Raven without support momentarily. She didn't realize she was leaning into him. Bracing herself she sat up in her chair.

"I don't know what you are thinking, but I'm not going to let you send my wife on a fool quest." The intensity of Joseph's voice hummed with vibrant energy. "We left Montana because it was becoming too dangerous to live there. I'm not going to let you send my wife headlong into danger."

Raven put her hand on Joseph's arm, pulling him back to his seat. Bear looked slightly startled, but he regained his composure quickly.

"No, no." His tone was reassuring, almost condescending. "We don't want to send your wife into danger. Listen, a few of us here have had military training, but we don't have the skill to train others. What happened today showed us we need to start. But," he paused and took a deep breath before continuing, "it's going to require sacrifice on both of your parts. Raven, we want you to stay here during the harvest and give us combat training. You would train anyone who stayed here and train the men when they came back to do guard duty. After harvest we can go into intensive training. You could even train any of the women who are interested."

Raven's heart was drumming in her chest. Her mind raced as she analyzed the implications of Bear's request. She would be providing military training and tactics to a possible subversive group. The same people she and Joseph were spying on were asking her to provide the skills to assault the nation she was sworn to protect. She tried to read Joseph's expression, but he wasn't giving anything away.

"There's more." Raven turned her attention back to Bear. "We need Joseph to work the harvest with us. It would help if we could use your belongings as well. Your tent would sleep six and your bicycles would help us transport supplies. We're not trying to steal your belongings and Joseph will be with us the entire time. I know it would be hard to be away from each other, but we have at least another month before we leave and harvest is only a few months."

So many thoughts were roiling through Raven's head, she couldn't sort out what was happening. The community was so well organized it wouldn't be difficult to incorporate a training regimen into the routine. Deciding who to train and how to provide the training without creating an entire new threat was throbbing in her head.

Joseph's expression changed slightly. The corner of his eyes tightened and his lips thinned. The change was almost imperceptible, but it was enough for Raven to feel a momentary flash of relief. Joseph would be the one to make the decision and he didn't look as if he had any desire to be parted from her. Raven wanted to jump in and start training all the members of the community, but doing so would be defeating the entire purpose of the mission.

Joseph took Raven's hand. "My wife and I need to talk about this. We're not concerned about our belongings. You've accepted us as part of your community so the supplies belong to everyone. It will be up to the Elders of the community to decide how to best use them. I know my wife can protect herself while I'm working the harvest. I just don't know if I can be parted from her for that long."

Joseph's hand was warm, causing Raven's fingers to tingle as he gently rubbed circles on her palm with his thumb. A slight shock went up her spine as she studied the blue veins and tendons creating a tree pattern standing in ridges against his pale skin. The dark skin of her hand had its own branching design of veins and arteries. Joseph's hand traced the scar dissecting across her palm and Raven pulled her hand away.

"I think it would be a good idea if I stayed here." She kept her voice low and her eyes downcast as she spoke. "There needs to be a defensive perimeter established around the community, I can help with that. It's going to take more than one person to train units to fight and I'm not sure training women and children to be soldiers is going to be the best way to protect us. It would be better to teach them self-defense. We can start classes tomorrow."

Bear didn't respond for a moment and Raven wondered if he was going to turn down her offer or demand more of her, but when she made eye contact with her he smiled.

"I hope we can all benefit from your knowledge." He stood up from his chair and motioned for Emily to step forward. "I think your aunt should help you go through our clothing stores and find you a few pair of pants. The boys are still talking about the show you put on in the field, and the conversations aren't centered around your fighting skills."

Raven could feel the heat in her face and she ducked her head before anyone could see the darkening of her cheeks. Smoothing her hands over the folds of her skirt, she made sure the folds covered her legs. The meeting broke up and the council members milled around for a few minutes. Joseph pulled Raven to the corner of the room.

"Are you sure about this, Raven?" His voice was a low hum as he whispered in her ear. "I can't protect you if I'm out on harvest."

"I think it's going to be the best way to get what we need. We've built up trust to get in to their inner secrets." Raven kept her voice to a sibilant whisper. "I can take care of myself."

Emily approached, taking Raven's elbow. "We should go to storage now. Tomorrow we're going to start going through the supplies and prepare for market. Everyone is going to be busy from now until the end of harvest. Let's get this taken care of now."

Raven walked into the gathering dusk, following Emily to the storage sheds behind the kitchens. The sheds were packed full of supplies the community had been working on all through the year. Emily led her past the first three sheds. Raven know the contents of these sheds, having had helped pack them full of the fluffy, white wool of sheep that had been sheared in the fall. The fourth shed held the clothing, bolts of cloth and sewing supplies. Raven detested this shed. She had never learned to sew and didn't have the patience to sit over a machine trying to force a tiny string through an even tinier needle eye. When the women gathered in the workroom to make smocks and skirts Raven always made sure to find another task to keep herself occupied.

Emily moved over to the rack holding stacks of pants and started pulling down options for Raven to try on. All of the pants came from second-hand stores or the large marketplace put on in the early spring. They were worn, but clean and in good condition. Seams had been reinforced and patches had been sewn over holes and worn spots. The pants were all structured to fit men's bodies and lacked the flexibility to conform to Raven's curves. She finally managed to find a couple of pairs that fit over her hips although they were too loose at the waist. Emily used a couple of safety pins to put in some darts so the pants wouldn't slide down Raven's hips. Raven changed out of the pants and wrapped her skirt back around her waist, straightening the fabric across her knees. The women would be gathering in the work room the next day to mend and tailor the clothes needed for the summer and Emily said she would include the pants to be fitted. Emily gathered the three pairs of pants Raven finally settled on into her arms.

"Do you think these will get you through the summer?" Emily was fingering the fabric of a beige cargo pant.

"They should be fine," Raven responded. She was working on putting the pants they had pulled off the shelf back where they belonged. "They're loose enough in the legs to move around in and the material is sturdy so they should last. I just hope they're not too hot to train in during the heat of summer. It would be nice to have some light cotton pants."

"I'll see what I can find when I go to market next week." Emily positioned herself between Raven and the door. "Raven, are you sure you want to do this? It's extremely risky. Summer is the worst time for us on the settlement. Raids are more common and the community doesn't have the manpower to offer complete protection to the residents who stay at the compound."

"That's why I'm doing this," Raven said. "I can help this community build defenses and teach the members to fight." Raven wasn't sure exactly what her aunt wanted from her and she was starting to feel cornered. She shifted her weight to the balls of her feet, not quite sure what she was going to do if Emily didn't move out of the doorway.

Emily stepped away from the entrance. "I worry so much about everyone when they go to harvest. I worry about the people left on the compound. Now I have to worry about you, too. I thought you and your mother would be safe enough at Haven."

"Emily, I can take care of myself." Raven struggled to keep her voice controlled. "Mom is safe enough at Haven. I can't stay behind stone walls when so many people are suffering." Raven stepped past Emily and walked down the path to her home.

Twenty-Nine

EMILY RETURNED FROM MARKET WITH a stack of cotton drawstring pants. Raven felt almost wicked as she walked around the compound in her new clothes while other women were wearing their long, wraparound skirts. She decided to bring it up to Emily one day when they were in the clinic alone.

"Emily, do you think I should wear a skirt when I'm not training the units?" she asked.

Emily looked up from where she was placing bandaging materials in drawers. She studied Raven for a moment before responding. "No matter how many feathers you try to put on to cover who you really are, it will never work, Raven. It's not hard to tell you don't fit in with the rest of the members of the community. The women in the community wear skirts because they are easy to make and the material is cheap and easy to find. They're not trying to make a fashion statement. It's a matter of convenience, one you should be familiar with coming from Haven."

The mention of Haven brought a lump to Raven's throat. She was surprised by the well of emotion flooding her when she thought of the complex where she grew up. Haven wasn't home any more, but her mother and her children were still there and she missed them. There hadn't been much opportunity to talk to Emily about Haven. Her aunt managed to steer any conversation away from any talk about the shelter. Raven decided to take a chance and ask her aunt the questions burning in her mind.

"Emily, why did you do it? Why did you take my mother's embryos?"

"I was wondering when this was going to come up." Emily seemed unsurprised by the question and actually smiled a little. "Do you think your mother would have been able to carry all the embryos she created? I helped bring nine of your mother's children into the world. Nine lives with her perfect DNA to pass on to future generations. They're out there Raven, your brothers and sisters, scattered between here and Arizona. I started when you were nine and finished when you were fourteen. I'm sure the oldest one is preparing to have a family of her own by now. She's almost twenty-one, now." Emily paused, ducking her head and speaking to the floor. "Do you think your mother would ever forgive me? I'm getting older and I would love to return to Haven to live out the rest of my life."

Raven shook her head. "I haven't talked to my mother for a long time. She was still looking for you and the children you took the last time I saw her. A whole section of her lab is dedicated to testing DNA of any likely candidates. She's trying to bring her children home."

Emily didn't mention Haven much after that day. Raven gathered the women and older children who were willing to learn and started training them. Her summer was spent working with the residents who were still at the compound, taking them through fitness training and self-defense exercises. She wanted to spend some time working on perimeter defenses, but she didn't have the manpower to build the bulwarks she had in mind. Once a week members of the community would return with transports loaded down with produce from the fields. There would always be four or five people coming in with the supplies. The group would stay for a week of training and then return to the fields at the end of the week. Raven had barely enough time to give each group the rudiments of physical training before they headed back to follow the field work. Working in the fields for twelve hours gave very little time for actual practice. Although there was no doubt the physical labor provided plenty of opportunity for conditioning, it wasn't the same thing as developing the muscles and reflexes for fighting. She needed to get her hands on all the able-bodied members of the community and drill and train them until the lessons stuck in sensory memory.

Raven made a list of every member of the community and divided them into units. She spent weeks studying the lists and developing a plan for training each group. By the time the late harvest foods started coming in, foreshadowing the return of the main body of community members, Raven had a training program outlined and prepared to implement. She marked the area she wanted to use as training fields and made a list of everything she needed to build the proving grounds.

The program had to be put on hold during the tail end of harvest as all attention turned to food storage. A handful of men returned from the harvest route to bring in crops and work the claims. Everyone worked together to process the food and prepare it for storage. Cold weather descended on the compound, bringing with it the harvesters and a flurry of activity. It took nearly two weeks for everyone to settle in and a new routine to be established. Joseph returned with the rest of the work crews and Raven outlined her plan to him. The new family unit was no longer unoccupied. A smaller community had joined with theirs while they were working the harvest. Raven and Joseph welcomed their new bunkmates with grace and dignity, but Raven was a little disappointed in the loss of privacy brought about when the new residents moved into the empty rooms.

More bodies meant more work and the need to process more food, but it also meant more hands to help with building defenses. Women still greatly outnumbered the men in the community and it was sometimes difficult to convince the women they needed to help with building the defenses and the new training grounds. The main complaint of the women as a whole was they joined the community to get protection from attacks and they weren't expecting to have to learn to protect themselves. Raven tried to convince them to join in the defense training, but at best she was only able to get some of the teenage girls to join the groups and that was mostly because that's where all the boys were.

Despite these setbacks Raven was able to make strong inroads in building defenses around the property defined by the community. Two of the newest members of the community filed claims on the neighboring plots and increased the community's entire acreage to three hundred and twenty. Raven had to adjust her defensive perimeter plans to incorporate the new acres. It was going to be tricky to build living structures on the furthest acreages, but Raven wasn't going to worry about that detail. Her job was going to be building a defensible perimeter and that was going to be her focus.

The southeast boundary of the community was protected by a swiftly running creek with high banks. Defending that border was as easy as planting a row of blackberry brambles at the stream edge. It would take a few years to completely overrun the banks, but in the meantime those far fields would be planted with alfalfa to discourage raiders. Most raids were a slash and grab operation, designed to crash in, grab as much product as possible and make a clean getaway. Any defensive quarter created would delay the possibility for quick getaways.

Raven built the bulwarks into the existing landscape as much as possible. The community only had two working tractors with limited attachments to do the heavy lifting, making it difficult to get the bulwarks in place. She had to work with the equipment she had.

Overseeing the construction of the fences and border defenses was exhausting enough, but Raven was also overseeing the training of the able-bodied men, women and young adults, all of which wore on her body. It was hard to motivate the units to train in the winter, but a few attempted raids at the height of the cold season were enough to convince most of them to work.

The few winter raids weren't too effective. A few desperate, hungry men tried sneaking onto the property and encroaching on some of the outbuildings, but Raven's soldiers managed to chase them away. From the glimpses Raven saw of their retreating backs it appeared they were more desperate than dangerous. As winter melted into spring the threat of raids increased. Raven increased patrols around the border of the property and worked on shoring up the hillocks and walls that had been built to reinforce the fences.

Raven used the natural contours of the land to build up the defenses around the edge of the property. The entire community spent weeks building up hills and piling rocks to create barriers for motorized vehicles. Between motion detectors, regular patrols and the defensive barriers, the community was turning into a fortress. Raven rotated the patrols to cover any weaknesses in the defense perimeters, allowing a greater protection of workers as the community started the spring field work.

By the time spring market rolled around Raven was feeling confident in the ability of her units. She was able to build a strong core of leadership and had four men acting as her seconds. The entire community consisted of two hundred fourteen souls, all of whose safety was now Raven's responsibility. She still couldn't shake the feeling she was creating the exact type of insurgents both she and Joseph were supposed to sniff out.

In the quiet moments they could find alone, Joseph reassured her they were doing exactly what they needed to do. Already, Bear had been approached by other groups about training units and banding together. Joseph had been invited to attend meetings and had met the leaders of other communities. He was slowly insinuating himself into the upper echelons of the subgroups and learning names of the leaders of each group.

Late night discussions were no longer possible, with couples on either side of the walls. Everyone in the community worked from dawn to dusk, either with farm work or defense training and it was physically draining on Raven. Her body ached and her mind wouldn't settle from the events of the day. It was difficult to shut out the murmur of voices seeping through the walls. Joseph tucked his data pad under her pillow and turned the music down low, allowing the gentle rhythms to soothe her to sleep.

Raven was deep in sleep when an alarm klaxon sang through the air, jarring her awake. She threw back her blanket and flew toward the door, pulling on her shoes as she went. All around her she heard doors fly open and the soprano cries of women and children singing through the structure. Bodies flooded the hall as Raven tried to make her way to the door. Fortunately, her room was close to the door and she was able to make it out of the building before the hallway filled up. Most of the men and some of the women had followed her out onto the front porch. The gun safe stood open and one of the men was handing pistols and rifles into outreached hands. Raven felt the cool smoothness of a gun belt slide across her palm and she quickly slung the strap around her hips, buckling it over her tunic, low on her hips. The gentle hum of a motor assailed her ears and she could see the lights of the cycles flashing in the darkness.

The full moon lit up the landscape casting the fields in an eerie glow. Raven scanned the landscape, trying to sense what set the proximity detectors off. She could smell the tang of sweat and fear in the air as she moved around the side of the building and scanned the fields. The cows and goats were all in the fields near the main compound and a quick scan didn't show any uneasiness there. A bleating cry drew her attention to the south field. Nearly a hundred head of newly shorn sheep, many of them ewes with dewdrops at their side, were grazing in the fallow acres near a small stream and Raven could make out the shape of dark figures creeping amongst the flock.

"They're in the sheep!" Her voice sang out in the darkness. She wasn't sure exactly how many people heard her but it didn't matter, her cry was repeated by voice after voice and the entire community turned towards the field. The cycles pulled alongside the group, racing towards the now bleating sheep, and pulled slightly ahead. Raven could feel the vibrations of a motor coming up behind her. She glanced over just as Bear pulled up beside her. He slowed down just enough for her to jump on the back of his cycle. She could feel the back wheel slip in the dirt and she grabbed Bear around his waist, allowing her body to move with his as he turned and found the bike's balance.

Raven could feel the speed of the bike as Bear gunned the engine and roared towards the field. She was flung forward as he rolled to a stop in front of the scattering flock. Bear swung off the bike and Raven allowed his momentum to carry her to the ground. All around her figures were racing through the darkness and she was having a hard time distinguishing invader from defender. Sheep were milling around, bleating and crying. Dewdrops were seeking their mothers, strangled cries singing across the fields. A body slammed into Raven, nearly knocking her off her feet. She grappled with the form for a moment before she realized it was one of the boys from her unit.

"Tim," she grabbed him by the front of his tunic. "Start gathering the sheep. Herd them toward the north end of the pasture. Get the dogs to help."

The boy nodded his understanding and gave a sharp whistle. Two of the broad-headed Akitas perked up their ears and ran at the boy. Raven watched as Tim gave a few sharp commands and the dogs started nipping at the heels of the sheep. It didn't take long for the other dogs to figure out what they needed to do and soon the sheep were bunched together and were being moved up the pasture.

Once the sheep were out of the way, Raven turned back to the mêlée. A few sheep were on the ground among the fighters, but their bleating and movement showed they were only hobbled and were still alive. A few shadowy figures broke away from the main group and attempted to bolt across the field. Raven darted towards the closest one and, with a running leap, managed to pull him down. Her momentum caused them to roll around in the dirt for a moment, but Raven came out on top and managed to subdue the man, wrapping her arm around his neck and forcing her knee into his back. Joseph approached with a rope and together they hobbled the man.

Raven pulled herself up and brushed the dirt off her pants. Her hand brushed the butt of her gun and she realized she hadn't even thought of pulling her weapon. All around her she could hear barks and cheers and she realized the fight was over. Once again marauders had attempted a raid on the farm and once again Raven had helped prevent the loss of life and livestock.

Chapter Thirty

THE FIVE INVADERS WERE CAPTURED, hobbled and forced into a group in the middle of the field. When the sheep they had captured were released they went crying back to the flock, bleating for their young. The approaching dawn was streaking the sky with fingers of red and gold, allowing Raven to clearly distinguish the features of the men huddling on the ground. They were all sharp angles and bones. Grey skin stretched over sharp cheekbones, giving them a slight alien cast. The men all hunched over, pressing their bodies close and shivering in the damp morning air. One of the men coughed continuously, his body arching as spasm after spasm racked his body. Raven watched as pink foam flecked his lips and he spit bloody mucus on the ground.

The air was thick with victory, but Raven could feel another weight circling the group. The sun continued its ascent on the horizon, but the rest of the community was still shut away in the buildings. Raven wouldn't let anyone sound the all clear signal. She sent patrols to check the borders and they had come back with a nearly empty hand cart. The frame was badly warped and the wheels were loose on the axle. She wanted to search through the few rough sacks and boxes scattered in the bottom of the cart but the man's hacking cough worried her and she didn't let anyone go near the contents of the rickety cart.

As the defenders started to gather, Raven motioned them to stay away from the invaders. She had taught her guards many of the hand signals she had developed from the language she learned as a child and most of the time she didn't even have to verbalize her orders. Bear moved to stand beside her, his rifle slung casually in his arms. Joseph stepped to Raven's other side draping his arm around her shoulders. Raven followed the direction of Bear's gaze as he stared at the coughing man.

"Do you think he has it?" Bear asked.

Raven didn't need to ask what Bear was talking about. The man was bent over, coughing up another bloody mucus plug. She gave a quick, sharp nod before turning to the rest of the crew. She motioned for them to gather around and stepped away from the captured men. A whirlwind of thoughts went through her head as she contemplated this new situation. Locked away in the buildings were nearly two hundred souls, waiting to be allowed out to start on daily chores. Releasing the entire community to be exposed to the one man's tuberculosis would be unconscionable. Raven had to weigh the health of the residents against the need to care for the animals calling to be milked and fed.

Joseph thrust a data pad into Raven's hands. She sent a message to Emily telling her to contact the authorities and to have them meet her on the road. It took some prodding and effort, but she managed to get the captive men to stand up and move to the handcart. She had the prisoners assist the sick man into the cart and push and pull the cart to the access road. The men were so weak she seriously doubted they would be able to manage the five mile walk down the road to the main intersection to meet the sheriff.

The four men pulling the cart struggled and stumbled as they made their way up to the main road. A small pile of food: bread, cheese, dried fruit and jerky was sitting in a crate by the side of the road. Raven allowed the men to stop and eat some of the food and drink some water. She had them place the remaining food in the cart to take with them. The concave nature of their chests and pale, twiggy arms and legs attested to the reason for their desperation. Raven doubted they would survive much longer, even with the food she had told the women in the community to leave by the side of the road.

The men only made it another mile up the road before exhaustion wouldn't let them go any further. Raven could see their legs quiver as they tried to push the cart, only managing to go a few inches. She finally stopped and had them sit by the side of the road to wait for the sheriff. The men huddled together, pulling their legs to their bodies and wrapping their arms around their bony knees. Their pale, translucent skin had almost a bluish tinge and Raven could actually make out the trace of their veins bulging through the skin. The men all hunched over as their breath came in gasping sobs. Raven was thankful when she heard the hum of the motor presaging the arrival of the sheriff department's vehicle. Joseph handed her a strip of cloth and she quickly wrapped it around her head and covered her face.

The sheriff's truck had a gold star emblazed in the white door. Raven was surprised at the stark cleanliness of the vehicle. She was used to the slightly grungy, used appearance of the community vehicles. The community vehicles were washed on a regular basis, but they were used so often to do laborious work they always seemed to be coated with dust and grime.

The two sheriffs' deputies disembarked from the cab of the truck. They were both decked out in protective gear-white hazmat suits, gloves, medical masks- and they seemed hesitant to approach the men sitting on the side of the road. Raven kept her men back as the handcart was loaded in the bed of the truck and tied down. She watched as the five invaders were cuffed and roughly loaded into the bed of the truck, crammed against the rough wood of the handcart. A few of them broke down and sobbed piteously as the sheriffs got back in the cab and drove away. Raven waited until they were a safe distance away before turning to face her men. All of them stared back at her, their faces pale in the bright morning light. Raven mentally steeled herself as she prepared to address this new threat against the community.

"We need to wait here while the other community members set up tents and supplies in the south field. It's laying fallow this season so we can camp there for the next four weeks." Raven watched the faces of the men carefully as she set the quarantine restrictions. She didn't want to have any backlash or mutiny if the men didn't agree with her. "We need to burn our clothing and anything else we used to restrain the men. I don't want anything from the fields getting back to camp. We'll move the sheep to another pasture and build a fire in the place where we were holding the men. I don't know how virile this strain of tuberculosis is and I don't want to take any chances. I'll have Emily bring some test kits and we'll run TB tests in a couple of weeks. If we all come back clean we'll be able to go to the market and make the harvest cycle like everyone else. If not, we'll spend the summer building a quarantine lodge and we'll all take a cycle of antibiotics while living in the quarantine quarters. As long as we stay isolated from the rest of the population they should be okay."

Raven didn't see any dissention in the eyes of the men. They all seemed to be taking the restrictions in stride. She pulled her head cloth through her fingers. The cloth rippled and snagged on her rough, dirt covered hands. She looked at the dirt embedded under her fingernails and shuddered.

"We need to take baths and scrub every inch of our bodies with strong soap," she said. "We can use the springs. I don't want any of us going into the bathhouse until I'm sure we aren't contagious. I'll have Emily leave us some soap and towels."

By the time Raven and her team made it back to the compound, tents had been set up in the fallow field and supplies had been delivered. Raven recognized the refrigerator unit and generator from her and Joseph's initial camp site from before they joined the community. It was sitting beside their old tent. A water purifier was set up on the table and new clothes and bedding was resting just outside the tents. Raven and her unit moved past the new encampment and skirted the far edges of the community. Most of the residents had left the structures in the main compound, but Raven and the men following her gave everyone a wide berth as they headed down the hill to the hot springs.

Wooden crates had been set up on the water's edge, beside bars of soap and soft white towels. Raven stepped away from the path to the main springs and headed for the slightly smaller, hotter pool. She knew she wouldn't be able to soak as long as the others in this pool, but at least it would get her clean. Emily must have been thinking the same thing because a small box and some soap and towels had been laid out beside the pool. There was also a plastic medical basin already filled with water and cooling by the side of the pool. Raven stripped and used a towel to scrub as much dirt off her body as she could. Slowly, she stepped into the steaming pool of water and ducked down until it came to her neck. Using the strong lye soap she scrubbed every inch of her skin until it was red and raw. The heat of the water was making it hard to breathe so she stepped out of the pool. Soap still covered her, but her body couldn't handle the heat any longer. Using the medical basin she scooped out water, let it cool for a few minutes and then poured it over her head. By the time she finished her skin was red and tingly and she felt raw, as if she had a mild sunburn. But she was clean, all the way down to her fingernails and toenails. Raven couldn't help grinning when she picked up the sandals Emily had left for her to wear in place of her shoes. They were hand-woven slippers made of hemp, similar in design to the ones she was given when she was a child by the kind woman by the burning fields so many years ago. She tied the sandals to her feet and picked up the crate, making sure to hold it, and its contents, far away from her body.

The men were waiting for her when she came back up the trail, lugging her crate of contaminated clothing. An old wooden handcart from the community stores was loaded down with crates of clothing and towels. Raven put her crate amongst the others and placed the plastic bin on top; she wasn't taking any chances.

They pulled the old wooden cart to the center of the field where the invaders had just been held captive a few hours before. The dogs had kept the sheep in the corner of the field, so it didn't take much effort to open the gates and force them into the next pasture over. Once the animals were corralled and the gates locked, Raven moved to the center of the field. The men had stuffed paper in the crevasses between the boxes in the cart and poured a little bit of kerosene over the contents. Flames darted over the top of the crates, lighting up blue at the base before changing to a cherry red. The wood crates were dry and caught almost immediately, sending crackling notes into the sky, with ash glowing first red and then darkening to black and finally grey as it crumbled to the ground. Smoke billowed, sending white, soot-filled clouds into the air. The fire cleansed the ground and burned away some of the fear lingering in the air.

Raven sent the rest of her unit to the tents to set up the camp while she, Joseph and Bear stayed and watched the cart burn. One of the boys brought a breakfast of bread, cheese and fruit to the field. She didn't realize how hungry she was until she bit into the warm, crusty bread, smeared with creamy white goat's cheese.

Raven and her team were in their self-imposed quarantine for four weeks. The rest of the community went about their business as if nothing changed, preparing the fields, caring for the animals and planning the annual exodus to the fields. Joseph's data pad kept them connected with the day to day happenings of the community. Raven was surprised to discover he had thought to grab the palm-sized device during the midst of the attack, but carrying the device seemed to be a deeply ingrained habit and Raven rarely saw him without it in his hand. He had even created a solar panel pack he wore strapped to his back so he could charge the pad without it ever having to leave his possession.

The four weeks in the fallow field were the longest of Raven's life. She tested every person who was part of defending the compound and had close contact with the invaders and any of their equipment. Many of the fields had been plowed and planted by the time she felt safe in removing the restrictions she had placed on the men. When she did finally allow the unit to rejoin their families the entire community seemed to breathe a sigh of relief. It appeared none of the defenders suffered ill effects from being so close to someone who was infected. Raven couldn't shake the feeling they had dodged a bullet this time. They were fortunate Emily had been able to maintain the health of the community and obtain vaccinations for the residents. Raven still didn't know who her source was or where her supplies were coming from. Emily was keeping that information completely under wraps.

By the time the unit rejoined the rest of the community, plans for the transient season were well under way. The council decided there was a need to keep a stronger presence at the now highly productive farm and Raven's trained troops were ready to defend the property without her guidance. She rankled at the idea of spending another summer trapped on the property, not knowing if Joseph was finding the information he needed to report to his contacts. There were too many people around to discuss what he was finding without running the risk of being overheard.

The crops were all in the ground and the spring repairs were completed. All attention turned to preparing for the transient field work season. Raven helped load bundles of fluffy white and grey wool into the trucks, buses and carts. Sacks of seeds from the previous year's harvest, along with bags of wheat and beans, were packed amongst the fleeces. Nearly thirty head of goats and an equal number of sheep were gathered and marked to take to market.

Crates containing chickens and their fluffy yellow broods were attached to the sides of the carts, their metal frames left to sway with the motion of the handcarts. The members of the community who would be herding the animals, walking with the hand and goat carts, or riding bicycles would be leaving for the Spring Market the next morning. It would take this group nearly a week to walk the forty miles to the Market grounds just outside of the city. Those travelling on the trucks and buses would be leaving the day before Market to meet with the others and they would all process through the medical clinic together for their first monthly health check-up to gear up for harvest.

This was going to be the first time Raven actually went through the entire harvest season as a traveler in the community. The council had decided she needed to be with Joseph and Bear as they met with harvesters and discussed training options for members of other communities. There was still land available in the bottoms for claims and the community wanted to make sure whoever moved into those claims was either willing to work with the community or were at least compatible with the community's goals. Raven had a feeling they were going to be meeting more than just potential community members. Bear had shown her the plans he had drawn up for the building of walls and barracks for what looked like a complete military compound. He had made a list of skills he was looking for in new residents for the community and, although he wasn't specific in details, it looked like he was looking for members with a military background. It looked like Bear was gearing up for war, building a fortress in the wilderness.

Chapter Thirty–One

THE MARKET WAS LOUD AND disorganized as veiled women walked in and out of booths, fingering wares and bargaining with vendors. Men stood between the booths, guarding the women as they went about their business. Groups of merchants wove amongst the crowds paying special attention to the bales of wool, quality of grains and quantity of product. Raven watched as Bear and Emily bargained shrewdly with the crowds filtering through their spaces. The community booth was small and only held a fraction of the goods they had brought with them. The rest of the goods were stacked in the camp, waiting for merchants to make offers and cart away the bundles and bags.

The late afternoon sun warmed the sheltered space of the booth, making it almost unbearable. Raven could feel droplets of sweat trickling down her neck and creeping down her spine. Five merchants were standing at the edge of the booth arguing and flashing hand signals to each other and Bear. The men rolled tufts of wool in their fingers or chewed on samples of wheat or beans. The subtleties of the bargaining were difficult to follow at first, but Raven's knowledge of sign language and non-verbal communication allowed her to pick up the meanings of most of the signs and she was actually starting to enjoy the banter.

A deal was reached with the five merchants. They would be by the camp in the morning to pick up wool and bags of beans and wheat. The community camp was situated in a deep meadow on the outskirts of the market. Raven posted sentries around the edges of the meadow and spent her nights walking the perimeter. By the end of the week there was a well-worn track surrounding the two acre lot on which the community had built their temporary camp. Raven slept an hour or two at a time, only allowing herself the time to doze and get a burst of energy. The milling crowds made her anxious, especially when she saw the cold, hungry look in many of the other campers' eyes.

The last day of the market left the community with very few of the goods they had brought with them. The bales and bags were gone. Livestock had been sold off and carted away by their new owners, but Raven couldn't relax her guard. She paced the camp, watching the older children herd the remaining goats into the livestock trailer and attach chicken cages to the sides of carts. Stacks of supplies were piled in the trucks and sent back to the compound. Raven had wondered how the community survived without access to the financial resources of the mainstream population. Watching the bartering at the market opened her eyes to a whole new world of options outside of the government-controlled neighborhoods.

The community had the supplies they needed to get through the harvest season. Nearly seventy members were going to be following the harvest this year, allowing most of the residents of the compound to stay and protect the fields and animals. Raven joined Bear and Joseph as they moved with deliberation and purpose through the market. They met with land owners and discussed exactly what each of them needed and what the community could bring to the fields. Deals were made and commitments to coordinate field work were developed. Raven could see the power Bear held in this environment. Nightly councils were held and Bear reigned supreme.

Joseph was Bear's second as they moved around the camp and this allowed Raven the freedom to go with them. Women and children were expected to stay in the defined borders of the encampment unless they were escorted by one of the men. Raven could have walked the market by herself. It wasn't completely taboo for women to be out on their own, but Raven was unsure of how she would be received. She still felt a little awkward walking around in pants when all the other women were wearing skirts.

Raven was watched everywhere she walked. At first she thought people were staring because of Bear's size but more than once she caught men staring after her long after Bear moved past. She wondered what the men were thinking as their cold eyes followed her around the market. Most of the goods were displayed in open air booths with vendors loud voices calling for customers to buy or trade. Every once in a while Bear would lead Joseph and Raven into tents or wagons controlled by furtive looking men. The weapons being traded by these brokers barely bordered on the right side of being legal.

There was an expectant hum around the camp as most of the supplies were gathered, cleaned and stored away in carts. The only things left out were the food that would be eaten cold in the morning and the tents and sleeping bags, even the sleeping pads were packed away. The final bus was loaded. It would be leaving in the morning, taking Emily and a few other women and younger children back to the community compound. Everyone else was anticipating the long walk to the campgrounds in the morning. Even the goats seemed agitated. Raven could hear the ringing in the bells as they gamboled in the field. Dusk was just beginning to fall when a small group of people approached the edge of the camp. Raven walked with the sentries to greet the strangers as they stood just outside the boundary line.

For a moment Raven stood and stared at the man and two women, no, the frames were too small. The man was standing with two girls. Veils obscured their faces and the shapeless quality of their dresses hid the size and shape of their bodies and Raven could not discern their ages. One of the girls shuffled to stand behind the man, while the other clutched at his hand. The man drew the girls close to him, briefly, and then gently prodded them forward.

"You're the warrior women we've been hearing about, aren't you?" His soft voice had a throaty quality and Raven realized he was holding back tears.

Raven didn't respond to the man's question. She had heard the whispers about her as she walked through the market. The raids on the community compound had buzzed from camp to camp. It was hard to keep Raven's role out of the gossip as the stories gained their own momentum. It was hard to shift the truth from the rumors and at times Raven didn't even recognize the actual events. No one approached her and asked what actually happened and there seemed to be an aura of mystery and sense of awe following after her. A cloud she couldn't seem to shake. She sensed steps coming up behind her and felt, more than saw, Joseph and Bear move to stand beside her. The man seemed to shrink a little into himself but didn't retreat.

"Please, I'm not here to cause problems." His knees were actually shaking and his face went three shades paler. "My daughters, Karen and Lacey." He tried to push the girls forward but they both clung even harder to their father. Swallowing, he started again.

"Their mother died this winter. We lost our land because we couldn't prove up and I can't take care of all of my children. My boys are old enough to work the fields with me, but my daughters, they will starve." Raven watched as tears actually formed in the corners of his eyes. "I heard you and your husband don't have any children and you have a responsibility to pass your land to the next generation. My daughters are young. If you take them they will be just like your own children. I promise you, they are good girls."

The gravity of the situation was slowly sinking in as Raven stared at the two girls clinging to their father. The longer she stared the more the girls tried to hide behind their father. Slowly Raven turned and faced Bear and Joseph. Both men had a slightly stunned expression on their faces. Raven knew Bear was impulsive and often wanted to allow the many supplicants who pleaded for help to join the community. This impulse was usually curbed through the efforts of his mother, but the Matriarch wasn't joining the harvest this year. Her age had finally caught up with her and her knees were so painful she couldn't get around easily any longer. The children's haunting eyes bore into Raven's soul but she knew there was no way she could take care of the two girls and still fulfill Joseph's mission.

Raven could see the crowd gathering behind her. Most of the camp seemed to want to know what was happening just beyond their border. A few sharp hand gestures and Raven had everyone back to work. Emily stepped out from among the tents and made her way across the camp. Raven recognized the tight expression on her aunt's face as she strode across the grounds. The decision to bring the girls into the community was about to move out of Raven's hands and land in her aunt's. Raven stepped back and allowed her aunt to take her place.

"Who are you?" Emily's voice carried a heavy dose of authority and the man actually took a step back this time.

"I...I'm Greg," he was barely able to stammer out his name.

"Do you have your health papers?" Emily asked.

·Greg's hands shook as he reached into his shirt and pulled out the card dangling from the cord around his neck. He removed it and handed it over. Emily studied it for a moment and handed it back.

"And the girls?" Emily asked.

A sheen of sweat sprung up on Greg's forehead and his face went even paler. "The girls are too young to work the fields. They don't have their health papers yet. Please, I can't take care of them. They'll die unless you take them."

"We can't take the chance of them bringing illness to our camp." Emily was angry. Raven could hear the tension in her aunt's voice. "They need to have their vaccinations and health checkups before they are integrated into any community."

"I can't." Tears escaped from his eyes and poured down his cheeks. "We're barely making enough to keep those of us in the fields fed and healthy. Please, you're my girls' last hope."

The girls' hiccupping sobs joined their father's melodic pleading. Raven could feel the desperation vibrating in the air. The man fell to his knees and pulled the girls close to him.

"I'll take them." At the sound of Samantha's voice Raven turned and faced the woman.

Emily stepped between Greg and Samantha. "We aren't going to allow the girls into the camp until they are vaccinated and have a health check up," she said.

"I can take them to the clinic." Samantha stepped up so she could stand beside Emily. "I have enough in my account to pay for their visit. I've worked hard for this community and I deserve to have children, too."

Raven could tell the woman wasn't going to give this up. Samantha wanted children and she was willing to do whatever it took to have them. She took a step towards the man and his daughters, but Emily's restraining hand held her back.

"We can't risk the children bringing disease into the camps. You know that, Samantha." Emily gestured and Raven and Bear moved to pull Samantha back.

Samantha shook off their restraining hands and took another step towards the man. "What if I left the community?" Her mouth took a determined set. "I can take what's coming to me and leave. There would be enough to get the girls their health checkups and support us for a few months until I can get work."

Bear stepped forward and put his arm around Samantha's shoulders. "No one is leaving the community, Samantha." He turned toward Greg and the children. "Where are your boys?"

Greg dragged the sleeve of his shirt across his eyes and cleared his throat. "They're at my camp. We're getting ready to leave in the morning. I have two boys, fourteen and fifteen. We just hope we can compete with the larger communities working the fields."

"Bring your tent to the edge of our campground. You can't bring the children into the camp until they get their health papers." Bear gently turned Samantha and pushed her towards Raven and Joseph. "Samantha may not be the only woman in the community willing to adopt your children. You may join us for the harvest and if you and your boys prove to be good workers and are willing to follow our rules we will allow you to live with us." Bear's decision settled the matter and everyone settled back to their routines.

The majority of the community members started their journey as soon as it was light enough to pack the tents and safely walk the trails to the new campsite. Raven decided to stay with Emily and the few others who were taking the community's motorized vehicles. One bus was going back to the community and the other two would be driven to the campsite to meet with the rest of the transient tribe later in the day. The delay allowed Samantha and Greg to bring the girls to the clinic and get their immunizations and checkups. When the bus left for the compound the girls joined Samantha and Emily and the others who were returning to Winter Quarters.

Raven was moving to board the second bus when two men crossed the boundary stones and walked towards the center of the camp. She didn't recognize them, but they approached as if they were comfortable with the community members. Joseph stepped down to stand beside her as the men stepped to the door of the bus.

"Joseph." The men nodded their greeting as Joseph took a casual, relaxed stance against the door of the bus. "Is everything set for our meeting?"

"We'll meet at the camps." Joseph crossed his arms across his chest. It looked like he was taking a relaxed position, but Raven could see the tension in his body. "We can be prepared to offer training to your units as soon as harvest is over, as long as we can find a training ground."

The taller of the two men stepped forward and studied Raven. "I heard she's the best. I hope she can give us what we need."

"She can train your men." Joseph actually took a step to position his body in front of Raven. "We'll teach you how to defend your people."

"We need to be able to do more than defend," the man said.

Joseph gestured for Raven to get on the bus. "We won't train people to raid and steal from other communities. We've learned to protect ourselves and our property."

"We're not thieves." The man's voice went up an octave. "We want to protect ourselves just as much as you do. If your wife can give our men the training they need to protect our families your entire community will never need to work the harvest again."

The men walked away and Raven and Joseph both stepped onto the bus. Greg was staring at them as they took their seats. Raven leaned close to her husband, putting her head on his shoulder. Joseph pulled her close, wrapping his arms around her. Raven knew the others on the bus would think they were just cuddling. No one would pay attention to the whispered conversation.

"What was that all about?" Raven breathed her question into Joseph's ear.

"It's the evidence we need." Joseph's lips were right against Raven's ear. "It's all going to be over by spring."

Chapter Thirty-Four

THE END OF HARVEST BROUGHT everyone back to the compound and the established routine. Those who had stayed had brought in nearly as much food as the ones working the harvest and the storage sheds were nearly bursting with supplies. Greg and his two boys, Greg Junior and Samuel, had made enough money to pay off the debts they had incurred trying to prove up their land. Bear encouraged him to completely pay off the debt and put another claim on the plot next to the community property. To no one's great surprise, Samantha divorced Bear and married Greg. She seemed happier in her choice and enjoyed having the children around to care for. The entire community pitched in to build a house for them. The house was a long, narrow structure consisting of a kitchen, two bedrooms and a bathroom. It was a simple wood structure, lacking the defensive elements of the community housing. Greg started attending the community meetings and even hinted he would be willing to make his property part of the compound and become part of the community, as long as the members were willing to help him build a more defensible structure.

Two weeks after everyone returned Bear called Joseph and Raven to the community hall for a meeting. The Matriarch was sitting at the head of the table and Bear's first wife was sitting beside her. Elias had died during the summer and since then the Matriarch's health was steadily failing. Bear and his first wife were taking over much of the daily decision making for the community. Raven and Joseph took the same position, sitting in chairs before the council, as they had when they were first invited to join the community. It was hard to believe she had been here for three years. Lakota and Marwa were both ten. It wouldn't be very long before they would be moving into their own quarters at Haven. A lump started to grow in her throat at the thought of her children. Always before she could receive messages or talk to them through video conference. She didn't realize how much she missed her children until that moment.

Bear smiled as Raven and Joseph took their seats. He glanced over at his wife, who was busy wiping drool off the Matriarch's chin. Joseph wrapped his arm around Raven's shoulders, a habit he had developed while they were living in the community. Raven couldn't get over the feeling he was staking a claim on her as much as the community was carving out a claim on the land.

"Joseph," Bear started. "We can't even start to tell you how grateful we are that you and your wife joined our community."

Raven squirmed a little in her seat. The deception they were practicing on this obviously trusting man rankled her. Joseph squeezed her shoulder, briefly, assuaging her nerves.

"We are more than grateful to you and to the community for taking us in and providing for my wife and me." Joseph's response was genuine. Raven wondered how he was able to keep his voice steady as the lies slipped out.

"There are two things I want to talk to you about, today." Bear nodded at his wife and she stood and wheeled the Matriarch out of the room. "Our conversation doesn't need to be heard and repeated throughout the entire compound." Bear waited until the door closed before he spoke again. "Joseph, there is a compound on the Snake River we're going to use for training. The town there was hit hard by the plagues and many of the residents died. Those who were left moved away into the city or into other communities. There are a few structures left, but most of the town is gone. We think it would be perfect for training grounds. Units are already there building and laying claim to the land. It'll be ready and stocked by the time you and Raven get there."

"Is it okay if I go check it out next week?" Joseph had straightened in his chair and his arm dropped from around Raven's shoulder. "I want to make sure it is safe before I bring my wife out there."

"Yes, actually I think that's a good idea." Bear paused for a moment and shifted in his seat. He looked uncomfortable and Raven wondered what else was on his mind. "I wanted to talk to you two about something else, though. I... I mean we are concerned about your property. We don't like to think about this, but we're all concerned about our mortality. If you die without apparent heirs your land will revert back to the government and anyone can come in and stake a claim. We're still a year away from proving it up and we don't want to lose it. I know this is a very personal decision, but in order to protect our community, you need heirs."

For the first time since they started this mission a concerned expression crossed Joseph's face. "I don't know if it's a good idea for my wife to conceive right now."

Bear held up his hand to forestall Joseph. "We know your situation very well. But, just because your wife can't have children it doesn't mean you can't. Joseph, there are a number of women here who have approached me about becoming your second wife. They would provide you with heirs and protect the community's investment in your land. You have already proven you have enough resources to care for more than just your wife and in order to protect your lands you will each need to take a wife. You have to think of the greater good here."

Raven turned and studied Joseph's face as Bear spoke. A warm, red blush started behind his ears and crept up his face. Joseph was usually pretty good about thinking his way out of problems, but Raven could tell he was struggling with this one. She turned back to the big man sitting across the room.

"I can't share my husband with another woman." Raven stared Bear down, refusing to break eye-contact. "And I can't take a wife myself."

Bear broke first, blinking and glancing down. Two bright spots appeared on his cheeks. "Raven, I know you understand we live differently here. You wouldn't have to share your husband in the sense you are thinking of." Bear's face burned even brighter. "The women would be your wives in name only. The marriage certificate gives the women the right to the land to hold in trust for your children, if anything should happen to either of you. It would be your decision on how you want to have the children. Emily has the equipment to do in vitro or artificial insemination."

Raven recognized his argument took the legs out from under her excuses she had for not wanting to be in a polygamist marriage, especially since she was supposedly a product of these types of communities.

"Bear," Joseph was squirming in his seat. "Even if I took a second wife I don't know I have what it takes. I mean…" Joseph trailed off, leaving Bear to draw any conclusions about Joseph's fertility.

"It doesn't matter," Bear waved off Joseph's stammered excuses. "The marriage contract can easily be ratified to allow any child born of the women to be your legal children and heirs. You can have a family and the community will be protected."

It seemed Bear had everything completely figured out. No matter what objection Raven and Joseph came up with, Bear had a solution. Thoughts were flying through Raven's head so fast it was hard to grasp on to one.

"This is a big decision." Joseph radiated a calm aura and Raven realized he has an idea. He took Raven's hand and they both stood up. "We need to spend some time thinking about this and talking some things over."

"Of course," Bear said. "It's a big decision. I don't expect you to make it right away. You still have two weeks until you're expected at the training grounds. I'm sure everything can be taken care of before then. I know there aren't a lot of opportunities for privacy here. I will give you privacy in this room to talk about it. I promise no one will disturb you."

Joseph and Raven sat in silence after Bear left the room. Finally Joseph stood and started pacing the room. Raven sat in stunned silence, mulling over the problem in her mind. She couldn't figure an easy way out of the situation. If they wanted to maintain the illusion they were invested members of the community it was only logical they would want to ensure the future of their property. Joseph finally stopped pacing and stood in front of her.

"I think we're going to have to do it," he said.

Raven stood up and took his hands in hers. 'I know. We're both going to need to take a wife. I never imagined being married after Billy. Now, I am going to have a husband and a wife and a husband who has a second wife. This is too confusing for me. We'll have to make them the beneficiaries and let them hold the land in trust. Any children they have will be taken care of by the community so, after this is over, we won't have any loose ends holding us back. I know living here has only been a means to an end, but these are good people and they deserve to have a little security."

Raven wrapped her arms around Joseph's waist and allowed him to pull her into his embrace. She rested her head on his chest, listening to the vibrant strumming of his heartbeat.

"I don't know if I can stand the thought of leaving one of my children behind." Raven could hear the doubt in Joseph's voice.

"We don't need to use our DNA." Raven pulled away from the embrace, but didn't move away. "No matter what happens, the children will be taken care of by the community. I know these women well enough to know they'll do anything to have a family. The women and the children will be fine."

Once the news spread that Raven and Joseph were looking to add two new wives to their family, Raven didn't have a moment of peace. There were nearly thirty single women living in the community and nearly all of them approached Raven about becoming the wives. It was unusual for a family to take two wives at one time since the entire purpose of a marriage was to make sure families were provided for. Few families were able to prove they could care for a such a large increase in the number of their family at once.

Despite extensive pressure from the community, Joseph and Raven had only picked one potential woman to act as a second wife by the time Joseph needed to leave to assess the new training site. Trish was in her early thirties and had never been married nor had children. Her situation wasn't unique to the women in the community. The gender imbalance was creating an entire generation of women without the opportunity to marry and have children. The day before Joseph left, two commitment contracts were drawn up to be presented to the community. A decision needed to be made before Joseph left in the morning. Since this decision was more about the Community's future than Raven and Joseph's relationship they let Bear pick the candidate for Raven's wife. He chose another thirty-year old woman named Charity. Charity had been married and already had one child. Her husband had been killed when the community had been attacked the year before Raven and Joseph joined.

The contracts were signed and sealed. Joseph and Raven promised to provide for the two women, making them the stewards of the land to hold in trust for any children. Any child born to the two women during the duration of the marriage contract would be considered Joseph's children. Raven declined the right of the first wife to claim the first child born of each woman. Any children these women might have would belong to the community. Bear made sure every member of the community was well taken care of and Raven knew the women would have ownership of the claims once she and Joseph left the compound.

Joseph and Raven took the night shift guard duty. They discussed this newest development, making decisions on how to handle it. Neither Joseph nor Raven wanted to leave a child with their DNA with the community. To complicate matters, both of them would be moving to the training center. Joseph explained this was the break they were looking for and anticipated finally being able to put a face to the mole. If they timed the discovery right, they might even be pulled from the community before the women had a chance to get pregnant. The use of in vitro and AI was still tricky and women rarely conceived in the first six months of trying. Their extraction was already planned and if everything went as anticipated the community would have no idea what actually happened, leaving them with the land in the hands of the two women and any future family they might have.

Joseph left to finish setting up the training grounds, leaving Raven to put things in order with the community. Rather than try to find two separate rooms for the women, Raven had the larger bed removed from the room she and Joseph had been sharing and put in two twin beds. It was a tight squeeze, but the women seemed happy to be out of the women's dormitory and in a little more private space. Charity's five-year-old daughter was placed in the girl's dorm at the end of the hall. In the end, all Raven was left to do was decide which residents were coming with her to receive more training and which ones were staying to guard the facility. By the end of the week she had identified thirty-four residents who were going with her, all of them volunteers. Raven was surprised almost half of them were women.

In the days leading to her departure Raven slept in the women's dorm. Deep in her heart and mind she knew she would be leaving the compound and never returning. She had known this day was coming from the first moment she had joined the community and had tried not to become close to the residents, but it was impossible to work side by side with such giving, caring people and not grow to love them. Bear was so open and compassionate, despite his large size, and Raven knew he would never deliberately hurt anyone. Samantha was so happy. Since her marriage to Greg she just exuded joy, especially in the quiet moment when she confided to Raven that, despite Emily's warnings, she was pregnant and was going to have a child of her own. Raven had a moment of doubt when Samantha told her this. She wanted to stay at the compound and help Samantha through the coming difficult pregnancy.

It was still dark when Raven and her new force boarded the bus. They intended to make it to the new training center before sunrise, disguising their numbers. The women were all dressed in the same drawstring pants and tunic shirt and were wearing black hoods with a strip of cloth covering their faces. The look was reminiscent of the ancient ninja warrior class and Raven couldn't help feeling she was building an elite soldier class just as powerful as the ancient secret society.

Chapter Thirty–Five

THE WELCOME TO PARMA SIGN was faded and peeling, making it barely legible as the bus drove into the town. It wasn't much of a town. The buildings stared out with windows like empty eyes, eaves sagging and overgrown yards. Raven watched a skinny, half-starved dog slink from an alley between two decrepit buildings. As the bus rolled passed, the dog darted back into the shadow of the alley, disappearing from sight. Raven wondered how many feral animals had taken up residence in the empty buildings. There wasn't an intact piece of glass in any of the store fronts or windows and most of the usable building materials had already been scavenged away. The skeletons of burned out husks of houses sat stark against the night sky. Raven could see the glowing eyes of creatures peering out of the darkness.

The bus crept through the deserted streets, jolting over the shredded pavement. She knew entire towns and cities were deserted and falling into ruin. This town was just one of many returning back to the earth. These shells of towns were scattered all over the landscape, silent testaments to the shrinking population. Parma, like so many other towns, had been abandoned nearly thirty years before, when most of the residents had died from the plagues. Those who lived did not have the strength or manpower to protect the remaining buildings and property from raiders. The survivors fled the town, trying to find shelter in any way possible. Parma was just another broken town.

The bus rattled on through the town and into the stark countryside. Here and there Raven saw signs of life amongst the ruins. Heavily fenced and guarded acreages delineated the borders of farms. Raven could see the shadowy figures of men pacing between the barns and houses, eyes flashing as the bus past. Finally the driver turned the bus onto a narrow road, hardly more than a goat trail.

The bus past under the canopy of overgrown trees and through the shadows cast across the overgrown path. Sunrise was still hours away, but Raven could see just as well in the dark as if it was the brightness of day. As the headlights scattered through the trees she could see the glowing of eyes illuminated by the lights. The undergrowth shook as small creatures scattered away from the rumble created by the motor. Finally, the bus broke through the underbrush and rolled into a clearing. Grass crunched under Raven's feet as she stepped into the meadow from the steps of the bus. A thin, white coating of hoarfrost covered the ground giving the meadow an ethereal quality in the moonlight.

Joseph was standing in the middle of the meadow, the flashlight in his hand creating a small circle of light, penetrating the darkness. Raven avoided looking directly at the bright light, shielding her eyes from the glow. Although she could see well in any kind of light it always took a moment to adjust and she had developed the habit of avoiding drastic shifts between light sources. It was obvious from the ferocious blinking and shuffling from the others disembarking from the bus they had not received the same training. The others stood milling around the meadow apparently trying to adjust to the tiny bit of light filtering down from the full moon.

Raven picked up her backpack and strapped it on. The forty pounds on her back was strangely reassuring, like an old friend she hadn't seen for a long time. Her companions picked up on her signal, pulling on their packs they stood staring at her. Joseph turned and silently walked towards the trees. Raven had no problem following once they crossed over the tree-line, but she could hear the stumbling feet of her companions. She could just imagine the work she had ahead of her turning this ragtag group of refugees into an elite force. Then she started thinking about what would happen if she did turn this group into an army. There would be enough people with a military background in the group she would be caught if she tried to sandbag the operation. She just hoped Joseph would have the evidence he needed before too long and they could shut down this operation.

The trees cleared again and Raven could see the gleam of the moonlight shimmering on the surface of water. The sound of rushing water assailed her ears. The volume let her know they were close to a river. It was her best guess for which one. Geographically they could be anywhere near the Payette or the Snake. A cluster of metal-sided buildings huddled a few yards from the bank of the smooth flowing river, their cool, silver sides gleaming in the iridescent moonlight. Dim yellow lights illuminated the grounds in front of the buildings and in the meadow, standing at stark attention, was a group of men and boys watching as Raven led her team into the clearing.

Raven assessed the men standing at attention as she walked across the bare ground of the meadow. The lines were ragged and she could see many of the younger soldiers fidgeting and squirming as she approached. The tension in the air was almost palatable as she moved down the rows. One young boy nearly dropped the rifle he was holding as she approached. His face blossomed red as he clutched the weapon to his chest and Raven could actually see his knees trembling as he bravely tried to look her square in the face. She finished inspecting the rows of soldiers and took her position beside Joseph. He was standing with the two men she had met the last day of the Farmer's Market.

"The boys need to get rid of their guns." Raven kept her voice low enough so only Joseph and the men could hear. "Take the weapons from all of them. When they learn how to use them they can have them back."

The men moved forward to commandeer the weapons as Raven studied the compound. There were five metal structures in the meadow. Their low, sloped roofs shimmered with frost, reflecting with an ethereal glow as the sun's rays were peeking over the horizon. The screech of metal on metal filled the meadow as Joseph peeled open a door to one of the buildings. Raven watched the men move single file into the structure. She moved across the meadow so she could watch as each person deposited their weapons into the arsenal. Tables, walls and racks were filled up as each person deposited guns, knives and other weapons in stacks. She kept her eyes blank as weapons were pulled from places where things with sharp, shiny blades shouldn't go. Here and there one of the men would turn to the side or refuse to make eye contact as they walked out. Raven would make them turn around and take out whatever weapon was hidden under their clothes and stack it on the table. One man tried to slip by her three times. On the third pass he stood in front of Raven refusing to turn back. Raven could almost feel the aura of challenge emanating from his pores.

"I'm not going to let you strip me of all my defenses." Anger sang in his voice, giving Raven the first challenge of her authority.

"As long as you have your brain and your hands you will never be defenseless." Raven never broke eye contact with the man, but she made sure the notes of her voice could be heard across the entire meadow. "I will teach you how to defend yourself and your land, but if you don't like the way I work you know how to get home." She turned and walked away, not allowing the man to respond.

Raven walked around the edges of the clearing, looking into each building. In addition to the armory there was a hospital, a mess hall and two dorms. She didn't enter any of the buildings, just giving them a quick visual inspection. There would be time for an inspection later. As she was passing the second dorm she spotted a low, squat building hidden behind the others. It looked like a storage shed, but Raven could see a bed and a desk through the open door.

Hanging above the entrance to the building was a board with the words *In defense of our God, our land, our freedom, our wives and our children.*

By the time she had finished her circuit around the meadow, the makeshift army had finished depositing their weapons in the armory and had lined up again. Raven looked at the faces of the crowd before her. Anxious eyes and gleaming faces peered back. Seventy-nine men, women and children all waiting to take their place as guardians of this world. She didn't see evil peering back at her, all she saw were people trying to make their way in a world of turmoil and strife.

The barracks were a mess. Personal belongings were scattered over unmade cots and dirty clothes were bunched in piles on the floor. Raven stood in the doorway of the first building, surveying the conditions, her hands planted firmly on her hips. As she walked through the mess she kicked empty cans and shell casings out of the way. When she turned, Joseph was standing in the doorway.

"The first order of business is to get this mess cleaned up." Raven stripped a sheet off the bed. "A mess like this is just waiting for germs and disease to fester. If the men aren't taking care of their dorm they aren't taking care of their equipment. Equipment failure in the field is a good way to get killed."

All it took was for Raven to show the men once what was expected and they all immediately stepped up their act. It took two days to clean the barracks to her expectations. When one of the boys asked why the women couldn't be responsible for the cleaning she made him do fifty push-ups and march in place for twenty minutes and then she stripped his cot and made him re-make it until she could bounce a work token off the taut bedding.

Raven learned the two men who had approached Joseph at the market camp were named Seth and Casey. Both men had served their required two years in the army and were under the assumption their experience made them the logical choice to be Raven's sergeants. Joseph had spent the week he was at the camp making sure it was defensible and hadn't focused much on the quality of men in the troop. Seth and Casey had assumed command of the men and had even made themselves separate quarters in the armory. Raven made them break down the cots and set them up in the barracks. The entire time they were working on their space Raven could hear them muttering under their breath. There wasn't a separate barracks for the women so Raven had the men build a dividing wall in the second structure. They had to march the five miles into Parma and hump back the materials. Raven didn't let anyone stay behind, watching each person as they marched across the fields. It wasn't hard to see who needed to pick-up the PT time.

Raven yelled herself hoarse over the weeks. She pushed the men and women to the brink of physical exhaustion, waking them in the darkness of the early morning hours, making them march, run, do push-ups, pull-ups, jumping jacks, obstacle courses, ropes courses. She divided them into squads and units and gave them work. Every day the men and women were given a menial task to be completed after morning calisthenics and chow. Duties were rotated through each unit so every group experienced chow-line duty, latrine duty and any other laborious task. There were a few murmurs of dissent, mostly from Seth and Casey, as she pushed the units to the brink of exhaustion and still made them work, but for the most part the men and women were willing to do their jobs as Raven directed them. By the fourth week, the entire troop was able to easily make the ten mile trek to Parma and back without straggling in at the end. She started weapons training then.

Seth and Casey were the first two in line when she turned the key to unlock the armory. Raven could see the excitement in their faces when the sunlight flooded the interior of the storage room, glinting off metal blades and the glass lenses of scopes. The two actually took a step forward before they seemed to realize Raven wasn't moving from her position in front of the door. Seth's dark face actually clouded over and a scowl pinched his features together. He reminded Raven of a sneaky rodent trying to get past a cat to get to a crumb of food.

"We need to understand the equipment before we use any of it." Raven stepped down from the doorway. "We are going to sort, clean and inspect every weapon we have in the armory. You are going to learn to take apart, put together and operate every weapon in this arsenal."

"We already know how to use a gun." Casey's challenge vibrated around the meadow.

"You're here to learn from me." Raven made sure her voice carried as far as Casey's. "If you don't like it, you can leave. You're not obligated to stay."

Casey moved back in line, but his expression didn't change. Raven began to wonder if she was going to have trouble with the man. She was also starting to worry about the contacts Joseph was supposed to be meeting. This ragtag group of soldiers was starting to look like a real army and Raven was afraid that if the contacts did show up and a raid happened there would be a real battle. Joseph kept reassuring her everything was under control and for her to keep up with the training.

As winter set in, Raven stepped up the physical exercise. She knew the hazards of sedentary life and wanted everyone to be in shape when the spring raids started. When it came time to train in hand-to-hand combat Casey and Seth joined in enthusiastically, a little too enthusiastically. Both of them enjoyed exerting physical pain on their opponents and tried to pair up with weaker or smaller team members. Raven finally pulled them out of their unit and moved them to a unit with much stronger and bigger men. After they had been thumped on a few times they stopped deliberately trying to harm their opponents.

The deep cold of winter set in during the months of January and February, but Raven didn't let up on the training. It was cold, but there was very little snow on the ground and the drills kept the trainees warm. She pushed the men and women to develop their defensive skills. Early spring was the high time for raids, even more than in the late fall. She wanted to be able to send the units back to their communities with the skills to defend their lands against raiders.

Chapter Thirty–Six

JOSEPH'S WHISPER IN HER EAR woke Raven from a deep sleep. "Raven, you need to take the unit into the forest. They can't be here when Seth and Casey's contacts arrive."

Joseph left the room while Raven pulled on her clothes and laced her boots. Most of the unit was hunkered down in town preparing for the next day's drill, but there were still ten members of the unit in camp. The troop in town had been left with the task of creating a fortress and preparing for an attack from the rest of the soldiers, one of the many training drills Raven was having her units develop.

As Raven stepped out of the tiny office where she and Joseph slept she could see the others coming out of the barracks, hair sleep-tousled and clothes being fastened. Joseph was approaching from the far side of the meadow. The unit fell in behind him as he walked towards her.

Joseph motioned for the others to continue into the trees behind the shed as he stopped in front of Raven. He waited until they were a good distance away before he spoke.

"They weren't supposed to be here until tomorrow." Raven didn't even need to ask who he was talking about. "Casey and Seth are with them. They separated from the main force when we sent them to town yesterday and met with their contact. I don't know who they're bringing in so I think it would be best if you took the rest of the unit to the field by the river."

Raven could hear the rumble of a truck motor vibrating through the trees and she knew there wasn't much time to get away. Turning, she made her way through the meadow and moved deep into the trees. Her unit was waiting for her and they fell into line behind her as she led them into the darkened tree-line. Raven could hear the crunch of the undergrowth as the ten men and women behind her tried to make their way through the undergrowth in the fading light. It was darker under the trees as the canopy filtered out most of the radiant light emanating from the full moon.

The hum of the truck motor vibrated in her ears as she moved under the shelter of the trees. A few hand motions slowed her group and sent her unit into the thick undergrowth around the base of the trees. The river was only a few yards away so she led the group to the water's edge and guided them along the shore. Their footsteps were barely audible, a change from the first time she walked with this group.

With quick hand motions she gestured for her team to skirt around the edge of the river and head towards the tree-line. If they stayed within the trees they could follow the river to an old bridge and cross to an old field with stone walls to hide behind. It was only about a two mile trek and the undergrowth was too thick for vehicles to travel through. She led the men and woman to the rickety footbridge and had them cross two at a time. The other bank of the river was completely overgrown. As she watched their backs disappear into the undergrowth she fervently hoped they made it to the field in time. The river was cold and swift this time of year and the undertow and whirlpools were hidden under the subterfuge of still water. If they were caught there was a chance they would try to make a get-away by jumping into the cold waters and be swept away. She waited for the last member to cross before she turned her face back to camp.

Raven crept to the edge of the trees and hid herself behind a clump of bushes. A supply truck completely dominated the meadow. Three people were standing near the truck, their backs to the forest. Casey and Seth were busy unloading the truck as Joseph stood, facing the trees, talking to the strangers. Raven could just barely make out what they were saying to each other. It was obvious the people were not part of the migrant community here for training. Their clothes lacked the ragged edges and worn look so prevalent in the fringe communities. Raven didn't know if it was just her years of experience as a soldier or the stance of the group, but she knew these people had an overwhelming military bearing, one that only came with years of military service.

Raven crept forward to try to hear what was being said. A familiar female voice carried over the meadow and Raven discovered if she stayed very still she could barely make out the words.

"You're going to need to get together a stronger force than this if you're going to take over the surrogate units." As the woman spoke she removed her hat. Bright red hair shone in the sunlight and suddenly Raven realized it was her old captain, Gabrielle Egan. "The Gen units greatly outnumber Naturals right now and we need to supplement our numbers."

The realization slowly dawned on Raven that this was the contact Joseph had been waiting for. The corruption in the forces ran deep if Egan was the main contact for the insurgents. Raven slowly edged back into the trees and lowered herself to the ground, half burying herself in dead leaves and undergrowth. Her head and face covering were in place. All of the soldiers, male and female alike, had developed the habit of wearing the hood and mask. Not only did it hide the identities of the soldiers from the few residents still trying to create a living in the area, but the layer of cloth kept their faces warm during the bitter cold.

Raven was listening for the sound of the truck leaving, but to her surprise, she heard another sound instead. The engines were almost silent, but there were more than just one or two trucks coming down the road. Throbbing of motors drummed against her ears and she realized, whoever they were, they were approaching the compound fast. Pulling herself up from the coolness of the earth, she slipped through the trees barely making any noise as she moved to the edge. Joseph looked up and spotted her just as she reached the tree-line. She ducked behind another clump of undergrowth, waiting to see if he needed anything. Egan must have caught on to the motion because she turned and stared at the trees.

"What's going on here?" Her hand was on her pistol. Raven felt safely hidden, but she didn't know if Egan would send anyone into the trees.

"It might just be an animal." Joseph's voice was amazingly calm. "Or my Commander might be sending a runner in from maneuvers."

"Go check it out." The order was directed at Joseph but Egan's voice held a note of concern.

Raven saw Egan's thumb move as it unfastened the snap holding her gun in place. Quickly assessing the situation, she realized there was no way she was going to make it across the meadow before Egan drew her gun. She pushed her body into the ground and waited for Joseph to approach.

Joseph stepped away from Egan, moving across the meadow towards Raven. Casey and Seth finished unloading the truck and lifted the tailgate back in place. Raven started to stand but Joseph motioned for her to stay at the edge of the grove. She stopped in the shadow of a thick willow stand, allowing Joseph to come to her. The thrumming of the motors was coming closer but Joseph didn't appear nervous. He positioned himself between Raven and the three soldiers, blocking his hand motion with his body. Joseph's hands were telling her to go back into the trees and stay down.

A sense of foreboding filled her as she slipped back into the trees. She could hear the sound of animals slinking back into their lairs. Somewhere in the distance an owl hooted. The symphony of sounds filled her heightened senses. She could still see Joseph's back as she settled herself at the base of a tree. He raised his hand and twisted it before closing it into a fist. The ringing of metal doors slamming shut filled the air at the gesture. Raven heard Egan's shout and then other sounds filled the meadow. Joseph started to run towards the buildings but his body gave a swift jerk and he fell to the ground. Raven leapt from her hiding place and ran towards where she saw Joseph fall. Her first reaction was to get to him but as she approached the edge of the trees she realized running into the open field into the midst of unknown enemies wouldn't be the smartest move. She dropped to the ground and pulled herself forward on her elbows.

Icy cold stabbed through her body and wet leaves and earth clung to her clothes. Fighting back the urge to shiver, Raven brought her rifle over her shoulder and set it up in front of her. She used the scope to bead in on the soldiers by the truck.

Egan was on the ground, her whole body twitching. The two who had been beside her were crouched beside the truck. Their guns were out and aimed at the outskirts of the camp. She saw the flash of the muzzle before she heard the report of the shot as one of the men pulled the trigger. A yelp and a sigh, far to her left, let her know the bullet found a mark. Bullets drilled the ground around the truck, spitting up dirt and smoke and pinning down the two men. Joseph was sprawled out on the ground halfway between the trees and the truck. Raven could see his chest rise and fall, but he wasn't moving. She wanted to go to him, but the bullets bouncing around the meadow made it impossible. The doors to the armory were sealed and Casey and Seth were nowhere to be seen. Raven knew she had to end this showdown before anyone else got hurt. She had to get to her husband and find out what happened. Her belly rolled and she bit back the nausea threatening to overwhelm her. *Not now.* She pushed the all too familiar sensation down, forcing the bile back in her throat.

Head or heart. The thought flashed as she took aim at the men behind the truck. Shooting to wound just gave you an angry man with a gun. The only way to truly keep herself and her people and, now that she knew for sure, her unborn baby, safe was to aim for the head or the heart. Eyeing the target she slowly squeezed the trigger. Smoke curled from the barrel and, as it dissipated into the air, she watched one of the men crumble to the ground. Her second bullet nearly missed the mark as the other man turned to see where the new threat was coming from. The impact with his right pectoral spun him around and pushed him to the ground, face first. All was silent. Even the animal sounds in the grove had stopped. The volley of bullets ended and it seemed even the wind had ceased whistling through the trees.

The sound of metal doors sliding open broke the spell. Shouts announcing the occupants were coming out unarmed filled the meadow. Shadowy figures ran forward forcing Seth and Casey to the ground. She could hear voices calling for her to come out of the woods with her hands up. Lowering her gun she eased herself from the ground and placed her hands above her head.

"I'm coming out," she called. "I'm unarmed."

Raven barely reached the edge of the trees when bodies collided against her with enough force to pull her down. Relaxing her muscles, she allowed her captors to pull her arms behind her and cuff her hands behind her back. She was pulled to her feet and her hood was violently ripped from her head and face.

"Bring her over with the others."

Raven easily recognized Captain Grey's voice. She went willingly with her captors to kneel with the others. Keeping her head down, she avoided looking anyone in the eyes. She was kneeling between two armies, two groups she had fought for, fought with, trained and came to care for. Each side was fighting for what they believed was right. Each side had something worth fighting for.

She could see Joseph as medics worked on him. He was strapped to a back board and placed on a gurney. The medics loaded him on a truck with Raven's second victim. Egan was loaded next, the white probes from the taser still sticking from her chest. Raven's first victim was laid out in the field, a white sheet covering his body. The truck raced from the meadow. Raven could hear a chopper in the distance and she realized Joseph was about to be flown out to God knew where and she had no idea if she would ever see him alive again. Her heart started racing and she felt pressure behind her eyes. Blinking rapidly, she forced the pressure back.

The meadow was a flood of activity. Raven watched as Grey's force moved through the buildings and stripped them. Weapons were carried from the armory and piled in the back of a truck. Bedding and clothing were thrown to the ground, mattresses flipped and shredded in the madcap search. During the entire process she could feel eyes boring into her from either side. Casey and Seth didn't even disguise the anger in their faces as they watched their belongings being spread over the ground.

"We could have held them off if you hadn't sent the rest of the team away." Seth's whisper carried easily to Raven's ears.

"The fight didn't involve us." Raven hissed her answer as quietly as she could. "They'll let us go when they realize we're not a danger to them. We only want to protect our lands and families."

Seth's mouth curled into a snarl but a sharp word from a soldier silenced his retort. Grey paced in front of the prisoners, his eyes darting back and forth as items were piled on the ground. Finally he stopped pacing and stood in front of Raven. He motioned her to stand. It was a struggle with bound hands, but she made it to her feet.

"We're taking you all in for questioning." Grey motioned to his men and they lifted Seth and Casey off the ground. The two were loaded in a transport truck, kicking and hissing as they tried to escape their captors. As soon as the truck drove out of sight Grey motioned to one of his men. The man moved behind Raven and she could feel the cuffs being removed. She stood in front of her commander, rubbing the circulation back into her wrists.

"Well, Lieutenant," Grey grinned. "It looks like we caught our man, or woman in this case. I suspected Egan was the one bleeding equipment off the base, but I could never catch her at it. This is actually the first time she left base with a delivery. Usually trucks would leave base with supplies and either disappeared or were attacked on the road. Hopefully taking out Egan will shut down this hub."

Raven looked to the liquid pool darkening the grass of the meadow where Joseph had lain. There was so much of it, just shining up at her in the moonlight. All that blood, it should have been inside his body not slowly seeping into the ground watering the grass. The sun was still hidden behind the horizon, but it was sending feeble rays over the hills, brightening the sky to a hazy blue. It was difficult to see all the supplies and weapons disappear into the trucks to be carted away. The people being left behind needed to have supplies to survive the journey back to their communities. Grey wasn't concerned about the pawns in the game, he just wanted the leaders. Raven was thankful they all had their packs and some weapons. She knew everything in this meadow would be taken, but the others would be allowed to return to their homes. Grey had found the rebels he was looking for.

Chapter Thirty-Seven

JOSEPH WASN'T DEAD. IT WAS the first thing she was told when she walked into Grey's office. Joseph was in a hospital in Portland, Oregon. Egan had shot him as soon as she realized the situation was going south. Joseph was fortunate she didn't have time to draw a good bead on him and the taser shots had hit her before she could do any significant damage. Raven had given her debriefing and shed the clothing she had worn for the past three years. The Surrogate program uniform was snug around her hips, but, despite its form-hugging contours, it didn't show her pregnancy. It was going to be a few weeks before she would have to tell anyone about the baby. For some perverse reason she wanted to tell her mother before she told anyone else. She wanted to tell her about Emily and the missing children. Grey told her he sent a unit to the community to arrest Emily, but they had been told she had moved away not long after Joseph and Raven left for the training center.

Raven was concerned about the friends she had made while she was with the community, but Grey said they all seemed to be adapting well. Carefully controlled information had been released to the press: a raid on an insurgent compound, two men captured, a man and a woman killed. The names of the captured were being withheld until further investigation, but Raven saw her and Joseph's names on just about every newsfeed scrolling on every screen. Grey informed her the community members were all in deep mourning for her and Joseph, but the marriage contracts were being upheld. To Raven's surprise, Grey told her both of the women in the marriage contract were pregnant. She wondered whose genetic material Emily used to impregnate them, but was relieved the community had the chance of protecting their claim with legal heirs to both her and Joseph.

Raven paced the confines of Grey's office while she was waiting for him to come back from Haven. Even though the main campus was only a few miles away, she hadn't quite made it back there yet. She wasn't quite sure what she was going to say to her mother about everything, or anything for that matter.

The door hissed open and a crowd of bodies flooded into the room. She stood in startled silence as she was pulled into the warm embraces of her family. Raven looked through the gaps between the shoulders of the crowd around her to find Grey grinning at her sheepishly.

"You know I can't keep anything from your mother," he said. "She insisted on bringing the whole family here as soon as she heard you were back."

Raven allowed herself to be drawn to the couch to sit with her family. Savanna was sitting almost on top of her with an arm around her shoulder. Travis leaned against the wall, his arms folded, giving the appearance of being completely relaxed. Caleb stood next to him. Raven looked at her tall, handsome brother, noting the hardened look in his eyes and the careful stance he took next to his father. A glint of metal shone from the bottom of his right pant leg. Obviously he left part of himself behind on his last mission. Marwa was sitting as close to Raven on one side as Savanna was on the other, resting her head against Raven's shoulder. Raven was surprised to see both Lakota and Marwa were wearing Haven uniforms and not the typical soft green tunics of the children living in the shelter. Marwa was dressed in the blue of the medical corps while Lakota was wearing the black uniform of the security force. He was sitting in a chair on the far side of the room, his long, lanky legs stretched out and crossed in front of him. Raven stared at him, but he refused to make eye-contact, instead stared at the floor, a tic twitching in his cheek and his arms crossed across his chest. His bearing and aura exuded his lack of desire for being part of the group. Hamasa and Asal were so tall. They stood behind Lakota, staring with bright, wide eyes at Raven. Her smile obviously put them at ease, but Raven knew the two children considered Savanna their mother while Raven was some omnipresent concept of an older sister who flashed in and out of their life like so many strikes of lightening; storming in quickly, making a lot of noise and leaving a wake of destruction behind.

"This has to be the strangest family reunion I have ever seen." Grey moved across the room and took his seat behind his desk. "It's nice to have Raven back in one piece this time."

Raven could feel her mother's arm tighten and draw her closer. She was starting to feel smothered, but she knew better than to shrug it off.

"How long is it going to be until we get Joseph back?" Raven tried to stare Grey down, but he turned his focus to the data pad on his desk.

"Egan's bullets severed his spinal cord." As Grey spoke a number of scans and medical charts appeared on the screen behind his chair. "It's going to take him some time to recover. He's going to have to go through multiple surgeries and rehab before he can come back to Idaho."

Raven stood up, finally shedding the trappings of her mother and daughter. "Can I go to him?" Grey looked up sharply at her simple plea.

"He'll be fine." Grey eyed her shrewdly. "I know you both were embedded for a long time. Is there something you didn't tell us in your debriefing?"

Raven didn't want it to come out like this, but with all eyes on her she didn't really have much of a choice. She glanced at Grey and then looked back to the floor.

"Joseph and I decided we wanted to make a commitment." She could feel the tightness in her cheeks, but realized she didn't have anything to be ashamed of. Her love for Joseph may not have been exactly the same as her love for Billy, but she did still love him and wanted the same level of commitment to him as she did her first husband. "We're having a child."

Silence. Raven finally looked up, taking in the expression in her family's faces. They were stunned, she could see it in the tightness of their jaws, the drawing together of the brows, but there wasn't condemnation in their eyes.

"Well, this sure throws a wrench in the works." Grey's voice finally broke the silence. "I needed you at Mountain Home. Now that Egan is gone, I need someone to run the base."

"Being pregnant isn't going to keep me from doing my job." Raven immediately regretted her words as soon as they past her lips. Grey had just dumped a massive managerial headache on her head and by blurting out she basically accepted the position.

Moving to Mountain Home was as much a trial in patience as learning the responsibilities of the new job. She wanted her family with her and sent to Haven for Lakota and Marwa. At first Lakota dug in his heels and refused to leave Haven. He wanted to learn security from Travis, but when Marwa expressed her desire to live with Raven, he grudgingly gave over. Raven could literally see him dragging his feet as they made the move to the base. She was promoted to Captain and was given the responsibility of managing the base. No easy task as it turned out. Raven was essentially in charge of running a small city.

Raven was deeply entrenched in her duties at the base when Joseph was released from the hospital. The ambulance delivered him to the front door and Raven watched him struggle into the house, his crutches drumming on the porch. He refused all help, despite the difficulty he had negotiating the three steps leading inside. A nurse, pushing a wheelchair, followed him inside. Raven could feel the sweat from the effort it took him to get in the house when she embraced him and then helped him sit in the wheelchair. He smiled and pulled her into his lap. Marwa was standing just inside the door and giggled uncontrollably at the gesture.

"I knew I could do it." Joseph smiled as Raven disengaged herself from his embrace and stood up. "Not bad for a man who wasn't supposed to ever walk again."

Joseph wouldn't let Raven help him in and out of bed, insisting the nurse wouldn't have anything to do if Raven took care of him. His legs were ice cold all through the night no matter what temperature it was in the house. Every morning the nurse would come in and attach an electronic brace to the metal disk creating a star pattern on his back. The device gave him almost complete range of motion, but he needed to relearn how to walk and strengthen his muscles to hold the weight of the metal contraption. His physical therapy had to be grueling, but he never gave any indication of the pain he was feeling.

Egan's trial was one of the most publicized events Raven ever experienced. She knew her mother had been in the media spotlight for most of her life, but her mother finding the source of disease and creating vaccines was nothing compared to the firestorm Egan produced. No matter how hard the government tried, they couldn't keep the media away from Egan. And the woman was fired up.

Joseph was sent to Washington to testify in her trial, leaving Raven to try to manage her way through the sludge-pile Egan left behind. Raven wouldn't allow the children to watch the trial, blocking any access to the feed on their data pads. Egan's lawyers didn't want her to take the stand in her own defense, but she refused their advice and defiantly took her place on the witness stand. Raven couldn't help watching the ginger-haired woman recite her diatribe. She kept a careful eye on the soldiers at the base as her words rippled across the barracks.

"They're all in on it." Egan's face was pale, but her voice was strong in her conviction. "Taylor, Smith, Grey. They're creating a race of genetically altered creatures, half human, half animal and turning them into killing machines. Us natural bornes need to arm ourselves. There are millions of these monsters being created in the mountains of Idaho. That's all Haven is, a monster factory. Do you really think Smith is locked away in a prison somewhere wasting away his life? He's out there, creating more genetically altered freaks and creating more diseases to kill off natural born citizens. If we don't do something to stop them, they'll wipe us all out."

Insurgent attacks increased, especially among the border of the western states, and the base was always on high alert. Raven had to double her security on transports to and from the base, and even then it sometimes didn't help. Perhaps the most prominent indication of changing sentiments was the segregation of troops. Natural born soldiers no longer fought beside genetically altered surrogate troops. They weren't even stationed at the same bases. All the troops at Mountain Home were genetically altered. Many of the soldiers in Egan's units were either transferred to Virginia or discharged from service for assisting in her treason.

Raven barely felt any ill-effects through the course of her pregnancy. She was in peak physical condition and was able to work and exercise all the way through her third trimester. The only reason she took maternity leave was because her mother insisted she take time off to recover from the birth. Savanna actually travelled from Haven near the end of Raven's pregnancy and stayed to deliver the baby.

Giving birth to her daughter was as easy as her first delivery. It was painful. She would have been fooling herself if she didn't say it was, but in the end she delivered a healthy, beautiful child. Meaghan was a joy to hold and care for. Raven didn't know why this child felt so different in her arms than her first child, but she almost hated giving her over to the nurse when the woman came in to take her for her first bath. The nurse gave her a data pad with the birth certificate to fill in the name and Raven realized her daughter was born on Christmas Day. She gave the girl the name Meaghan Noel, Meaghan for the woman Joseph remembered from his early childhood and Noel in celebration for the day of her birth.

Everyone at home doted on the child; even Lakota lost some of his resentful aura when he held and rocked his little sister. Joseph was strong enough to take care of the house while Raven took care of the ins and outs of the base, managing the facility in much the same precision as her mother ran Haven and her programs. With the help of Travis's security force and her mother's Haven graduates, the base became a miniature Haven in itself. The few raids attempted on its perimeter and in the Little Haven community on its edges were woefully unsuccessful and soon insurgents knew the base was a force to be reckoned with.

Managing the base became a huge balancing act as Raven worked through her days. Raven watched as troops came through the proving grounds and moved out to parts unknown. She still had to deal with the detention center, but the work she had put into cleaning up the hospital extended to the quarters, reducing the number of illnesses and infections in the detention ward. Casey and Seth spent a brief stint in the detention center before they were sent to Virginia to stand trial next to Egan. Every time a new unit came in Raven felt the same sense of excitement she had when she first joined the service. As the troops were scattered to different fronts Raven couldn't help but yearn to go with them.

Joseph continued to gain strength as he adapted to his body armor and it wasn't long before he joined her in managing the base. Raven couldn't deny they made a good team. She just missed being in the middle of the action and wanted to go back to the front line.

More than anything Raven wanted to go back to the front, any front, and fight the battle.

Meaghan was nearly three years old when Raven was summoned to Grey's office. She brought the child to Haven to visit with her Grandmother and actually walked the two miles to Grey's headquarters at the center of the surrogate unit. As she entered his office, Raven's eyes were drawn to the three-dimensional topographical map hovering above the cherry-finished briefing table in the center of the room. She recognized the mountainous region of the Sierra Nevada's slashing across the Nevada, California border. The area was rich in precious metal mines and a well-known insurgent stronghold. A knot started to grow in Raven's belly and her heart started racing as adrenaline sang through her system. She pulled her eyes away from the map and looked towards the two men sitting in the chairs on the opposite end of the table. Sitting next to Grey, in a high-backed cushioned chair, was a two-star General. Whatever they had for her had to be important if such a heavy hitter was involved. Raven offered her salute and Grey motioned for her to take a seat.

"Captain Taylor, let me start with introductions." Grey gestured to the man sitting beside him. "This is General Jackson; he's in charge of security deployment in the hot zones of America."

Raven's eyes were drawn to the map now rotating in slow motion above the table. A red dot hovered in the center of the mountain range. She had a strong feeling she was going to be heading for that red dot.

"Captain," General Jackson's voice brought her back to the men sitting at the head of the table. "There's a hydraulic gold mine near the borderland between Nevada and California. The mine is currently under our control, but it has been constantly threatened by insurgent operatives. We need to make our presence known in the area."

Raven had a hard time keeping a straight face. She knew it wouldn't be good form to grin like a Cheshire cat at the thought of going into a hot zone. Knowing she had to do something to keep calm, she focused on her heartbeat. Tying the rhythm of her heart to the beat pounding in her temples, she was able to slow her breathing and control her facial expression.

"We're sending a unit to the mine to protect our interests." The general waved his hand over the top of the table and the map zoomed to show the ragged topography of the mine. "You're going to command the unit. It is going to be up to you and your team to protect the mine."

A screen on the table in front of her lit up and started scrolling a list of names. She recognized most of them as the men and women who had been part of her unit during her last tour. All of the soldiers who had been with her in the retrieval of Smith were on the list, including Sandoval. All together there were nineteen names. Her name at the top made it a squad of twenty. Not a very long list, if the expectation was to protect the entire mine.

"Your unit will work with the security team already in place." Grey had taken over the debriefing. "In addition to the nearly five hundred mine workers there are approximately a hundred private sector security personnel guarding the mine. Your team will protect our interest in the mine and train the locals in tactics and combat. Most of the guards and workers are natives and know the area. They also know where all the insurgent spider-holes are. Most of them are too afraid to speak up because of threats of repercussions. Their families and livelihoods have been threatened and insurgent attacks are a constant threat."

The map continued to develop more details as it zoomed towards a tiny village clinging to the side of the mountain. Raven could make out the details of the tiny shanties scattered across the mountain. A few yards away, a set of structured buildings, lined up in military precision, denoted where Raven and her squad would reside.

"It'll be up to you and your squad to train the locals and help them root out the undesirables." General Jackson tapped the console, bringing up a series of yellow dots, scattered through the hills. "We suspect these are the strongholds of insurgent operatives, but we can't confirm anything. The caves and tunnels running through these mountains are extensive and the insurgent groups know more about them than we can even imagine. We need to build up this stronghold in the mountains. That will be your job now, Major."

It took a moment to realize the general hadn't made a mistake, he was actually telling her she was being promoted. Raven ducked her head to hide the smile creeping around the corners of her mouth. She was going back to battle. To hide her rising emotions, she studied the names on the list. She was familiar with most of the names on the list except for one. Private First Class Marcus Anderson didn't ring any bells for her. There was a symbol beside his name denoting his status as an engineer. Her unit was coming back together. She just hoped Sandoval had overcome his weaknesses and would be an asset to the team.

"You'll be deployed within the week." Grey pushed an icon on his monitor, shutting down the topographical map. "You'll also need to say your good-bye's to your family. Communication is going to be spotty at best. We need to be careful about the messages sent out of this camp, there's a risk messages can be intercepted by the insurgents."

A sudden sharp twinge stabbed Raven's heart. The excitement of being deployed pushed the idea of being away from her family out of her mind for a moment and now the images of those she loved flooded over her. She had become used to having her children around her when she worked and she hadn't really thought about leaving them behind. It wasn't unusual to be on communication lockdown when on assignment, but not being able to even call home on a regular basis was going to be trying, especially since she was going to be so close to home this time.

"This is a long-term assignment, Major." Raven looked up at the General's words. "We intend to send your team up there for two years to train and organize the local militia and then slowly wean them off our assistance over the next year. You won't see your home for the next three years."

Raven waited until she and Joseph were in bed to tell him the news. She wanted to talk to him before sitting down and explaining to the children. Meaghan was too young to understand, but Lakota was finally starting to trust her and now she had to leave again. It was hard to know what Marwa was feeling. She always seemed so calm and happy. Raven knew much of Lakota's demeanor was influenced by this quiet child of the desert. Joseph didn't say much when she told him, he just held her through the night. The children reacted much like she expected. Lakota's face tightened in a scowl similar to the one he wore the first six months after she returned from the community.

"I'm not going back to Haven," he stated.

Joseph placed his hand on Lakota's shoulder. "You're all welcome to stay here," he said. "I'm taking over as Commander and we can keep the home-fires burning."

Leaving was harder this time, but Raven was filled with a sense of purpose as she boarded the carrier. She was going back to the battle.

Chapter Thirty-Nine

IT WAS MUCH COLDER IN the mountains than in the lowlands, Raven decided. She was used to the dichotomy of desert and mountain climates growing up in Idaho, but it had never gotten this cold. The drive in the open-topped jeep, even the short distance between the base and the tiny village, was almost more than she could handle, but she needed to make the trip at least once a week. She had such a small crew at the base there wasn't much for her to do there. Supply manifest sent once a month, daily reports to read and sign, eat, work out, sleep, make sure everyone was obeying orders, train the local militia and make sure the locals were protected. Despite the warnings about insurgent operatives and threats against the mine, Raven saw very little action and she had been at the base for close to six months.

The village was a collection of poorly built huts, each clinging to the side of the mountain. Raven drove the jeep into the center of what would have been the town square of a real village. Instead there was a poor, squat, tin building resting at a slant in the middle of the square. Dark, black smoke billowed from the roof, attesting to the use of a coal burning stove used for heat. As Raven came to a halt in front of the makeshift schoolhouse the door swung open and children flooded onto the steps, running towards the jeep. Tiny hands reached up to take packages as Anderson stepped out and started to unload the jeep. Raven didn't have any concerns about what would happen to the contents of the packages as the brown boxes disappeared into the shanty. The children knew they needed to share the bundles of food contained in each of the packages.

Sister Eugenia appeared at the door, sidestepping the mass of children as they scurried into the building. Raven looked the tall, lithe woman up and down. It looked like she had lost even more weight over the past month, weight the woman couldn't afford to lose. A simple olive pants and sweater draped over her willowy frame, hiding her growing leanness. Raven had treated the nun for pneumonia at the beginning of winter and had nursed the woman through a few tough nights. Despite Raven's warnings to take it easy and allow her body to heal, Sister Eugenia continued her work at the village school and hospital. She was adamant that if she didn't do it no one else would.

Raven was impressed with the work the nun did, especially working to provide education and medical supplies to the children of the village. God knew her job wasn't easy, as she had told Raven many times. Despite the assistance Sister Eugenia received from her order, there were never enough supplies to care for everyone. The mine barely paid workers enough to survive, not nearly enough to care for a family. It wasn't unusual to see children as young as eight slogging through ankle-deep slag heaps, shoveling grey-white silt into buckets. The scrap-heapers, as they were called, were paid based on the weight of the materials they brought into the secondary processing plant. Sister Eugenia had tried to recruit Raven to help her get the children out of the mine, but when the money the little ones brought into the homes could mean the difference between food on the table and empty cupboards, there was no way Raven could keep them away. Child labor laws didn't seem to mean much here on the fringes of society. It was all Raven could do to keep the border of the mine property protected. The best way Raven knew how to help was to work the contacts she had through her mother.

A fifteen minute conversation with her mother was all it took, which was good because fifteen minutes every few months was all she got. She could write letters and receive packages, but video conferencing and sending messages was out of the question. Despite these constraints, Savanna managed to send a plethora of supplies and even some equipment. By far the best piece of equipment her mother had sent was a refurbished S290. The compact robot, modeled after the one Raven remembered from her childhood, was a huge asset to the tiny village. It was completely useless in the mines. Dust and grime stirred up by the blasts and massive earthmovers would tear up the sensitive cogs and gears in the more delicate components of the machine. There was nothing preventing the compact robot from laboring around the village, though.

The S290 had a number of subprograms designed specifically for the work needed to eke a living out of the mountainside. Anderson loved the squat little machine. It wasn't unusual for the soldier to be out in the fields beside it, tweaking programs and adding hardware in an attempt to improve the machine's performance.

Anderson lowered the transport platform attached to the back of the jeep, bringing the robot to the hard-packed clay. The children cheered and ran past Raven, towards the shiny, steel contraption. She couldn't help smiling as Anderson pointed out the new equipment he had attached to the back of the robot. He was having a hard time convincing the children not to touch the sharp blades he had fabricated and attached to the rear of the machine. She watched as he brought the robot to the wide field just beyond the collection of low huts.

Raven turned back to the schoolhouse, allowing Anderson to lead the children to the field to test out the new plow system. Sister Eugenia was leaning against the door frame, her arms across her chest. Even though she was smiling, Raven could see the lines of exhaustion in the woman's face. The nun looked much older than her thirty-two years. Raven walked to the door and took the nun by her arm as the woman turned and they walked into the building together.

The low-slung building was dark and smoke hovered on the ceiling, creating swirls and clouds around the light source. Raven had to blink to clear her vision. Low tables and cushions were scattered around the room. Textbooks and paper was scattered across the surface of the tables. Pencils had been dropped and left to roll across the slanted surfaces and fall to the floor. Obviously the children had been interrupted in their school work when the jeep pulled up to the building. Raven allowed a smile to play around her lips at the thought of the chaos she probably caused in the classroom. Sister Eugenia moved silently around the room gently cleaning scattered supplies.

"I'm sorry; I didn't mean to interrupt your lessons." Raven made her way towards the boxes stacked in the middle of the floor.

Sister Eugenia gathered books from where they had fallen on the floor. "It's okay, Raven. The children need a break every once in a while. I can only do so much for them before the mountain claims them."

An easy friendship had developed between the two women over the months Raven had been stationed at the mountain base. Sister Eugenia was the only person around who used Raven's civilian name. Raven leaned over and picked a pencil up off the floor. She studied the implement for a moment. The wood and graphite device was similar to the stylus she had grown up using, but until she was transferred to this village she had actually never seen a pencil. Placing it on the desk, Raven turned back to the woman and the boxes stacked in the center of the room.

Sister Eugenia was opening one of the boxes, using a pair of scissors to slice through the extra layer of packing tape across the box. It was obvious the boxes had been opened and resealed, probably at one of the many stops they made on their voyage from Haven. Raven was always surprised by the amount of resources her mother was able to send to the village.

"Are these the seeds your mother promised to send?" Sister Eugenia started pulling paper-wrapped packages out of the boxes.

"Yes." Raven opened another box and started pulling out the contents. "The seeds are heirloom. My mother sent some instructions on how to grow and harvest the plants. She designed the instructions to fit into your lessons so you can teach the children."

Raven pulled the jars of crystallized fertilizer out of the box she had just opened. "Once the soil is prepared you're going to need to add these nutrients. There are instructions on how to rotate the crops and use mulching to enhance the nutrient quality of the soil. If we can produce enough food in the village, we may be able to convince parents to keep their children out of the mines and in school and growing crops."

Sister Eugenia gave a noncommittal nod as she continued to unpack boxes. "Your mother has done more for the members of this village than most people have done for this entire nation." Raven didn't miss the frustration in the woman's voice.

"It's hard to get supplies through all the check-points." Raven stacked seed packets on the table. "It's fortunate no one is really interested in the seeds and fertilizer in these packages. I'm sure if this was food, these packages would never have gotten this far. These seeds are genetically modified for the shorter growing seasons in the mountains. It may take generations, but my mother is determined to save the world."

Sister Eugenia reached over and put her hand on top of Raven's. "Isn't that what we are all trying to do? We all have our callings, Raven. I wondered why God would call me to this place in the mountains. I was working in a refugee camp across the border with an entire order of nuns when I had a dream about this place. I knew I needed to be here. The work we have done here will save hundreds of lives and perhaps the lessons we teach will save thousands more. Once we teach this village to be self-reliant we can move to the next and then the next."

Raven stopped opening boxes and turned to study the nun. There was a zeal glowing from the woman's eyes, a glow Raven recognized all too well. It was the same glow her mother had when Savanna talked about Haven.

"Sister, how can you think helping just these few can even make a dent in the horrors of this world?" Raven tried not to let frustration creep into her voice, but it was hard to keep it out. "This is such a tiny handful of people compared to the billions suffering every day. It breaks my heart to think my children have to grow up with so much loss and pain surrounding them."

Sister Eugenia placed her arm around Raven's shoulder and pulled her close. "Your children aren't suffering, Raven." Raven could feel the warmth radiating off the woman and she had to work hard to blink back tears. "From everything I've heard of your children, they are happy, healthy and well-sheltered with your mother. You're the one who is suffering, child. I see how much you miss your husband. I see how much you care and worry for the soldiers in your trust. You're making a difference in the world. Cast your bread upon the water and it will come back to you ten-fold. We're making a tiny ripple in the sand here, but it will spread. You'll see. It will spread and soon it will become a tidal wave."

Raven suppressed the shudders that threatened to overwhelm her senses. She could feel her defenses beginning to crumble and she didn't want to cry in front of the nun. A sudden klaxon sounded, startling Raven and causing her ears to ring. She hated the higher bell tones. They always made her implant hum. Raven pulled away from Sister Eugenia and ran to the front door. Anderson was running from the fields, followed at a slightly slower pace by the S290. The children were arriving from all corners of the village and disappearing through the school house doors. Raven knew they were going to disappear out the back and into a shelter carved in the side of the mountain. The shelter was one of the first structures built in the town, predating Raven and her team's arrival at the base.

Anderson was already behind the wheel when Raven made her way to the jeep. As she took her place in the passenger seat the S290 wheeled its way up the ramp and locked itself into position. The jeep was already in motion as Raven strapped herself into the safety harness.

"The motion sensors have been tripped at the southwest corner of the mine property." The S290's voice had a slight electronic cadence, barely noticeable. "It appears to be a caravan of some sort. Whoever they are it appears they have stopped moving. It does not appear to be a large caravan but the mine guards are moving to intercept."

Raven didn't need to order Anderson to speed up. His foot was already pushing the accelerator to the floorboard. The local militia was fairly heavy-handed when it came to trespassers and Raven wanted to get there in time to prevent any clash. Dust billowed around the jeep, tossing grit into Raven's teeth. She pulled a cloth out of the pocket of her shirt and wrapped it around her face and head. A cloud of dust, four times the size as the one being kicked up by the jeep was approaching from near the mine. Raven and Anderson were so far ahead of the others it was easy to see they were going to make it to the edge of the field first.

The jeep slammed to a stop in a spray of gritty sand. Raven pulled her automatic weapon out from the bin beside the seat, unstrapped her harness and rolled out of the seat, keeping the jeep between her body and the small crowd of people gathered at the edge of a stream. She counted about twenty people, all involved in various activities designed to set up an extensive campsite. A few of them stopped and looked in the direction of the jeep as Anderson rolled out and took a position beside Raven. Reaching across Raven and into the cab, he grabbed the mouthpiece for the sound system and addressed the crowd.

Raven focused on the group ahead of her, barely registering the words he was saying. He was warning the group they were trespassing on private property and if they didn't move on they would be in danger of being arrested or killed. His words caused a sudden commotion in the tribe. Women and children started running towards tents and gathering items from the ground. One of the men approached the jeep, his arms outspread in a non-threatening gesture. Anderson's barked order to freeze was accompanied by the roar of engines as the security detail from the mine arrived and pulled into position. Armed guards spilled out of the back of the trucks and, dropping to their bellies in the sand, pointed their weapons at the now terrified group of travelers.

Raven waved the guards down, trying to concentrate on the words being yelled across the open space. The gist of the conversation seemed to be the tribe was looking for a place to set up camp for the night. They had seen the stream from the roadway and decided to stop here to eat and drink. Anderson convinced the tribe it would behoove them to move on to avoid any possibility of a misunderstanding. The tribe begged to be allowed to fill their water containers before leaving. Raven nodded, focusing the S290's camera sensors on the activity as the tribe filled plastic and metal containers. The stream was fast moving and not a vital water source to the village, so there really wasn't any danger of the tribe adding toxins to the stream, but Raven wanted the extra protection of being able to watch their activity. Once the water containers were filled, the tribe loaded their vehicles and sped towards the road. The situation resolved, Raven ordered the guards back to the mine and back to duty. The siren sang the all clear as she returned to the village. She could see the children slowly filtering out of the school house, but she had Anderson drive past without stopping. She had to return to the base and finish her daily reports.

Chapter Forty

WINTER BLOOMED INTO SPRING AND the mountainside turned into muddy slop. Raven helped Sister Eugenia in the greenhouse, planting seeds and starts to get a head start on the gardens. The responsibility of building the greenhouse and the raised bed for the community gardens fell on the shoulders of the children of the village, but with the help of the S290 and the soldiers from Raven's unit, the construction was completed quickly. Sporadic relief supplies would arrive in the village, from Haven when her mother could send them, or from Sister Eugenia's connections with charitable groups in California and Nevada. These donations were enough to keep many of the children fed until a crop could be put in the ground.

Over the course of the summer Raven brought textbooks on growing, harvesting and preserving food to the school. The children reveled in the knowledge and the community garden benefited from their hard work. Sister Eugenia gained health and strength over the months and it wasn't unusual to see her working in the garden, her olive-drab pants and shirt standing in stark contrast to her bright, white head scarf. The community custom of wearing headscarves and veils carried over to the traditions of the village and dictated all women had to keep their heads covered when in public, even the ones in Raven's unit. The women had been issued camouflaged head scarves with their uniform and were required to wear them when they were off compound grounds. Raven liked using the head covering to contain her tightly braided mass of rich black hair. She was required to keep her waist-length mass braided and pinned above her collar. Tying it in to the head scarf helped keep the weight off her neck and alleviated some of her headaches, as mild as they were.

By early fall the underground cellar was built and, with the help of the village children and the S290, stocked with freshly preserved vegetables from the community garden. Although there wasn't enough of the preserved food to last the entire village through the winter, it was enough to take away the fear of starvation, especially for the children. Plans were already under way to expand the garden the next spring. With the guarantee of food to last through the winter, Raven and Sister Eugenia were able to convince the adults of the village to keep the younger children out of the mine. There was no way to convince them to keep all the children away and many of the older children would spend long hours digging ore-rich clay from the ground and bringing it to the slurry pits for processing. Raven's authority ended at the mine entrance and there was little she could do to keep the children away from the pit.

Another growing season and a larger harvest this time brought excitement to th village. Winter came early and hard, again. The last of the harvest was barely processed and stored away before the harsh, cold winds rolled down the mountain. More often than not, Raven would find the entire school in the greenhouse on her frequent visits to the village, reveling in the warmth of the glass covered walls. Care packages and relief supply deliveries were still sporadic and letters from home were even more infrequent. Her mother's letters were always filled with love and hope, but Raven detected a hint of fear underlying the simple news reflected in the letters. Lakota rarely wrote, but Marwa made up for his lack of communication with long, detailed filled letters.

Once the weather started to warm, the children started to work the fields plowing and spreading fertilizer and composted vegetable matter. An occasional tribe would meander away from the road and cross the borders of mine properties, but the show of force from the mine guards were enough to send them on their way. The training Raven gave the guards was sufficient to give the mine owners the confidence to turn guard duty over to the locals. Her team had orders to spend the next year slowly phasing out their support and preparing the local militia to take over guard duty. Raven was concerned about leaving Sister Eugenia in the border lands, but the woman kept insisting her calling was here and Raven was not to concern herself over the people of this village.

Another harvest came and this time the fields produced a bounteous crop. Some of Raven's concerns were assuaged, but she still had an overwhelming fear for the children of the village. Winter locked the mountain up hard. The cold, frozen mine produced very little gold as the ground was rock hard and was almost impossible to work. Children came into the hospital with blackened fingers and toes and, although Sister Eugenia and Raven tried to save the little frostbitten digits, often amputation was the only answer.

Eventually the cold grip of winter loosened its hold on the mountain and warming breezes softened the ground. Any day Raven was expecting the orders to prepare to return to the Idaho. Her unit's term of service was scheduled to end in three months.

The cool spring day was winding to a close, giving a beautiful red and golden sunset the chance to breathe a cool breeze across the mountain. Raven ducked into the school building and moved to take her place in the circle of people gathered around the felt cloth on the floor. A feast was spread out on the gray cloth, consisting mostly of shoots of fresh greens, grains and a few platters of sliced meat Raven didn't recognize but suspected was one of the small goats the village children were responsible for herding.

A few village children were walking around the circle with ceramic bowls and fresh towels. One of the girls placed a bowl in front of Raven and handed her a towel. Raven held out her hands and allowed the girl to pour the warm water over them and wash away the dust of the mountain. The children gathered the bowls and the towels and faded into the background.

Someone handed Raven a piece of flat, unleavened bread and a bowl of flavored rice. Raven had participated in these village feasts often enough to know what to do. Making sure to take at least a portion of everything, Raven filled flat bread after flat bread until she was beyond satiated. She avoided the slightly fermented fruit juices she knew had been brewed in tubs behind the huts opting instead for fresh, sweet tea. The meal was eaten in almost total silence; the only sound being the smacking of lips and the slurping of liquid. After the food was gone, everyone reclined on cushions while some of the men pulled out cigarettes and cigars to smoke. The women huddled in a corner, whispering in low voices, glancing at the men in case one of their husbands called for something more to eat or drink.

Raven realized she was the only woman still at the table. It wasn't unusual for her to be sitting with the men, discussing mine operations and security procedures. The men still didn't trust her. If anything they merely tolerated her presence.

She wanted to loosen the collar of her shirt, but her flak-jacket was fastened all the way to the top and it would take a lot of effort to get under it. Regulations mandated she keep her protective gear on whenever she left the shelter of the base and even here, among the leaders of the village and the company representatives, her helmet was only a few inches from her hand. Raven reached for a sweet fruit tart and popped it in her mouth. It was one of the delicacies she enjoyed and knew was going to miss when she went home.

The door swung open, bringing in a cool, fresh breeze. Anderson ducked into the building. His normally jovial smile was replaced by a worried frown. Raven knew something was wrong and she stood to move towards him. He motioned for her to move outside before he spoke. Guiding her to the middle of the street so they could talk without being overheard, Anderson leaned down, speaking in low tones. Raven could hear soft music playing from the confines of the school.

"It's Sandoval," he whispered. "He freaked out. Started yelling about not wanting to go home and being sick and tired of being led around by the nose and being told what to do. We tried to talk him down, but he grabbed his gun and started walking away from the base. The twins wanted to follow him, but I told them I wanted to come get you. You could follow him much better with the S290 and your vision than we could."

Raven sent Anderson back to the base in her jeep and took the truck he brought down. The S290 was already in the pilot's seat, its computer tied directly into the navigation system of the truck. Raven activated the robot's voice control so she could focus on the sub-dermal tracking device showing Sandoval's location. The sky was glowing with the last few rays of sunset as the jeep followed the path down the mountain. She could make out the glowing form of Sandoval as he hunched into the wind. Directing the S290 to pull up beside him, Raven stepped out and stood in front of the man, forcing him to stop.

Sandoval barely looked up as Raven moved within inches of his face. His dark eyes were flashing, nostrils flared and his breath was whistling through foam-flecked lips. Raven kept her voice low as she spoke, but there was no doubting her intensity.

"Get in the truck," she growled.

Sandoval flinched, but didn't move. Raven could see the corner of his eyes soften as he started to realize the severity of the situation. The cold wind cut through Raven's uniform, causing goose bumps to spring up on her arms. She shivered and pushed in closer to the man standing in front of her.

"Get in the truck now!" She spoke through clenched teeth. "I'm putting you on the next transport home. You're cracking up and I'm not going to allow you to put these people at risk with your immature behavior."

Sandoval's eyes tightened and glistened from unshed tears. Raven couldn't tell if he was scared, angry or becoming defensive. The muscles between her shoulder blades tightened and she felt as if eyes were watching her. Turning, she scanned the hillside looking for tell-tale heat signatures. She didn't see anything, but the feeling didn't go away. She swung back to face Sandoval. He hadn't moved any closer to the truck and was staring off into the distance.

"I'm not going to allow you to get us killed with your childishness." Raven grabbed the man by the collar and tried to drag him back to the truck. Sandoval didn't budge. In fact, he seemed to dig his heels deeper into the sand. Raven used her leverage to bring him down to the ground and put her knee on his chest. "Get in the truck before you get us both killed."

Sandoval stopped struggling, closed his eyes and turned his head. "Who would care if we died?" His voice cracked. "The test tubes who were our parents? You at least have a mother at home who cares for you and misses you. I have nothing."

Raven stood up and pulled Sandoval to his feet. "If you don't get in the truck right now I'm going to order the S290 to put you in there, and it won't be gentle." Raven had no idea if the S290 could force the man into the truck, but she was willing to give it a try. She knew the robot had the capacity to lift a two ton vehicle, having used it as a jack when one of the trucks had a flat tire.

Sandoval seemed to collapse in on himself. Hanging his head, he turned to the truck. Raven followed close behind in case he decided to bolt. A sudden crack followed by a whistling resounded from the hillside. Raven tackled the man in front of her, pulling her arm over his head attempting to protect him. Gun-fire cracked over her head. An impact against her flak-jacket knocked the wind out of her, causing her to gasp for air. She lifted her eyes, looking for the location of the truck. It was a few yards away. She knew she could make it, but Sandoval didn't have the protection of a helmet and a flak-jacket. There was no way he would make it to the truck.

Shadowy figures were appearing from behind rocks and holes in the side of the mountain. All Raven could think about was if the insurgents captured the truck and the S290 they would have access to technology beyond their current capabilities. She pulled her data pad out of the pocket on her sleeve and pushed the communication icon.

"S," Raven called the machine by the moniker given it by the village children. "Return to base. Turn the truck around and return to base."

The wheels on the truck spun, kicking dirt into the face of one of the encroaching invaders. One of the shadow figures grabbed at the truck. He caught hold of a strap dangling off the back. Stumbling, the man took a few steps before he fell and was dragged a few yards before dropping to the ground. Raven dropped the data pad to the ground, picked up a rock and smashed the screen. Sparks arced across the internal workings, frying the inside of the device. Throwing a few handfuls of dirt over the open wound of the screen, she ground the device into the grit. There would be no recovery of data from this device.

Raven used her body to cover Sandoval the best she could. She felt his body quivering as he curled into the fetal position. She could hear the click of guns over her head. Her first reaction was to close her eyes and duck her head so she wouldn't see it coming, but she didn't want the enemy to see her last moment of life to be one of fear. Lifting her head she saw the barrel of a gun inches from her nose.

Looking past the AK-47 she looked into the dark eyes of a young soldier. The boy's jaw dropped letting her know her eyes caught the light just right. It was an effect she liked to use to her advantage, so far her glowing eyes seemed to be working. The boy took a step back and looked over his shoulder to the man behind him. A spatter of orders assaulted her ears. She put her hands on top of her head and rolled off of Sandoval.

Hands grabbed at her, pulling her arms behind her back and tying them. She felt almost weightless as she was yanked from the ground and forced into a kneeling position. Sandoval was being given the same treatment. Once he was pulled to his feet, the men deposited him next to her. The boy who had held his gun on Raven reached down and picked up her smashed data pad from the dirt. A bright shot of electricity sparked from the device and he dropped it, shaking his hand and rubbing it as if to stop a strange sensation. Despite the fear making her heart race and the number of weapons trained on her, Raven couldn't suppress her smile. There was no way anyone was going to be able to retrieve any information or salvage the hardware from the device.

The sun set completely and shadowy darkness covered the mountain, giving everything a grayish haze. Someone grabbed her arms while another man forced a rough, scratchy cloth sack over her head. The smell inside the sack almost made her gag, but she swallowed the bile back in her throat. Sound was muted, but she could still hear voices shouting orders around her. Hands grabbed her and she felt herself being lifted from the ground. The wind was knocked out of her when her stomach came in contact with a bony shoulder and it took a moment to get it back. Gasping, she tried to take a deep breath, but it wasn't until she was lying on the cold, metal bed of a truck that she was finally able to suck in any air. She could smell the burning exhaust and feel the jerking of the vehicle as it went over the rough terrain. A bitter feeling started to roil in her belly as she realized the seriousness of her situation. She needed to figure out how to get herself and Sandoval out of this situation alive.

Chapter Forty-One

IT WAS DARK. FOR THE first time ever in her life it was dark and all sound was muffled. Raven could only rely on the sensations she could assess from her sense of touch. The truck had rolled to a stop and she was pulled out into the elements. Cold wind buffeted her and she shivered despite the layers of her uniform. Hands on her arms kept her upright as she was forced to walk. Obstacles caused her to stumble, but the hands kept her moving with forward momentum. The wind suddenly dropped off, but the cold became even deeper. They must have entered shelter of some sort, but Raven couldn't tell what kind. Usually the shelters in the area, even the tents, carried with them a degree of warmth.

Raven was forced to walk. She took short, probing steps, attempting to avoid stumbling over any more obstacles. Either the men holding her had become more adept at helping her negotiate around debris, or the ground had fewer items in her path. Her feet didn't connect with anything to cause her to stumble and fall. It seemed as if they had been walking forever, but finally the men forced her to a stop. Raven could hear shouting all around as she was forced to her knees. The floor beneath her knees felt like rock and the air around her was heavily laden with moisture. They had to be in some type of subterranean cavern. a deep, God-forsaken hole in the ground with little chance for escape or rescue.

Not being able to see was frustrating beyond belief. Raven could feel her heart drumming in her chest. She needed to calm down, but not being able to see terrified her. She tried shaking her head and using her shoulder to push at the bag, but it wasn't budging. A sharp pain shot through her head as if something hard hit her from behind. She couldn't afford to lose herself. She needed to stay strong and allowing them to hurt her would just weaken her defenses. Raven slumped, hoping she wouldn't feel any more blows.

Her arms were jerked and stretched until her joints strained and a hand in her back forced her into a bowed position. She couldn't help gasping for breath. Every movement was agony and she ground her teeth to keep from crying out. She tried moving to alleviate the pressure on her shoulders but a booted foot to her ribs caused her to stay her movement. The bag was ripped from her head and her scarf came with it. Her long, black braid had burst from its constraints and fell over her shoulder to coil on the floor.

She lifted her eyes to shadows dancing in firelight. Despite the darkness, Raven could make out the contours of a cave. Her head swam as she lifted her eyes to try to locate Sandoval. Her position made it painful to look around, but she had to find him. He was her responsibility.

Sandoval was kneeling with his back to her, almost within arm's reach. His hands were tied behind his back and his head was bowed as if in prayer. The effort to keep her head up against the strain in her shoulders was too much and Raven let her head drop. Closing her eyes, she tried to center herself, biting back the pain. Voices cried out around her. Angry voices calling in a language she didn't understand. Pain shot through her head as someone grabbed her braid and pulled up her head, forcing her to make eye-contact with the man crouching in front of her. The small, dark face crinkled as he smiled at her, revealing yellowing teeth. Raven estimated the man was in his early fifties, but his sinewy body belied strength younger than his years.

"So, the infidel commander is so confident in her abilities she decided she didn't need the protection of her unit." The man's fetid breath washed over her, almost making her gag. "Are you surprised to find yourself in the nest of insurgents? Isn't that what your people call us? Well, we have a name for ourselves. We call ourselves loyalists. You are without the protection of your stone and metal walls, creature. Your altered DNA can't help you here. I don't know why you and your man were wandering out in the middle of our lands, but we have you now. What will your people give to get you back?"

The man grabbed the sack and placed it back on Raven's head, cutting off her sight. Despite the muffled sounds she could still hear shouted orders. Sudden cries assaulted her ears. Recognizing the cries as those of pain, Raven struggled against her ties. They had to be torturing Sandoval. It was his cries she heard. A sudden, sharp pain in her side cut off her breath and she stopped struggling. Another blow in the same area caused her to grunt in pain. She stopped moving, but the blows still came. Gritting her teeth, she refused to cry out. She wouldn't give them the satisfaction.

After a time the blows stopped. Raven strained to hear something from Sandoval, but everything was too muffled and sounds overlapped. It was impossible to distinguish Sandoval's voice from the rest. Her eyes ached from the pressure of unshed tears, but she blinked them back. She knew at any moment the bag could be ripped from her head and she didn't want her captors to see her in a moment of weakness.

The pain was excruciating, beyond anything she had ever experienced. Raven tried to draw in breath but a sharp pain flashed through her ribs and her shoulders protested the pulling action as her lungs tried to fill. The best she could do was draw in short, quick gasps. The sack felt moist and sticky against her face, but she couldn't tell if it was from condensation from her breath or blood pooling from injuries inflected by fists and feet. Her head was swimming and she could feel consciousness slipping away. The voices disappeared completely and Raven welcomed the darkness.

The sweet oblivion of unconsciousness didn't last long. She awoke gasping and gagging as water soaked the sack and filled her nose and mouth. Her lungs felt ready to burst as she tried to draw in life-giving oxygen. The bag was ripped from her head, again, and strands of hair were stripped away leaving her scalp tingling. A man was standing directly in front of her. All Raven could see of him was his scuffed boots with buff colored pants tucked in the top. Strands of her hair brushed against the leather of his boots, leaving streaks of water mixed with a pink tinge of blood, darkening the leather. Raven tried to lift her eyes, but the pain overwhelmed her senses, forcing her to lower her head.

Coughing and sputtering, water and bits of food spewed from her spasming stomach and splattered on the ground. The feet jerked back and for a moment Raven was afraid he was getting ready to kick her again. No pain from blows followed, so he must have just been avoiding the sick. Voices were raised in the tone of command and water splashed over her head, soaking the dirt floor of the cave. Her hair felt like a mass of weight, pulling her face closer the muddy filth below.

A heavy hand grabbed the mass and pulled her head back, exposing her face to a sharp blow from someone's fist. Bringing her face back to front she spat blood at the man's feet. The fist was still tightly wound in her hair, stretching her head back, causing her shoulders and arms to scream in painful protest.

Raven blinked, trying to focus her eyes and clear her vision. The man in front of her was holding a palm-sized device close to her face. It took her a few minute to realize he was recording her. She heard the words, "gen freak", but the buzzing in her ears wouldn't let the context of the words penetrate her mind. Suddenly the man moved right in front of her, putting his face next to hers.

"Genetically altered freak," his voice carried an angry snarl. "You come in here with your filthy genes, rape our land, enslave our children and steal our natural resources. Your lust and greed brings you into our world and, like a scorpion, we lie in wait. You and your friend fell into our trap. Your lives are forfeit."

Raven could see spittle forming at the corner of the man's lips as he spoke. The rage behind his words caused shudders to roll down her spine. His eyes carried her death and she knew this man intended to kill her.

Shuffling and thudding noises approached and a heavy body was dropped to the dirt beneath her. The man handed the recorder to one of his men and grabbed a knife. He stepped close, hovering over her head.

"All must know you are a freak," he screamed.

His hand replaced the one holding her hair, the blade in his hand flashed in the light as it came closer to her face. Raven wanted to close her eyes so she wouldn't have to see death, but she didn't want the pain to surprise her. She looked at the knife with a steady, unwavering gaze until the shine disappeared behind her head. A sharp pain flashed across the nape of her neck, then it was gone. Strands of hair whispered past her ears as the hand loosened its grip. Raven dropped her head and closed her eyes. She was still alive. She could draw air into her tortured lungs. Closing her eyes she relished the sensation of taking a deep breath.

A cool breeze skimmed across the nape of her neck, causing goose bumps to form on her arm. It was an entirely new sensation and she opened her eyes with a start. On the ground, just inches from her face, was a thick pile of long, strait, black hair. Her hair. It took a moment to make the connection to the breeze on her neck and the pile of hair in front of her. A roiling feeling developed from the pit of her stomach and rolled into her chest. At first she thought she was going to be sick, but as a cloud filed from her mind she realized it wasn't nausea filling her stomach; it was a much stronger emotion. An incoherent rage. Blinding madness. She wanted to rage and scream and rip the rope from her wrist. Bringing her eyes up she searched for the man who had shorn the hair from her head.

She felt heat in her eyes and a glottal growl developed deep in her throat.

A thick, dark body blocked her line of sight. Boots thudded on the hard-packed dirt and taut scuffling noises assaulted her ears before the body fell to the ground in front of her. The man rolled onto his back, groaning, before lying still. Despite the swelling and bruising on his face, Raven could easily identify Sandoval. The man was barely stifling sobs and tears liberally smeared his face. Raven glanced down his body, assessed his breathing, looked for deformities or posturing. Despite the bruises on his face and the arms crossed over his ribs, he was breathing and conscious. The distraction of assessing Sandoval calmed her and she was able to focus on something other than her rage.

A shadowy form crossed in front of her and more scuffling noises told her the person was moving to take a position behind her. Now that the rage was gone a cold fear started to grow in her vitals, coiling around her bowels and causing her stomach to clench. She heard a slithering above her head and suddenly the rope holding her arms went slack. Without the assistance of the rope she had no way of keeping her balance and she collapsed, her head hitting Sandoval's chest. She heard his grunt and low moan of pain, but she didn't have any strength left in her muscles to prevent her body from falling. She couldn't find stamina to even lift her head a few inches. Pain throbbed through her tired muscles as circulation roared back into her veins. She wanted to scream out, but she tightened her lips against any sound.

She felt herself being pulled to her feet, but her arms were so numb she didn't feel the hands encircling them. Men were on either side, bracing her up, since her legs couldn't support her weight. Despite her attempts to control her physical response, she couldn't stop her legs from trembling. Her knees refused to lock into a standing position and she had to rely on the two men to carry her weight. The air breathed against the back of her neck and tingled against her ears, leaving her feeling more vulnerable and exposed than at any other time in her life.

Sandoval cowered at her feet, quaking, as men moved to stand in front of her. Raven dragged her head up so her eyes drilled the man in front of her. He dragged his sleeve across his mouth, wiping the spittle from the corners of his lips. Grabbing her chin, he brought his face close to hers.

"Your eyes are brown, now." Raven could feel the spray of saliva against her face as he spoke. "But I heard about the demon shining from within. You do not scare me, creature."

Raven saw the fist coming and she tried to turn her face to lessen the impact, but the pain still flashed across her jaw and she heard a snapping sound as it connected. Tasting salt, she spat onto the ground, not wanting to swallow the blood pooling in her mouth. Lifting her eyes, she felt her lip curl but she cut off the snarl before it escaped her throat. Another flash of pain and this time when she spat she saw a chip of white floating in the pool of red liquid.

"Tell your creators to meet our demands and we will let you go. If they do not, we will kill you where you stand."

It was difficult to focus and her ears were ringing. The pain was everywhere, taking her breath away. Coughing and spitting, she tried to clear the blood from her mouth. After a few more blows the men couldn't even support her and she felt her legs crumbling. She kept her lips tightly sealed against any sound, even when fists were traded for heavily soled feet. Blissful unconsciousness took her long before the blows ended.

Chapter Forty-Two

SOUND CAME BACK FIRST, THEN the pain, erasing any thought of the far away sounding voices. It radiated into all points in her body and a gasping groan emanated from her throat before she could tighten her jaw against it. No hands grabbed her and the voices didn't get louder. Raven swallowed any more sound and slowly took stock of her body. Not wanting to draw attention to any movement, she cautiously moved her fingers and toes, one at a time. They all worked, despite the sharp pain in the last two fingers on her right hand. She was barely able to move the pinky and suspected it was broken. From the pain in her chest and shoulder she suspected her pinky wasn't the only thing broken.

Warmth radiated from the form beside her. Shivering, she realized she had been stripped down to the skin-tight body suit all soldiers wore beneath their uniforms. The extra thin material was an added layer of protection against the cold and the elements, but alone it did little to protect from the draft and chill of the cave. Moving as slow as possible so as not to draw attention to herself, she positioned herself closer to the huddled mass. Tucking her arms to her chest, she pressed herself against Sandoval's back, drawing in his warmth.

The body heat helped a little bit, warming her enough she was able to stop shivering. Once her body stopped shaking Raven realized Sandoval was quivering. She could hear his low, choking sobs. For a moment she wanted to hit him and tell him to shut up, but she knew it wouldn't change anything and just draw unwanted attention. Carefully, she pulled her hand from where it was curled against her chest and wrapped it around his shoulder. She pulled her head as close to his ear as possible.

"Shh, Shh." She hissed in his ear, trying to soothe him. "It's okay. They know where we are. You have your locator chip. As long as we can stay together they will find us." Raven wasn't sure if she believed what she was saying, but it seemed to calm the man huddled on the floor. She didn't dare say anything more, but the sound of her voice actually calmed her a little and she didn't want to completely lose the connection she had with the man.

A song was reverberating in her head and she started humming a few bars. It was a song she loved to listen to for its chorus of halleluiahs. The first few lines of Cohen's *Halleluiah* skimmed through her mind as she hummed. In her mind, she could see the young, future King David, kneeling before the tortured King of Judah as the young shepherd played to assuage the ruler's tortured soul. She couldn't figure out why this song came to her now, but the humming seemed to keep Sandoval calm and her heart slowed its frantic rhythm. She kept up her breathless humming, the words of the song burning in her mind. The swelling halleluiahs leading to the second verse continued and suddenly she realized why she was thinking of this song. The girl, she tied him to a chair and cut his hair. She stripped him of his strength and dignity. The breeze against her neck caused goose bumps to spring up on her arms.

They cut her hair. The cold air against her neck and shoulders breathed this reality into her soul. Her waist-length straight black hair, her one connection to her mother. Her long hair. Her connection to Haven, safety and her mother. Now it was gone. On a deep level Raven knew her hair should be the least of her concerns. The aching in her ribs and the pain she felt in her chest every time she drew in a breath terrified her. She couldn't control the trembling of her body and soon the pain forced her back into darkness.

Raven was ripped to awareness when she was grabbed by her arms and dragged to her feet. This time they tied her hands and stretched them above her head. Someone leaned down and placed something at her feet. Her mind felt hazy and she had to blink multiple times to clear her vision. After a moment she could make out the huddled form of Sandoval cowering at her feet. His choking sobs assaulted her ears and she tightened her throat against the sound she wanted to make. It was shameful enough to be captured by his stupidity; the least he could do was face death like a man. Her head swam as she raised it to face the men who were tying her arms. The red light of the camera wavered before her, creating a glowing trail.

"Oh, ho, it looks like the kitty has come out to play." The man behind the camera had a sardonic smile on his face. "Tell your associates we will release you if you pull your little garrisons out of our lands. If not we will do to you what we are going to your man here."

The man nodded to another person standing near the back of the cave. Raven saw a shadowy form appear and the glint of metal. Sandoval's scream was cut off with a strangling cry and dark red blood spurted from the stump of his neck. It was over in a matter of seconds. Sandoval's eyes blinked up at her despite the fact his head was a good three feet from his body. His mouth moved as if he was trying to speak, but no sound escaped the pale lips. Raven swallowed the bile back in her throat and stared at the man holding the camera.

"As long as there is evil like you in the world I will never stop fighting." Raven could hear the deep growl in her voice as she spoke. "You rule with pain and fear, but I do not fear you."

Raven's words were cut off by a blow to her stomach. She could feel the muscles in her stomach spasm as she gasped for air. Coughing and sputtering, she drew air into her tortured lungs. A ringing blow across her face caused her eyes to blur and she welcomed the blackness.

Someone was screaming. A loud popping noise sang off the cave walls. Raven wanted to open her eyes, but she couldn't find her way to complete consciousness. Her shoulders protested against the straining weight of her body. She tried to open her eyes and managed to open her right one a slit. Everything was fuzzy and dark and none of the sounds made sense. Pain wracked her body and she quivered and shuddered as she tried to pull herself upright. Her shaking legs wouldn't support her, despite all her efforts. She kept collapsing, pulling on her shoulders as her joints protested. Her knees were almost touching the ground, but her arms, stretched above her head, wouldn't allow her knees to connect with the dirt floor beneath her.

Raven wanted to allow the blackness to take over again. Her body was fighting to pull back from the edge and wouldn't let her slip back into unconsciousness. A sudden warmth surrounded her as arms wrapped around her waist. Raven gasped and bit back a scream, anticipating more pain. Instead the rope slackened, allowing her arms to fall down as her body was gently lowered to the floor. Raven could feel a sob bubbling in her throat and she couldn't bite it back. The arms were gentle and soothing, filling Raven with a sense of peace. Pain overwhelmed her senses and tears poured from her eyes, unstaunched despite her efforts to hold them back. Raven closed her eyes as tightly as she could, but the tears kept flowing. Fingers gently brushed tears from her check and Raven could feel the warmth of someone's breath against her neck as comforting words were whispered in her ear.

"Shh, Shh. Your friends have come for you." The rich, masculine voice gently caressed her mind. "We have drawn most of the men away to allow your people to come for you."

Raven tried to force her eyes open. She wanted to see the face of the man holding her in his arms. Stabbing pain caused her eyelids to twitch and close before she could make out his features. He looked young. It was all she could see before her eyes closed again. His hands were on her wrists, releasing the ropes holding them together. Pin-pricks of pain scattered to her fingertips as blood rushed back to the tortured digits. Raven flexed her fingers, trying to stimulate the blood flow, reaching up, she tried to feel for her savior. His face was smooth, free of any facial hair and deformities.

"Who are you?" Raven had to force the words from her throat and even then she couldn't get the volume past a whisper.

"Don't try to talk." The voice was still so close she could feel his breath on her cheek. "You will be safe soon. Hold on. You're strong enough for this."

Raven felt her throat tighten up and a cough was forced from her chest. She tasted the metallic bitterness of blood in her mouth. Turning her head, she opened her mouth and allowed the hot liquid to spill from her lips.

"No, no, little one." The voice said. "You need to stay with me."

She could feel his hand on her head. Warmth spread from the top of her head, across her face and scattered across her shoulders. Breathing didn't hurt as bad and her eyes opened a little more. The face started to come together. Dark brown eyes, dark skin, a flash of a smile. Black eyebrows showed the color of his hair, despite the white cloth covering his head. She didn't recognize him, so she knew he wasn't one of the locals.

"Are you with the embedded troops?" Her voice was stronger, but it was still just barely above a whisper.

"Not in the way you think." Raven caught a glimpse of a smile before her eyelids started to droop. "I need to leave you now. You need to be strong. They will be here soon."

As he left he took his warmth with him, causing Raven to shiver. She became aware of the sounds again and the smells. A strong smell of urine permeated the air and assaulted her nostrils. Raven realized the smell was coming from her. She didn't know when she lost control of her bodily functions and she had never felt so helpless.

The noises were coming closer, Raven could hear voices reverberating off stone walls, feet scrambling and an occasional rapid fire gun. It took some effort, but she managed to open her eyes enough to look around. The cave opening was close enough she could see daylight streaming from outside. There wasn't anyone near her, in fact she couldn't see anybody standing near enough to stop her if she could get to her feet and run. She rolled to her side and tried to pull her legs under her body to stand up. Suddenly her head started to swim and a wave of nausea overwhelmed her causing her to collapse back to the sandy ground.

The crunch of wheels on the sand brought Raven around again. She lifted her head and stared directly at the thick-treaded tires of her S290. Raven reached out and grabbed the base of the machine and pulled herself forward. The broad wheel base created a small platform and she was able to pull herself up enough to get to her knees. Nausea crept up and she had to stop and allow her head to stop spinning and her stomach to settle.

"Major, get on. Hurry." A disembodied voice, so different from the machine's normal tones, sang from the vocal processing port of the robot.

The voice coming from the sound processors was not the normal digitized voice. Instead, Anderson's deep voiced timber was singing through the speakers. Raven pulled herself to the platform and turned to sit on the cold, hard metal. As she turned, her knee hit something solid. She looked down, expecting to see a rock. Instead, Sandoval's blank, clouded eyes were staring up at her. She reached out and curled her fingers into his black curls, pulling the head into her lap. The S290's arms raised and a pair of shields blossomed around her, cocooning her in metal. The S290 spun around and shot forward, leaving Raven's lurching stomach to catch up with them. It wasn't doing a very good job.

"Hold on, Major, we'll have you out of here soon." Anderson's voice carried a triumphant note.

The world was hazy and dark. The jerky motion of the S290 was more than she could handle and she started heaving. There wasn't anything in her stomach and she could taste the bitterness of bile mixed with the coppery flavor of blood in the back of her throat. Spitting, she tried to get as much of the taste out of her mouth as she could.

Raven could hear the ping of bullets against the shields surrounding her. There was no way to keep her body from flinching, despite knowing the shield would protect her from anything short of a rocket attack. The smell of smoke, blood, spent shells and hot metal assaulted her nostrils and she could see light shining through minuscule gaps in the shield. A clanking and a hiss followed by the smell of burning sulfur attested to the release of a rocket from the launcher mounted on the S290's shoulder. The resulting blast pushed the machine forward, causing Raven's stomach to lurch again.

Despite the light seeping into the machine Raven was in almost complete darkness. She could hear the whistles of missiles flying through the air, but she couldn't trace where they were coming from and where they might land. Raven felt the motor strain as the S290 tipped up a short incline. The short, jerky motion stopped and Raven felt an increase in speed. They had to be travelling in a truck. The sound of bullets and rockets faded as she felt the speed increase. Blackness was flirting with the edges of her mind. Resting her head against the vocal processor, she allowed the hum of the machinery to soothe her and she closed her eyes to the blackness.

Chapter Forty-Three

THE WORLD WAS QUIET AND still. Raven allowed the silence to swallow her up and swaddle her in its warmth. She could feel the solid weight of Sandoval's head in her lap, but she kept her eyes closed. The S290s digital processor was humming in her ears and she wanted to close her mind to anything else. Unfortunately, the pain was keeping her away from the warmth and security of the darkness. It was coming over her in waves, creeping up her legs, hips, stomach and chest. The heat seeping through the metal of the shields was stifling and Raven was finding it difficult to breathe. Stretching out, her feet touched the metal and she tried to push against it. Nothing moved despite her efforts. She pulled her leg back and kicked at the shield. Pain shot through the sole of her bare foot, sending shockwaves up her leg.

"Calm down, Major." Anderson's voice was coming from outside her cocoon instead of through the vocal processors. "The shields are jammed. We'll have you out in a minute."

There was a hiss and the shields parted, allowing light to flood over her, stabbing into her eyes and blinding her momentarily. Arms reached out to lift her off the platform but Raven pulled away and tried to block them from reaching her. She was suddenly aware of the filth coating her body. The odor of her own bodily fluids and the feel of the dirt and sand coating her was stomach churning and she didn't want anyone to touch her. She didn't have the strength to resist for long and the arms lifted her and pulled her up from her resting place. Sandoval's head slid from her lap and landed on the ground with a thud. Raven opened her eyes and stared at the head as Anderson lifted her. Jesse was standing over the globe, his twin behind him looking over his shoulder. Raven tried to gesture to the head, but Anderson turned to carry her away.

Medics made quick work of her remaining clothes and expert hands started probing her injuries. Pain rippled from every point of her body. She clenched her teeth, biting back gasps of pain. The sting of an IV assaulted her senses and she looked down her arm to the clear plastic tube dripping fluids into her body. The bright lights above her were starting to become fuzzy and dull. Closing her eyes, she allowed the darkness to take over.

Memories came back in flashes. She remembered the desperate flight of the medevac chopper over the mountains. Yellow lights flashed overhead as her gurney was wheeled down long hallways. The surgery suite was cold and the metal operating table was hard beneath her body. There wasn't much more to her memories until she woke up with a dry mouth and an overwhelming sense of nausea creeping up the back of her throat.

Raven tried to call for water, but her throat was so dry no sound came out. She tried to swallow, but there was no moisture in her mouth. Bright lights were shining in her eyes, causing everything to glow with a hazy mist. A form came into view, seemingly hovering over the space between her bed and the lights. Raven blinked to clear her vision and the face of the doctor changed its configuration. The man still had a hazy white glow around his head, but Raven could see the blue eyes surrounded by light brown eyelashes. It seemed unfair that such long, beautiful lashes should be found on a man's face. It was a strange thought and it faded quickly from Raven's mind as she drifted back to sleep.

A nurse was holding ice chips to her lips the next time she woke. She eagerly sucked the cold moisture into her mouth. It wasn't enough to provide the liquid she needed. Her tongue felt heavy and thick. Straining her head off the pillow, Raven tried to reach for more. The plastic spoon holding the chips drifted away and Raven collapsed back onto the pillow.

"Relax, Major," the nurse's hand gently caressed Raven's shoulder, bringing with it a sense of warmth. "I will give you some more in a minute. You've been through the ringer and you need to take it easy."

Raven looked down the length of her body trying to assess the extent of her injuries. Both arms were swathed in white bandages and a thin tube was dripping fluid into her left hand. Her left leg dangled from a sling contraption rigged above her bed. A thin blanket covered her from the chest down and a hospital gown was draped loosely over her body. The odd angles of the blue cloth attested to the number of bandages, tubes and wires hidden beneath its folds. Something was binding her chest, making it difficult to take a deep breath. Not that she wanted to take a deep breath. It hurt too bad to do more than to draw in shallow gasps. The oxygen tube in her nose was helping to keep her SAT levels up, but Raven could feel a headache coming on.

The screeching of the privacy curtain drew Raven's attention. She barely recognized the doctor from her hazy remembrances. The smile on his face reflected his recognition and Raven couldn't help but respond to the gentleness in his blue-grey eyes.

"Welcome back, Major." His voice had a note of triumph in it as he spoke.

"Back from where?" As far as Raven knew she had not left her hospital bed.

"You've had a pretty rough time lately, Major Taylor." He pulled out a light and flashed it in and out of Raven's eyes. "We've had you in a medically induced coma for three days. It took us three surgeries to put Humpty-Dumpty back together again and your heart stopped twice on the operating table, but we brought you back."

Raven tried to lift her arms, but the weight of the bandages kept them to her sides. "Tell me."

The simple statement was all that was necessary. The doctor pulled a rolling stool over and sat beside her bed.

"It could have been worse." A muscle ticked in his cheek as he spoke. "Your team got you out just in time. You had two broken ribs on your left side that punctured your lung causing a partial collapse. The kicks bruised your kidneys and nearly ruptured your spleen. It was close. Any more internal bleeding and we wouldn't have been able to save you. You have a concussion, we're going to need to keep a close watch on you for that one. A slight dislocation of the right shoulder radial joint and some tearing of the muscle. Two broken fingers on your right hand, both wrists had fractures and rope burns. We had to do some reconstructive surgery on your right hand. Mostly you have bruising and internal bleeding. We managed to save your spleen, but it was close."

Raven allowed her body to sink back into the bed. She realized the only reason she wasn't writhing in pain from her injuries was because of the massive amount of narcotics flowing through her veins. Her throat was still dry and without even thinking about it she signed for a drink of water. The nurse brought a cup with a narrow straw protruding above its rim close to her lips. It took almost too much effort to draw the lukewarm liquid into her parched mouth. Closing her eyes, she dropped her head back on the pillow and tried to relax. Her eyes popped open when she realized the nurse had recognized the sign language.

Raven studied the face of the woman standing above her bed. Blue eyes shone brightly amid a riot of fading, blond curls trimmed in short bob. Molly, but Molly was dead, killed in the Taliban raid when they attempted to retrieve Dr. Smith. Blinking, she tried to clear the cobwebs from her mind. It didn't work.

"Close your eyes, Raven," the woman signed. "We'll talk later."

Raven tried to shake her head, but she couldn't make her mind focus. Finally giving up, she closed her eyes and allowed her mind to clear. She heard the rhythmic timbre of medical machinery and the low tones of the doctor as he gave orders. It wasn't long before she was lulled to sleep.

Raven lost track of time as she slipped in and out of drug-induced sleep. She woke when the nurse came in to bathe the sweat from her body and change her bandages. Her body craved sleep as it battled her injuries and she allowed herself to float on the hazy cloud the drugs induced in her mind.

Molly was back. Her gentle fingers worked over the sore spots as she changed bandages and washed away sweat, blood and tears. Raven couldn't believe she was actually crying. Molly didn't say anything as sobs wracked her body and tears flowed down her cheeks. Sleep eventually overwhelmed her senses and she slipped away from the pain.

Opening her eyes to the darkness of the room was almost a relief. It was the soft darkness she was used to. She was able to make out the soft shapes hidden in the shadows and hear the gentle music of the machines monitoring her breathing and heartbeat. The deep aching pain was fading and she was actually able to take a few deep breaths without feeling a stabbing pain in her chest.

"Light," Molly's gentle voice warned her and she closed her eyes as the room was flooded with a bright light. "How are you feeling today, Raven?"

Squinting against the brightness of the light, Raven tried to work words around the dryness of her mouth. She tried to swallow but her mouth felt like it was full of sand. Molly brought a straw to her lips and Raven drew cool liquid into her parched throat.

"I'm better, Molly." Her voice sounded harsh.

"You'll be going home soon," Molly whispered. Her gentle voice soothing Raven's trembling heart. "As soon as you're stable enough to move we'll get you on the next transport."

"My team?" Raven whispered the question, almost hesitantly.

"Safe." Molly's gentle response was all Raven needed to hear.

"How did you get here?" Raven had meant to ask her the question a long time ago, but there always seemed to be something else on her mind when Molly was around.

"I almost didn't make it." Molly worked with simple efficiency as she talked. "The refugee camp was between the Taliban and the base when they tried to retrieve Smith. They threw everything they had at the base and rolled over the camp as if it wasn't even there. It was the worst fifteen minutes of my life, but the attackers were only interested in getting to the base and once they got past the camp we were able to escape into the hills until the attack was over. The invaders had more bravado than bullets and it didn't take long for them to be beaten back. We were rescued from the hills and sent back to the states."

"Where are we?" Raven looked around the room, trying to see if she recognized anything in the sterile space.

"We're at a compound on the southern border of California and Mexico." Molly pulled up a stool and sat beside the bed. "The private security agency that runs this base is in charge providing security for the mining and drilling companies. There aren't many military forces left in this part of the country. Individual State defense is all being turned over to the local governments. We're being called home."

Raven slipped back into a deep, drug-induced sleep, letting her body's natural strength heal itself. Her body was strong and healthy and it wasn't long before she was able to get out of bed and, with Molly's help, was able to shower and brush her hair. Molly offered to trim the ragged lengths, but Raven refused to let her come anywhere near her head with scissors. The right side of her hair was longer than the left and the back was shorn all the way to the nape of her neck. A long, thick strand still touched her hip, the last remnants of the black waves her mother loved so much. Raven wrapped her head in a scarf and refused to let anyone touch it.

It took nearly three weeks for Raven's body to build enough strength to sit for any length of time, despite the vitality of her body. Molly helped Raven sit in a chair and adjusted pillows around her body to help her sit in a comfortable position. Raven just wanted to sleep, but knew her muscles would atrophy if she didn't work them. Her daily therapy included walking the halls between her room and the nurse's station, a task she almost didn't feel up to. The first time Molly strapped the belt around her waist and guided her down the hall her legs felt quivery and she was got a charley horse in her calf although she only walked the length of the hall once. After her walks, Molly would bring her back to her room and helped her sit in her chair. Once Raven was positioned comfortably, Molly would kneel on the floor and started rubbing thick, creamy lotion into her feet and legs.

Her team finally arrived at the base and everyone, including Molly, was scheduled to fly out in the morning. She sure hoped their flight out would be less exciting than the last one. Molly was gently humming, her hands were soft and soothing and Raven could feel her eyelids getting heavy. The light reflected off Molly's yellow curls creating a slightly ethereal glow. It reminded Raven of the man who had cut her down in the cave.

"Molly," the woman looked up at Raven's drowsy tone. "Did they ever find out who helped me when I was in the cave?"

Raven could see the confusion in Molly's eyes. "Raven, there wasn't anyone in the cave with you." Molly's voice was slightly condescending. "That young sergeant, Anderson, fit two personal shields and a rocket launcher onto that little robot of yours and sent it in after you. I don't know how you found the strength to climb onto the wheel base and hold on until you were retrieved and we still can't figure out why you brought Sandoval's head back with you."

"Because I couldn't bring all of him." Even saying it now didn't make sense. She knew Sandoval's head had been sent to the crematory and the rest of his body wasn't able to be retrieved, but she at least wanted to make sure the man had the dignity of a funeral with his unit.

Raven wasn't allowed to go back to Idaho right away. Instead, her team was brought to a base in Southern California. When the unit got off the plane they were herded into a courtyard far away from any buildings, given tents and cots and told to set up camp. It seemed to take forever to go through processing. All she wanted to do was get home to her family. She wanted to hold her children and see her mother. She wanted to dig her hands into the dirt and taste the fruits of her labors as it grew from the ground.

The entire unit was kept in California for six long weeks. Sitting in the counseling sessions was almost as torturous as being kept in the cave. At least with the cave it was all physical-she could shut out the physical pain. A hush settled over the compound and Raven watched as soldiers were filtered through the base. There seemed to be a wildness expressed in the tightness of the men and women's eyes as they passed through the compound. There was a different feel to these soldiers. They just didn't seem to have the same sense of oneness as she did with her unit. It seemed to take forever, but one day she was finally called to Command. She left the segregated courtyard where she and her unit had been camped out and made her way through the compound. As she wound her way around the maze of buildings she could feel the eyes of the soldiers following her. More than once she heard the whisper of "Gen" or

"Freak" as she past a group of men or women. By the time she made it to headquarters a tension had developed between her shoulder blades and a painful throbbing was threatening behind her eyes.

A short, balding man was sitting behind the desk when Raven entered the Command office. He motioned her to a seat at the far side of the room.

"Major, I'm not going to mince words here," he said. "Your unit is being sent back to Idaho. We know you're not a Gen and we want to know if you would like to stay here, or if you would like to go back with them."

It seemed a strange question to Raven. This man didn't even tell her his name, he just blurted out the question. A cold, creepy filling began to settle in her chest and Raven knew something was wrong. Her mind travelled the far distance to Haven and the shelter keeping her family safe. As for as she was concerned, there was only one answer she could give.

"I belong with my family and my unit," she said. "I want to go home."

Raven wasn't even allowed to stop at the base when the plane landed in Mountain Home. She was loaded in a truck and immediately brought to Grey's office outside of Haven. Grey was waiting for her when she opened the door. He stood up from behind the desk and moved to embrace her. It seemed strange he was so demonstrative. Usually he was fairly reserved and unemotional.

"Welcome home, Raven," he said.

Grey moved across the room and sat behind a newly commissioned desk. The high shine of golden-yellow polish glowed around the seal of a golden eagle in flight, clutching a snake in its talons, emblazed across the front of finish.

Raven moved to a chair and sat down, not because she needed to particularly, but because she wanted to avoid any more uncomfortable moments. "Why am I here, Grey? I want to be home with my family."

"You will, Raven." Grey sat down behind his desk. "Some things have happened, though, and I want to prepare you for it." Grey paused and took a deep breath. "We're no longer the United States of America. We need to defend our ways against all enemies, foreign and domestic. Our borders have been redefined and our world has changed. Leadership has changed. No longer will we listen to dictates from a far-away leader who doesn't understand the struggles we are going through here. The Idaho territory is its own entity. We're responsible for governing ourselves."

"Who's going to lead us if we are no longer ruled by Washington?" Raven asked.

"I am," Grey's answer was succinct and not quite unexpected. "I've been elected Governor of the Idaho Territory. It was a fair and legal election and our troops have already been stationed at the borders. Everyone within the borders of the Territory have the option of joining us and swearing an oath of allegiance to the new government or being relocated to a new territory. They're either with us or they're against us. The United States is now the East, the West and the rest."

Chapter Forty-Four

GREY STOOD FROM HIS CHAIR and crossed the room to sit beside Raven. They sat in silence for a few moments. Raven was trying to process the information Grey had just dropped into her lap. She had just spent the better part of half her life defending a country that no longer existed. Now she was sitting in the office of a man who was essentially the leader of the new, free world. After a few minutes she looked up to confront him.

"I want to be with my family, Grey." It wasn't a request.

Grey's brow furrowed at Raven's demand. He stood up and moved across the room, forcing her to follow. "Your family is fine, Raven." Grey didn't slow down as he opened the door and led her out to the hallway. "Besides, we need you here. I have the perfect job for you."

"My term of service is over." Raven was trying to slow her walk and force Grey to turn to face her. It wasn't working. "I've been through enough. I want to be with my family."

"You can be with your family." Grey finally stopped walking. "You'll have your own home and your children will come live with you. I need someone to run my training facility. I'm putting you in charge."

"I don't want this, Grey." Raven didn't know how she could make him understand.

"Come with me, Raven." Grey led her to the courtyard outside and across the breezeway to a doorway of a solid looking structure. He waved his hand in front of the sensor and the light flashed from red to green. Opening the door he motioned for her to enter. She did so, reluctantly.

He led her down a corridor to a wide metal door. A quick wave of his hand over the chip sensor and the door slid open with a hiss. She stepped into the room and was immediately assaulted by warm air and the scent of antiseptic. The soles of her boots rang against the metal walkway as she walked the length of the room. She couldn't quite figure out what she was looking at. Row after row of containers were suspended from the ceiling. The bottoms of the containers rose from the floor in columns. An orange, gelatinous mass bulged out from between the towers rising from the floor and the caps attached to the ceiling by cords, tubes and wires.

While Raven watched, two women, bedecked in white lab coats and surgical masks, approached one of the masses. One typed some information on a data pad and then nodded to the other. The second woman took out a laser scalpel and used it to carefully split the orange mass open. She reached in and struggled to pull out the contents. Whatever was inside the gelatin squirmed and wiggled as the women stepped back and pulled it from the orange mass. It took a moment for Raven to realize the woman was holding an infant in her arms. The first woman entered some information in a data pad and a clear plastic, egg-shaped pod descended from the ceiling. The infant was placed inside and with a few more taps the pod was sent along a track to a door on the far side of the room. Stepping to the next unit, the two women repeated the process. This time the infant came out screaming, its cries reverberating off the metal walkways and ringing through the rafters.

Grey led Raven down the rows of pulsating containers, but he walked so quickly she could only start to make out the forms inside. She caught glimpses of fetuses in various stages of development through the orange, translucent gels. The women continued their work as Grey led Raven past them on the walkway and through the far door.

Hundreds of bassinets were crowded into the room, each one containing an infant. Dozens of nurses walked between rows, gently tending each tiny being. Grey bent over one of the bassinets and picked up the baby. Raven's arms curled instinctively around the form as Grey placed it in her arms.

"This is the future, Raven." He loosened the swaddling cocooning the infant. "We no longer need to rely on the frailties of the female body to produce children. Even now the technicians are resetting the artificial wombs from the twenty infants delivered today. Those wombs will spend the next nine months growing children."

Raven studied the perfect features of the infant in her arms. The child's face was half hidden behind a pacifier, but her blue eyes seemed to peer deep into her soul and struck a resonant chord in her heart. A shaft of light reflected off the metal of the ceiling and caused the infant's tuft of red hair to glow. It was almost with a sense of regret that Raven gave up the infant when a nurse approached and took the baby from her arms.

"You want me to run this facility?" Raven kept her voice low, but she managed to give it intensity.

"No," Grey motioned for her to follow him out of the room. He continued to explain as they walked the corridors. "Dr. Omoto manages the infant ward. I need you to manage the education and training center."

Grey opened a door and led Raven to a courtyard. The sounds of children's screams and laughter assaulted her ears as soon as she stepped out on to the terrace. Raven watched as children of all ages roiled around the courtyard. Grey pulled a whistle from his pocket and gave three short blasts. The children became a blur of motion as they darted across the courtyard and lined up in perfect squares. Not one child was out of place, not one squirmed in their perfectly straight lines as Grey led Raven down the stairs and through the crowds of children. The children stared straight ahead, their eyes unwavering as Grey and Raven passed by them.

Grey led her across the walkway and into the building on the far side breezeway. His form seemed to melt a little as they progressed and Raven recognized the signs of pain and exhaustion in the slope of his shoulders and slight limp. He waved his hand in front of the door sensor and, as the door opened, he turned to face Raven. She tried to school her features before he saw, but she wasn't fast enough.

"We're all dying a little bit every day, Raven." The simple statement was said without emotion. Grey led Raven through the door and into the building. "I'm seventy-nine years old. It's time I passed this work on. You're going to help me make sure this world has a future."

"General," Raven decided it was time to give the man the respect he had earned over his lifetime. "You're asking me to take over the training center for the genetically altered units. These children deserve to have choices in their future. You know my mother and I don't agree with this program."

"Once you've worked with these children you'll understand." Grey's tone held no apology. "Your grandfather and Doctor Smith were the progenitors of this program, but I don't even think they knew what we could do with their research. We've tied our future to these children. They're designed to not just survive in the world we have destroyed, but to thrive in it."

Raven was silent as Grey led her through the corridors of the building. He showed her the nurseries and dormitories filled with hundreds of children. Everything was lined up with military precision. Even the toys on the shelf were clean and spaced perfectly. The white, austere walls lacked any sense of individuality and personality. Raven didn't even bother counting the number of children in each room. Music was being piped through the building. Each room had a different song with tempos and beats to match the function. Children as young as three were sitting in desks in front of computers, screens flashing words or algorithms as they worked through the problems. Everything the children needed to thrive and develop was provided within these walls.

Grey led Raven out of the building and into a second courtyard. She could see acres of fields and trees spreading to the mountains in the distance. Across the lawn was a simple, white-washed structure stood out against the melting softness of the mountains.

"It will be your home, Raven." Grey spoke in a hushed, reverent tone as they looked across the valley. "Your family is inside, waiting for you."

Her mother and Travis were sitting on a couch in the large circular room when Raven walked inside. Lakota and Marwa were standing by the window. Raven noticed they were holding hands. Meaghan was nowhere to be seen, despite the emptiness of the space. Marwa peeled her hand out of Lakota's and flew across the room nearly knocking Raven off her feet with her exuberance.

"I'm so glad you're home." Marwa's voice was choked with tears.

Raven gently peeled the child off her neck and took a step back. It was hard to believe this young child-woman was the little girl she rescued from the desert so many years before. Savanna rose from the couch and slowly approached. Her limp was much more prominent and the grey wing streaking her blond hair at her temple was wider and silver streaks liberally graced her hair. Raven allowed her mother to draw her into an embrace. Her normally self-possessed, strong, mother was actually trembling.

"Don't ever leave me again." Savanna's whisper was barely audible. "You're home, Raven. This is where you belong."

The only person who did not move across the room to embrace her was Lakota. He stood with his arms crossed, leaning against the wall, a blank expression on his face. Raven started to move across the room when the sound of tiny feet on the hardwood floor drew her up short. Her little Meagan Noel stood on anxious toes, her tiny hands fidgeting and tugging at her long, dark curls. Joseph was standing behind the child. His smile drew her in and warmed her heart.

"Are you really my Mommy?" the child asked.

The child's innocent question pierced her heart and nearly brought tears to her eyes. Lakota finally moved away from the wall and picked up the child.

"She's the woman who gave life to us, Little One." Raven could hear the anger in her son's voice. "I don't know if I would exactly call her mother."

"Lakota!" Savanna's voice was harsh and shocked.

Raven waved her mother back when she would have approached. "Lakota, I know it seems strange for me to be back after so long, but I'm home to stay now."

"It's a little too late, now." Lakota put Meaghan down and pulled Marwa close to him. "I'm leaving for basic in two weeks. When I come back Marwa and I are going to be married. I'll be nineteen by then and able to make my own decisions. Marwa and Meaghan will stay at Haven in the meantime."

Marwa moved forward and placed her hand on Lakota's shoulder. "Lakota, I don't want to stay at Haven." Marwa's voice was gentle, but there was an underlying strength in her tone. "I'm going to stay here and Meaghan needs to be here, too. Now, let's go see the rest of the house."

Despite Marwa's gentle nature and quiet ways, Lakota didn't lose the hard edge of anger he projected the entire two weeks before he left for basic training. Raven tried to make overtures to her son, but he resisted any attempts to draw close. It was wrenching to send him away knowing he didn't understand just how much she loved him. Every battle she fought, every sacrifice she made was to make the world a better place for her children. She wished there was a way she could make him understand what she did for him, but no matter how hard she tried she couldn't break through the hard shell he had built up around himself.

Raven spent most of her days getting to know the daily operation of the training facility. With a sense of regret, she gave up her tags and had a new microchip implanted in the palm of her hand. It was easier to access the sealed facility through the information programmed in the tiny chip. The children in the program were born with an ingrained sense of purpose and commitment to their unit. She was amazed at the progress the children were making in their learning and training. They were light years beyond anything she accomplished in her childhood.

When Lakota returned from basic training he and Marwa had a quiet commitment ceremony. Not long after the ceremony Lakota was deployed to the borderlands. The territories between Nevada and Arizona were rife with friction and illegal border crossings were turning the land into a war zone. Grey was considering tightening the border lands and cutting Nevada off entirely, but the natural resources in the state made it necessary to keep it as part of the protectorate.

Raven studied the map in the war room faithfully. She needed to know what was happening with her son. The newly outlined borders flashed red, denoting the boundary lines of the new countries. The Northwest Territories consisted of the former states of Idaho, Washington, Oregon, Northern California, Nevada, Wyoming and Montana. It was the biggest territory carved out of the former United States of America. It was also the wealthiest. The natural resources provided just about anything necessary to keep the residents of the territory healthy and thriving.

Joseph went back to the community and recruited Bear and his family to work in the new government. The community became the new model for living in the territories. As long as residents were willing to swear allegiance to the new government they were allowed the freedom to protect their land and way of life. Raven was happy to learn the Community was thriving and had been allowed to maintain their way of life. Emily had never returned, but her clinic was still operating and, according to Joseph, the Community members were all in good health and happy. He told her about the two children who had been born to their wives. Both boys, both thriving in the agrarian society.

The body armor Joseph sported weighed almost as much as he did. Raven couldn't help thinking how much Anderson would love to get his hands on the metal framework sprouting from the disk in the middle her husband's spine and the web of wires and metal framework wrapping around his hips and spreading up his back, over his arms and down his legs. Joseph was paralyzed from the middle of his back down without the brace. His legs were still cold to the touch and were limp and lifeless when they lay in bed at night.

There were still contingency forces out there refusing to swear allegiance to the new government. Many of them refused to swear fealty to any form of government. These feral groups thrived in the mountains and wilderness left bare by the plagues. Raven didn't envy General Grey his role in protecting this new country. Everyone had their roles on the changing face of the world.

Lakota

LAKOTA WAS MISSING SOMEWHERE IN the Arizona Territory. The message had come across Grey's desk two hours before. His unit had crossed the border to assist some refugees who were trapped in a canyon without water and few supplies. Raven didn't even hesitate, as soon as she read the message she took one of the Haven bikes and raced towards the border. She didn't expect Joseph to follow her and she was halfway to Mountain Home before she even registered his voice ringing in her ear.

"I'm here, Raven." His voice assuaged the drumming in her soul. "Think about what you are doing. I'll help you, but you need to think this through."

Raven had hundreds of miles and dozens of hours to make a plan, but as soon as she approached the edge of the territory all thoughts of the plan faded away. Her only thought was going in, finding her son and bringing him home. A line of guardsmen confronted her at the border and she had to present her credentials before they allowed her to cross into Arizona. It took only a few seconds for the soldiers to scan the chip implanted in the palm of her hand. Waves of heat radiated from the roadway and sucked into her helmet, causing sweat to bead up on her forehead. She removed her helmet and wiped the sweat from her face. She had been on the road for twenty hours and she could feel the grit of the day's travel in every crease of her skin.

"Major Taylor, is that you?" Raven turned at the sound of her name. Anderson was loping towards her, his weapons and gear jingling as he approached. "What are you doing in this God-forsaken desert?"

Raven grasped her former team member's forearm and pulled him forward. The embrace was the typical comrades in arms contact.

"Anderson," she greeted him warmly. "I'm looking for my son. His team went after some refugees and they disappeared in the desert. I'm here to find him."

Anderson laughed a rich, booming laugh. "I have no doubt you could pick up this desert, shake out the spiders and scorpions, kick their backsides and force them to tell you where your son is."

"I'm hoping I won't have to go that far." Raven couldn't believe she was joking with the man. She must have been more tired than she thought.

"Raven!" Joseph was holding up a data pad and was motioning her over. "He sent a message. We have his coordinates."

Raven scrolled through the message. The coordinates were less than fifty miles from her current position. He was pinned down in a canyon with his team and thirty refugees. Raven was certain he was putting himself at risk to climb to a high spot to find reception. For a second she flashed back to home and Marwa. The girl was seven months pregnant and the same age Raven was when she lost Billy. A deep foreboding filled her heart as she thought of her son, lost in the heat of the desert.

"Let's go!" Anderson's voice rang out. At first Raven thought he was calling to her, but as she looked down the line she saw a group of people split off from the line and rally to the man. He made a few gestures, ones Raven taught her crew when they were stationed in Afghanistan, and the group fell into line behind him. "The Major has a mission for us."

Raven placed her helmet on her head and started her motorcycle. With Joseph following on his cycle and Anderson and his troop in the armored truck, the miniature convoy sped across the desert. The coordinates took them off-road and onto some barely recognizable tracks. Raven could barely see through the dust clouds being kicked up by the wind. Puffs of smoke and clouds of dust rising above the horizon signaled they were getting close. Raven stopped and gestured to the men behind her. According to the message, Lakota and his team were pinned down in the canyon just ahead. Signaling for the men to stay where they were, Raven rode to the top of a hill just to the right of the main trail. From this vantage point, she could make out the figures surrounding the narrow maw opening into the blind canyon beyond. The burnt husk of a transport truck stood near the mouth of the canyon, attesting to the raiders' original intentions. Raven could make out about half a dozen figures, each with their full attention focused at the opening of the canyon. The sun was just beginning its downward track, creating shadows in the backwash of the hills. Pulling out the data pad from her sleeve she sent quick orders to her men. Now it was just a waiting game.

Finally her pad beeped, signaling her team's readiness. She tapped an icon on her data pad and a missile shot out from the launcher on her bike. The heat from the thrust split the air and rippled across her back as the missile whistled towards its intended target. Sand and rock blasted more than fifty yards in all directions and the blast wave flipped the transport truck on its side.

The raiders immediately dove from their hiding places, running away from the blast site. They didn't get very far before they came up against Raven's force. Although the attackers were matched in numbers, they were greatly outgunned in fire-power. From her vantage point, Raven watched as they dropped their guns almost as one and raised their hands in surrender. By the time she made it off the hill and to the site, the raiders were bound and the embattled refugees were trickling from the canyon.

Raven stopped her bike right next to the Anderson's armored truck and peeled off her helmet. She studied each form coming out of the canyon, anxiously assessing each face, looking for signs of injury, looking for her son. Finally, a tall, graceful form stepped out of the shadows and into the fading light. Lakota was supporting a limping figure, his shoulders stooped beneath the weight of the man.

Curbing her first impulse to race across the desert and draw her son into her arms, Raven turned her attention to the raiders huddled beside the burned-out truck. There were six men and women, all with a half-starved, wolfish cast to their eyes. The wildness was almost beyond anything she had ever seen before. Shivers went down her spine as she realized the eyes reminded her of her captor's only a year before, right before he cut off all her hair.

A sudden snort drew her attention to the refugees. They were all settled in a group, huddling together to preserve body heat as a chill wind swept across the desert. The sun had set, bringing the cold, westerly winds to stir up the sand and bring the song of the desert to Raven's ears. As she studied the group she suddenly realized she recognized some of them.

"Grandfather!" she cried.

Etu's smile lit up his whole face as she ran to him and wrapped her arms around his shoulders. His frame seemed so thin and brittle, she was almost afraid to squeeze him. She could feel the trembling of his limbs as he drew away and took her face in his cold, arthritic hands.

"Oh, Raven, my child." Etu pulled her into his embrace and, despite his trembling body, Raven felt a strength flow from him all throughout her frame. Tears welled in her eyes as his warmth spread and enveloped her. All the pain and sorrow she had felt through the years dropped off her body and all she felt was love and strength. Stifling her cries, she buried her face in his long, grey hair and dried her eyes on its length. Finally, she drew away and turned to the crowd. Her eyes fell on another shriveled form.

"Figures," Kai's voice was filled with bitterness and scorn. "You're just like your mother, flying to the rescue as if no one else can save the world. I swear your entire family has a hero complex."

Raven couldn't even feel anger for the woman who had been so instrumental in giving her life. Pity welled up inside her as she looked at the tiny, crippled form huddled on the ground. She noticed a man sitting beside her. Despite his adult-sized body, his features seemed unformed, as if he wasn't complete.

"He's your brother, Raven." There was no compassion in Kai's voice as she spoke. "He doesn't have anyone to take care of him except for me and Grandfather."

Raven gestured to Anderson to start loading passengers in the truck. There wasn't going to be room for everyone on the first trip, especially since the six raiders needed to be in the first transport. It was almost completely dark and the transport wouldn't be able to return until morning. They were taking a risk being across the border as it was.

The transport was almost completely loaded when Raven moved to help Etu up from the ground. He refused to take her hand when she reached for his, instead pointing to the others on the ground.

"I will go with the next group." His soft voice held a note of resignation. "Take the others first."

"Grandfather," Raven crouched down to talk to him at eye level. "We need to take the weak and the sick first. The others will be fine here through the night."

Etu shook his head and pointed at the others. "They go first, I go last."

Raven knew she couldn't move the old man from his spot. Shaking her head she moved to where Kai was sitting.

"You and your son need to get on board." She reached for Kai's hand, helping the brittle woman from the ground. Kai's son stood and followed his mother, his eyes never leaving Raven. It took some effort to get the two in the back of the vehicle. Raven heard more than one grumble and groan as they made their way into the hollow area near the back. A sharp intake of breath and a high pitched curse denoted someone's fingers being stepped on.

Raven closed the door to the truck and moved back to the now reduced crowd of refugees. The burn of eyes followed her as she walked back to where her son was standing.

"Grandfather is in worse condition than those others." He kept his voice low, but Raven could hear the angry undertone. "Why didn't you send him?"

"It was his choice, Lakota." She couldn't keep the note of authority out of her voice. "Now, take my bike and provide an escort for the others."

"No." The sharp response gave Raven pause. "I'm strong enough. I'll stay here and help with defense. You're not my commander. You can't order me around."

Raven bit back her response. This was not the time to press her parental authority. Gesturing for one of the other guards to take the bike, she turned back to the refugees and guide them back to the canyon to wait out the night. The wind brought Etu's chant to her ears, blending with the music of the desert, welcoming the darkness.

About the Author

Lucinda Moebius grew up in the mountains of Idaho and Eastern Oregon. Her mother taught her to read when she was four years old and since that time books have been her constant companions. She has a Bachelors Degree in English Teaching, a Masters in Educational Leadership and is currently pursuing a Doctorate in Education. Lucinda supports her writing habit by teaching High School and College.

www.ingramcontent.com/pod-product-compliance
Lightning Source LLC
Chambersburg PA
CBHW021442240626
47153CB00001B/247